A TO IZZARD

A HARRY STEPHEN KEELER COMPANION

RAMBLE HOUSE

Proudly presents

A TO IZZARD

A

HARRY STEPHEN KEELER

COMPANION

Edited by Fender Tucker

Summer 2002

A TO IZZARD:
A Harry Stephen Keeler Companion
©2002 by Ramble House

The Harry Stephen Keeler Story and Introduction to Riddle of the Travelling Skull © by Richard Polt

Harry Stephen Keeler's Screwball Circus, Hick Dick from the Sticks: HSK's Quiribus Brown and The Skull of the Stuttering Gunfighter © by Francis M. Nevins

The Webwork World of Harry Stephen Keeler
© by Chris Mikul

Who in the Hell is Harry Stephen Keeler? © by Mark Allen

Harry's Home Page © by William Poundstone

Web Pages: How H. S. Keeler Wrote Certain of His Books
© by Ed Park

As the Plot Thickens © by John Marr

The Amazing Adventures of the Kracked King of Keelerland
© by Bill Pronzini

Z. Narvik: North Pole Manhunter © by Ken Keeler

The Cracksman with the Transposed Hands © by Jim Weiler

The Man with the Plastic Skull © by Fender Tucker

Keeler by Design and Selected Dust Jackets
© by Gavin L. O'Keefe

Selected Short Stories and Articles by Harry Stephen Keeler
© by Harry Stephen Keeler

ISBN 13: 978-1-60543-125-3

ISBN 10: 1-60543-125-7

CONTENTS

SORT OF LIKE HARRY

GREY-SCALE PLATES

BIBLIOGRAPHY

THE RAMBLE HOUSE STORY

Fender Tucker

Ramble House was inevitable. In the early 20th Century as soon as it became possible to record sound and pictures, people wanted this ability for themselves. Over the years the media changed (film, wire, acetate, reel-to-reel tape, video-tape, floppy disk, CD, DVD, etc.) but one thing remained the same: if a person bought something, he damn well expected to be able to make a copy so he wouldn't have to buy it again when it wore out.

But what about the oldest medium of them all? Books. Why can't people make copies of books they buy just as they can the other media? Well, it turns out that if you're a genius like Jim Weiler it's not much of a problem at all.

In the late 1990s, Jim and his friend Fender Tucker were languishing in Shreveport Louisiana at a software company, Softdisk, which used to be a major player in the early days of home computing. But the days when people would pay to have new software delivered to their door every month were numbered—the Internet provided way too much software for free—so Jim decided to look into other ways of making his computer expertise pay off. He tried e-books, which were barely in their infancy at the time. He started converting old public-domain books into electronic text and his project, The Naked Word, soon had over 100 classic books available as text files for PC users.

Since those early days of e-text the concept has come a long way and now major publishing companies are gambling that people will read books on electronic "palm readers". But for someone like Jim Weiler, the idea was too "logical", too "reasonable"; he preferred to look beyond the obvious and foresaw a day when people who love reading real books will insist on having backups of their favorites. And they'll want them on paper and handy to carry around—unlike e-books.

But surely the book-making technology is already in place? It's been around since Gutenberg. If you need a back-up book, just buy a printing press and learn the art of typesetting. Or call a Vanity Press and get 500 copies made for a few thousand bucks.

Well, what Jim had in mind was true *home-publishing*: the ability to make books, one at a time, using normal household items, for a reasonable amount of labor and expense. It took him three reams of paper, two laser toner cartridges, and scores of trials and errors, but by 1999 he figured out how to make a nifty paperback copy of any old book at home. Then he taught me how to do it.

I was the old man at Softdisk, veteran bookphile and posterboy for the proposition that too much reading can make a man dull and lifeless. I liked to read *about* writing almost as much as I liked writing itself, and I thought that I knew every old mystery author there was, from Edgar Allan Poe through Dashiell Hammett to James Crumley. But until I read about Harry Stephen Keeler in Bill Pronzini's *Son of Gun in Cheek*, I had never heard of him! That's what amazed me about him. How could he have been so forgotten? Was there a conspiracy among crime buffs against him?

And it wasn't just a lack of mention in the books about mystery writing. I was a used bookstore lurker. Whenever I'd stop in a strange town while driving across America, I'd check out the used bookstores. I still do and it drives my wife crazy. But as of June 20, 2002 I have yet to find a single copy of a Keeler novel on a bookstore shelf! And I've been looking for them for about five years now. Keeler has almost disappeared from the face of the earth.

So I turned to an old friend and ally in the quest for books not deemed reprintable for the modern masses: the local library. There were no Keelers there, of course, but through inter-library loans I was able to obtain a couple dozen of HSK's novels—beat-up, worn-out, re-covered copies that were 50 years old or more.

And this was at the same time that Jim figured out how to make copies of old books at home. We combined our various obsessive-compulsive neuroses and created Ramble House—the house that will not sleep until all of Harry Stephen Keeler's mystery novels are back in print for a reasonable price. At the time of this writing, Ramble House has 42 of Keeler's novels scanned, OCRed, typeset and proofread—available for anyone to buy. Since some of Harry's juggernauts are huge—several were over 500 pages long—we have had to break some up into volumes. It's no more fun binding a huge paperback than it is lugging it around. Ramble House books are made to fit into a pocket for easy carrying.

Each title requires the following processes:

(1) We scan each page of the book with a hand scanner, providing a TIF (black and white picture file) of the page. It takes about three solid hours.

(2) We use an OCR (Optical Character Recognition) program to turn each TIF into text, riddled with errors, which we fix a page at a time. Twenty mind-numbing hours.

(3) We edit the text into a printable format and print out copies of all of the pages, which we bind into a RH-like book. Five hours.

(4) We proofread the book, checking for any OCR, punctuation or formatting errors still there. Three hours.

(5) We print and bind each copy of the book, cutting it to size and adding the dust jacket. One hour per copy.

Our project would not have progressed as swiftly as it has without the help of the Harry Stephen Keeler Society, a group of Keelerphiles headed by Richard Polt of Cincinnati Ohio. Propelled by his excellent newsletter, *Keeler News,* the society brings together up to a hundred Keeler fans from around the globe. And it's quite a group of literati. Most are writers; some are artists; a few are well-known in television and academia. A quick glance at the Table of Contents of this book will give you an idea of the brainpower behind this madness.

But the goal of the Society and this companion book is to bring to the great unwashed masses an appreciation of the art of Harry Stephen Keeler. I've gathered some of the very best essays written about him and when you're through reading them, you'll know as much about the writer as any living person (except maybe Richard Polt and Francis M. Nevins). There is some overlapping of information—since all of the essays were written independently of the others—but the literary universe of HSK was so vast that you'll be surprised at how little redundancy there really is. Each essayist has his own personal favorite Keelerisms and when you've got a few Keelers under your belt, you will too.

The first part of this book are those essays *about* Keeler. The second part consists of some of Harry's own writings—short stories, articles, memoirs, etc. He wrote many short stories before he became a dedicated novelist, and this companion has some of his best and most famous. Probably the most important and telling is an essay called *My "Million Dollar" Plot-Inventing Secret,* which answered a lot of *my* questions about his writing style. Once you read it you'll have a much better idea of why his work seems so quirky. There was indeed a method to his madness.

Following Keeler's stories are some pastiches written by Society members for the annual Imitate Keeler Contest featured in *Keeler News.* One of the charms of Keeler's distinctive literary style is that it inspires—almost compels—readers to try their hand at it. See if it doesn't happen to you after plowing through one of his webwork mysteries. You live in his world long enough and you start seeing the same things he sees: skulls, strange wills, wily celestials, and the damnedest murder plots ever concocted.

And finally, to finish up the book—and this introduction which has wandered quite far off the point, as Harry was apt to do—a complete bibliography of HSK is provided. Thanks to Mike Nevins, whose research has made him *the* most valuable player in the Keeler game, we know of just about everything Harry wrote during his long literary life. We even know how much Harry was paid for each book: not much and not nearly enough.

And really finally, inserted into the middle of all of this Keeleriana are beautiful templates of some of the dust jackets that Australian artist Gavin L. O'Keefe has designed for all of the Ramble House editions. Gavin recognized how exclusive our editions are and volunteered his artistry to make them even better.

That's the Ramble House story. It shows what can happen when you blend the genius of a Harry Stephen Keeler with the healthy obsessive-compulsivenesses of a Weiler, Tucker, O'Keefe, Polt, Nevins, Mikul, Keeler, Poundstone, Pronzini, Allen, Park and Marr.

Read on—if you dare.

2005 ADDENDUM: You're reading the third edition of this book, printed on a professional Docu-Tech machine. In general, all that's changed from the first Ramble House edition, is the size, page layout and the cover pictures by Gavin O'Keefe. For this edition, the color plates have been replaced by greyscale plates. The bibliography has also been updated to show that Ramble House did indeed complete its five-year mission of bringing every damn novel Harry Keeler ever wrote back into print for a reasonable price.

A
TO
IZZARD

A
HARRY STEPHEN KEELER
COMPANION

Dedicated with Love and Gratitude from His Fans to the Man Who Wrote All Those Incredible Stories:
Harry Stephen Keeler

ABOUT HARRY

The Harry Stephen Keeler Story

Richard Polt

We are drawn to the unescapable conclusion that Mr. Keeler writes his peculiar novels merely to satisfy his own undisciplined urge for creative joy.

—The New York Times, 1942

Felt any undisciplined urges for creative joy lately? Ever wonder about the forgotten chambers of the American psyche? Can you appreciate literature that tenaciously disregards convention to form its own bizarre criteria of excellence? The rich and dreamlike world of Harry Stephen Keeler awaits you.

Keeler (1890-1967) lived all his life in Chicago, a city which is lovingly rendered, warts and all, in his scores of novels. In the teens and twenties Keeler published a stream of short stories and serials in the pulps. His first hardcover novel, *The Voice of the Seven Sparrows*, appeared in 1924. Keeler's early work developed and perfected the concept of the "webwork plot," in which several strings of outrageous coincidences and odd events end in a surprising and utterly implausible denouement. Keeler is also fond of the Arabian Nights device (used in such early novels as *Sing Sing Nights* and *Thieves' Nights*): he tells stories about people telling stories—a great opportunity to reuse that early pulp fiction! The result is intricate, verbose, thoroughly entertaining, and quite imaginative. In *The Matilda Hunter Murder* (1931), a novel of over 700 pages, an atom bomb is a main plot device. *The Box From Japan* (1932), an even more massive opus, is set in 1942 and features intercontinental 3-D color television.

By the mid-thirties, Keeler had reached some popularity (in 1934 *Sing Sing Nights* inspired two bottom-of-the-barrel movies from Monogram Studios, one starring Bela Lugosi as a Chinese bad guy). Keeler continued to produce some of the oddest and most original mystery novels of all time. The first two volumes of one Keeler tetralogy (*The Marceau Case, X.*

Jones—Of Scotland Yard, The Wonderful Scheme of Mr. Christopher Thorne and *Y. Cheung, Business Detective*) are "documented novels," collections of items such as telegrams, cartoons, poems by madmen, Chinese jokes, and photographs, including one of Keeler himself. A two-volume Keelerganza consisting of *The Mysterious Mr. I* and *The Chameleon* is narrated by an enigmatic protagonist who assumes 50 false identities.

In the late thirties, Keeler's style began to depart even further from normal prose. His books were dripping with outré elements (such as bordellos of freaks) and twisted into supremely convoluted webwork plots—but in many works, he removed almost all of the action from the immediate scene and presented it through dialogue. And often this dialogue consists of page after page of thick, artificial dialect. In *The Man With the Magic Eardrums* (1939), a bookie and a safecracker run into each other in a house in Minneapolis and spend the night talking. Oh yes, there are two phone calls, and another character comes into the house and talks for a while. This takes hundreds of pages. The direct action of *The Portrait of Jirjohn Cobb* (1940), which has to be one of the most astoundingly unreadable novels ever written, consists of four characters, two of whom sport outrageous accents, sitting on an island in the middle of a river, talking and listening to a radio, again for hundreds of pages. And these novels were only the first volumes of two multi-novel sequences! What do these people talk about? Well, it would really take hundreds of pages to explain. These works are the *Waiting for Godot* of the Keeler canon, drawn out to the length of *Finnegans Wake*. Oddly enough, a dramatic adaptation of the same story that formed the basis of *The Man With the Magic Eardrums* was used in one of the earliest television broadcasts, a program experimentally televised to 200 people in New York in 1940. Despite his exploration of television in *The Box From Japan,* this was the most TV exposure that Keeler ever got.

Keeler's U.S. publisher, Dutton, dropped him in 1942, not long after publishing *The Peacock Fan,* which includes a vicious satire on the publishing industry but which Dutton was contractually obligated to print. Harry now resorted to the obscure Phoenix Press, which published a series of relatively short Keelers such as *The Case of the Barking Clock* and *The Case of the Transposed Legs.* Keeler's beloved wife, Hazel

Goodwin Keeler, a more conventional writer herself, was now playing an increasingly important role in Harry's work: her short stories were inserted into his novels on the flimsiest pretext. Faced with the unmarketable weirdness of this stuff, even Phoenix Press—which had already been cutting Keeler's novels ruthlessly—abandoned him in 1948, and his British publishers, Ward Lock, printed their last Keeler in 1953. But Harry struggled on, publishing his works in Spanish and Portuguese translations. His novels published in Madrid by Reus include *El Cubo Carmesí* (*The Crimson Cube,* completed 1954, published 1960) and *La Misteriosa Bola de Marfil de Wong Shing Li* (*The Mysterious Ivory Ball of Wong Shing Li,* completed 1957, published 1961).

When Hazel died in 1960, it looked like Keeler was ready to give up. But in 1963 he was remarried, to his former secretary Thelma Rinaldo, and made a comeback—in spirit, if not in reputation. The ancient typewriter started clattering away once again, and Harry even collaborated with Thelma as he had with Hazel. Many HSK creations of the fifties and sixties, such as *The Case of the Two-Headed Idiot* and *The Scarlet Mummy,* have never been published anywhere in the world. Keeler hoped they would appear in print, but the fact is that he was working, indeed, "merely to satisfy his own undisciplined urge for creative joy." Keeler is a true rarity: a man devoted to the end to his unique vision of art.

Who the Hell is Harry Stephen Keeler?

Mark Allen

"Mark, who in the Hell is Harry Stephen Keeler?" you ask?

Why I'm glad you did! He was only one of the most fascinating American writers who ever lived! Harry Keeler was born in 1890 and lived until 1967. *He wrote novels such as The Man With the Magic Eardrums, Finger! Finger!, The Barking Clock, The Skull of the Waltzing Clown* and *The Case of the Transposed Legs.*

Haven't heard of those?

Well, he published countless other colorfully titled books all over the world during his "heyday". He wrote mystery novels or, more specifically, "whodunits"—or, well... he liked to call them "webwork" novels. Remember that never failing writing device from literature class? No? Well, a "webwork plot" makes a story by taking characters that should have nothing to do with each other and events that are completely unrelated and then somehow connecting them by using totally implausible coincidences. Sound like a headache? Sometimes it is! Oh but a really FUN headache! And the characters and events he came up with were either brilliant or just ridiculous, depending on where you're coming from. Take a look at this great list of 6 plot devices I completely ripped off from William Poundstone's great HSK website.

A man is found strangled to death in the middle of a lawn, yet there are no footprints other than his own. Police suspect the "Flying Strangler-Baby," a killer midget who disguises himself as a baby and stalks victims by helicopter. (*X. Jones of Scotland Yard,* 1936)

Someone killed an antique dealer just so he could steal the face—only the face—from a surrealist painting of "The Man from Saturn." (*The Face of the Man from Saturn,* 1933)

A woman's body disappears while taking a steam bath. Only her head and toes, sticking out of the steam cabinet, remain. (*The Case of the Transparent Nude,* 1958)

Because of a clause in a will, a character has to wear a pair of hideous blue glasses constantly for a whole year. This is so that he will eventually see a secret message that is visible only with the glasses. (*The Spectacles of Mr. Cagliostro,* 1929)

A poem leads the protagonist to a cemetery specializing in circus freaks and the grave of "Legga, the Human Spider," a woman with four legs and six arms. Legga was born in Canton, China, and died in Canton, Ohio. (*The Riddle of the Traveling Skull,* 1934)

A disgruntled phone company employee calls every man in Minneapolis, telling him the morning papers will name him as the secret husband of convicted murderess Jemimah Cobb, who runs a whorehouse specializing in women with physical abnormalities. (*The Man With the Magic Eardrums,* 1939)

Harry Keeler had an overly colorful imagination that was perhaps a little too creative for his own good, especially when it came to coming up with names for characters and places. Check out this list of character names:

Philodexter Maximum (a poetry publisher)
Screamo the Clown (a dead clown)
Scientifico Greenlimb (a science fiction writer)
Sophie Kratzenschneiderwümpel (husband-baiting temptress)
Marchbank, Marchbank and Marchbank (a law firm)
Kinkella MacCorquodale (a mafia boss)
Furbelly Wavetail (a cat)

His hyper-drive brain often got ahead of him when trying to set "mood" or establish a character's personality. Take the following passage from *The Man With the Wooden Spectacles*, in which Harry is introducing a young female attorney named Elsa Colby. Elsa has a shy disposition and is about to find herself blackmailed by a crooked judge into representing a peculiar criminal in a fixed trial:

Elsa Colby was so small—at least as compared to the giant quilt cover which, on its slightly inclined rack, covered almost one wall of her cramped office—and which office, fortunately for it's own size, was never crammed with clients and seldom with even a client!—that at times she had to mount a small stubby stepladder stool to ply her skillful needle. The bright red of Elsa's hair—made even brighter, seemingly, by its contrast with the knitted mouse-grey one-piece dress that she wore—was of the exact color as the great scarlet poppies which lay at each corner of the quilt; her blue eyes were precisely the blue of the pond which lay at its middle—at least of the one experimentally completed ripple on that pond; and the freckles on her face—and most particularly on her nose—were like—but no, they were not like anything on the quilt proper at all, but were like the spattering of brown ink from an angry fountain-pen on a sheet of white paper.

Her quilt, it might be said, lay exposed in entirety upon its huge rack for the simple reason that it held, here and there, throughout its entire area, certain flecks which must be done in green; and Elsa, having been able to pick up a huge amount of green silk thread—but green only!—at a discount, had to do that color first, and fully, just as independent shoestring movie producers, with little or no money to rent locations or put up settings, have to complete, in one rented setting, all the scenes for two or more "quickies,"—before negotiating a new setting!

Elsa, this day, had just completed a single leaf of those several million green leaves yet to be done, and had climbed off her stool to survey it from a distance—when her phone rang. She did not answer it immediately, however, for her point of surveyal of her quilt happened to be alongside her one broad window and her surveyal thereof had transferred itself instead fascinatedly to the street far below where some kind of local political parade was going by, the band music coming up almost thread-like through the glass pane of the window, the obviously green-coated musicians seeming, from above, like small green rectangles mathematically spaced apart, and all flowing onward in unison—and a real elephant!—Republican, therefore, that parade!—looking from above, like some grey wobbling paramoecium—and scarcely any bigger! From the old-fashioned windows of the 9-story Printography Building across the way, ink-smeared printers' devils were leaning out and gesticulating to each other—and Elsa, who loved elephants passionately—even when shrunken a hundredfold as was this one!—was assuredly just now torn between love and business!

See how his brain seemed to almost be leaping ahead of his typewriter-bound hands, daring them to keep up? Harry seemed to go off on all kinds of irrelevant tangents and inappropriate analogies without once looking back. Take a gander at this humdinger of a "sentence" from The Steeltown Strangler:

> Now, local-colourist, we can eat up-town at an air-cooled place—rather half-way *de luxe,* too, for a town like this—or we can eat at a joint outside the gates where a hundred sweat-encrusted mill-workers, every one with a peeled garlic bean laid alongside his plate, will inhale soup like the roar of forty Niagaras, and crunch victuals like a half-hundred concrete mixers all running at once. Which—for you?

Or look at this sentence (OK, I promise, only one more) from *The Man With the Magic Eardrums.* Even though I have barely dipped my toe in Keeler's immense body of work, this is, so far, my favorite Keeler-ism to date:

> For he was to become now, as I was shortly to find, as coldly calculating as an adding machine sitting on the North Pole!

Harry Keeler also had a fondness for writing in phony foreign dialects or, more specifically characters who spoke English but whose heavy accents left no mystery to their ethnic origins. This allowed Keeler to go hogwild with commas, apostrophes and hyphens as he took full liberty as to the spellings and phonetics of ahh-soo-solly Chinese and "Harlem jive" African American-isms. Take this passage from *The Man With the Wooden Spectacles,* where Aunt Linda is reciting an important story (titled 'The Kidnapping of Wah Lee') to Elsa Colby that reveals a clue as to one of the other character's motivations:

"On'y aftah de gang dey has stringed him along wid fish-sto'y aftah fish-sto'y as to w'y de boy ain' retuhned. An' finally he sees he is gettin' stringed by—by expuhts!—an' so den he tell de po-leece. An' de po-leece, investigatin', fin' ev'dences dat Wah Lee's convuhsation wid his papa, dat day, wuz listen' in on. An dat de gang knew dat way dat Wah Lee wuz goin' into de pahk 'roun' dusk. And so lay fo' him. An' dat wuz de end ob dat chapter. Boy gone! Moneh gone! All ovah! Not one man cotched."

Try and guess what nationality this character from The Riddle of the Traveling Skull is:

"Well, wot' the bloomin' idea back o' all this confab, anyw'y? You shoot me—an' you've shot yoursel, your pop-in-law an' your woming all into the p'ypers. For this 'ere w'ite silk badge wot I'm wearin' says as 'ow I'm a delygyte from Lime'ouse to th' British H'Isles an' Colonial Possessings Convenching o' Skyte-an'-Chips an' Jellied Eeels Purveyors, to be 'eld in Vancoover, British Columbiar, three weeks from tomorrer. An' seein' as oo' I am, shootin' me wouldn't be good-like. No! For I've left a few notes in me 'otel drawer—an' me delygyte's pypers—in case o' accident like wot. So wot's keepin' us from gittin' down to business? You s'y you got that twenty tousand dollars? Orl right. P'y it over—like as 'e towld you you was to do."

Sometimes Keeler would write entire strings of chapters in this thick, clichéd dialect. Sometimes whole novels would be written in it! In *The Portrait of Jirjohn Cobb,* which Harry Stephen Keeler Society founder Richard Polt calls "...one of the most astoundingly unreadable novels ever written", the "action" is portrayed in long, drawn-out yarns told between four characters—two of whom sport page after page after page of impossible-to-decipher accents.

And there's another device Keeler loved to use; the Arabian Knights method of telling stories about people telling stories. Entire novels could take place in one room of a house between two characters telling each other what they had done that day and who they had talked to and what those people had said about others (*The Man With the Magic Eardrums*), or maybe between four characters sitting on a island while talking and listening to the radio (*The Portrait of Jirjohn Cobb*), or a protagonist coming across news clipping after news clipping in a person's secret drawer and reading the contents out loud. But, the stories that the characters would tell, or the news items they would read to get to the real story that Keeler was trying to tell were never boring. It's just a delightful mystery as to why Keeler liked to work this way.

Harry's writing was so strange that it often crossed into the territory of science fiction. Though he did write many short stories and a few novels that were officially classified as such, his strange "mysteries" often blurred the lines between the two genres. A few of his books were some of the most mind-bending metaphysical stuff this side of Phillip K. Dick. But where as Dick's speculative fiction about alternate realities was trippy and often contained sophisticated, satirical humor, Keeler's version of another space-time was more "kooky" or, "wacky" for lack of a better phrase. Check out this exposition of the detection theories of Xenius Jones, hero of Keeler's mad, multimedia opus *X. Jones—Of Scotland Yard* (1936) that Richard Polt highlighted on his Harry Stephen Keeler Society home page:

> So, Jones says, for all practical purposes, in a world of space and "time," the "wrinkles" resulting from the "crime-stress" appear, in reality, as "deviations." Deviations in human conduct: deviations from normal habit, custom, and be likened to an explosion, or concussion, the force of which radiates out in all directions—not just into the future, he cautions—but also into the past!—definitely deviating the paths and conduct not only of the chief actors—but of all those who have intimate contact with them—and who, by that very relationship, are thus displaced in 4 dimensions from the chief actors. The maximum possible "deviation" in a murder is, Jones points out, that of the murdered man—whose course is deviated, for the first time, from living to being dead!

Harry Keeler had a brilliant, fire-brained and creative mind that was mixed with a child-like, okay I'll say it, an almost insane way of wrapping words around an idea. Despite their migraine-inducing complexity and complete disregard for plausibility, Keeler's "webwork" plots do indeed make sense (well, for the most part they do). It's kind of hard to peg him into any genre—or even into the "good" or "bad" categories. His work is certainly like no other. Although he has been dismissed by many as a hack it must be said that it takes an intelligent mind to untangle one of his novels. His immense body of work, though long out of print and very hard to track down (in more ways than one), is inarguably worthy of further study, speculation and enjoyment.

I could go on for hundreds of pages and take up tons of bandwidth talking about Keeler, but why go on and on when others have explained his work so well? Absolutely check out William Poundstone's excellent introduction essay to Keeler and his work at the Harry Stephen Keeler Home Page then, plunge into Richard Polt's awesome Harry Stephen Keeler Society (of which I'm a member—heh heh). Founded in 1997, Polt has been valiantly uniting Keeler fanatics (whom are sprouting in ever growing numbers) worldwide and striving to "...maintain the memory of a man whose tangled dreams are part of the American heritage—whether America knows it or not!"

The Webwork World of Harry Stephen Keeler

Chris Mikul

"Probably no writer has ever lived whose work can compare to Keeler's..."

Publisher's blurb

I'd like to think that nothing really good in the way of culture ever dies. That no matter how obscure a book or film, a comedy sketch or piece of music, there will be some mad enthusiast out there somewhere keeping its memory, and the memory of its creator, alive. Sadly, I know this is not the case. Things disappear all the time. Virtually the whole of silent cinema is gone. TV stations routinely wipe the tapes of precious programs to save storage space. Songs which were once on everyone's lips are forgotten. And books slowly disintegrate as their authors' reputations fade.

Which brings me, in a roundabout way, and when dealing with the subject at hand, roundabout is the only way to go, to Harry Stephen Keeler, one of the oddest writers, and certainly the oddest writer of mystery stories, ever to sit down in front of a typewriter to, as he put it, blacken paper. Keeler, who produced a hundred or so supremely unlikely works, both published and unpublished, over five decades, is someone who almost —almost, thank goodness—slipped through the net.

How to convey the unique, the ineffable flavour of a Keeler novel? You could start with some of the titles. *The Skull of the Waltzing Clown*, *The Man with the Magic Eardrums*, *The Case of the Barking Clock, The Defrauded Yeggman*, *The Case of the Transposed Legs* or, a personal favourite, *Finger, Finger!*

Or the names he gives his characters. Opening *The Book with Orange Leaves*, we find Dr MacLingo Summerdyke, Come-Unto-God Whipplesecker, Isberian Jones, Scientific Mike

Gorgo, Professor Acors Persoon, Orcott Renfrew and Stefan Czeszcziczki (the Polish 'rapid calculator').

Or his subject matter. At first glance it looks like a normal mystery story, but there's something not quite right. Here is the dustjacket summary of *The Riddle of the Traveling Skull* (1934).

> Roger Pelton, wealthy manufacturer and with a beautiful daughter, was trying to be happy. But he could not rid himself of a corroding memory of his youth; and all his worst fears were confirmed when suddenly he came face to face with a human skull that was on travel.

Or perhaps just this aside, also from *Traveling Skull*.

> *I was thinking deeply in the meantime. My forehead was so corrugated, as I could sense by feeling alone, that an Eskimo's fur coat, sprinkled with nothing but Lux, could have been washed on it.*

The man whose forehead must have become equally corrugated thinking all this up, Harry Stephen Keeler, was born in 1890 and spent most of his life in Chicago, the setting for many of his novels. His career got off to a less than promising start when, as a young man, his mother had him declared insane and committed to an institution, an experience he writes about, with considerable effectiveness, in *The Spectacles of Mr. Cagliostro* (1926). Having secured his release from the asylum aged 22, Keeler studied engineering and worked briefly as an electrician in a steel mill. He began to submit stories to magazines, making his first sale in 1913. His first novel to see publication was *The Voice of the Seven Sparrows* in 1924.

Judging by the number of editions Keeler's early novels went through, he must have had a considerable following at one point (one of his most popular books, *Sing Sing Nights*, became the basis for two—reportedly excruciating—films released in 1934 and 1935, the latter, *The Mysterious Mr. Wong*, featuring Bela Lugosi). The quintessential Keeler novel is a densely plotted affair which he called a 'webwork', in which the seemingly disparate stories of numerous individuals weave and interweave, all eventually coming together at the book's climax as the mystery is solved in a thoroughly implausible yet meticulously crafted way. Rarely do his books begin with anything so mundane as a murder. *The Spectacles of Mr. Cagliostro*, for example, starts with the hero attending a reading of his father's will, in which it is stipulated that he must wear for a year a pair of ponderous leaden spectacles with oblong blue lenses (wills with absurd clauses were a favourite Keeler device). Often it is not even clear until well into a book what the central mystery is going to be.

Coincidences do not pop simply up in Keeler's novels, they are the engine which drives them. Keeler throws all the normal rules of logic right out the window, and after them goes any idea that the mystery writer should play fair with the reader, introducing the criminal early in the story, providing all the information necessary to solve the crime and so on. God help anyone who actually tried to solve a Keeler mystery. In one celebrated example, the killer in *X Jones—of Scotland Yard* isn't introduced until the very last line. (This is, incidentally, one of two 'documented' novels Keeler produced, in which the story is told through letters, police reports, newspaper clippings, diagrams and photographs, including one of a bearded lady and another of Keeler himself!)

Keeler's characters are cheerfully two-dimensional. His typical hero is a young man full of vim and pep and other qualities not generally associated with young men today, who falls into a wicked plot spun by a Machiavellian villain, but eventually wins out, often with the help of a pretty but resourceful girlfriend whom he'll be marrying soon after the last page. The chief function of a Keeler character is to talk, and talk, and talk. Sometimes almost an entire novel takes the form of a conversation between two characters who, in their own sweet time, elaborate the enormously complicated plot with endless digressions. Keeler sometimes sinks beneath the weight of his own verbiage (and his predilection for having his characters speak in completely unconvincing dialects doesn't help) but then he'll come up with a detail or incident so thoroughly outrageous that you remember you couldn't be reading anyone but Keeler. Raymond Chandler used to say, when in doubt, have a man come through the door with a gun. Keeler's more likely to send in a Chinese half-man.

> *The door opened, revealing as it did so, a strange figure—a half-man, no less, seated on a "rollerskate" cart—framed*

against the bit of outer hallway. But no ordinary half-man, this, for he was a Chinaman; quite legless, indeed, so far as the presence of even upper leg stumps went; but amply provided with locomotion of the gliding kind, anyway, in the matter of the unusually generous rubber-tired wheels under the platform cart. Suspended from his neck was a tray containing shoestrings, pencils, safety-razor blades, what not. In age he was about 44 ... his oblique eyes would have been declared, by an expert in Chinese faciology, to have been the obliquest in all New York.

—from *The Case of the 16 Beans* (1944)

Two of Keeler's obsessions are present in this passage—Orientals (and in particular Chinese) and physical deformity. One can only speculate about the reasons behind Keeler's love of freaks, who have walk-on parts in many of his novels, although it seems reasonable to suppose that Keeler's early spell in an institution inspired in him a sympathy for society's misfits (in *The Green Jade Hand*, for example, the mystery is solved in spectacular fashion by Simon Grundt, the mentally retarded fellow who mops the floors of the local police station). Other Keeler obsessions include skulls and trepanning (the ancient practice of drilling holes in the cranium), antique safes, skulls in antique safes, circuses and the fourth dimension.

Like Charles Fort, the pioneering chronicler of anomalous phenomena, Keeler scoured newspapers for odd stories which he could weave into his plots. Fort, who sported a prose style every bit as eccentric as Keeler's, spent years in libraries in the US and UK, ferreting out accounts of mysterious and paranormal events. He viewed the world as one vast organism, all of its parts interconnected in ways we can barely imagine. Here is Fort in *Wild Talents* (1932).

Sometimes I am a collector of data, and only a collector, and am likely to be gross and miserly, piling up notes, pleased with numerically adding to my stores. Other times I have joys, when unexpectedly coming upon an outrageous story that may not be altogether a lie, or upon a macabre little thing that may make some reviewer of my more or less good works mad. But always there is present a feeling of unexplained relations of events...

> *In Hyde Park, London, an orator shouts: "What we want is no king and no law! How we get it will be, not with ballots, but with bullets!"*
>
> *Far away in Gloucestershire, a house that dates back to Elizabethan times unaccountably bursts into flames.*

Compare this to Keeler, in *The Skull of the Waltzing Clown* (1935).

> *People—and everything they do—all lie in a webwork affair of some sort. In other words, as poker players would probably put it: The cards are always stacked. A man picks up a toothpick in Havana, Cuba, at 4:31½ P.M. on April 30, 1927—and for no other reason whatever owns the Empire State Building in New York City at 9:26¾ A.M. February 29, 1942.*

Fort's view of the universe is more obviously metaphysical than that of Keeler who, like the good engineering student he was, saw the world as a sort of vastly complicated machine which can be taken to pieces. What they share is a love of fantastic explanation. Fort delighted in spinning absurd theories to explain his anomolies. Keeler, in explaining the surreal situations his characters face, builds ever higher towers of invention.

As Keeler's webwork plots grew more complicated, his novels grew longer and longer. *The Box from Japan*, a phantasmagoria published in 1932 but set in 1942, clocks in at a whopping 765 pages. He was soon writing vast works on continuous rolls of paper, which had to be split into several novels for publication. Like a biologist transferring cultures from one Petri dish to another, he'd cut a chunk of text from one book and grow another one around it. This means that certain characters and situations recur in different books, although always seen from a slightly different angle. Keeler also loved to throw into his novels stories by his wife, Hazel, an illustrator and writer of romantic fiction whom he married in 1919. She was a conventional writer compared to him (though that's not saying much) but he thought she was wonderful and once created a whole novel sequence around one of her short stories.

Keeler's sales began to slide in the late '30s and he was dropped by his American publisher, Dutton, in 1942. A small publishing house named Phoenix issued a further nine—ruthlessly edited—Keeler titles, the last in 1948. His British publisher, Ward Lock, stuck with him a little longer, issuing his last book to be published in English, *Stand By—London Calling*, in 1952. After that, the only new Keelers to appear were in translation in Spain and Portugal, where he had a small following. Keeler put his dwindling sales down to the fact that he wasn't serving up the sex and violence that readers now seemed to want, but he could not and would not change his style, and, published or not, he kept churning out novels.

In 1960 Hazel died, an event which completely devastated Keeler. He gave up writing, sold hundreds of copies of his books in English and other languages (he had inscribed them all to Hazel) and sank into a deep depression, but somehow managed to pull himself out of it. In 1963 he married his former secretary, Thelma, and sat back down in front of the typewriter again.

Keeler remained dedicated to his own peculiar muse right to the end, all the time convinced of the importance of his work. In a letter to fellow writer T.S. Stribling, one of a number written in the wake of Hazel's death, he writes:

> *No one ever thinks of a novel as something written to enrich some single lone reader somewhere who* needs *that novel badly at a critical time in his life. And who, reading it, and changing the current of his thoughts, thereafter makes altered decisions, and his altered decisions cause altered decisions in people connecting to him in space-time, and their decisions alter those of others, and lo, the pattern of the whole world is altered, i.e. it becomes World X-143-a instead of World Y-243-b. All from a single book!*

Clearly, Keeler conceived his own life as part of a webwork plot.

Harry Stephen Keeler completed his final novel, *The Scarlet Mummy*, in 1966, and died the following year, leaving behind enough unpublished manuscripts to fill twenty books.

And that was very nearly that. Keeler, for all his surpassing strangeness, made little impression on critics of crime fiction, and would almost certainly have been forgotten had not the writer Francis M. Nevins taken an interest in him. In 1972

Nevins began publishing a series of articles in the *Journal of Popular Culture* which introduced a new generation to Keeler. William Poundstone was inspired to seek out Keeler's widow, Thelma, helped rescue Keeler's remaining manuscripts, and set up a Keeler home page on the Web. This in turn inspired Richard Polt to found the Harry Stephen Keeler Society, which issues the excellent bimonthly *Keeler News*.

It is the Internet, which was once supposed to sound the death knell for books, that is most responsible for rescuing Keeler—and countless other authors—from obscurity. Previously, you could have spent your life fruitlessly searching secondhand bookshops for out-of-print Keelers. Now they regularly turn up on the book search services, although be warned, prices have been rising steadily of late. And if you can't afford original Keelers, Fender Tucker's Ramble House has embarked on the ambitious project of issuing all of the master's works in paperback, including novels which had previously been published only in Spanish or Portuguese, and others which have never seen the light of day at all.

Of course it's quite fitting that the master of the webwork novel has been saved by the World Wide Web. I'm sure that Keeler, who loved gadgets and wrote about intercontinental 3D colour TV in *The Box From Japan*, would have heartily approved.

William Poundstone's

HARRY STEPHEN KEELER
Home Page

It was like trying to think about the square root of minus zero.

—Harry Stephen Keeler

HARRY STEPHEN KEELER (1890-1967) is one of the strangest writers who ever lived. In his time, he was pegged as a mystery novelist who also wrote some science fiction. Today, if you've heard of him at all, it's as the Ed Wood of mystery novelists, a writer reputed to be so bad he's good. Actually, no genre, nor "camp," can much suggest what Keeler is all about. Take some typical Keeler situations:

~ A man is found strangled to death in the middle of a lawn, yet there are no footprints other than his own. Police suspect the "Flying Strangler-Baby," a killer midget who disguises himself as a baby and stalks victims by helicopter. (*X. Jones of Scotland Yard*, 1936)

~ Someone killed an antique dealer just so he could steal the face—only the face—from a surrealist painting of "The Man from Saturn." (*The Face of the Man from Saturn*, 1933)

~ A woman's body disappears while taking a steam bath. Only her head and toes, sticking out of the steam cabinet, remain. (*The Case of the Transparent Nude, 1958*)

~ Because of a clause in a will, a character has to wear a pair of hideous blue glasses constantly for a whole year. This is so that he will eventually see a secret message that is visible only with the glasses. (*The Spectacles of Mr. Cagliostro*, 1929)

~ A poem leads the protagonist to a cemetery specializing in circus freaks and the grave of "Legga, the Human Spider," a woman with four legs and six arms. Legga was born in Canton, China, and died in Canton, Ohio. (*The Riddle of the Traveling Skull*, 1934)

~ A disgruntled phone company employee calls every man in Minneapolis, telling him the morning papers will name him as the secret husband of convicted murderess Jemimah Cobb, who runs a whorehouse specializing in women with physical abnormalities. (*The Man With the Magic Eardrums*, 1939)

~ Every resident of "Idiot's Valley" is mentally retarded and packs a gun. (Several novels; Idiot's Valley is Keeler's Yoknapatawpha County.)

Keeler's plots are so go-to-hell weird, they sound like a certain type of "serious" literature. But they're not!

Biography

Who was Harry Stephen Keeler? After modest commercial success in the 1930s, Keeler all but vanished from the literary universe until his rediscovery by mystery novelist, critic, and attorney Francis M. Nevins, Jr. Starting in 1969, Nevins wrote an excellent series of articles on Keeler in the *Journal of Popular Culture*. These articles (to which this discussion is much indebted) were virtually the only sources on Keeler's life and oeuvre until recently. Nevins wrote of Keeler:

> His universe is full of the grotesque, the deformed and the rotten, but is not less amply stocked with the wildly hilarious. His targets—the military, the state, capitalism, racism—and his special interests—the occult, Eastern philosophy, science fiction—make him specially relevant to the nightmarish Sixties and Seventies which have forgotten him, while his meticulous crafted and joyously zany stories render him at the same time delightfully irrelevant to the mess and horror of the real world. Engaging and escapist at the same time, a gray mouse to the public world but an outrageous exuberant maniac behind the typewriter, he was always his own man, there was never anyone like him before or since, and I doubt that the planet could produce another to match him. He was the sublime nutty genius of American literature, and as long as boundless creativity is cherished, so will Harry Stephen Keeler be.

Largely because of the Nevins articles, Keeler acquired a cult following among those who could find his books. That was no given, for everything Keeler wrote had been out of print for years. Editions issued by E.P. Dutton and Phoenix Press are prized collector's items among the few who know, or care, who Keeler is. Only about 2,000 of the later Phoenix Press titles were printed. Only a fraction survive. Keeler never made it into paperback. Many of the Keeler books you find are hardcover reprints for the commercial lending library market (way back when, people paid to rent books the way they rent videos now).

Harry Stephen Keeler was born the same year as Agatha Christie (1890) and lived in Chicago most of his life. His mother committed him to an insane asylum when he was a child. This experience doubtless accounts for his affection for insane asylums, mental illness, and characters who are unjustly committed to an asylum in his fiction. Keeler went to work as an electrician for a steel mill at the age of 22. He began selling stories to the pulp magazines and edited one such publication (*10-Story Book*). Eventually he published novels (first in Britain, then in the U.S.) He churned out over 70 novels, plus many shorter pieces.

Keeler cannot easily be pigeonholed as an "outsider." He was published by big houses internationally, and he was a pulp magazine editor as well. Keeler is usually called a mystery writer. He did write plenty of sure-enough mysteries. Be warned, though, that his work bears no more relation to Christie or Hammett than does the phone book of Idiot's Valley. Although much of Keeler is steeped in the tradition of classical puzzle mysteries, woe to the reader who thinks he is going to guess the denouement. *The Ace of Spades Murder* is a whodunit in which the character who will be revealed guilty is introduced, for the first time, on the third-to-last page of the book.

Incredibly, Keeler tops that in *X. Jones—of Scotland Yard*. The guilty party is not mentioned until the last sentence of the last page of this 448-page story. The culprit is . . . well, to "play fair," I'm going put it in a footnote.[1] But face it, *X. Jones of Scotland Yard* is out of print—permanently. Unless you're planning to haunt libraries and rare book stores until you find it, you might as well read the footnote.

Keeler wrote other genre fiction: thrillers, historical romances, and science fiction. In the latter category is a remarkable short story, "John Jones' Dollar." The premise is that a guy puts a dollar in a savings account where it grows, through compound interest, to such a fortune that, centuries later, it is used to found a socialist utopia. This is possibly Keeler's best-known story and would rate extensive anthologization if the writing wasn't so bad, even by stiff Keeler standards of badness. I don't know enough about the history of science fiction to say if this clever idea was original with Keeler, but he wrote it in 1914 and the idea is now a sort of s-f cliche (Douglas Adams spoofs it in *The Restaurant at the End of the Universe*).

Even Keeler's publishers didn't know what to make of him. The jacket copy of most of his books is not much different from that of any mid-list detective novel. They certainly didn't try to sell Keeler as being camp. The only concession to Keeler's extreme strangeness is occasional language to the effect: "a story such as only Keeler could write." Amen.

Keeler created, and was seemingly the sole practitioner of, a genre he called the "webwork novel." This is a story in which diverse characters and events are connected by a strings of wholly implausible coincidences.

That's interesting because, well, you're not supposed to do that. Most Western literature avoids coincidences. The author is permitted a single unlikely premise, and then everything is supposed to follow inevitably from that. Keeler's stories are coincidence porn. Coincidence is very much the *raison d'etre.*

Towards the end of the novel, all the subplots mesh together to produce a stunning surprise ending. In order to achieve that effect, Keeler throws plausibility out the window. He uses what amount to plot "wild cards." A crazy clause in a will requires a character to [fill in the blank!] in order to inherit a fortune. An obscure religious cult believes such and such. A

---

[1] Editor's Note: Bill Poundstone is nice enough to reveal the murderer's identity, but I'm not. You'll have to buy the Ramble House edition.

nutty law requires something else. Now don't think that Keeler worried himself about whether there really was such a law or belief, or whether the will could stand up in court.

Keeler took the webwork novel seriously enough to turn out a detailed manual on webwork plotting, complete with insanely confusing diagrams. Did anyone actually read this and try to use it?

Keeler's narrative style is no less incredible than his plots. Indeed, the two can scarcely be distinguished, for his writing is essentially all plot. Characterization, description, dialog, and use of language hardly exist in the conventional sense. Every paragraph hits you over the head with new and implausible information. There is little room for anything else.

In many of his later works, Keeler takes this daft aesthetic a step further. Despite this total concentration on plot, almost nothing happens within the time-frame of the narrative. It's all digressions about what happened off stage! Again, that's not something they advise you to do in writing courses. The effect is so baroque that it goes way beyond usual notions of "bad writing." It is more in the spirit of Oulipo than commercial fiction, good or bad.

Keeler's characters are mechanical contrivances. I mean that not, particularly, in a pejorative sense. It is simply the way a Keeler story works. Each character is a compressed spring poised to serve its role. Free will hardly exists. The perfect Keeler character is a clockwork automaton; the perfect Keeler plot is a pinball machine.

In one novel, there's a character named Suing Sophie. Sophie goes on transpacific cruise ships, striking up an acquaintance with a single man on board. When the ship gets into port, Sophie bids her male friend farewell by loudly exclaiming, "Yes! I'll marry you!" then rushing off. Now the man has not proposed marriage. But Sophie has made sure that there are plenty of witnesses to her farewell. Soon afterward, the man is greeted with a breach of promise lawsuit for failing to marry Sophie. In the settlement, Sophie collects a huge award, which she then uses to travel to the cannibal isles of the South Pacific; specifically to islands whose inhabitants have recently been converted by Christian missionaries. There Sophie convinces them of the errors of their recent conversion, and reconverts them as practicing Jews.

You know all this and more about Sophie; before it's over, Keeler probably gets more plot mileage out of Sophie than Flaubert does out of Emma Bovary. The difference is that Sophie does not appear in the action of Keeler's novel at all. Other characters just allude to her.

In Agatha Christie at her sharpest, everyone is a suspect. In Keeler, everything is a McGuffin, that is to say, an essentially meaningless token that drives the plot. Because the webwork novel is so fundamentally phony, everything is, sooner or later, revealed to be irrelevant. A typical Keeler plot is a fractal shaggy dog story, filled with digressions, and digressions within digressions, that are themselves shaggy dog stories.

As in a shaggy dog story, the truest synopsis of a Keeler plot is: Never mind.

These webwork novels tended to be long. *The Box from Japan* is 765 pages, and it's set in awfully small type. Some novels were so long that his publishers insisted on breaking them into more manageable chunks. What was originally a 350,000-word novel was issued in three volumes as *The Marceau Case* (1936), *X. Jones of Scotland Yard* (1936), and *The Wonderful Scheme of Mr. Christopher Thorne* (1937). In *The Matilda Hunter Mystery*, the publisher inserted a coupon the reader was supposed to fill out his guess as to the guilty party and return. The coupon appeared toward the end of the book, after all the necessary clues had been revealed. Dutton did that for all its mysteries back then. The difference was that, in Matilda Hunter, there was still a couple hundred of pages after the coupon.

How did Keeler create such a volume of densely plotted fiction? According to Nevins, Keeler was an avid collector of newspaper clippings of bizarre events. When he started a story, he would grab a handful of clippings at random and try to figure some way of linking them all together. That sounds like something the Dadaists might have talked about doing, and maybe tried once. Who knew that in Chicago Harry Keeler was turning out novel after novel that way?

Another part of Keeler's "method" was recycling. Many Keeler novels are shamelessly padded with undigested inclusions of short stories or novellas that, not surprisingly, Keeler had sold to the pulps long before he started working on the novel (classic advice to free-lancers: sell your material to more than one market!)

This happens in more than story: A character turns out to be a writer and asks another character to read this story he's written to tell him if it's worth publishing. Sure, I'll take a look at it, he says. And the next chapter is the story.

Possibly the oddest thing about Keeler's writing is the odd subject matter. In novel after novel, skulls keep cropping up—human skulls—which are not incidental but are rather the center of gravity of the plot. It's one thing to use a skull once. Then you'd figure, all right, I'll find something else for the next book. Not Keeler. Skulls are so important that they end up in some Keeler titles: *The Riddle of the Traveling Skull, The Skull of the Waltzing Clown*.

Trepanning—the obsolete practice of drilling holes in the skull for supposed therapeutic purpose—well, that keeps cropping up, too. It makes you wonder if Keeler had the procedure done (as far as I know, he didn't).

Bizarre racial themes are another of Keeler's obsessions. *The Case of the Crazy Corpse* begins with the police dredging a coffin out of Lake Michigan. Inside is a nude body, the top half of a Chinese woman, the bottom half of a black man. The two halves are joined with a green gum. In The *Ace of Spades Murder*, a black man is stabbed to death with a jeweled dagger on which is impaled the ace of spades. The detective has to solve the crime before a law placing a statute of limitations on the murder of a black person takes effect. Interracial marriages are a great deal more frequent in Keeler's world than in the America of the 1930s, and Keeler has a positive mania for linking a black person to an Asian (by marriage, green gum or otherwise).

Incredibly, there are political passages in Keeler's writing. These make it clear enough that Keeler was a critic of racism. Perhaps he even thought of these screwball race plots as having a "message." That said, Keeler shared his contemporaries' politically incorrect affection for dialect.

Mainstream fiction limited dialect to minor, Step 'n' Fetchit characters, who provide comic relief and then surrender the stage to the white people. In Keeler, one is aghast to find that a character who talks like this—

> *Yassuh, Ah ca'ied a boxed telumscope to de 'spress comp'ny fo' de man whut usta fix 'em in dah.*

—will be narrating a substantial portion of a very long novel. Any reader mad enough to attempt to guess the murderer in a Keeler story has to sift "clues" from Keeler's guaranteed inauthentic versions of Harlem jive, dialect-comedian Yiddish, and flied-lice Chinese.

I suppose the quintessential Keeler obsession is freaks, and especially, the whorehouse of freaks. There is hardly a Keeler novel that does not have at least one character who is a circus freak or a civilian with a notable physical abnormality. A couple of stories share the specific element of a bordello specializing in a multicultural assortment of hunchbacks, bearded women, and polydactls. It is not much of a stretch to imagine a literary writer using such a motif today. But again and again and again? In the Keeler universe, it would seem, these bordellos are common.

Much of Keeler's writing is genuinely hilarious. You are never given the luxury of being sure it is supposed to be. Take some of his character names:

- Criorcan Mulqueeny [corrupt political boss]
- Screamo the Clown [dead clown]
- Scientifico Greenlimb [science-fiction writer]
- Wolf Gladish [evil circus impresario]
- State Attorney Foxhart Cubycheck
- Or try this one [name of a "man of the future" in a time travel story]:

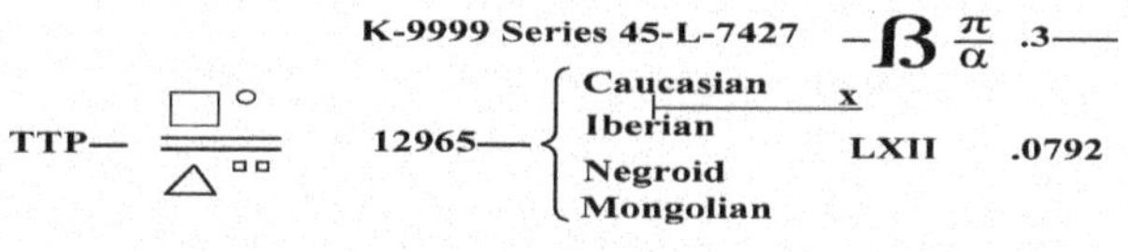

K-9999 Series 45-L-7427 —ß $\frac{\pi}{\alpha}$ .3—

TTP— □ ○ / △ □□ 12965— { Caucasian / Iberian / Negroid / Mongolian } x LXII .0792

These are funny in a subtle way: You get the impression that if a stupid person was trying to come up with "funny" names, he might come up with these names—which are funny because they fail to be funny. You're laughing at the idea that someone would think these names are funny, rather than at the names themselves.

Of course, in a larger sense, these names are funny, for the reason above. The question is whether Keeler is the true naif, or the comic impersonating a naif. It's hard to say, and the answer may not be 100 percent either way.

Keeler sometimes supplies detailed road directions or family histories and has the characters recite them in full several times during a novel. Often this ends up being marvelously funny. That's tough to pull off, and I suspect that the humor must be intentional.

I am pretty sure that Keeler did not see himself as being in the business of turning out parodies of the mystery genre, though. He took his writing seriously enough. Some of what strikes us as funny (skulls in novel after novel) almost surely wasn't intended as such. Likewise numerous memorable passages of bad writing:

> Pardon me, my son, if I use the shenjiji dialect, almost as different from regular Japanese as Welsh is from English.

> Redwayne TerVyne, known to the Chinese of America, because of his passion for Chinese items in his nationally syndicated column, as "The Great White Prynose," and to New York in general as "The Keyhole," hopped out of his luxurious $10,000 purple car in front of the row of de luxe art shops on Fifth Avenue.

> And Angus MacWhorter, left alone with his colourless ascetic furniture, and his diorama, stroked his chin in helpless futility.

Yet another part of Keeler's charm is his unmitigatedly bad titles: *Finger, Finger!, The Yellow Zuri, The Amazing Web, Find the Clock,* and *The Face of the Man From Saturn.*

Keeler collaborated with both his wives. His first wife, Hazel Goodwin (married in 1919) was a professional writer, a competent purveyor of pulp fiction. Keeler adored Hazel's writing. Many of his books incorporate short stories of hers.

There is always a note telling you which chapters are Hazel's and which are Harry's, but you don't need it. For us Keeler fans, the story stops dead when Hazel takes the baton.

> Coroner Bowers was a stocky man in a wrinkled brown suit, and his face was ruddy and seamed. He had hair like sifted ashes . . .

(This from Hazel's first full page in the collaboration, *The Strange Will.*)

There's nothing at all wrong with Hazel's writing. It's easy to see why some critics preferred her to her kooky husband. It's just that lots of people did what Hazel Goodwin did, and some did it better. Harry was the only one who's ever wanted to do what he did.

One of more unaccountable obsessions of Keeler's life was Hazel's short story, "Spangles," (originally published 1930). Keeler liked it so much that he built six novels around the story's eminently forgettable central character, circus owner Angus MacWhorter. Now if you read "Spangles" (which, for ease of reference, is included as a chapter in two of the six novels), it's perfectly ordinary. From this unlikely beginning, Keeler constructed a series around MacWhorter (who, in Keeler's hands, is every bit as paper-thin a character as everyone else in Keeler).

Most critics didn't like Keeler much. A New York Times critic once said "All Keeler's novels are written in Choctaw."

Two Z-movie versions of Keeler's work were produced. Bottom-of-the-line Monogram Studios made *Sing Sing Nights*, based on Keeler's novel of the same name, in 1934. *The Mysterious Mr. Wong* (based on a story from the same novel) appeared the year later and starred Bela Lugosi. I found the latter on videocassette. It's awful—not amusingly awful the way Keeler might be said to be, just plain awful awful.

Some of Keeler's books were dedicated to pet cats. One is dedicated to one of his own fictional characters.

Keeler's Last Years

In mid career, Keeler's readership dried up and blew away. His relationship with Dutton deteriorated. Conceivably, part of the reason was *The Peacock Fan* (1941), which might be considered Keeler's Pierre, with its fantastically paranoid depiction of the publishing industry. Publishers Simon and Dolliver Vinnedge not only write trick clauses into their authors' contracts but actually impersonate various characters in an attempt to get one of their authors sent to the gallows. *The Peacock Fan* was Keeler's last book with Dutton.

Keeler moved to Phoenix Press, now remembered as a publisher of last resort. But even Phoenix dropped him in 1948.

Keeler was publishing in Britain until 1953. *Stand By—London Calling* was the last Keeler book to appear in English. Keeler's later works were published only in Spanish and Portuguese translation (!)—or finally, not at all.

Why was Keeler published in Spain and Portugal? Did Keeler strike some responsive chord in the Iberian soul? Probably not. Keeler had been published in Spain and Portugal during his salad days. Nevins speculates that Keeler continued to be published there mainly through editorial inertia. Under Franco, novels published in Spain had to pass a censorship board. In that regard, Keeler's lack of sex may have been a plus.

Thus such gems as *The Case of the Crazy Corpse* saw print only as *O Caso do Cadaver Endiabrado*.

Hazel died in 1960. Keeler was so devastated that he stopped working. He took all or most of his books to a used book dealer to sell.

Keeler bounced back in 1963, when he married Thelma Rinaldo. Thelma had been his secretary years earlier, and in fact Keeler had once contemplated leaving Hazel for her. Keeler began writing again,, even though American publishers were no longer interested in his work. He left 16 complete unpublished manuscripts at his death, and a dozen in various stages of completion.

By the accounting of Nevins, the completed but unpublished-in-his lifetime works of Keeler amount to 1.3 million words, enough to fill about 20 average-sized mystery novels. The later works published in Spanish or Portuguese translation account for another 1.1 million, or about 16 volumes. In his later years, Keeler also published a mimeographed newsletter for a very small circle of friends. It contained biographical notes, philosophical musings, and cat lore. Keeler died in 1967.

My Search for Keeler

I'm not at all sure what it would have been like to meet Harry Stephen Keeler. A photo which appears in one novel show him as a pale, fiftyish, blonde man, looking like a high-school shop teacher.

Keeler was long dead by the time I heard of him, but a few years back, I found a "Thelma Keeler" in the Chicago phone book. I told the friend who had first told me about Keeler. We got in touch with Thelma. She was living in Chicago, in a housing project according to Nevins. We corresponded for a couple of years. Thelma was almost blind by then and had to have another person answer her letters.

My friend and I told her we had founded a "Harry Stephen Keeler Appreciation Society." This was a white lie. We had tried to interest friends in Keeler, but no one was. We voted another friend in as treasurer of the "Society." She hated Keeler.

It turned out that Thelma had a library of Harry's books and was willing to sell them. My friend purchased them. These weren't Keeler's original copies of his books (which he had sold after Hazel's death) but books he had acquired since. Some were signed with a dedication to Thelma. Many were in Spanish or Portuguese. Thus my friend acquired what has to be the finest Keeler collection on the West Coast.

We learned a few biographical facts from this purchase. Based on dedications, "Chirp Chirp Chirp" was Harry's "pet" name for Thelma. One dedication mentions "John Barleycorn" with the implication that Harry had had a battle with the bottle.

Harry's books included a clipped ad for a catalog of marital aids. This read: "Complete mutual satisfaction for men and women/Enjoy complete and fulfilling martial pleasures. There's no need NOW to lose out! True satisfaction for both men and women." This advertised a 12-page catalog of Universal Sales of Hollywood, CA.

Thelma mentioned that she still had some manuscripts of Harry's and asked if we wanted to see them (!!!) She sent them to us. They included a rough manuscript and notes for an unpublished novel titled "Murder of a Giant." We promised to try to write a treatment for a screenplay—in fact this was one of our society's goals—but we never got around to it.

The manuscript package included a letter, or maybe a script, in which Harry was trying to convince his wife (the first wife, Hazel?) to contribute material for "Murder of a Giant."

My friend and I tried our darnedest to promote Keeler. Bill Pronzini had just written a popular book, *Gun in Cheek*, about "bad" detective writers. Keeler rated a short mention. It was practically the first time Keeler had been mentioned anywhere since the Nevins articles. So we sent off a letter to Pronzini. He responded with a very nice letter. He said he would direct any queries about Keeler to our society. We got one. It was from a guy who said he had tried to interest publishers in a biography of Keeler. No takers.

We corresponded with Francis Nevins, and met him when he was in Los Angeles. He said he had tried to interest publishers in reprinting Keeler's works with no luck. He doubted that Keeler would ever be published again.

We asked Nevins if he had been influenced by Keeler in his own writing. His answer was a slightly shocked, "I hope not."

I wrote letters to several members of Congress, trying to get support for a postage stamp commemorating the centennial of Keeler's birth (HSK 1890-1990). Not that it would ever happen, of course, but I thought it would be swell to read their responses. It was. Several wrote back—all favorably. One was Jesse Helms. (Piss Christ, no. Keeler commemorative, yes!) Another was Alan K. Simpson. The Simpson letter was particularly good because he said quite a bit about Keeler, calling him a "great American author."

No Keeler commemorative stamp has been issued—so far.

We nonetheless gave a party to celebrate the Keeler centennial on November 3, 1990. About forty people came. Only a few had read Keeler, and no one besides my friend and I liked him. To get people to come, we told them that it didn't matter that they hadn't read Keeler, and the party really wasn't about Keeler. Of course, this was a lie worthy of Suing Sophie.

We took pictures of groups of people holding up Keeler books and pretending to read them. The plan was to send these photos to Thelma to show her that, yes, today's young people still read and discuss Keeler. We never got around to sending them. We were afraid that she would ask what ever happened to that screenplay treatment.

Anyway, I thought that Keeler, as master of the webwork novel, ought to have his own web page. So here it is, Harry.

The Keeler Revival

A Keeler revival, of a scope that would have seemed fantastic just a few years ago, is underway. It started with the founding of a Harry Stephen Keeler Society by Richard Polt in

1997. Thanks to the Web, the membership spans the globe. Members receive a subscription to a handsomely produced Keeler News. The Society's website includes links and cover art from nearly all of Keeler's published works.

Even more incredibly, Keeler is back in print. Ramble House, run by Keeler aficianado Fender Tucker, has issued paperback editions of dozens of Keeler titles, including those left unpublished at Keeler's death. (A downside of the Keeler "rediscovery" is that used book dealers often ask outrageously high prices for the old hardcovers.)

In recent years, Keeler has been profiled in the *Village Voice* and *The Wall Street Journal.*

Keeler's papers are at Columbia University.

Web Pages: How H. S. Keeler Wrote Certain of His Books

Ed Park

Harry Stephen Keeler (1890-1967) wrote prose the only way it should be written, that is, ecstatically. Perhaps too ecstatically for popular tastes; though Dutton published him until the early '40s, by 1954 his books were appearing only in Spanish and Portuguese translations. His ostensible whodunits contain tales within tales, digressions on everything from the halftone process to Ouspenskian philosophy, and detours into the outer districts of dialect. (His 765-page *The Box From Japan,* by some lights the longest mystery novel ever written, features a monologue by a German-Mexican descendant of a Russo-Japanese War hero.) Even his plain English—the sturdy phonemes of his beloved Chicago—is none too plain. A typical sentence from The Mysterious Mr. I (1938) reveals certain punctuational fondnesses:

> And here was I—at 4:20 in the morninq—with not less than the tail-end—if not the tail itself—of certain information by which $100,000 might be made to change hands—if and maybe, to be sure!—sitting in the office of MacLeish MacPherson, M.D.!

Yet there was method to his madness, if one believes his extended 1928 study, "The Mechanics and Kinematics of Web-Work Plot Construction." Serialized in eight numbers of The Author & Journalist, it may be the most impractical how-to ever written, a reminder that those; who can (and do) shouldn't necessarily teach.

The piece has its outrageous charms. In technicalese that betrays his engineering background, with illustrations that look like geometry proofs or parsing sticks gone haywire, Keeler explicates his "web-work" theory, anatomizing the "15 elemental plot combinations," from a simple two-thread affair (a Venn diagram close-up) to the Scheherezade plot (a sort of runic hootenanny). A brief account of a character diverted from a route is rendered unhelpfully as "His path has changed from B-B' to B-B"." He decrees the "Keeler Law" (protagonist must have numerous interactions from start, thus providing threads for later weaving). On a metaphysical level, Keeler (depicted as a spider on one A&J cover) suggests that the doing of web-work "fills the gaps in one's spirit which rebels at the looseness of life as it apparently is."

The showstopper is a two-page graph of *The Voice of the Seven Sparrows* (1924), his first published novel. This skeletal representation looks like a subway conductor's nightmare—timetable and station chart rolled into one.[2] Lines—parabolic or straight, solid or dashed—represent characters ("Sarah Fu") or objects ("Sheet of carbon paper"). Though the narrative clocks in at roughly four days, Keeler considers its chronology to begin with Confucius—and thus locates the left margin 500 years in the past. A detailed key to the 80 intersections ("And then Absalom!" roads plot point 76—did Faulkner subscribe to A&J?) itself reads like the short story of some itemizing postmodernist.

The public response could be characterized as one of irked bewilderment. (Perhaps Keeler sensed this earlier; in installment four he states, with a hypnotist's conviction, "Your reading this very article is changing your course and mine by measurable degree: either your ideas are being modified and shifted to some extent, or else you are evolving antagonism toward my theories.") Keeler does point out, albeit in the very last chapter, that he himself didn't actually diagram his stories in this way—a pedagogical misstep, to be sure. Professional authors piped up in later A&Js, with the aptly named Oscar Friend tendering an olive, branch entitled "How About a Compromise?"

What's absent in "Web-Work" is the author's motivation for writing in the first place—the Jamesian *donnée,* Nabokov's "cosmic synchronization." What got Keeler's silk glands spinning? In 1947, he revealed "My 'MillionDollar' Plot-Inventing Secret!" to Writer's Digest; it involved extracting a sizable "chunk" from a finished story and weaving a new book around

---

[2] Editor's Note: The webwork diagram is reproduced in full in an Afterword to the Ramble House edition of *The Voice of the Seven Sparrows.*

it—a potentially endless cycle of self-borrowing, the literary equivalent of a sourdough starter. The writer and law professor Francis M. Nevins, a seminal Keelerite, told the Voice that this practice is quite visible in Keeler's manuscripts—long passages lifted from one novel appear, sometimes nearly verbatim, in a later MS.

But the question of how there came to be chunks in the first place is not addressed. Legend has it that Keeler drew randomly from news clippings and wove the disparate accounts together. (If this is true, his artificial method resembles the *procédé* of Roussel, who would take two sentences, nearly identical in spelling but not sense, and write the only story that could link the first to the last.) In his novels, this possible aleatory origin is not always well hidden; a Keeler chapter has enough coincidences to make Paul Auster blush.

A critic of an earlier version of "WebWork" called his m.o. "the last word in formula." But Keeler's best novels are his most audacious, freaks of homegrown modernism in which the formula lies buried beneath a barrage of sheer (if spastic) style. *The Marceau Case* and *X Jones—Of Scotland Yard,* both from 1936, offer divergent solutions to the same murder case—one with such improbable details (lawn mower, flying dwarf) as to border on slapstick. You can tease out the interconnections, develop them into a web-work chart if you like, but you will have wasted the better part of your youth. The books have an irresistible drive, a capacity for invention that borders on stream of consciousness, except that there's no single narrative voice. The books, dossier-like, consist entirely of cablegrams and letters, diagrams and vaudeville ads, scraps of shoot music and penny dreadfuls and ersatz Winchell columns—not to mention photos, including one of Keeler himself, smiling as if caught breaking his own laws.[3]

---

[3] Ed Park's Note: And, perhaps, sharing the proto-Oulipian orbit of Roussel. According to Mark Ford's Raymond Roussel and the Republic of Dreams, "While, on one level the *procédé* reveals all words—or fragments of words—to have potential double meanings, on another it imposes on them the strictest possible laws of connection." The Marceau books hinge—or do they?—upon a single line of a manuscript, which reads: " 'Blimey, 'Erb! Little?' Lu Caslow's dreary eyes". Is the culprit Meyer B. Li? Or a midget funambulist named Little Lucas?

If the multimedia onslaught of the Marceau books suggests an unhinged U.S.A., then *The Mysterious Mr. I* and *The Chameleon* (back in print after over 60 years, thanks to a small press called Ramble House) weigh in as a lower-brow Ulysses. For "ineluctable modality of the visible," read "$100,000 reward!"; for a single Dublin day, an October 13 Chicagoland of 22-word newspaper headlines and meticulously rendered humor-magazine offices. Our hero, the *ne plus ultra* of unreliable narrators, gives a different name (med student George Spelvin; guest lecturer Scopester Glendenning) to everyone he meets; the catch is that even the reader can't pin down his identity. Like an amphetamine Penelope with her daily shroud, he builds up each persona, only to unravel it a few minutes later; Keeler, master of the web-work, reads best when he seems to be falling apart.

As the Plot Thickens

It's Time to Rediscover Harry Stephen Keeler, the Ed Wood of Mystery Literature

John Marr

Since Edgar Allan Poe invented the modern mystery story in 1841, everyone from functional illiterates to Nobel Prize winners have tried their hands at the form, creating everything from brilliant literature to unreadable tripe. But few stories have even remotely resembled the works of Harry Stephen Keeler. In his 50-odd—make that quite odd—mysteries, Keeler created a madly hysterical alternate universe populated by eccentric characters, peculiar events, and seemingly random insanity.

Keeler has been out of print in English since 1953, but a small, growing cult keeps his memory alive. Still, Keeler is not to be confused with a brilliant writer. His style is weird, idiosyncratic, occasionally incomprehensible, and often idiomatic to the point of idiocy. A typical character is described as having "an eternal bump of investigative fervor, if not a downright hypertrophied curiosity." Everyone always does things "A to Izzard." His books are flawed by lengthy digressions into crackpot philosophy and archaic technology and by pages of unintelligible, wretchedly inauthentic phonetic renderings of ethnic dialogue that confound even his staunchest supporters.

His characters are pure cardboard, embodying plenty of derogatory racial and ethnic stereotypes (although Keeler, a Fabian socialist, apparently was mocking American racial attitudes). Except for the surprising verisimilitude of the frequent asylum scenes, mood and atmosphere are conspicuous only in their absence. When one of his foremost champions, mystery critic and writer Francis Nevins Jr., was asked if Keeler had influenced him, he replied, "I hope not."

But those flaws only bother narrow-minded nitpickers who Just Don't Get It. Keeler aficionados read the master for the plot. And what plots! His novels are nothing but pure plot, a dozen or more disparate strands woven together into a single gloriously goofy tapestry. It's pure eccentric genius.

Keeler transcended *deus ex machina,* deploying regiments of metaphorical robots to keep things moving along all sorts of bizarre tangents. The seemingly rickety labyrinth is held together by a fantastic agglomeration of weird wills, lunatic laws, kooky contracts, idiotic oaths, and some of the most outrageously beautiful multi-layered, interlocking coincidences ever devised by the human mind. The mystery is ultimately resolved by an exquisitely unreal solution with all the wacky ingenuity of a flawlessly conceived Rube Goldberg device.

If one can adopt an appropriately offbeat frame of reference, the pleasures of Keeler are sublime. The standard Keeler novel opens with the squeaky-clean protagonist (invariably thrifty, reverent, brave, ambitious, and penniless) caught up in a hysterical pickle that makes *Catch-22* pale by comparison. His creditors are baying on his doorstep, with his enemies not far behind. He may be the unwitting victim of a nefarious capitalist plot to foreclose on his mortgage, steal his inheritance, or defraud him of his patent. Through a bizarre chain of coincidences, he finds himself implicated in some crime. His alibi is worthless, for his witnesses are invariably dead, abroad, or otherwise incommunicado. He is deeply in love, but his fiancée can never simply tie the knot. She has pledged to stay single until some rare book is stolen or a one-act vaudeville play is produced.

Happily, he may be the beneficiary of a will, but he never just gets the money. Inevitably he has to do something strange, like wear a pair of weird glasses for a year or decipher the meaning of a bag of beans, before he can come into his. And then chaos ensues, as the hero and various minor characters career about Chicago like pinballs in their efforts to untangle the twisted web.

Standard subplots involve weird curios, circus freaks, concealed identities, and mysterious (but not sinister!) Chinese laundries. It's the stuff of pure pulp fiction, but zanily transformed as if it's gone through the looking glass once too often.

Keeler was that rare bird: the unaffected yet totally self-aware eccentric. He is often pigeonholed with Plan 9 director

Ed Wood; they share a common wacky appeal. But where Wood took his films and his writings quite seriously and achieved his most memorable effects by accident, through sheer ineptitude, Keeler put considerable, albeit goofy, thought into his books. It's easy to picture the man sitting at his typewriter chuckling madly as he concocted even more goofball plot twists.

Keeler was born in Chicago in 1890 and lived in the city virtually his entire life. Most of his books were set there, and he passionately described the city as the "London of the West." He filled his books with local color, down to streetcar directions. Action bounces all over town, from well-known locales like the Loop and Bughouse Square (a Keeler favorite) to obscure spots like Goose Island.

His childhood wasn't the most stable. His father died when he was five, and his mother was forced to convert the Keeler home into a theatrical boardinghouse. This exposed the young Keeler to a steady stream of characters. Stepfathers changed almost as often as roomers; Mrs. Keeler had a knack for marrying the short-lived and wound up burying three more husbands.

The result wasn't the most stable young man. When Keeler was 20, his mother committed him to an asylum for a year or so for vague reasons. The experience forever embittered him against the mental health profession. In later years the mere mention of psychiatry was enough to send Keeler into a bitter rant. His novels would always be filled with sane people committed to asylums, where their protestations would get crackpot diagnoses like "Auto Hypnotic Pseudo Paranoia."

After being released from the asylum, Keeler picked up a degree in electrical engineering and took a job working in a steel mill as an electrician. But his true passion lay elsewhere. He started pecking out short stories and serials for the pulps on evenings and weekends. The pulp magazines of the 1910s and '20s were a far cry from the bloodcurdling titles of the '30s and '40s. Keeler's stories were always mannered in style and tone, even as they were outrageous in plot and incident. His works were well received. One magazine, *10 Story Book,* thought highly enough of Keeler to hire him as editor, a position he would hold until the magazine folded in 1940.

Keeler's first book, *The Voice of the Seven Sparrows,* was published in England in 1924. Several more Keeler titles appeared in Britain before he finally cracked the U.S. market with *Find the Clock!* in 1927. It was an appropriately odd beginning for one of the more unusual careers in American letters.

Keeler was fascinated by The Arabian Nights, and many of his early novels followed its format of a few characters engaging in storytelling contests. This enabled him to assemble a book out of little more than a framing sequence, a few of his pulp stories, and some white paste. This simple formula allowed plenty of room for the inimitable Keelerian touch. In his most successful book, *Sing Sing Nights* (1928), three men, unbeknownst to one another, simultaneously hide in the room of a notorious cad, each intending to shoot him. As Nevins notes, this sort of thing "happens every few pages in a Keeler novel, and anyone who can't see a certain loony beauty in it is not the reader Keeler requires."

When the smoke clears, the cad is dead of only two bullet wounds. Because none of the trio will admit to not firing and ballistics is an unknown science in Keeler, all three are convicted of murder. The night before the execution, the warden makes a sporting proposition. He'll give a pardon to the prisoner who can tell the most interesting story. Each of the three tales that follows is pure Keeler, involving such things as two men showing up at a costume party in identical moth suits, a mysterious set of ancient Chinese coins, and some poor fellow whose brain is transplanted into the skull of a gorilla.

Keeler always loved the bizarre; he was perhaps the first American novelist to routinely use trepanning as a plot device. He loved to populate his books with flocks of circus freaks; rare is the novel without at least a midget or two. "Keeler's fixation with physical abnormalities rivals Todd Browning's," said author William Poundstone, creator of the first Keeler Web page. You can be sure Keeler caught *Freaks* during its first run.

But his passion for the odd and unusual went beyond mere content. Keeler had a passion for weird narrative and structural devices. Typical is *Thieves' Nights* (1929), wherein the protagonist picks up a manuscript and starts reading. The story he reads—which is quite lengthy, taking up more than half the book!—is about a guy entertaining the governor with a series of stories about "Bayard DeLancy, the King of Thieves."

Naturally, all the DeLancy stories are repeated verbatim. That makes for three, count 'em, three levels of narration. It's easy to forget that you're actually reading a story-within-a-story-within-a-story. When the action finally returns to the protagonist of the outer level of the story (who is involved in a typically wacky imposture plot triggered by the ubiquitous weird will), the effect is startling. And then in walks Bayard DeLancy himself!

Keeler novels abound with such literary tomfoolery. When a character picks up a magazine to read a story, Keeler obligingly inserts a story (generally a recycled pulp tale), regardless of relevance. Every once in a while, his characters discuss "that author fellow" Harry Stephen Keeler's latest book. In a supreme act of reflexiveness, Keeler managed to work a photo of himself into *X. Jones of Scotland Yard* as an illustration! Keeler was probably just trying (and succeeding) to be outré, not artistic. But in many ways he quite innocently anticipated postmodernism. Keeler scholars are diligently trying to establish a link between the master and Thomas Pynchon.

Most of Keeler's novels fall into the category of "webwork," a subgenre he invented, christened, and apparently was the sole practitioner of. According to legend, Keeler started a webwork novel by plucking a dozen or so newspaper clippings from his files at random. He would then use the events described, no matter how disparate, as "nodes" in his plot. This certainly is consistent with the Keelerian spirit, but probably not with the reality. The incidents his plots revolve around—a thief stealing the face, and only the face, from a surrealist painting; a burglar breaking into homes to play a violin in front of the safe; a disgruntled phone company employee calling up every adult male in Minneapolis—are simply too strange to have originated anywhere but in the slightly cracked "cerebellum" of Keeler himself.

One of the best introductions to the Keelerian universe is one of his earliest fully conceived webworks, appropriately titled *The Amazing Web* (1930). Without graphical aids, a concise, much less coherent, summary of the multiple plotlines of even a short webwork is impossible. The major action here revolves around the efforts of the protagonist, a young lawyer, to win a case. He needs the fees to buy a boat so he can search every desert island in the South Pacific. It seems his beloved has fled to Australia and assumed a new identity. The only clue to her new name is in her purse, which was snatched by a man later marooned on some unnamed desert island. Somehow, Keeler manages to interweave this with more than a dozen equally outlandish strands, not the least of which involves a mysterious man hiring a cyclist to perform a "double loopless loop-the-loop" for 1,200 men carrying empty suitcases.

Keeler described his webwork plotting technique in detail in a lengthy essay titled "The Mechanics and Kinematics of Web-Work Plot Construction." It reads suspiciously like an advanced engineering textbook, complete with bewildering diagrams and pages of intricate, detailed analysis of such Keelerian structural devices as the "triplicity incident" and the "quadrangular polygon." As an exercise, he dissects his first book, *The Voice of the Seven Sparrows.* In a foldout diagram, he shows no less than 18 plot threads woven together in a fantastic pattern. The strands intersect at such enigmatic incidents as "Wicks forwards to New Orleans a cryptic deuce of spades with Chinese writing on it" and "Ng Yat, mastering Yeng San, wins his way by the game to becoming the Rockerfeller [sic] of the Orient." Fortunately for American literature, "Mechanics" languishes in obscurity.[4]

Keeler's literary fortunes peaked in the 1930s, when he burst beyond the confines of the mere webwork novel to create what he called "mega-novels." First came massive works such as *The Matilda Hunter Murder* (1931, 741 pages) and *The Box from Japan* (1932, 765 pages), two of the longest single-volume mystery novels ever written. Keeler happily described the latter as "perfectly adapted to jack up a truck with."

Then came the multi-volume mega-novel epics, huge madcap masterpieces wherein Keeler achieved the acme of his nutty art. One of the best of Keeler's mega-novels, and perhaps his "hyper-super-vital" masterpiece, is the story of "The Aeronautic Baby Strangler Case." The main saga is told in *The Marceau Case* (1936) and *X. Jones of Scotland Yard* (1936), but tangents pop up in three other novels. (The Keeler bibliography is itself a webwork.) The action centers on the murder of reclusive millionaire Andre Marceau, who is found garroted in the center of a freshly rolled croquet lawn. Childlike foot-

---

[4] Editor's Note: *On Webwork,* an 84-page booklet that includes "Mechanics" is available to HSK Society members for $10.

prints are found near the corpse, but they don't reach the edge of the lawn—as if their maker had vanished into thin air! A mysterious stolen autogiro (a primitive ancestor of the helicopter) is spotted hovering over the lawn at the time of the murder. By coincidence (of course), all the neighbors are out of town that evening. The only witness is a blind man who heard Marceau shout, "It's the babe from hell." A midget is suspected, as Marceau many years ago wrote a letter to the London Times warning of the perils of "nanism" and advocating that all "dwarfs, midgets, and cretins" be strangled at birth lest the human race shrink and be devoured by insects. A note is found among Marceau's papers indicating that the name of his killer can be found in this sentence: " 'Blimey, 'Erb! Little?' Lu Caslow's dreary eyes actually glistened." Strange clues abound. What significance, for example, should be attached to Marceau's insistence that the publisher of World Humor magazine excise the "Chinaboy Chuckles" column from his subscription copy before mailing it to him?

Multiple mazes unfold as various parties—a private detective with a private agenda, a scoop-minded American newspaper syndicate, an eccentric Scotland Yard inspector applying a weird crime-solving technique based on a four-dimensional space-time continuum—rush to solve the case. Red herrings abound as solution after solution is proposed, each concurrently more absurd and yet more logical than the previous. Even the red herrings have red herrings! One "solution" implicates a six-toed midget tightrope walker who appeared briefly on the Australian stage under the name Little Lucas; another blames Meyer B. Li, a Chinese Jewish giant. (Careful readers will note that both names appear in the "Blimey, 'Erb" sentence.) Or was Marceau really done in by a rare genetic disease that merely made him look like he'd been garroted as he faked a set of childish footprints? In the world of Keeler, each is perfectly reasonable and equally likely.

Particularly delicious is the incident of the Astro-Extensionists. The trail of one suspect seemingly ends in a farmhouse in New Zealand where he lived years ago. In consensus reality, a dead end. In conventional mystery fiction, time to trot out the neighbor who never forgets a thing. But for Keeler, this is an opportunity for a signature coincidence. The current tenant of the house happens to belong to the Astro-Extensionist Church. As Keeler explains in detail, one of the church's basic tenets is that a person's soul is the aggregate of his or her actions and possessions. Thus, Astro-Extensionists carefully preserve any items left behind by old tenants lest they destroy part of the previous occupant's soul. The suspect left behind but one item, a half-burned envelope. This frail clue is enough to link him to a troupe of Japanese aerialists, all of whom (save the suspect) were wiped out when their native island sank into the sea during an earthquake. The case is all but solved! Well, maybe.

In many ways, Keeler seemed to be mocking the conventions of the mystery genre. He routinely lampooned the art of deduction and was always manifestly unfair to the reader. In one novel, he devotes some 40 pages to an elaborate solution to the murder, with the names of the suspects being deduced from little more than a circled date on the dead man's calendar. The impeccable reasoning collapses when an observer points out that the marked date is, in fact, the deadline for the dead man's tontine payment. Ultimately, a half-wit discovers that the "murder" really was a case of accidental death. Keeler surely enjoyed it when one of his publishers started inserting notices in his books, sometimes hundreds of pages from the end, announcing, "Stop ... at this point all the necessary characters and clues have been presented to make it possible for you to determine the guilty person." It made tricks like introducing the killer in the final chapter all the sweeter.

The 1920s and '30s were Keeler's golden age. Major publishers in both the United States and Great Britain put out his books. First editions were often followed by reprints and cheap "popular price" hardback editions, the paperbacks of the day. He was reviewed widely and often. Befuddled as they were, critics usually gave him positive notices. The London Times Literary Supplement devoted the same attention to the new Keeler as they did to the new Agatha Christie, praising him for his "extremely complicated and highly ingenious narrative." On the negative side, the New York Times accused him of writing his novels in "Choctaw." Esteemed mystery critic Anthony Boucher, a loyal Keelerite, probably summed it up best: "His fabulous fertility could make Keeler the greatest writer in the business—if only he could write."

Monogram even made a few films based very loosely on *Sing Sing Nights*. One, *The Mysterious Mr. Wong,* starred Bela

Lugosi. Ironically, these films, available on video, are the most accessible items in the Keeler canon today.[5]

Keeler's decline began in the 1940s. E.P. Dutton, his American publisher, dropped him. Judging from his novels, it was not a happy separation. In *The Peacock Fan,* one of Keeler's last Dutton titles, an evil publisher conspires to have an innocent author executed. The only American publisher Keeler could find was Phoenix Press, a small, poorly paying outfit specializing in cheap genre fiction for the rental libraries that then dotted the country. It was the literary equivalent of going from major theatrical releases to the straight-to-video market.

Gone were the sprawling mega-novels, but not the surrealism and the outlandishness. In fact, Keeler novels like *The Case of the Barking Clock* and *The Case of the Transposed Legs* were even more extreme. Finally, Phoenix Press dropped him, in 1948, leaving him without a publisher in his native land. But, just as the British publishers had picked up on him before the American houses, so they stuck with him after America forsook him. Still, even the British were losing their taste for Keeler. His last book published in Britain, *Stand By, London Calling,* came out in 1953.

This would have been the end for most ordinary writers. But Keeler was no ordinary writer. During his salad days, he had surprising success overseas. His works were translated into at least a dozen languages. And though English-language readers forsook him, his books kept selling on the Iberian Peninsula. Keeler kept on cranking out books that were translated directly into Spanish and/or Portuguese. At least 10 Keelers only appeared in Spanish, and another four were only available in Portuguese translations. According to the lucky handful of bilingual Keeler collectors, titles such as *The Man Who Changed His Skin* and *The Case of the Transparent Nude* showed that Keeler hadn't lost his touch. Even after those markets also dried up, Keeler wrote on. At the time of his death, in 1967, Keeler was totally forgotten and utterly convinced that one day the world would rediscover him. He left some 1.3 million unpublished words behind, which, from all reports, live up to the bizarre standards he'd set.

---

[5] Editor's Note: Try Sinister Cinema, P.O. Box 4369, Medford OR 97501-0168, 541-773-6860.

Today, a small cult of Keeler fans keeps the memory alive through the Harry Stephen Keeler Society and its lively newsletter, The Keeler News, as well as various Web pages. Although many of his later novels are rare and highly sought after, copies of his classics of the 1920s and 1930s still pop up in mystery specialty bookstores, unfortunately at prices that are rapidly becoming unreasonable. But it should be only a matter of time before some daring publisher takes the Keelerian plunge. With Mystery Science 3000 wrapping up a successful run, Raymond Scott CDs in the record stores, and Ed Wood biopics playing the malls, America is finally ready for Keeler.

The Amazing Adventures of The Kracked King of Keelerland

Bill Pronzini

The man who came in...was about 35, and exceedingly dark of skin, though by no manner of means a Negro; indeed, his blue-black hair was as straight as hair could be; his jet eyes were a cold black, and there was a scar on one cheek. Dressed in green-striped trousers of almost dandified cut, he was in his shirtsleeves, which, patterned with pink stripes and interlocked green flowers, were the final touch that proclaimed plainly his Sicilian blood.

—Harry Stephen Keeler
The Case of the 16 Beans, 1944

He turned back in the direction he had come, and walking rapidly eastward soon passed under the same viaduct from which he had descended a short while before, and Chinatown now lay in his rear.

—Harry Stephen Keeler
The Green Jade Hand, 1930

One of his publishers said of him: "This master-mysteryman writes baffling, fast-moving yarns [whose] odd plots relate some of the strangest things that ever happened to man." The San Francisco Chronicle challenged readers to "just try to worry about your own trials and tribulations when you're working on [one of his] conundrum[s], slinking down dark alleys, trailing Oriental and Occidental villains, examining curious lethal devices employed by the Portuguese, the Armenians and the Greeks to say nothing of the Chinese!"

The Baltimore Evening-Sun offered one of many dissenting opinions; "He writes in a strange jargon which eschews the distinctions between the parts of speech, and employs such a system of punctuation as no other writer save perhaps Gertrude Stein ever dared."

The New York Times put it even more succinctly: "All [his] novels are written in Choctaw."

Critic Art Scott opined that his "preposterous tales might best be described as the sort of story you might expect to get had W.C. Fields ever managed to spin out to full length the tales he was always beginning: 'Yas, my dear, I remember once when I was 2,000 miles up the Umbobo river, armed only with an assegai...' "

He himself, in a letter to a fan, cheerfully admitted that "some people have claimed (librarians) that the author is certainly insane." And Francis M. Nevins, Jr., perhaps the most passionate of his champions, eulogized him thus: "When they made [him] the mold self-destructed. For close to half a century he stomped through the staid precincts of the mystery story like King Kong crossing a country churchyard. His... novels form a self-contained world of monstrously complicated intrigues, half farce and half Grand Guignol, half radical social criticism and half a labyrinth in which he hid himself... He was the true original of Kesey's R.P. MacMurphy and Vonnegut's Kilgore Trout, the sublime nutty genius of the mystery genre."

The subject of all these comments is, of course, Harry Stephen Keeler. And a nutty genius he indeed was. More to the point of this narrative, he was also the first great alternative writer—and one of the three or four greatest of all time.

Some Keeler devotees might take exception to the last statement. He was *sui generis,* they might say; he transcended any labeling of bad or good; he and his work stand aloof. Ah, but you can say the same about Michael Avallone, Michael Morgan, Florence M. Pettee, Anthony M. Rud, or any of the other alternative behemoths. Indeed, you can also say the same about Doyle, Hammett, Christie, Carr, Spillane, and others at the opposite end of the criminous spectrum. Fact is, we live in a world of labels and categories and everybody's got to fit someplace. I say Harry Stephen fits here better than anywhere else, so at least for the duration of this chapter I lay claim to him and his fifty-odd (very odd) novels published in the English language.

Dissenters may skip to Chapter 5. The rest of us will proceed.

Harry Stephen Keeler was a Chicago native, born in 1890. He spent most of his life in the Windy City, where he worked as an electrician, in a steel mill, as a pulp magazine editor

(10-Story Book, one of the lesser pulps, from 1919 until the magazine's demise in 1940), and of course as a freelance writer. He wrote his first short story in 1910, made his first professional sale in 1913, and published his first criminous story in 1914: "Victim Number Five," in Young's Magazine (reprinted thirty-eight years later in the 1952 Mystery Writers of America anthology, Maiden Murders). In 1919, the same year he began working for *l0-Story Book,* he married Hazel Goodwin, also a pulp writer, who specialized in light fantasy and love stories of the forgettable variety. It seems to have been a perfect union, in that Goodwin not only encouraged Harry Stephen's literary endeavors but collaborated with him on numerous manuscripts and evidently inspired more than one of his screwball plots. Three years after Goodwin's death in 1960, Keeler married a second time, to his long-time secretary, Thelma Tertza Rinaldo, who also collaborated on his novels. This second marriage ended with Keeler's death in February of 1967.

His first novel, *The Voice of the Seven Sparrows,* was in fact one of many magazine serials he penned between 1919 and 1924; it was first published in book form by Hutchinson in England in 1924, and didn't see print here until four years later (E. P. Dutton). His third book, *The Spectacles of Mr. Cagliostro,* seems to have been his own personal favorite among his early work; he once said in a letter that it was "scornfully rejected by nearly every publisher in the U.S.A., none even vouchsafing me a letter on it, and then issued by a firm [Dutton] which turned it down (as optional book) and did mighty damned well." Two other early titles, *Sing Sing Nights* and *The Amazing Web,* were also well received in both England and this country. In *Blood in Their Ink,* British mystery writer and critic Sutherland Scott said of *The Amazing Web;* "It would be quite impossible to attempt to analyse the plot, which darts hither and yon with quite indescribable abandon. Yet it remains a truly great mystery story." On the other hand, Francis Nevins, in an article for *The Armchair Detective,* called it "the worst legal mystery in the world."

All in all, Keeler published some forty-nine novels in the English language between 1924 and 1953. Numerous other novels appeared only in Spanish and/or Portuguese throughout the 1950s and into the 1960s; still others exist only as unpublished (and mostly unpublishable) manuscripts. Keeler's particular brand of lunacy, reasonably popular in an era (the twenties and thirties) that embraced the likes of Doc Savage, the Shadow, and entire magazines devoted to stories about zeppelins, was not met with favor by the serious-minded folk of the post—World War II years. Keeler's last novel to appear in the United States was *The Case of the Transposed Legs* (in collaboration with Hazel Goodwin) in 1948. And its publisher—in fact, the publisher of the last nine of his novels to appear here, from 1943 to 1948—was that colossus among alternative houses, Phoenix Press. Just what is a Keeler novel? those of you who have never read one might be asking at this point. The answer to that question is by no means an easy one. "A Keeler novel," Art Scott says, "is a stupefyingly complex skein of multiple interlocking plots and subplots, the whole mass structured according to a scheme of Keeler's own devising." Harry Stephen labeled this complex skein a "web-work plot" and early in his career wrote a treatise on the subject: "Mechanics and Kinematics of Web-Work Plot Construction," which was published serially in *The Author & Journalist* between April and November of 1928. Here is Francis Nevins's explanation of the web-work plot novel, from a four-part article on Keeler and his work in *The Journal of Popular Culture:*

> The web-work novel may be defined as a book of pure plot which bears not the slightest resemblance to real life but which is so meticulously constructed that regardless of the book's length—and Keeler's lengthiest run over 1500 pages—every absurd complication turns out to make blissfully perfect sense within the author's zany terms of reference. Keeler intensifies the deliberate and gleeful artificiality of his novels by using certain devices much as wild cards function in poker; among these devices are lunatic laws, nutty religious tenets, wacky wills and crackpot contracts, but his most famous and most characteristic ploy is the system of interlocked back-breaking coincidences.

Keeler's other favorite "wild cards" include rare books of one type or another, most of which have elaborate titles and histories of his own devising; oddball curios such as human skulls and ancient pieces of Chinese jade; cryptograms and puzzles; quasi-science-fictional devices and situations; and a seemingly inexhaustible storehouse of esoteric information on such topics as literary incunabula, politics, safes and safecracking, clocks, electricity and neon signs, steel mills, mathematics, horse racing, Chinese history and philosophy, lunatic asylums, lighthouses, circuses, embryonic television, and Nicaragua. He owned a "private morgue" of thousands of newspaper clippings which he kept in a series of little drawers in a huge filing cabinet, each marked after the fashion of an encyclopedia. When he was ready to embark on a new novel, according to bibliophile and fellow mystery writer Vincent Starrett (who knew him well), Keeler "would grab a hatful of [these clippings], stir them together, and select anywhere from six to a dozen at random; and these became the basis of his story. However disparate in time or place or circumstances, he welded them into a continuous narrative and forced them to 'click.' "

Another of Keeler's favorite ploys was to recycle his own and Hazel Goodwin's magazine fiction, using it whole or in part, revised or unrevised, expanded or compressed, as the foundations of some novels and as web-work plot elements in many others—making him the champion self-plagiarist of this century. In some cases he included complete stories, word for word and with their original magazine titles, plunking them into the narrative anywhere from near the beginning to near the end; these stories always have some integral plot function, although that function may not be clear to the reader at first. In *The Face of the Man From Saturn,* for instance, an enthusiastic paean to socialism (one of Keeler's pet causes, along with such others as political corruption and the evils of capital punishment), there is a long science fiction story called "How Socialism Finally Arrived in the World," set in the year A.D. 3235 and featuring a professor of history at the University of Terra. A pulp gangster story, "The Search," concerning a pickpocket known as the Eel, can be found in *The Man with the Magic Eardrums. The Vanishing Gold Truck* contains what Keeler, in the novel's dedication, calls a "beautiful little circus story" ("silly" and "unreadable" are more appropriate descriptive adjectives) by Hazel Goodwin entitled "Spangles," which first appeared in *Best Love Stories Magazine;* Keeler so admired it that he used its central characters, the circus folk of MacWhorter's Mammoth Motorized Shows, in this and five subsequent novels. Two other Goodwin stories, "Slim Decides" and "20 Minutes," appear verbatim in *The Case of the Mysterious Moll* and *The Case of the Barking Clock,* respectively. And an unintentionally hilarious Keeler "Chinese fable" called "The Murder of Chung Po: The First Detective Story: The Fable of the Murdered Hermit, the Assortment of Variegated Eggs, the 3 Superficially-Thinking Wisemen, and the Cogitating Magistrate" graces the pages of one of Harry Stephen's alternative masterpieces, *The Case of the 16 Beans.*

Still another of his stocks-in-trade was a positive Dickensian flare for endowing his characters with unusual names—so unusual in some instances that they are downright chucklesome. Here are just a few of his more inspired *noms-d'absurdité:*

Rudolph "Blue-Bow" Ballmeier (lawyer)
Nyland "Golden-Tongue" Finfrock (lawyer)
Mulchrone KixMiller (writer)
Mingleberry Hepp (writer)
Charley Squat-in-Thunderstorm (Indian)
Ebenezer Sitting-Down-Bear (Negro Indian)
"Poke-Nose" Hohoff (reporter)
Judge Fishkins Dollarhide
Count Ritzenditzendorfer
Pfaff Hufnagel
Bucyrus Duckstone
Hutchcock McDolphus
Isdale Archdeacon
Bogardus Sandsteel
Ochiltree Jark
Balhatchet Barkstone
Jeronymo Ashpital
MacAngus MacWhiffle
Abner Hopfear
Oswald Sweetboy
Joe Czescziczki
Maltby Lawhead
Scientifico Greenlimb

As for his characters, they are like no other in fiction. Their speech, relationships, and behavior are so bizarre that they might exist on another planet only approximating Earth—a planet where freaks and screwball ethnic minorities abound, mostly for the amusement of the "normal" white majority.

Keeler thought nothing of introducing a major character one hundred pages or more into a novel, or of totally abandoning a major protagonist two-thirds of the way through one. He also thought nothing of using an object rather than a person as a novel's main character. A mythical rare book of Chinese aphorisms entitled *The Way Out*—a book, we are told, that contains "all the collated wisdom of the Chinese race"—gets people into and out of hot water in five novels published between 1941 and 1944: *The Peacock Fan, The Sharkskin Book, The Book with the Orange Leaves, The Case of the Two Strange Ladies,* and *The Case of the 16 Beans* (the "Chinese fable" mentioned above is supposedly from *The Way Out*). About his "Way Out" stories, Keeler once said that he "had a hell of a damned time trying to slant each to a bit of Chinese wisdom and then write the bit of wisdom to fit the story. I had to be brief, pungent, Chinese in flavor and where possible, with a bit of humor. And I nearly busted my cerebellum making them up." Those who read the "Way Out" stories, in particular *The Case of the l6 Beans,* may be inclined to believe that Keeler did indeed bust his cerebellum in making them up.

Gangsters run rampant in his novels—toughs with such names as Al "Three-Gun" Mulhearn, Two-Gun "Polack" Eddy, Louis Rocco, Scarface Scalisi, and Driller O'Hare. Most of the nonethnic ones speak in a strange, slangy patois that would have had Dutch Schultz and the boys, had they ever read any of it, out of their chairs and convulsed on the floor. For instance:

> "2 and 2's [statistics] collected by this lone hustler through casing the court convictions over 20 years shows that in 81 percent of acquittals there's always one hustler that's well heeled with scratch, and conversely 76½ percent of convictions shows a mob without a cent of coin back of anybody. And why am I handing you this fakealoo? Because, Kid, always work in a mob where there's one geezer handsome-heeled; in catching the best mouthpiece money can buy he has 81 percent chance of a kiss-off from the jury. Then you'll catch his kiss-off at the same time, 2 and 2's, boy, are never a shill." (*The Green Jade Hand*)

> "Okay! Ask 'em, then—one question each—and one only—and in a low voice—because any minute now he'll be up on this level [of the building]. And I don't want nobody's bazooing to drown out his approach. For I want him safe in here—beyond all three doors and beyond yonder bolt—so's I can be putting that rod on his spine and letting him know it's a snatch." (*The Case of the 16 Beans*)

Ethnic characters, gangsters and otherwise, also run rampant in Keelerland. As Nevins says, "Everyone in a Keeler novel, including the hero and the heroine and even Keeler himself in the third-person narrative portions, is a blatant racist; every conceivable race and nationality is systematically and uproariously libeled over and over again." But in spite of this, Nevins contends, Keeler was not in fact a racist: "[He] knew he lived in a racist society, knew that he couldn't do a thing to change it, hated racism deeply, but refused to be solemn about the subject and insisted on his right to express himself in a way that could be misinterpreted." Nevins bases his defense of his hero on a handful of scenes, characters, and plot elements in the Keeler canon; but the overwhelming volume—and not-occasional viciousness—of racial slurs, jokes, and stereotyping also to be found in the canon would seem to make that defense insupportable. Harry Stephen may not have been a card-carrying white supremicist, but neither was he an advocate of the NAACP or the Italian Anti-Defamation League. At best his racial attitudes might have been ambivalent.

Not only did he and his WASP characters regularly refer to ethnics as "niggers," "wops," "Hunkies," "Heines," "Chinks," and so forth, but anyone and everyone with an ethnic surname was made to speak in some of the most shamelessly awful dialect ever committed to paper. In such novels as *The Vanishing Gold Truck* and *The Case of the 16 Beans,* dialect of one kind and another takes over the narrative and goes on for page after page after page, until the deciphering of all the elided, bastardized, and phonetically misspelled words becomes a mind-numbing chore to tax the patience of the most dedicated cryptographer. Any reader who attempts to pursue either of these titles (and a few others) would do well to lay in a supply of Excedrin-Plus before beginning.[6]

Here are a few illustrations of Keeler's brand of ethnic dialect, all from *The Case of the l6 Beans*:

> Black: "An' he say, kinda jokin' lak, 'Soun' to me lak dey's a Shylock Home aroun' dis place—on'y he is a punk Shylock Home, 'kaze he don't obsarve nothin'. Now huccombe, Shylock Home, Ah could go 'way downtown to Six' Ab'noo yistidday, wid you traipsin' all obah Alb'ny? Somebody hatter tek keah dis house, an' get de th'ee 'potent tel'phone calls I 'uz 'spectin', an' dat somebody wuz me! W'y, Ah lak to have die wid bo'dom.' Den ob co'se Ah say, stubbo'n lak—'kaze I 'uz puzzle 'bout dem 16 seeds—'Well, 'twuz day befo' yistidday, den, dat you wuz dere.' An' he grunt an' say: 'Seem lak Ah cain't call my own doin's mah own in dis town! An' he add: Yassuh, Shylock Home, 'twuz day befo' yistidday, an' Ah picked up a crooked pin on Broadway an' buyed mahse'f a malted milk on Fo'th Ab'noo—now you know ebberting 'bout my movements. Is you satisfied? If not, whut else mebbe you lak know?' "

> Chinese: "Gleetings, Mistel Palladine. I makee big mistook las' ni'te, w'en I sellee you shalt shoestlings, 'stead of long shoestlings like you wan'. But I no likee bothel you this molnin' fo' to le' me extsange—you plob'ly lots busy in molnin's, yes, no?—but allee lite!—come I now, aftel you' lunch, to makee extsange."

> German: "Bod afder dot, Roggo, vy nod we boomp him off ride avay? Unt schnake his potty aud-d-d-d tonide bevore—?"

> Sicilian: "Bat wance we catch thoz' ransome monee, Loo-ee—you no mebbe gonna try order us for to mak' beeg scatter—weeth heem knowin' 'oo we are."

---

[6] Editor's Note: Ramble House recommends Darvocette, or, if you can get it, Percodan.

Keeler's narrative prose is often enough in the same headache-inducing category. Art Scott says that his style is "florid, gramatically knock-kneed"; and so it is. It may also be described as a savory goulash of Edwardian verbosity mixed with the color purple, spiced with slangy words and phrases both generic and Keelerian, and leavened by jawbreaking sentences and confounding paragraphs of such awesome composition as

> Not only had the safe quite evidently been cast in days before the modern combination dial had been thought of, but it had moreover been through a fierce fire at some far-gone day, for its door was warped as though the most intense of flames had played over the entire mass of metal, and it could be seen that the door no longer fitted snugly into the framework machined for it. Indeed, it was evident that the very lock itself must have melted in those flames, and that the original owner had had to chisel away both lock and site to operate the single sliding bolt and gain access to the charred remains of his papers and, perhaps, Civil War currency, for a square of powerful steel containing a single milled slot—literally a section of armor plate a half-inch thick—had been riveted by four rivets over the site of the old lockwork; and that newer, and no doubt more thief-proof, mechanism had been installed in the open orifice back of this steel plate was indicated by the long-stemmed but powerful key which Jech at last succeeded in extracting through his shirt-bosom to the extent that the long leather thong holding it around his neck permitted, for the key's complicated notches and prongs suggested from the extreme intricacy of their pattern that if the safe and lock makers of several decades back could not construct an impregnable strong-box, they could at least create an unpickable lock. (*The Green Jade Hand*)

> Ironically he gazed at himself—gay, yet penniless, bird of plummage as he was—with his striking driver's costume of short-sleeved green flannel shirt, belted into black trousers with red stripes on edges, the legs of the latter buckled into shin-high thong-laced yellow cowhide boots, his short bullwhip—mere symbol, no more, of old

> circus-wagon days—swinging, by a snap-catch, from his side; then tilting back on his head the flat broad-brimmed Australian-like grey hat, with brim rolled up on one side, that was part and parcel of the costume, he swung his troubled gaze in a great arc across the desolate countryside region where the wagon stood—a region of uncultivable knolls, becoming apparently bigger and bigger toward the south, or left of him, with here and there, in all directions, patches of malignant-looking weeds, and here and there, too, clusters of scrub oak—and more patches, like actual woods of the same, in the distance, left, right, and forward—and no fences anywhere, because of apparently nothing that had to be kept in or out; after which troubled surveyal, he dourly regarded the lonely store that stood off from his wagon. (*The Vanishing Gold Truck*)

> Glumly he gazed out of the broad window next to the capacious chair in which he sat, which looked down on the morning traffic pouring, this sunny June morning, past 47th and Broadway, far far below, then, withdrawing his gaze, he contemplated himself glumly, across the thickly green carpeted and mahogany-furnished office, in the cheval mirror fastened to the closet door in the opposite wall, seeing only, however, just a young man of 28 or so, with steel grey eyes, who, not so terribly long ago, as it seemed to him, had been wearing a blue naval coast patrol uniform, but who today, now that the war was over and gone, was dressed in a brisk pepper-and-salt suit, and four-in-hand tie with a colorful plaid of just such a degree as the modern New Yorker might safely wear. (*The Case of the 16 Beans*)

Harry Stephen's fine hand with ethnic dialogue has already been demonstrated. Here is an example of how he handled more conventional dialogue between two supposedly intelligent WASP characters—and of his unique method of dispensing pertinent facts to the reader through colloquy.

> "What on earth do you mean, Boyce? About knowing 'smart-alecky wisecracks'—and handing them out free gratis? Just because you've run your grandfather's poky, stodgy little real-estate business for 6 years, there at the

> 242nd Street station of the Broadway Subway—or 6 years minus your year-and-a-quarter time out while serving on that Navy coast patrol vessel—doesn't mean you can't speak—as a young man might—any longer. Real-estate men aren't supposed to be old fogies, are they? And besides, the matter has nothing whatsoever to do with your grandfather's will, so far as I see it."
>
> "Oh, no?" was Boyce Barkstone's sepulchral rejoinder, the while he gazed oddly, in turn, at the other. "Well, listen to this little incident then...The last time I saw Grandfather alive—which, according to the date on this will, was the morning of the day he drew the will—I said, inadvertently, and not knowing I was addressing him—it was a beastly comedy of errors, understand—a ghastly mistake—a case of—of two other men, as you might put it—anyway, I said to him—inadvertently and unwittingly: 'Nuts to you, you old fool!' " (*The Case of the 16 Beans*)

But it is not in his prose that Keeler's real genius lies; it is in his plots. Most of them defy synopsizing at any but great length. Some defy synopsizing at any length, among them such massive single-volume works as *The Box from Japan* (l932, 765 pages) and *Finger, Finger!* (1938, 536 pages). At 360,000 words, *The Box from Japan* is the longest single-volume mystery novel in the English language—a book which Keeler himself, with puckish humor, described as "perfectly adapted to jack up a truck with."

What I can do to give you an idea of the nature of his web-work plots is to list the essential characters and plot ingredients in some of the more memorable ones. Keep in mind that these are the essential, not the only ones, and that they interrelate and interlock by means of manipulation, massive coincidence, and all manner of literary pyrotechnics.

The Green Jade Hand (1930)

A stolen book of exquisite rarity and value, the "De Devinis Institutionalibus Adversum Gentes" a.k.a. the "Vindelinus de Spira," which likewise bears the weighty title of Lucius Caecilius Firmianus Lactantius and which was published and bound by Wendelin of Speier in 1472; a couple of unscrupulous Chicago bibliophiles; a venal—and deaf—curio shop owner named

Casimer Jech; an excon cracksman whose entire savings of over three hundred dollars (earned by working extra hours in the machine shop at Joliet) is stolen on the day he is released from prison; a panhandling hobo who finds a tiny, carved, six-fingered green jade hand in a bowl of chop suey; two "colored women safeblowers" who turn out to be former circus acrobats and "strong-arm women" once known as the Indian Sisters from Rangoon; a conniving Cleveland rooming-house owner called Sadie Hippolyte; "the biggee king of Chinatown," Wah Hung Fung; the only male descendant of a master jade-carver of the Ming dynasty, who happens to be an embezzler of bank bills and unregistered American Liberty Bonds; another Chinese thief, this one a coolie with a cork leg; a pair of young Caucasian lovers named Dirk and Iolanthe, Dirk being the inventor of the Mattox Noiseless Platen for typewriters; Iolanthe's long-lost black-sheep brother; a feeble-minded police-station janitor, Simon Grundt, who fancies himself a great detective; a foppish, eccentric "scientific investigator," Oliver Oliver (a.k.a. "old Double-O"), who is fond of "exposing his super-brilliant private detective badge" to cab drivers, among others; a bejeweled bracelet in the form of a golden snake with its tail in its mouth; a thousand-year-old Chinese book entitled The Sayings of Tu Fu (a forerunner of *The Way Out*); a weird reward offered by the Bohemian Society of Chicago and matched by the Archeological Museum of Evanston, Illinois, involving the determination of a person's sex; a scheme to raise funds for a plainclothes policemen's ball at the Fireman's Hall (?) by selling tickets to a bogus investigation conducted by a half-wit inside a murdered man's shop; a "diabolical burglar trap"; some crackpot policework, based on all sorts of illogical and erroneous assumptions; and the most outrageous, vaudevillean (literally) unmasking-of-a-"murderer" scene in all of crime fiction.

The Man with the Magic Eardrums (1939)

A rich Minneapolis racetrack bookie, Mortimer Q. King, a.k.a. "Square-Shooter" King, a.k.a. "Camera-Shy" King, who is ostensibly married to a well-to-do ex-Southern belle but who is actually married to "the world's most notorious Negress" as the result of a "noxious lost chapter" in his life; the degenerate Negress, Jemimah Cobb, owner and operator of a London whorehouse populated by freaks (a woman with seven fingers on each hand, a female Quasimodo), who is presently awaiting the hangman's noose in Pentonville Prison, London, for murdering her rich Chinese lover, Mock Lu, and who has vowed to reveal, as soon as she steps onto the gallows, the identity of the white American to whom she is legally married "as a revenge against the entire white race"; the baffling "Mulkovitch Riddle," in which a bearded Russian was known definitely to walk into Jemimah's dive but never to have walked out again, with no trace of him having turned up when the police shortly afterward searched the place; King's present wife, Laurel, who is on a three-day "novena" in sackcloth and ashes, praying for her dead father, Catholic prayer-book publisher Ignatius van Utley, in the Convent of St. Etheldreda in Milwaukee; a burglar named Peter Givney, whom King catches trying to break and enter his home and who wears a pair of artificial eardrums called the Cromely Micro-acoustic Sound-Focusing Auricles; a freak in the manufacture of these hearing aids which provides Givney with supersensitive hearing that enables him to open burglar-proof safes, not to mention "hear a lady fly sighing after her gent fly has kissed her [and] a dago eating spaghetti in Naples"; a telephone call and eventual visit from a Buffalo lawyer who offers to buy a human skull King uses as a good-luck talisman; a "Senatorial Investigation Toward Abolishment by Federal Statute of All Race-Track Booking in America, by Machine, Oral and All Other Recording Devices or Systems"; a lawsuit brought by a Chinese laundryman against the Buffalo Trust and Savings Bank, claiming he owns the land under their skyscraper; a Polish doctor, Stefan Sciecinskiwicz, who has been dating King's maid and who is the brother of a "notorious mankiller" called Two-Gun "Polack" Eddy; the human skull (Mr. Skull, King calls it), which was given to Mortimer by a Wisconsin farmer who dug it up in one of his fields and which he (King) has loaned out to a friend for a pre-Halloween party; some other gangsters, one of whom is a one-eyed gigolo named Blinky who is beheaded by his pals; some dazzling legalistics and some even more dazzling misinformation about the effects of marijuana cigarettes (e.g. "If you smoke one, atop any kind of alcohol—let alone absinthe—you'll just tell your whole family history"); a limping crimple-minded Negro windowwasher; a short story written by still another gangster, this one known as "Big Shoes," who is trying to crack the New York fiction markets; a train called "the famous Minneapolis-Chicago Non-Stop Perishable Through Freight"; a seven-foot traffic cop; one hundred thousand dollars in diamonds; a racehorse named Who-Was-Greta-Garbo; a British Negro odds-figurer known variously as "Horses," "Milkwagon," and "The Clock"; an old gentlemen who secretly collects emeralds; a disgruntled ex-newspaperman who broke into the Multi Connection Room of the new Minneapolis Telephone Exchange, threw a switch ringing at least half a million Minneapolis telephone bells, and then delivered a speech stating that each subscriber was to be named Jemimah Cobb's white American husband; an explanation of the Mulkovitch Riddle that involves transvestitism and a bearded lady; and a perfect *deus ex machina* resolution of Mortimer King's problems with Jemimah and her vow to expose him. All of this takes place over the course of a single night, inside King's Minneapolis home, and is told primarily through dialogue.

The Case of the 16 Beans (l944)

A wacky will in which sixteen beans of various types and colors comprise the entire bequest from a rich eccentric, Balhatchet Barkstone, to his young nephew Boyce; a cryptic accompanying note written by Balhatchet urging Boyce to "find a good spot—the right soil, in short!—to plant all his beans in, where, growing simultaneously, they may grow him a valuable crop"; a crazy misunderstanding; a lecture at the Philosopher's Club entitled "Continuation of Proclivities and Talent the Only True Basis for Calculating Legal Family Descendancy"; a copy of *The Way Out*, the book of Chinese aphorisms; another rich eccentric, Gilbert Parradine, owner of (among other things) the Parradine Moderne Motion Picture Theatre and the Parradine Tower; "the most diabolical and policeproof kidnap plot ever invented by gangsters'; a film starring a British comic named Broom Sherwood; a secondhand book-dealer, one Ochiltree Jark; a deceased upstate New York farmer who had such an anti-Chinese complex that he bought up dozens of Manhattan chop suey restaurants and canceled their owners' leases, with the idea that the poor devils would then "go off and blow their brains out, or something"; an intellectual Chinese exlawyer who lost his legs in a train wreck, turned to selling shoestrings on the streets of Chicago, travels by means of a platform cart outfitted with "strange water-encased paddle-blades," and is known as "Half-a-Chink, King of the Roller-Skating Rink"; a micro-brained, book-collecting dealer in animal hides called Hutchcock McDolphus; a European opera singer with a voice of "cool, molten gold"; a scientific specialist in beans, i.e., a "beanology professor"; the aforementioned Chinese fable entitled "The Murder of Chung Po: The First Detective Story"; the working out of what may well be the weirdest cryptogram ever invented in or out of fiction; a miraculous rescue utilizing the marquee of the Parradine Moderne Motion Picture Theater; and the revelation of a demented "family history" in which generations of Barkstone patriarchs bequeathed their male heirs increasingly more elaborate puzzles and cryptograms that the heirs must solve in order to "earn" the family fortunes.

The Marceau Case (1936), *X. Jones of Scotland Yard* (1936), *The Wonderful Scheme of Mr. Christopher Thorne* (1937)

This is the first of several multi-volume Keeler "mega-novels"—a tour-de-force that runs more than 1400 pages in its three volumes and that Nevins says is "beyond the slightest sliver of a doubt one of the great goofy masterpieces of world literature." He'll get no argument from me on that score.

All three books are based on a single "impossible" murder case, in which yet another rich eccentric, this one living in England and named Andre Marceau, is found strangled by an acid-soaked wire garrote in the middle of his newly rolled croquet lawn. His dying words were "The Babe from Hell!" which leads to the case being called the "Aeronautic Strangler-Baby Case." Other salient facts: A stolen autogiro apparently piloted by a child was seen to hover over the Marceau house at the time of the murder (Marceau, who was an airplane enthusiast, had placed a fifteen-foot, red-neon-lighted arrow on his roof, pointing toward London); a set of tiny footprints leads up to and away from the body, but doesn't reach the edge of the lawn; Marceau's ascot had been removed and stuffed into his pocket, and smells oddly of fish; and many years before, Marceau had written a letter to the London Times advocating the extermination of all Lilliputians, i.e., dwarfs and midgets, because their genetic defect, "nanism," would eventually cause the entire human race to shrink in size and thus all of mankind would be devoured by voracious insects.

The All-American Press Service, in the person of American detective and dissolute womanizer Alec Snide, embarks on a race against Scotland Yard sleuth Xenius Jones to solve the case. Snide wins out (sort of) in The Marceau Case by using his wits and by concocting an elaborate ruse to befuddle his opponent; Jones triumphs (sort of) in X. Jones of Scotland Yard by means of a fourth-dimensional method of detection he calls "Reconstruction of the Complete Invisible Stress-Pattern in a Medium Lying in a 4-Dimensional Continuum, by Analysis of the Surrounding Rimples." Keeler spends a dozen pages explaining this theory, but most of the explanations seem to make little or no sense, and in fact appear to be written in a language only approximating English. Choctaw, perhaps, as the New York Times suggested?

These first two books in the trilogy/mega-novel are comprised of literally hundreds of letters, telegrams, newspaper columns, photographs (one of a bare-breasted woman, another of Keeler himself), advertisements, cartoons, courtroom transcripts, and humorous booklets called "Chinaboy Chuckles." The third entry, *The Wonderful Scheme of Mr. Christopher Thorne,* is done in "straight" narrative form and not only offers yet another explanation of the Marceau murder but also stops every so often, as Nevins says, "to interpolate a disquisition on Oriental philosophy, or a brain-teaser riddle on how to get oil, water and gas pipes into three adjacent houses while drilling no more than 18 holes and having no pipe cross over or under any other pipe."

Among the solutions to the Aeronautic Strangler-Baby Case offered in the three novels are ones involving a cabal of enraged midgets plotting revenge against Marceau for his attack on Lilliputians, and the theory that Marceau was not murdered after all, but that he died of a rare hereditary disease called tetanoid epilepsy imagined as he was expiring that an evil baby was flying the autogiro above his croquet lawn, and earlier placed the acid-dipped wire around his own neck as a home remedy to prevent a skin rash from spreading upward to his face. Among the strange characters who appear and disappear in astonishing ways are a religious cult of astroextentionists (folks who believe you must never throw away anything left in a house by a previous owner or tenant), and a midget circus performer known variously as Little Lucas, Guy Ezekiah, Yogo Yakamura, The Juggling Jesus, and the Six-Toed Polish Dwarf.

So there you have Harry Stephen Keeler—or as much of him as I can give you in a single chapter in a single book. If you'd like to take a trip to Keelerland on your own, his books, though long out of print, can be found with a little diligence. But I warn you, just as Nevins and the eminent critic Will Cuppy warned me and others before me—a warning whose validity I can personally attest to. Once you've spent a couple of hours with the Kracked King of Keelerland, you'll never be quite the same again.

HARRY STEPHEN KEELER'S SCREWBALL CIRCUS

Francis M. Nevins

If ever there was an author unappreciated in his lifetime it was Harry Stephen Keeler. His outlandish plots and outrageous prose and people were so far removed from the conventions familiar to mystery reviewers that critics, when they bothered to take notice of him at all, loved to use him as a dartboard. "All Keeler's novels are written in Choctaw," commented the New York Times (before Anthony Boucher's tenure). "He writes in a strange jargon which eschews the distinctions between the parts of speech, and employs such a system of punctuation as no other writer save perhaps Gertrude Stein ever dared," said the Baltimore Evening Sun. "Keeler's wife, Hazel Goodwin, writes beautifully," reported Townsfolk Magazine, adding: "As for Keeler himself, the less said the better." Another wit remarked: "We look forward to the day when one of his novels is translated into English."

Will Cuppy of the Herald-Tribune was closer to the mark when he said: "There is nothing quite like Keeler in the mystery field; read any one of his works, and you're never quite the same again." But really Keeler was no more a mystery writer than he was a science-fiction or fantasy writer. Keeler was Keeler. When they made him the mold self-destructed. In a four-part series published long ago in the Journal of Popular Culture I tried to provide an overall survey of HSK's wild and woolly world, but since THE SIX FROM NOWHERE is part of a series, in this introduction I'll concentrate on the series this book belongs to.

Keeler in fact created several series. One has a book as its protagonist, another has a skull, yet a third revolves around a house (after which the publisher of this volume has named his enterprise). Among HSK's human series characters are Quiribus Brown, a 7½ foot tall mathematical wizard from the Indiana boondocks, and Tuddleton Trotter, an aged and bedraggled universal genius and patron of homeless cats. But the longest Keeler series with continuing human characters is the Circus Septology. At the center of these books, immovable in his office trailer while the world turns cartwheels around him, sits Angus Milliron MacWhorter, owner and proprietor of MacWhorter's Mammoth Motorized Shows, the Biggest Little Circus on Earth.

MacW, as his employees call him for short, also owns one of the longest faces in history, a great sad old-fashioned face, seamed and brooding like a late portrait of Lincoln. His business dress includes silk hat and long frock coat but after sundown he prefers a pink-striped nightshirt, the more comfortably to sit in the privacy of his trailer and peruse his great morocco-bound Bible or the latest number of the Weekly Ecclesiastical Review. But when a knock sounds on that trailer's outer door the time for tranquil theologizing is over. Something Crazy Has Happened. Not that a lunatic event disturbs MacW's habits: he continues to sit like a benevolent lump throughout all his adventures.

MacWhorter and his circus were not created by Keeler. His first wife, Hazel Goodwin Keeler, dreamed them up as the background for her short story "Spangles" (Best Love Stories, 26 June 1930). Keeler fell in love with this inane and unreadable story, wove his septology around the MacWhorter circus and even included "Spangles" as a chapter in two of the seven novels. Anyone who reads the books today will be flabbergasted at the astronomical difference in quality between Hazel's stone-cold-dead chapter and the crazy whirling universe Harry built around it.

The first MacWhorter novel is THE VANISHING GOLD TRUCK, completed in 1940 and published in this country by Dutton in 1941 and by Ward Lock in Britain a year later. The scene is Keeler Country, somewhere in the Bible Belt and probably not too far from the Kansas-Oklahoma-Missouri-Arkansas borders although Harry will cut out his tongue rather than tell you what state the circus is passing through at any given moment. A map of the area will demonstrate in the wink of a gnat's eyelash that it's like nothing in any atlas anywhere.

Up in the metropolis of Southwest City a fanatical anti-liquor clergyman named Rev. Zebulon Q. Holowynge has been trying to keep delivery trucks from servicing the local package stores and bars. This man of the cloth is convinced that the circus no less than the bottle is an enemy of God and plans to close down the MacWhorter show as the book opens. The circus has just completed its journey through the serpentine coils of Old Twistibus and is camped in the town of Foleysburg, which is totally sealed off from the outside world because its founder believed that electricity was the devil incarnate and insured that no telephone, telegraph, radio or other diabolical device should ever darken the precincts of the town.

Meanwhile back at the east end of Old Twistibus, one lone circus truck is pulling up at Elum's Store, and unless this truck rejoins the circus by a certain hour The Sky Will Fall In. This is a pattern we'll run into several times in the septology. Since driver Jim Craney and the lioness in the rear of his vehicle will never make it in time through Old Twistibus—especially since MacWhorter's elephant has knocked down the bridge across Bear Creek—Jim uses Elum's telephone to try and persuade Sheriff Bucyrus Duckhouse to let the truck use the Straightaway, a completed but not yet officially opened superhighway on pillars that tunnels through Smoke Ridge and cuts hours off the trip to Foleysburg. Meanwhile Al "Three-Gun" Mulhearn and his gang are about to steal a load of gold bars from the Cedarville Bank and make their getaway to Southwest City via the same straightaway. At the high point of the novel, both the Craney circus truck and the truck containing the robbers are reliably reported to be on the Straightaway while Duckhouse sits with his shotgun at the west end of the tunnel, waiting to nail the robbers. The Craney truck comes through the tunnel and its driver tells Duckhouse that another truck is indeed on the road behind him. But the robbers' truck never comes through, and it's physically impossible for it to have left the road! Here is a miracle problem worthy of John Dickson Carr, and the outrageous solution makes it clear that the Carr locked room novel is precisely what Keeler is here lampooning. MacW has little to do with the plot or its climax, whose prime mover is Sheriff Bucyrus Duckhouse. Even in Hazel's story "Spangles" which is printed as a chapter of this book, old Angus is little more than a walking lump.

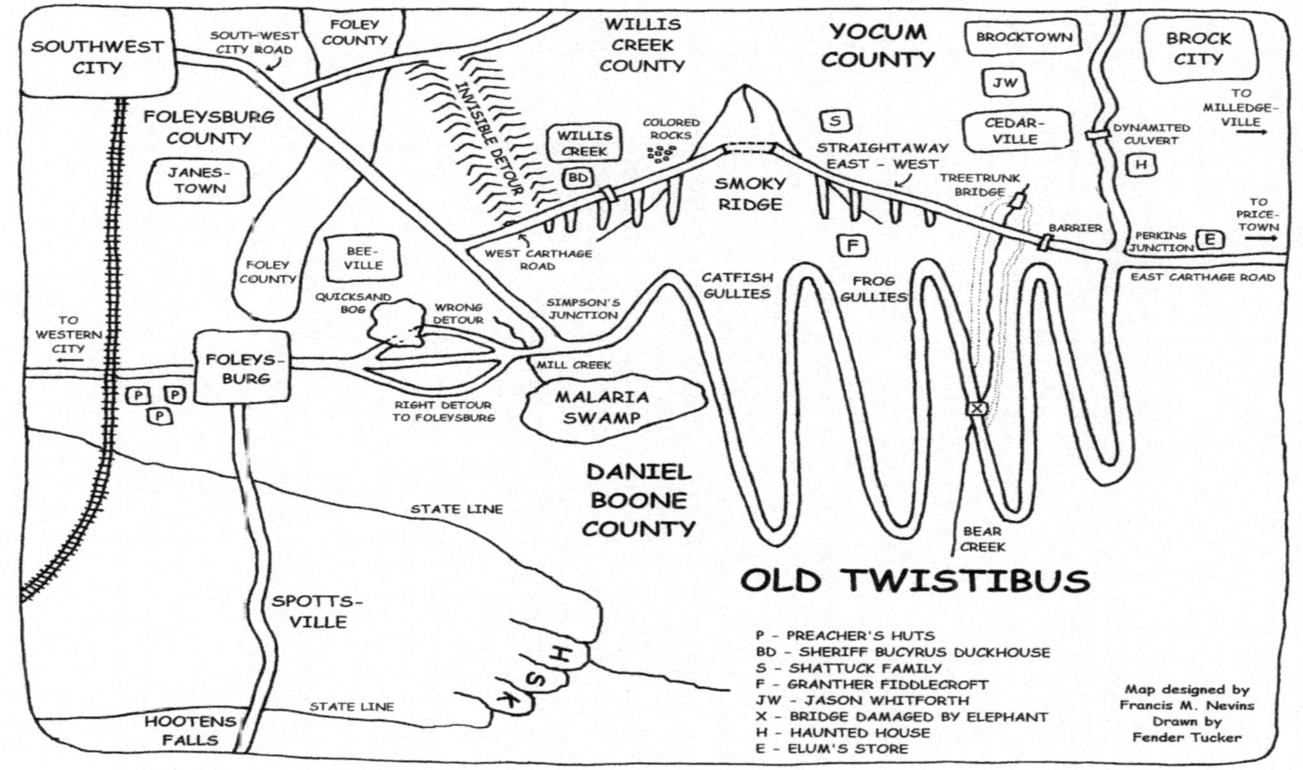
SOUTHWEST CITY
SOUTH-WEST CITY ROAD
FOLEY COUNTY
WILLIS CREEK COUNTY
YOCUM COUNTY
BROCKTOWN
BROCK CITY
FOLEYSBURG COUNTY
JANES-TOWN
INVISIBLE DETOUR
WILLIS CREEK
BD
COLORED ROCKS
S
JW
CEDAR-VILLE
TO MILLEDGE-VILLE
DYNAMITED CULVERT
STRAIGHTAWAY EAST - WEST
SMOKY RIDGE
TREETRUNK BRIDGE
H
TO PRICE-TOWN
BARRIER
PERKINS JUNCTION
E
WEST CARTHAGE ROAD
BEE-VILLE
FOLEY COUNTY
F
CATFISH GULLIES
FROG GULLIES
EAST CARTHAGE ROAD
QUICKSAND BOG
WRONG DETOUR
SIMPSON'S JUNCTION
TO WESTERN CITY
FOLEYS-BURG
MILL CREEK
P
P
P
RIGHT DETOUR TO FOLEYSBURG
MALARIA SWAMP
X
DANIEL BOONE COUNTY
STATE LINE
BEAR CREEK
OLD TWISTIBUS
SPOTTS-VILLE
H
S
K
STATE LINE
HOOTENS FALLS
P - PREACHER'S HUTS
BD - SHERIFF BUCYRUS DUCKHOUSE
S - SHATTUCK FAMILY
F - GRANTHER FIDDLECROFT
JW - JASON WHITFORTH
X - BRIDGE DAMAGED BY ELEPHANT
H - HAUNTED HOUSE
E - ELUM'S STORE
Map designed by Francis M. Nevins
Drawn by Fender Tucker

In December 1946 Keeler completed the next MacWhorter manuscript, a 140,000 word gargantua he called THE ACE OF SPADES MURDER. Unable to get either his American or British publishers to issue the book in that length, he broke the manuscript down into five separate MacWhorter novels, adding new plot elements as he needed them. Only two of the five were ever published in English. The earlier of these was called THE CASE OF THE JEWELED RAGPICKER in this country (Phoenix Press, 1948) and THE ACE OF SPADES MURDER in its lengthier British version (Ward Lock, 1949). It's a rather short book, only 256 pages in the American edition, but has enough material for ten ordinary novels, including a cast of 65 characters (several of whom turn out to be the same person), a time span of more than thirty years, a plot with ramifications in ten or twelve different states, and enough screwball activity to choke a rhinoceros. The opening chapters are set three decades in the past in Chicago's fabulous Hotel de Romanorum, built by a classics professor who came into money, with Latin quotations engraved in the floors and Roman numerals nailed to the doors. In the broom closet of this quaint hostelry is found the body of a black ragpicker, an ace of spades pinned to his back with a jeweled dagger. Thirty years later the crime is still unsolved but Bill Chattock, wine chemist turned circus truck driver for the MacWhorter Shows, thinks he knows where the key to the solution lies. But the 30-year statute of limitations applicable to the murder of blacks (which Keeler calls the Negro Homicide Protection Statute) is about to expire, and the killer will be safe from prosecution forever unless within the next few days Bill gets hold of the evidence and presents it to State's Attorney Igl Carwardine who by Keeler Koinkydink is vacationing in Ramsbottom, 25 miles north of the circus camp in Foleysburg. Bill takes leave of absence from the circus and goes off on his quest, winding up in the hamlet of Moffit, Indiana and the home of a greeting-card salesman named Pentwire Hughsmith, where with the help of a rare pocket dictionary Bill not only unravels the secret of the ragpicker murder but reconciles Hughsmith with his ex-wife, an indigent cookbook saleswoman subsisting on one pork chop a day. But on his way back to rejoin the circus at Foleysburg, Bill gets word from MacWhorter that he is to bring with him across Old Twistibus a new show wagon, complete with a large sum of money in a secret compartment.

The topography of Keeler Kountry has changed since THE VANISHING GOLD TRUCK and the valley of Old Twistibus has sprouted some new growths, including at its western edge the Great Poison Swamp with its horrible man-eating starky fish. There are also several human hazards in the valley. A gun moll disguised as a lady novelist is intent on offering Bill some drugged strawberry wine when he passes by, and Spearfish Meldrum and his gang are waiting at the west end of Old Twistibus to relieve Bill of the money in the truck and throw him to the starkies. I refuse to reveal how Bill escapes these traps, but had it not been for Captain Gunlock Lanternman and his top-secret Supercopter the residents of Keelerland might have wound up nibbling bits of Chattock the next time they had barbecued starky for supper. At journey's end Bill tells MacWhorter not only the entire story behind the murder of Ragpicker Joe but also his reasons for not sharing the tale with the authorities.

THE CASE OF THE JEWELED RAGPICKER is a huge crazy canvas of inspired Keelerisms, bursting with outrageous characters and incidents that Keeler in his abundance puts before us for a few moments and then drops. His style as usual is so bizarre as to take the breath away. A person with many chores to do is described as "busier than a wet hen." At one crisis point Chattock "seized a mental pencil out of one lobe of his brain and jerked a mental sheet of paper out of a second lobe." Will Cuppy had it right: you can't remain the same person after you've read Keeler.

The third and last MacWhorter novel to appear in English was also the final Keeler book published in his native tongue while he was alive, although it appeared only in Britain. STAND BY—LONDON CALLING! (Ward Lock, 1953) recycles the same two-headed dilemma that pops up in earlier and later novels in the series: old Angus is threatened with the loss of the circus while one of his younger employees strives manfully to cross Old Twistibus and rejoin the show before the sky falls in at X Hour. We open as usual with the circus at the east end of Old Twistibus, on its way to electricity-less Foleysburg. At a time when MacW must raise $3000 to pay off a mortgage on the show, he receives a telegram from a New Orleans law firm offering a handsome sum for one of the circus's free attractions, a grotesque little diorama depicting the execution-by-hanging of a crowned and stuffed fish.

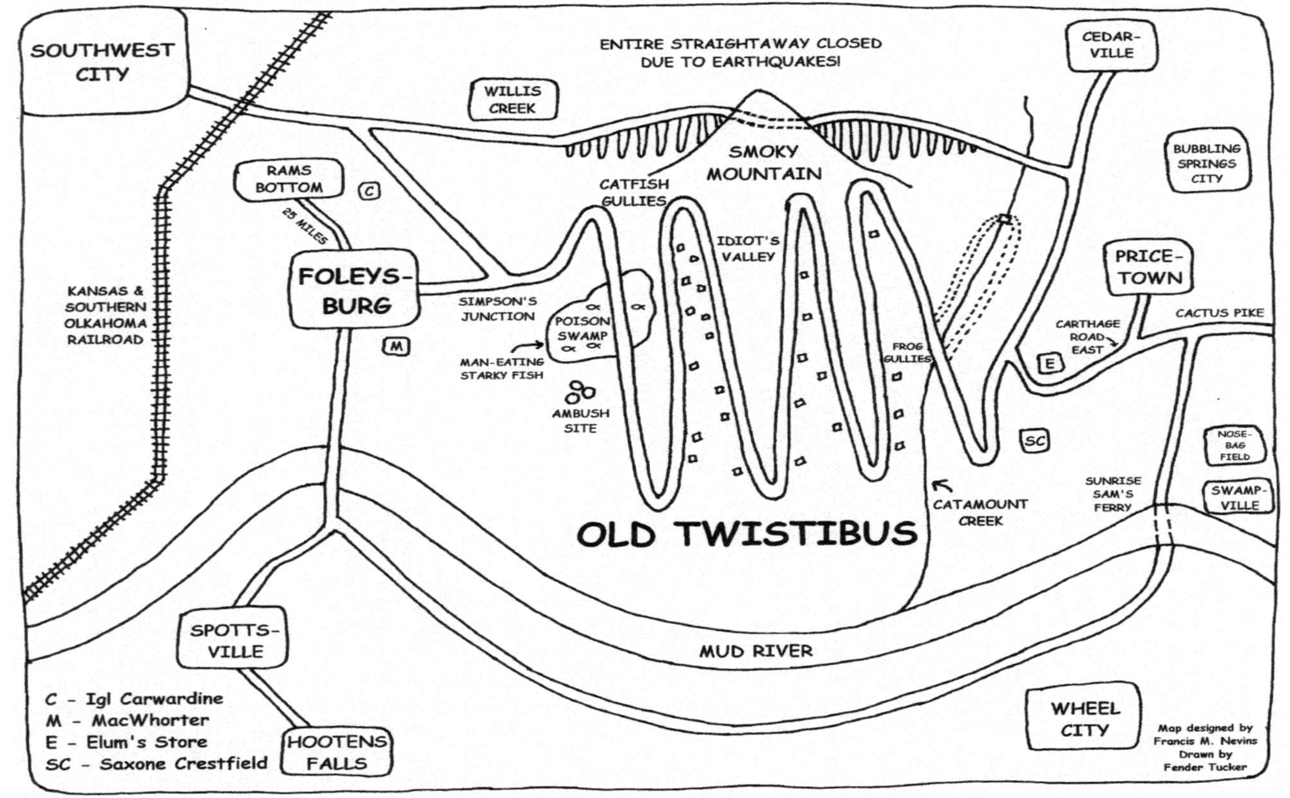

SOUTHWEST CITY
ENTIRE STRAIGHTAWAY CLOSED DUE TO EARTHQUAKES!
CEDAR-VILLE
WILLIS CREEK
RAMS BOTTOM
C
25 MILES
SMOKY MOUNTAIN
CATFISH GULLIES
BUBBLING SPRINGS CITY
IDIOT'S VALLEY
KANSAS & SOUTHERN OLKAHOMA RAILROAD
FOLEYS-BURG
M
SIMPSON'S JUNCTION
POISON SWAMP
MAN-EATING STARKY FISH
AMBUSH SITE
PRICE-TOWN
CACTUS PIKE
CARTHAGE ROAD EAST
E
FROG GULLIES
SC
NOSE-BAG FIELD
SUNRISE SAM'S FERRY
SWAMP-VILLE
CATAMOUNT CREEK
OLD TWISTIBUS
SPOTTS-VILLE
MUD RIVER
C - Igl Carwardine
M - MacWhorter
E - Elum's Store
SC - Saxone Crestfield
HOOTENS FALLS
WHEEL CITY
Map designed by Francis M. Nevins Drawn by Fender Tucker

Meanwhile one of Angus' drivers, young Pell Barneyfield, who is in the throes of an unholy and illegal love for his sister Erlys Janway, the circus "good-night girl," sets out on a cross-country quest to establish that a gargantuan mix-up took place in his infanthood and that he and the girl are not siblings. Unless he navigates Old Twistibus and brings proof of his contention back to the circus by a certain hour, Erlys will stifle her own passion for Pell by marrying sly Steve Octigan, the show's barker, who decides to take out a bit of insurance on his sexual conquest by bribing a family of feuding Idiot's Valley hillbillies to ambush Pell as he traverses the spaghetti-like trail. The outlandish plot element which both enables Pell to escape the trap and connects his quest with the hanged-fish diorama is a 75-year-old woolen suit that is incapable of wearing out. But the network of crazy coincidence that marks vintage Keeler never materializes in this adventure, which is rather feeble compared to the truly insane masterworks in the MacWhorter series. A dreadful short story by Hazel called "Lost—In This Block" contributes twenty pages to the book's length and not a milligram to the story.

STAND BY—LONDON CALLING is a disappointing finale to Keeler's English-language career, although he kept writing almost until his death. But unless you are multi-lingual or have access to his manuscripts your knowledge of the MacWhorter saga ends here. Of the remaining three books which Keeler carved out of the 140,000 word version of THE ACE OF SPADES MURDER, two were published only in Spain and the third was perused only by the Portuguese.

THE CASE OF THE CRAZY CORPSE was completed in April 1953 and published by Editorial Seculo of Lisbon as O CASO DO CADAVER ENDIABRADO. The book bears a very strong resemblance to JEWELED RAGPICKER, even to the point of both novels opening twenty-five or thirty years in the past with the discovery of a body under grotesque circumstances. In CRAZY CORPSE the body is fished out of Lake Michigan in its own coffin and turns out to be two bodies, the upper half belonging to a Chinese woman and the lower to a black man, the halves joined together by some kind of greenish gum. No sooner has Keeler set up this gruesome situation than he jumps ahead to the present and picks up MacWhorter brooding in his show wagon. Unless he gets some quick cash into his hands, the entire circus will shortly be taken over by the sadistic retired lion-tamer Geispitz Gmohling, who feels the urge to get back in the ring and "crack the old whip again over the big pussies' backs." Gmohling has bribed Flamo, MacWhorter's fire-eater, to spy on the circus from within, and Giff Odell, Angus' young assistant who has the sorely needed cash, is hundreds of miles away searching for the solution to the Crazy Corpse case and faces a rich assortment of obstacles in his race to rejoin the circus in time. By the end of the book Geispitz and Flamo have been banished into outer darkness, MacWhorter's young protege has found himself a wife and the mystery of the glued bodies has been solved, although the solution is markedly similar to that of JEWELED RAGPICKER.

THE CIRCUS STEALERS, completed in 1956 and published by Instituto Editorial Reus of Madrid in 1958 as LADRONES DE CIRCOS, covers the same familiar ground we've traversed before. The circus is in Pricetown and will shortly cross through Idiot's Valley along Old Twistibus, which is compared "to a giant strand of boiled spaghetti tossed down by a super-giant." The Poison Swamp and its starkies still sit at the west end of the road but this time every one of the valley's inhabitants is a mental defective and most of them tote guns. Foleysburg is still the stopping point at the other end of Twistibus and still survives without any electrical appliances but its laws have undergone some changes since our last visit. Checks are not legal tender in this community, the U.S. Supreme Court has just ruled that in Foleysburg midnight means 6:01 P.M., and a local ordinance makes it a crime to bring a prehistoric animal within the city limits. Out of these and other elements a villainous rival big-top entrepreneur named Wolf Gladish has hatched a scheme to snatch the entire MacWhorter circus out from under its owner's nose. MacWhorter learns of the plot and Gladish finds out that MacW has found out and the rest of the book is move and countermove, thrust and parry, except for an interlude in which we are treated once again to Hazel's unreadable story "Spangles." The last-minute arrival of a truck driven by a skeleton saves both the day and the circus for Angus. The young assistant who must cross Old Twistibus and rejoin the circus before X-Hour is named Rance Holly but this time around the track he hasn't been off in quest of the solution to a 30-year-old murder.

Ecology-minded long before it became fashionable, Keeler was determined to recycle every last particle of his 1946 ACE

OF SPADES manuscript, and the dregs of that 140,000 word effort were finally recast into the fifth MacWhorter novel, A COPY OF BEOWULF, which was completed in July 1957 and published by Reus as UNA VERSION DEL BEOWULF in 1960. This time the circus isn't in danger of being taken away from MacW and the entire book concentrates on the quest of Angus' young assistant for the titular volume. The results are horrendous. In forty years this is the only totally boring Keeler novel I've found, with no brainbusting coincidences or outrageous lines of description and dialogue to enliven the enterprise. Keeler's intention was apparently to satirize the conventions of 19th-century riverboat melodrama for his Spanish audience, which is why we find the villain over and over referring to the heroine as "me pee-roud bee-u-teh" and the heroine calling the bad guy "you willian" (sic). This is the limit of the fun in A COPY OF BEOWULF, which was the last MacWhorter novel to appear anywhere till now.

Later in 1957 Kealer completed REPORT ON VANESSA HEWSTONE, another circus novel much better than BEOWULF but never published anywhere. For some reason HSK decided to change the names of all his circus people in this book. The protagonist is Noah Quindry of Quindry's World-Colossal Motorcade Circus, a bald plump fellow who is round as a great dumpling and wears a black-and-white checkered suit with crimson derby rather than MacW's tophat and swallowtail coat, but for all practical purposes this is the same MacWhorter circus. This time however there is no Old Twistibus and no race to save the show from a Willian. Instead the problem is an unknown maniac traveling with the circus who insists on cutting out and stealing every specimen of the letter U he can lay his hands on, including a part of a poster advertising the movie UNION STATION, a segment of a banner welcoming the Unitarians to town for a convention, a corner of a Fu Manchu paperback, an engraved letter from the underground tomb of Ulysses the Talking Dog ("a dog of so many patterns of coat that he must have been the son of all dogs in history"), and even a letter forming part of a tattoo on the dead body of Screamo the Clown. Suspicion focuses on a mysterious young archery expert who has recently joined the circus and much of the book is almost a parody of the classic Cornell Woolrich pattern of oscillation between belief and disbelief in the man's guilt. The solution and the reason for the

U-nappings come out in one of the wildest Keeler denouements ever.

The MacWhorter circus first came to life in an old pulp magazine and another pulp is at the center of the last of Angus' adventures. THE SIX FROM NOWHERE, which was completed in 1958 but never published anywhere until now, boasts HSK's most juicily named villain, Gonwyck Schwaaa. (At the first appearance of his name in the manuscript Keeler adds a little footnote: "To Editor only: 3 a's. Author.") Gonwyck and his cohorts are plotting to steal a certain copy of the magazine Detective Narratives from MacWhorter's safe, and the intrigues over the pulp intertwine with the affairs of a British female mathematician, an educated hobo, the ashes of a corrupt politician in a Chicago crypt, and a pair of circus cats who have left 2,000,000 progeny across the United States. Among all the MacWhorter novels this is the wildest, and every publisher who rejected it in Harry's lifetime ought to be made to stand in the corner with a dunce cap.

MacW and his circus made one brief final appearance in a manuscript Keeler completed in 1960 but, although it's one of his daffiest late novels, never found a publisher for. In BREAKFAST AT THE WARINGS, alternately and more aptly titled THE CASE OF THE TWO-HEADED IDIOT, Angus receives a $3000 offer from a Chicago law firm in return for permission to let the firm's unnamed client have a private ten-minute session with a two-headed idiot child that had once been exhibited in MacW's circus. Angus sends his young assistant Brock Colburn to the Windy City to look into this offer but Brock happens to be an escaped convict wanted in Chicago for murder—a crime which of course he didn't commit. As one might expect in a Keeler novel, the first person he meets in Chicago holds the key not only to the idiot child mystery but also to Brock's little difficulties with the authorities and winds up becoming his wife too. But these lucky resolutions are reached only after we've followed Brock through 400 pages of deliciously intertwined subplots which demonstrate once again that even in his last years Keeler remained the great wack of American letters.

I don't think it's stretching things too far to say that the Angus MacWhorter series reflects a good bit of Keeler's view of life. If the grotesque and bizarre and casually monstrous people and incidents encountered along and at each end of Old

Twistibus represent HSK's view of how the world goes, then the MacWhorter circus must stand for his vision of the ideal society—personalistic, communitarian, nonacquisitive, noncompetitive, content to travel over and through the rocky absurdities of Old Twistibus, unpretentiously amusing those who wish to see—and MacWhorter himself must be Harry's self-portrait, benevolent and ineffectual and eccentric and without illusions. No other writer combines as Keeler did the unfettered delight in creation of a small child and the mathematical craftsmanship of a computer that has somehow programmed itself. He was the sublime nutty genius of the 20th century, and as long as boundless creativity is cherished, so long will Harry Stephen Keeler be.

HICK DICK FROM THE STICKS: Harry Stephen Keeler's Quiribus Brown

Francis M. Nevins

The origin and development of Harry Stephen Keeler's series characters are frequently as bizarre as the plots of Keeler's own novels, and the saga of Quiribus Brown is no exception.

During the latter part of World War II the editors of *Esquire* decided to launch a series of short detective stories and invited Keeler to create a new character for possible publication in the magazine. Miffed at the thought of being asked to "submit a sample like a guy with a tin cup," Harry told the editors that if they wanted him to go to the trouble of thinking up a new character they'd have to pay him $100 in advance. To his great surprise *Esquire* sent him a check immediately, although specifying that the advance was not a commitment to accept what he submitted. So Keeler sat down and proceeded to create a character. He strung together a typically outrageous plot about a barking clock and an astigmatic witness and dreamed up a 7½ foot tall mathematically-educated hick from the sticks as his new detective. At first the hick was named just that—Abner Hick to be precise—but before sending out this 14,000 word adventure Harry prudently changed his protagonist's name to Quiribus Brown. The name change made no difference. *Esquire* rejected the story. The new detective character chosen to grace its pages was Henry Kane's New York PI Peter Chambers, who narrates his own cases in a self-created idiom known as High Kanese which is worlds removed from Keeler's style but no less lovably eccentric.

With the rejected tale back in his hands Keeler decided to recycle it, but in bigger and better form. He blithely yanked poor Quiribus out of the plot, replaced him with that bedraggled old universal genius Tuddleton Travelstead Trotter who had starred in Keeler's mammoth extravaganza THE MATILDA HUNTER MURDER (1931), added 85,000 more words to the story and sold the result to his Spanish publisher Instituto Editorial Reus, which issued it in 1947 as EL CASO DEL RELOJ

LADRADOR. After its Spanish publication Keeler broke up the 100,000-word version into two separate and unrelated novels which his then American publisher Phoenix Press brought out as THE CASE OF THE BARKING CLOCK (1947) and THE CASE OF THE TRANSPOSED LEGS (1948).

That took care of the original story he had written with hope of publication in *Esquire*, but he still had an original and unused character on his hands. So during the late months of 1947 he proceeded to make Quiribus Brown the hero of another book.

A reading of the manuscript of this book and of some of Keeler's letters, combined with a bit of educated guesswork here and there, has helped me reconstruct what Harry's original plan must have been. Quiribus Brown, 7½ feet tall and weighing in at 360 pounds, has been raised on a small farm in the Indiana boondocks by his invalid father, Professor Xanrof Brown, who has trained him to be a mathematical wizard. But the Anglo-Saxon ancestry of father and son has earned them the wrath of their chauvinistic German neighbors and Quiribus has been the object of special hatred because of his outlandish size. Thanks to a conspiracy on the part of local officials—including prosecutor Gerhardt Drumheller, grand jury foreman Hans Flintkopf who has his eye on the Brown farm, and criminal court judge Herman Oberholm—it has come about that poor Quiribus will be tried for perjury, and inevitably convicted and imprisoned, unless within one month he can solve four criminal cases through mathematical reasoning. (I won't attempt to describe the conglomeration of happenings from which the frame-up was constructed.) So Quiribus takes off for crime-glutted Chicago in desperate hope that the big city will yield him the four cases he seeks. The rest of the book was to describe his quest for and solution of these cases.

That was the original plan. Then things started to happen to it.

First off, Harry grew so attached to one of Quiribus' four cases that he decided to cut it out of the original plan and expand it into a separate novel. This required him to reduce from four to three the number of crimes Quiribus must solve by mathematical means; and an examination of the manuscript shows that this change was indeed made, although Harry missed a few references to the necessity that four crimes be solved. Then he cranked out two of the remaining three episodes he needed. In "The Case of the Black Marbles" Quiribus is asked to determine whether there was anything unfair or fraudulent about the newly invented game of chance in which Chinese restaurateur Hung Fung Lee lost virtually everything he owned, including the Restaurant of the 99 Blackbirds Returning to Nest, to the unscrupulous Oriental gambler Lu Mong. Did I hear someone ask what was Quiribus' fee? One double helping of chop suey. In "The Case of the Hidden Munitions Plant Spy" the FBI, having no mathematical geniuses of its own, prevails upon Quiribus to visit Shelltown, site of an experimental armaments factory, and find out which of the industrial town's many inhabitants is actually a mathematics-loving spy who's passing on military secrets to Russia as a way of avenging Germany's defeat in World War II. (I'll leave the political implications of the story to Henry Kissinger or Colin Powell—or anyone else who wants them.) Neither story ranks among Keeler's best efforts but no one other than HSK could have written either.

At this point Keeler became sick of Quiribus Brown and unwilling to write any more about him. But the two stories he'd completed added up to only half the wordage needed for a full-length book. Harry resolved this impasse by bringing his wife into the picture. Years before, Hazel Goodwin Keeler had written a story about debonair English sleuth Josman Sheffield who operated in Chicago as a Holmes-like consulting detective with the assistance of a faceless Watson named Carter. Harry asked Hazel to pull Carter out of the story, replace him with Quiribus Brown and expand the tale to the length of half a book. Hazel complied, with the result that the last 90-odd pages of the Quiribus manuscript consist of "The Case of the Flying Hands," written by Hazel alone. This story is flat and unimaginative compared to the two written by Harry, and Quiribus plays not much more of a role in the plot than did the faceless Carter in Hazel's original version. Sheffield and Quiribus investigate an attempt to burglarize the apartment of lovely Orchid Fernleigh and her grandmother, discover the fingerprints of a criminal whom Sheffield knows to be dead, and are soon led to the hiding place of some stolen plans for a flying saucer. Although the case has no mathematical element and hence wouldn't help Quiribus avoid conviction for perjury back in Indiana, Sheffield takes time out for a side trip to his young assistant's home town where he nips the conspiracy in the bud; and the certainty that Orchid Fernleigh will be able to marry the young man she loves coincides with Sheffield's solution of the criminal problem so that all the virtuous characters have found happiness by the time the curtain falls. Hazel lifted the central plot gimmick of her story from "The Prints of Hantoun," the classic Professor Poggioli story by the Keelers' long-time friend T. S. Stribling. As Harry remarked in a letter: "What one will do to get a book-length!"

The Quiribus manuscript, whose overall title was THE CASE OF THE FLYING HANDS, now consisted of the framing story, "The Case of the Black Marbles," "The Case of the Hidden Munitions Plant Spy," and Hazel's "The Case of the Flying Hands." Keeler's English publisher Ward Lock accepted the manuscript in this form but soon had second thoughts, telling Harry that they wanted to drop his two episodes, get a ghostwriter to expand the "Flying Hands" story to novel length and issue the result as a new book by HSK. Harry hit the ceiling, and on returning to terra firma he fought the publisher's plan tooth and nail. Finally Ward Lock announced that they wouldn't publish the manuscript at all and after several years' delay returned it to Keeler, who had long since spent the advance money. Harry then shipped the book off to his Spanish publisher Reus, which purchased the manuscript and added it to their stockpile of unpublished Keeler originals. At Harry's death early in 1967 THE CASE OF THE FLYING HANDS had still not appeared even in Spain, and afterwards Reus switched to a policy of publishing nonfiction only and returned the manuscript. Since then it has remained buried, but now like a monster lurching out of the grave in a cheap horror flick it lives again, thanks to that wonderful loon sanctuary known as Ramble House.

The story which Keeler had removed from the original plan saw print much sooner, being published in its expanded book-length form by Ward Lock as THE MURDERED MATHEMATICIAN (1949). In this variant on the original premise of the manuscript, Professor Xanrof Brown has died leaving a wacky will which disinherits his son Quiribus unless the young giant solves *one* crime by the application of mathematical reasoning within a specified time. The corpse of the novel's title is Professor Lucius Munstergale, head of the mathematics department at Mid-West University. His nickname, Radical Luke, is based on his fanatical attempts to expunge Greek letters from mathematical symbology and on his flamboyant trigonometry examinations. [The novel includes one complete exam supposedly from Luke's pen, and a typical question deals with a rascally lightning-rod agent who erects a 267,824,729-foot-tall rod atop a 100-foot tower.] But what makes Munstergale a menace to the non-mathematical world is that he Knows Too Much about certain Chicago bigwigs. He can prove that Mayor-Elect J. Haverstock Unwynde is in reality the notorious escaped Nazi Rudolph Pfankuch, and he also has evidence that the Chief of Police's son-in-law, Alfonse Speirrl, is selling tainted food in his chain of restaurants. When Munstergale is shot to death in his home, he leaves behind as his Dying Message a set of mathematical symbols several galaxies beyond the comprehension of the crack-brained flatfeet of Chicago's Homicide Squad. Luckily Quiribus has just arrived in the Windy City in search of a crime with a math angle, and after a display of Keeler Coincidences our gigantic hero is asked by the police to work on the Radical Luke case as a special expert. HSK inflates his original short-story plot into a novel of more than 75,000 words with the help of all sorts of red herrings, side excursions and longwinded verbal perambulations. This is nowhere near his best book but as a bizarre parody of the Ellery Queen dying-message gambit it does have its moments (including a brief encounter with a young college student named F. Dannay!), and the gross insults aimed by the other characters at poor outsized Quiribus add up to another of Keeler's oblique jabs at America's treatment of its minorities.

The last traces of Quiribus are found in THE STOLEN GRAVESTONE (1958), one of the many late novels Keeler finished but never found a publisher for even in Spain. The protagonist this time is Saul Wing, a 6'4" Chinese who dresses like a North Woods lumberjack and speaks perfect Angry-Saxophonish just like Harry's earlier Asian hero Y. CHEUNG, BUSINESS DETECTIVE (1939). In the early chapters of the novel, where Saul wanders around Chicago's Gyp Row and gets picked up by an apparent prostitute who in reality is a serial killer targeting very tall men, several pages of manuscript are copied almost verbatim from the chapters of THE MURDERED MATHEMATICIAN where Quiribus wandered the same honky-tonk district for his own curious purposes. Among the many facets of Harry's wild genius was a genius for stealing from himself. Eventually we learn that Saul's burning ambition is to become a private detective, and he gets the chance when he's invited to solve the puzzle of "who stole the gravestone from the grave of F. Jansky, pastrymaker, and placed a pair of rubber boots thereon"—boots that were "cunningly ordered in an ossified man's name," "a poor devil lying rigid as a board, without hands or feet—a man who was once President of the Buffalo, New York, Ethical Society."

If Ramble House can resist publishing that one, I am Queen of the May.

The Riddle of the Traveling Skull: An Introduction

Richard Polt

If you are attuned to the unique, it won't take you long to realize that this novel has a flavor all its own. There is a clash of ingredients here that most readers will either love or hate: a wildly implausible plot combines with the particularities of real Chicago locales; silliness (Julu berries and the Billy Bulger Bulge) blends with a touch of genuine creepiness (the skull with an etched metal plate in it, the typewritten scrap reading "every hour is filled with fear for me"). As you venture forth into the tangles of *The Riddle of the Traveling Skull*, awaiting the arrival of Legga the Human Spider and the Great Simon, you will no doubt wonder: who was the man who concocted this odd tale?

Harry Stephen Keeler was born in Chicago in 1890, a few months before his father finished drinking himself to death. His mother managed to make a living by running a boarding house for vaudevillians; she was to marry three other men, only to be widowed again each time within a few years. Young Harry grew up in this colorful, unstable, theatrical atmosphere, drinking in the cheap thrills of dime museums and melodramas, in a Chicago that was overflowing with races and dialects. At age sixteen, he dressed a dummy in his own clothes and fooled a friend into believing that he had been shot. This incident was written up in the papers, and Keeler developed a taste for flamboyant trickery that is apparent throughout his fiction.

Shortly after earning a degree in electrical engineering from the Armour Institute of Technology, Harry was committed by his mother to the insane asylum at Kankakee, for reasons that are still obscure. Keeler spent most of 1912 in this institution, and got through the experience partly by taking notes on everything he saw; he was discharged as fully recovered, but retained a lifelong antipathy to psychiatrists.

Fresh out of Kankakee, the only job he could find was as an electrician in a South Chicago steel mill. Keeler rose before dawn every morning to sit before his typewriter before going to work—for he was full of stories he needed to tell. The stories began to get published, and Keeler's mother—perhaps to make up for the asylum incident—offered to support him if he wanted to try to become a professional writer. In their row house at 740 North State Street, Harry discovered a hidden room that he turned into his studio. A sign was placed proudly in a window: "Harry Stephen Keeler, writer of Detective Stories, Serials, Action Stories."

By 1919, Keeler's star was rising fast. In October of that year, he married the pretty and talented Hazel Goodwin, daughter of a prominent physician who was none too happy about the pairing. Keeler became the editor of the weekly *Chicago Ledger* and the monthly *10 Story Book*, both of which were outlets for some of his own tales, sometimes published under pseudonyms. He was to edit the *Ledger* until 1923 and *10 Story Book* (which was filled with short fiction, drawings by Hazel, and revealing girl photos) until it folded in 1940—in addition to doing a stint in the mid-twenties as the editor of *America's Humor*. But it was fiction to which Keeler devoted his main energies—first a stream of clever short stories, and then longer, serialized tales that he came to call "webwork plots."

Keeler constructed his webwork novels in what he called his workshop, which was dominated by a bank of filing cabinets containing notes and clippings on strange happenings, dialects, scientific facts, and peculiar names and places. On the wall was a pin-studded map of the city where his current tale was set (usually Chicago, "the London of the West"). On a blackboard, HSK would diagram the intersecting threads of his plot, sometimes mapping them onto a timeline divided into small intervals. He would type the first draft of a novel on his old L. C. Smith using a continuous roll of paper, so that he wouldn't have to interrupt his train of thought.

The classic Keelerian webwork is an intricate tangle of story lines, glued together by red herrings and outrageous coincidences, ending with a staggering surprise that forces one to reinterpret the entire story. The point is not to represent reality as we know it, or to delve into psychology, but to produce the unique pleasure that comes from getting narrated events to click into a pattern. As Keeler put it, "It is this artificial relationship, this purely fictional web-work plot, this bit of life twisted into a pattern mathematically and geometrically true, that fills the gaps in one's spirit which rebels at the looseness of life as it apparently is." The result of this aesthetic ideal is a genre that is closest to mystery, although Keeler, who never read a word of Agatha Christie, had little use for the conventions of murder mysteries. Often, as in *The Riddle of the Traveling Skull*, it is unclear for some time whether a murder has even been committed. Keeler novels are not whodunits, but what-the-hell-is-going-ons—weird whirlwinds that sweep their protagonists up and spin them around many times before depositing them at the ridiculous but happy ending.

Keeler developed an elaborate theory of plots in "The Mechanics (And Kinematics) of Web-Work Plot Construction," a series published in *The Author and Journalist* in 1928. These articles classify sequences of incidents into 15 different types and propose a recipe for generating a webwork: the main or viewpoint character must intersect four or five other threads (people or objects) in such a way that each encounter is the cause of the next one. The alert reader will find this kind of pattern at the heart of *The Riddle of the Traveling Skull*. Having generated a plethora of plot threads, Keeler proceeds to tie them together with maniacal precision, making sure that there is an explanation (no matter how far-fetched) for every occurrence. Normal standards of plausibility are abandoned: strange behavior is explained by an even stranger typographical error, or eccentric will, or obscure legal loophole; when the continued existence of a character would be inconvenient, he is promptly killed off in a railroad accident. The effect is the literary equivalent of a Rube Goldberg invention, in which everything happens for a reason, yet the rationality of the system only makes the whole thing more absurd.

Keeler often combines the intricacy of webwork with the multiple narrative layers of the Arabian Nights technique: one of a character's acts is to tell a story. This is not only a convenient opportunity to reuse some of Keeler's early short fiction, but creates a distance between narrator and reader—a distance that Keeler likes to exploit.

Keeler's writing injects a note of radical experimentation into popular fiction and anticipates later developments in American literature. The world of HSK is as complex and erudite as that of Thomas Pynchon or Don DeLillo, as self-consciously playful as that of David Foster Wallace, and as interlinked as the

Internet. (Is it a coincidence that the first page of William Gibson's 1984 novel *Neuromancer*, the founding document of cyberpunk, includes the word "webwork"?)

Starting in 1924, Keeler began adapting his serials to hardcover editions, first in Britain (with the publishers Hutchinson and Ward Lock) and then in the United States (with Dutton). The long list of Keeler titles testifies to his energy and to his compositional techniques: he was never shy about reworking earlier material, and often constructed new novels around "chunks" that had been excised from previous manuscripts. The Keeler canon is itself a sort of webwork, with stories that overlap the boundaries of single volumes, spin off into new stories, go through British and American variants, and refer slyly to each other. Among the highlights of the 1920s and 1930s—Keeler's most brilliant period—are several outstandingly idiosyncratic creations. (The dates given are those of the American hardback publication.)

Sing Sing Nights (1928) was constructed in just a few days from an Arabian Nights framework in which three convicts engage in a storytelling contest, plus three of Keeler's earlier pulp stories (including the Keelerian counterpart to Kafka's "Metamorphosis," a story in which the hero wakes up in the body of a gorilla). Krenwicz, one of the convicts, borrows from "Mechanics (And Kinematics)" to explain how to generate a webwork plot. This book sold surprisingly well; it was translated into many foreign languages, and in 1934 inspired two cheap films from Monogram Pictures ("Sing Sing Nights" and "Mysterious Mr. Wong," featuring Bela Lugosi attempting to play a Chinese villain).

Thieves' Nights (1929) is a more sophisticated Arabian-Nights-style tale, featuring four layers of narration in which one character—the thief DeLancey—recurs in both the outermost and the innermost layer.

The Spectacles of Mr. Cagliostro (1929), Keeler's darkest novel, draws on his own experience to spin a tale of a man driven into an insane asylum either by his enemies or by his own paranoia—the reader is long left in doubt as to which.

The Box from Japan (1932), at over 750 pages, is Keeler's longest single-volume novel and one of the longest mystery novels in English. Set in 1942, it features intercontinental three-dimensional television, sugar-producing cacti, and a

Japanese emperor who is under the delusion that he can turn his blood invisible at will.

The Marceau Case and *X. Jones—Of Scotland Yard* (1936) are arguably Keeler's masterpieces. These vast, surrealistic works tell the tale of the mysterious "dispatchal" of André Marceau, who collapsed in the middle of his croquet lawn croaking, "The Babe—From Hell!" For once, a Keeler creation is a whodunit and a parody of conventional crime fiction. The case is solved in the first volume by an American, only to be reinterpreted completely in the second volume by Xenius Jones, a British investigator who subscribes to a "four-dimensional" theory of detection. The Marceau books tell their stories exclusively by means of documents (often culled from the magazines that Keeler edited), including letters, telegrams, an astronomical chart, a poem by a madman, newspaper stories, a Bible verse, cartoons, photographs (including one of Keeler himself), a short story by Marceau, pseudo-Chinese jokes, and family trees.

Almost as remarkable are *The Mysterious Mr. I* (1938) and its sequel, *The Chameleon* (1939), where Keeler takes the concept of an unreliable narrator to a delightful extreme: the story is told by someone who assumes 50 different identities, leaving the reader mystified until the end. For good measure, while impersonating a professor of philosophy the narrator proposes yet another solution to the Marceau case.

While Keeler's earlier novels were received well, in the late thirties his popularity began a precipitous decline, due in part to the peculiar style that he developed when he began to run out of earlier material. Most late Keeler novels consist almost exclusively of dialogue—long-winded dialogue about events that happen offstage, heavily larded with exclamation marks, dashes, and dialect, and often written with a syntax that must be called aggressively unreadable. (*The Monocled Monster*, published by Ward Lock in 1947, includes the following immortal sentence: "Since it had been brought by her so belatedly with respect to his departure, use it Barry Wayne had not even bothered to do, for fully dressed he already had been by then—and combed, as well, through the sense of feel also, had been his hair.") Keeler's later novels for Dutton were printed in tiny editions and read only by diehard fans. After *The Book with the Orange Leaves* (1942), he was dropped by Dutton and had to turn to the obscure Phoenix Press, which put out nine Keelers destined primarily for the lending-library market. Several of these Phoenix novels incorporate short stories by Hazel Goodwin Keeler, which usually bear little relation to the main plot.

Phoenix published its last Keeler in 1948 (*The Case of the Transposed Legs*), and in 1953 Ward Lock put a stop to Keeler's British career with *Stand By—London Calling*. But Keeler soldiered on, writing exclusively for Spanish or Portuguese translation at the rate of $50 per novel. His stories from this late period return obsessively to a few themes: he wrote no fewer than nine novels about a traveling circus (inspired by Hazel's circus story "Spangles," which may in turn have been inspired by a silent movie by that name) as well as a series of verbose science-fiction novels featuring time travel and involving an old mansion known, appropriately enough, as Ramble House.

The Keelers had no children—only a rabbit named H. L. Mencken and many cats—so when Hazel died of cancer in 1960, Harry was left in solitude and deep despair. In a fit of depression, he gave away his personal copies of his novels by the taxiload to Chicago used book dealers. He was enabled, as he said, to grab "the tail of the greased pig called the will to live" by the reappearance in his life of Thelma Rinaldo, who had been his secretary at *America's Humor* in 1927. After a tumultuous courtship, Thelma and Harry were married in 1963. Returning to his typewriter, Keeler produced a few more manuscripts that have never been published in any language, including *The Scarlet Mummy* and a Ramble House novel titled *The S____ V____*.

Shortly after Keeler's death in 1967 his widow, Thelma, was contacted by Francis M. Nevins, a mystery connoisseur, writer, and legal scholar who was to become the foremost expert on Keeler. "The Wild and Woolly World of Harry Stephen Keeler," Nevins' series of articles in *The Journal of Popular Culture* (Spring 1970, Fall 1970, Winter 1971 and Summer 1973) laid the foundation for a small posthumous cult. Nevins has continued to contribute generously to the literature on HSK. In 1982, Thelma donated 34 boxes of Keeler's papers and manuscripts to the library of Columbia University, which is their home today.

The Riddle of the Traveling Skull is one of Keeler's most neatly crafted webwork tales, and one of his most successful:

it was issued by Dutton and Ward Lock in 1934, reissued in a cheap hardback edition by Triangle Books a few years later, and translated into German, Spanish and Portuguese. The story began in 1914 as a two-part, 18,000-word tale titled "The Trepanned Skull." In 1933 Keeler expanded it by 63,000 words, including what fans recognize as signature touches of High Keelerian prose: the references to the fourth dimension and Ouspensky, the setting in the near future (1940), and the delight in freaks and eccentrics. The sonnet by Hazel anticipates her more extensive contributions to Keeler novels of the 1940s and 1950s. As in much of Keeler's best work, one gets the feeling that in-jokes are bubbling beneath the surface. (One example: the character with the improbable name of Dr. George McBean was a real ophthalmologist who had diagnosed Keeler's own cyclophoria. When a fan in Akron with eye problems wrote to Keeler asking whether "you know of any such man as this Dr. McBean in real life," Keeler promptly referred him to the doctor—not without warning his reader to stay away from "that dismal swampy miasmatic world of neurology and neurologists.")

As for the ethnic caricatures in this novel, it's clear that Keeler felt no compunctions about stepping on the toes of African Americans, Chinese, or Czechoslovaks. Like most of his contemporaries, he drew freely on stereotypes in order to add excitement and (literally) color to his tales. What sets Keeler apart from his times on racial matters is the fact that in other stories, he took the issue of race seriously and dealt with it in a peculiar, but certainly anti-racist way. The hero of *Y. Cheung, Business Detective* (1939) is a sympathetic Chinese-American. *The Man Who Changed His Skin* (a 1959 novel published only in Spain [until Ramble House's 2000 edition]) deals with a white man who wakes up in a black body, and discovers that a black man's life is worth living after all. Keeler has a special fondness for mixed-race characters, such as Ebenezer Sitting-Down-Bear of *The Wonderful Scheme of Christopher Thorne* (1936), who is half American Indian, a quarter black, and a quarter white. Ebenezer lashes out against racism and economic injustice: "We starve to death—amidst plenty—if we don't play the game—as we find it." Keeler's solution to racism is a radical one: according to Krenwicz, his spokesman in *Sing Sing Nights*, racism will be overcome only when scientific advances such as plastic surgery and "giant air-liners" promote worldwide intermarriage and the actual destruction of the races.

With its dreamlike coincidences and startling reversals, *The Riddle of the Traveling Skull* is deliciously suited to make us suspect that "the human threads that make up the web called Life mesh together in patterns more startling and more bizarre than they even appear on the surface to do." It makes us question and requestion its events, searching for new interpretations—for "What are more deceptive in life than facts?" For me, the first sentence of this book was enough to send an unfamiliar tingle through my spine—enough to keep me reading until the mystifying end, and then to catapult me onto an insatiable quest for more Keeler. Within a few months of reading *The Riddle of the Traveling Skull*, I had founded the Harry Stephen Keeler Society (look for us on the Internet—we always welcome new members). A growing number of people around the world have been rediscovering Keeler in the last few years. Now, thanks to Ramble House, more denizens of the twenty-first century will have the opportunity to decide whether Harry Stephen Keeler was a hack, a lunatic, a genius—or a little of each.

BY
HARRY

My "Million-Dollar" Plot-Inventing Secret!

From Writer's Digest, April, 1947

Harry Stephen Keeler

My good friend Aron Mathieu, who has watched my published novels, over the last 17 years, grow from 1 to 60 in number, asked me if it is not time to reveal that "million-dollar" plot-inventing secret in some ten or twelve thousand words.

I have surprised Aron by saying that it can be revealed in no more than a couple of thousand words![7] I have even shocked him out of his next 10 years' spiritual growth by saying that I would even reveal the secret to the readers of *Writer's Digest.*

And here it is—for such as are base enough to wish to become mass-productionists in the field of the novel!

First of all, in building or inventing the plot for a proposed novel, I build it on sufficiently *giant or excess dimensions* that, when the resultant novel is finished, the novel *will come out materially greater than the length desired.*

Greater, if possible, by at least 20,000 to 30,000 words.

This merely involves developing *all* the possible plot issues, and allowing in the plot scenes and characters which ordinarily, from the strict viewpoint of economy, the author would leave out. Would perhaps present by mere mention, or in retrospective narration on the part of other characters.

This procedure naturally necessitates, at the completion of the resultant novel, a surveyal of it to see just *what* can be "by-passed" out. There are two ways of cutting a novel. One is by taking out words, phrases, sentences, and occasional paragraphs. The other—and it's ever so much easier—is by

---

[7] Editor's Note: 1422 words to be exact.

by-passing certain plot developments, sequences of action, whole stretches of narration covering such.

Now I don't throw away that 20,000-to-30,000-word "by-passed" stretch which, in this family composed of two writers, Hazel Goodwin Keeler and myself, we familiarly call "the chunk." I build a new novel—about that chunk.

Now don't go away! The great "million-dollar" secret is going to be revealed in a few minutes under a sudden dazzling flood of searchlights. Curtains will be drawn at the appropriate moment, from two sides of the stage, by gorgeously uniformed attendants. Martial music will be played. All will be copacetic. Stick around, cull—till the big show!

Yes, I build a novel about that by-passed chunk No harder, my friends, than building a plot "cold-turkey" from a notebook of pivotal plot-ideas.

The beautifully-typed chunk will not just be tossable into the new story at its eventual typing, as so many nicely typed pages. To be merely re-numbered. The setting of the scene may change: what may have been laid in an engraving office may turn out to be laid in an undertaker's casket factory! A new character or two may crawl in. One or two may quietly crawl out. Some new plot-angle may nose its way in. The chunk will, in due and final course, actually have to be re-typed, every bit of its way. But it has served its purpose.

The "generouser" the better, as Alice might have said. At the completion of my following too-big novel, we proceed again to lop off—amputate—enucleate—extract—slip out—bypass —one 20,000 to 30,000-word chunk.

What, you will all now accusingly ask—and quite rightfully, too!—happens when the bypassed chunk this time turns out to be the same chunk that we built the novel about; the same one by-passed last time. Ah me, my friends, weep not. None of the novels built about an isolated stretch of narration are ever the same. I once built five novels, in succession, about the same chunk which persisted in getting itself blithely by-passed out every time. Those five novels were as different from each other as an elephant is from a banjo.

Old Chief-Mushroom-Spore we began to call that chunk around the house; in final desperation, because I got tired of the chunk—not of the novels that were built from it—I demoniacally built a purposefully short novel about it that gobbled it up—held it—from which it could not be extracted. Good-bye, chunk! See you never, never again—I—hope!

But this naturally sets your next question.

What *do* we do when the resultant novel is not long enough for anything to be bypassed out of it.

In that case, we go to work exactly as you are working today, were working yesterday, may be working tomorrow. Yes, cold turkey! Pick and shovel on shoulders, ill-fitting striped blouse hanging from weary shoulders. Hep, hep, hep—and hey there, No. 22,378, last one on the line, stay in step, or you'll get bread and water. Hep—hep—. Yes, we dig up from somewhere our old notebook of pivotal plot ideas and fragmentary concepts that have occurred to us here and there, on street cars, crossing bridges, or while lying underneath tables at cocktail parties. We jiggle and we juggle, we pull and we tear, we transpose and re-transpose, we put and take and take and put, we flounder about, we flop this way and we flop that way.

We sweat, groan, drive plot nails, bite the heads off with our teeth, draw the stems out again—during all of which we toss fitfully of nights in our sleep—dream bad dreams—in daytimes snap at our wives till they are driven to the divorce courts—and finally come out, *Deo volente*—that means God willing—with one 17½-carat pure-brass plot. One that, as a result of the knockdown and drag-out wrestling match it took to give it birth, we haven't energy to write upon for some weeks.

And there's the great secret, my friends. The million-dollar secret! It was slipped you quietly, pure grape juice, no less, right in your castor oil! It was handed you, just for the fun of it, without music—without fanfare. Yes, the million-dollar secret. And which is this:

It's 100 times easier, from the point of mental work, and tax upon the inventive faculties, to derive a story to fit a stretch of narrative already written, than it is to invent one cold turkey. From scratch. From nuttin! The already-written-out stretch of narrative to which a new story is to be fitted acts as an amazing mental touchstone. A fuse. A divine stimulus.

How does it do this, asks you over there in the middle of Row 2?

I'll tell you how! And why. Because, like a skunk lurking in the bushes, I've watched the mental process that takes place, dozens of times. I've watched it cold-bloodedly—myself as subject—and found out exactly what goes on. Here's what does:

The chunk, of necessity, contains elements which are foci for the automatic evolution of "threads". These threads wave at, and toward, similarly helplessly waving filaments which *come toward them from a surrounding (or contiguous) structure which is being created by suggestion.* By a process of mind no different than that used in dreams—fusion—certain of the outgoing threads from the chunk become fused with certain incoming ones from the suggested surrounding structure, thread for thread—and lo!—in the twinkling of an eye, we have organic structure. An organism, no less.

This, I swear to you, is exactly what happens in a psychological way. I've watched it happen scores of times—taken notes on just what occurred at the second of occurrence. In brief, the chunk does all the work; about all you need do is to ride around and shout "gee" and "haw" at the appropriate points.

And if you will allow each novel which wraps itself about a chunk already written to come itself to the large and generous size it will try ever manfully, even malignantly, to come to, you will always have a final chunk that has to come out—you will never come to the end of your plot-building process.

I ought to know! I have produced, chiefly by this method, some 60 book-sized novels in 17 years. This is one about every 103 days. And when you subtract the time of writing, revising, and transcribing—I do all that myself!—the actual plot-building time must have been short indeed; no more, in fact, than about 4 days per novel.

So put away, on your shelf, for a short experimental time, your plot-wheels. Your patented books with strange flopping vertical half-pages carrying "A-clauses," "B-clauses" and "C-clauses!" Your cards that set one (1) strip-teaser in one (1) Timbuctoo nunnery, seeking one (1) missing musical note from one (1) apple pie.

Try—Chain-Plotting! Like Medieval Magic, it works when all else fails!

THE STRANGE STORY OF JOHN JONES' DOLLAR

Harry Stephen Keeler

THE STRANGE STORY OF JOHN JONES' DOLLAR
Or
HOW SOCIALISM FINALLY ARRIVED IN THE WORLD!

by "Socialisticus"

On the 201st day of the year 3235 A.D., the professor of history at the University of Terra seated himself in front of his Chromo-Visaphone and prepared to deliver his daily lecture to his class, the members of which resided in different portions of the earth.

The instrument before which he seated himself was very like a great window sash, on account of the fact that there were three or four hundred frosted glass squares visible. In a space at the center, not occupied by any of these glass squares, was a dark, oblong area and a ledge holding a piece of chalk. And above this area was a peculiar-looking microphone, suspended by two hair-like springs, toward which the professor directed his subsequent remarks.

In order to assure himself that it was time to press the button which would notify the members of the class in history to approach their local Chromo-Visaphones, the professor withdrew from his vest pocket, a tiny contrivance no larger than a quarter, which he held to his ear. Upon moving a tiny switch attached to the instrument, a metallic voice, seeming to come from somewhere in space, repeated mechanically: "Fifteen o'clock and one minute—fifteen o'clock and one minute—fifteen o'clock and one min—" Quickly the professor replaced the instrument in his vest pocket and pressed a button at the side of the Chromo-Visaphone.

As though in answer to the summons, the frosted glass squares began, one by one, to show—in absolutely perfect hue and tint and color and shade—the faces and shoulders of a peculiar type of young men; young men with great bulging foreheads, bald, toothless, and wearing immense square horn spectacles. One square, however, still remained empty. On noticing this, a look of irritation passed over the professor's countenance.

But, upon seeing that every other glass square but this one was filled up, he commenced his talk.

"I am pleased, gentlemen, to see you all posted at your local Chromo-Visaphones this afternoon. I have prepared my lecture today upon a subject which is, perhaps, of more economic interest than historical. Unlike the previous lectures, my talk will not confine itself to the happenings of a few years, but will embrace the course of ten centuries, the ten centuries, in fact, which terminated three hundred years before the present date. My lecture will be an exposition of the effects of the John Jones Dollar, originally deposited in the dawn of civilization, or, to be more precise, in the year 1935—just thirteen hundred years ago. This John Jon—"

At this point in the professor's lecture, the frosted glass square which hitherto had shown no image, now filled up. Sternly he gazed at the head and shoulders that had just appeared.

"B262H72476Male, you are late to class again. What excuse have you to offer today?"

From the hollow cylinder emanated a shrill voice, while the red lips of the picture on the glass square moved in unison with the words:

"Professor, you will perceive by consulting your class book, that I have recently taken up my residence near the North Pole. For some reason, radio communication between the Central Energy Station and all points north of 89 degrees was cut off a while ago, on account of which fact I could not appear in the Chromo-Visaphone, Hence—"

"Enough, sir," roared the professor. "Always ready with an excuse, B262H72476Male. I shall immediately investigate your tale."

From his coat pocket the professor withdrew an instrument which, although supplied with an earpiece and a mouthpiece, had no wires whatever, attached. Raising it to his lips, he spoke:

"Hello. Central Energy Station, please." A pause ensued. "Central Energy Stations This is the Professor of History at the University of Terra speaking. One of my students informs me that the North Pole region was out of communication with the Chromo-Visaphone System this morning. Is that statement true? I would—"

A voice, apparently from nowhere, spoke into the professor's ear. "Quite true, Professor. A train of our ether waves accidentally fell into parallelism with a train of waves of identical wave-length from the Venus Sub-station. By the most peculiar mischance, the two trains happened to be displaced with reference to each other one half of a wave length, with the unfortunate result that the points of negative maximum amplitude of one coincided with the points of positive maximum amplitude of the other. Hence the two wave trains nullified each other and communication ceased for one hundred and eighty-five seconds—until the earth had revolved far enough to throw them out of parallelism."

"Ah, thank you," replied the professor. He dropped his instrument into his coat pocket and gazed in the direction of the glass square whose image had so aroused his ire. "I apologise, B262H72476Male, for my suspicions as to your veracity—but I had in mind several former experiences." He shook a warning forefinger. "I shall now resume my talk.

"A moment ago, gentlemen, I mentioned the John Jones Dollar. Some of you who have just enrolled with the class will undoubtedly say to yourselves: 'What is a John Jones? What is a Dollar?'

"In the early days, before the present scientific registration of human beings was instituted by the National Eugenics Society, man went around under a crude, multi-reduplicative system of nomenclature. Under this system, there were actually more John Joneses than there are calories in a British Thermal Unit. But there was one John Jones, in particular, living in the Twentieth Century, to whom I shall refer in my lecture. Not much is known of his personal life—except that he was an ardent socialist—a bitter enemy, in fact, of the private ownership of wealth.

"Now, as to the Dollar. In this day, when the Psycho-Erg, a combination of the Psych, the unit of esthetic satisfaction, and the Erg, the unit of mechanical energy, is recognized as the true unit of value, it seems difficult to believe that in the

Twentieth Century and for more than ten centuries thereafter, the Dollar, a metallic circular disk, was being passed from hand to hand in exchange for the essentials of life.

"But, nevertheless, such was the case. Man exchanged his mental or physical energy for these Dollars. He then re-exchanged the Dollars for sustenance, raiment, pleasure, and operations for the removal of the vermiform appendix.

"A great many individuals, however, deposited their Dollars in a stronghold called a bank. These banks invested the Dollars in loans and commercial enterprises, with the result that every time the earth traversed the solar ecliptic, the banks compelled each borrower to repay or acknowledge as due the original, plus six one-hundredths of that loan. And to the depositor, the banks paid three one-hundredths of the deposited Dollars for the use of the disks. This was known as three per cent, or bank interest.

"Now the safety of Dollars, when deposited in banks, was not absolutely assured to the depositor. At times, the custodians of these Dollars were wont to appropriate them and proceed to portions of the earth sparsely inhabited and accessible with difficulty. Again, the banks, at times, tiring, presumably, of banking, failed to open their doors, facetiously notifying their clients that they were 'frozen': I say 'facetiously' because it is obvious that a bank in a tropical or semi-tropical clime could not suffer a calorific change amounting to a downright glaciation. But, be that as it may, they did not thereafter open up, and many of the Dollars deposited therein automatically ceased to exist, due to the vagaries of higher accounting. And, at other times, nomadic groups known as 'yeggmen' visited the banks, opened the vaults by force, and departed, carrying with them the contents.

"But to return to our subject. In the year 1935, one of these numerous John Joneses performed an apparently inconsequential action which caused the name of John Jones to go down forever in history. What did he do?

"He proceeded to one of these banks, known at that time as 'The First National Bank of Chicago,' and deposited there, one of these disks—a silver Dollar—to the credit of a certain individual. And this individual to whose credit the Dollar was deposited was no other person than the fortieth descendant of John Jones, which John Jones stipulated in a paper that was placed in the files of the bank that the descendancy was to take place along the oldest child of each of the generations which would constitute his posterity.

"The bank accepted the Dollar under that understanding, together with another condition imposed by this John Jones, namely that the interest was to be compounded annually. That meant that, at the close of each year, the bank was to credit the account of John Jones' fortieth descendant with three one-hundredths of the account as it stood at the beginning of the year.

"History tells us little more concerning this John Jones—only that he died in the year 1945, or ten years afterward, leaving several children.

"Now you gentlemen who are taking mathematics under Professor L127M72421Male, of the University of Mars, will remember that any number, such as X, in passing through a progressive cycle of change, grows, at the end of that cycle, by a proportion p, then the value of the original X, after n cycles, becomes $X\ (1+p)^n$.

"Obviously, in this case, X equalled one Dollar; p equalled three one-hundredths; and n will depend upon any number of years which we care to consider, following the date of deposit. By a simple calculation, those of you who are today mentally alert, can check up the results that I shall set forth in my lecture.

"At the time that John Jones died, the amount in the First National Bank of Chicago to the credit of John Jones the fortieth, was as follows."

The professor seized the chalk and wrote rapidly upon the oblong space:

1945 10 years elapsed $1.34

"The peculiar, sinuous hieroglyphic," he explained, "is an ideograph representing the Dollar.

"Well, gentlemen, time went on as time will, until a hundred years had passed by. This First National Bank still existed, and the locality, Chicago, had become the largest center of population upon the earth. Through the investments that had taken place, and the yearly compounding of interest, the status of John Jones' deposit was now as follows." He wrote:

2035 100 years elapsed $19.10

"In the following century, many minor changes, of course, took place in man's mode of living; but the so-called Communists still agitated wildly for the cessation of private ownership of wealth; the First National Bank still accepted Dollars for safe keeping, and the John Jones Dollar still continued to grow. With about thirty-four generations yet to come, the account now stood:

2135 200 years elapsed $364.00

"And by the end of the succeeding hundred years, it had grown to what constituted an appreciable bit of exchange value in those days—thus:

2235 300 years $6920

"Now the century which follows contains an important date. The date I am referring to is the year 2313 A.D. or the year in which every human being born upon the globe was registered under a numerical name at the central bureau of the National Eugenics Society. In our future lessons, which will treat with that period in detail, I shall ask you to memorize that date.

"The Socialists and Communists still agitated, fruitlessly, but the First National Bank of Chicago was now the First International Bank of the Earth. And how great had John Jones' Dollar grown? Let us examine the account, both on that important historical date, and also at the close of the 400th year since it was deposited. Look:

2313 378 years $68,900
2335 400 years $132,000

"But, gentlemen, it had not yet reached a point where it could be termed an unusually large accumulation of wealth. Far larger accumulations existed upon the earth. A descendant of a man once known as John D. Rockefeller, III, possessed an accumulation of great size, but which, as a matter of fact, was rapidly dwindling as it passed from generation to generation. So, let us travel ahead another hundred years. During this time, as we learn from our historical and political archives, the Socialists and Communists began to die out, since they at last realized the utter hopelessness of combating the balance of power. The account, though, now stood:

2435 500 years	$2,520,000

"It is hardly necessary for me to make any comment. Those of you who are most astute, and others of you who have flunked my course before and are now taking it the second time, of course know what is coming.

"Now the hundred years which ended with the year 3535 A.D. saw two events—one, very important and vital to mankind, and the other, very interesting. I shall explain.

"During the age in which this John Jones lived, there also lived a man, a so-called scientist called Metchnikoff. We know from a study of our vast collection of Egyptian Papyri and Carnegie Library books, that this Metchnikoff promulgated the theory that old age—or rather, senility—was caused by a colon bacillus. This fact was later verified. But while he was correct in the etiology of senility, he was crudely primeval in the therapeutics of it.

"He proposed, gentlemen, to combat and kill this bacillus by utilizing the fermented lacteal fluid from a now extinct animal called the cow, models of which you can see at any time at the Solaris Museum."

A chorus of shrill, piping laughter emanated from the brass cylinder. The professor waited until the merriment had subsided and then continued:

"I beg of you, gentlemen, do not smile. This was merely one of the many similar, quaint superstitions existing in that age.

"But a real scientist, Professor K122B62411Male, again attacked the problem in the Twenty-fifth Century. Since the cow was now extinct, he could not waste his valuable time experimenting with fermented cow lacteal fluid. He discovered that the old gamma rays of Radium—the rays which you physicists will remember are not deflected by a magnetic field—were really composed of two sets of rays which he termed the delta rays and the epsilon rays. These last-named rays—only when isolated—completely devitalized all colon-bacilli which lay in their path, without in the least effecting the integrity of any interposed organic cells. The great result, as many of you already know, was that the life of man was extended to nearly two hundred years. That, I state unequivocally, was a great century for the human race.

"But I spoke of another happening—one, perhaps, of more interest than importance. I referred to the account of John Jones the fortieth. It, gentlemen, had grown to such a prodigious sum that a special bank and board of directors had to be created in order to care for, and re-invest it. By scanning the following notation, you will perceive the truth of my statement:

2535 600 years $47,900,000

"By the year 2635 A.D., two events of stupendous importance took place. There is scarcely a man in this class who has not heard of how Professor P222D29333Male accidentally stumbled upon the scientific fact that the effect of gravity is reversed upon any body which vibrates perpendicularly to the plane of the ecliptic with a frequency which is an even multiple of the logarithm of two to the Naperian base 'e.' At once, special vibrating cars were constructed which carried mankind to all the planets. That discovery of Professor P222-D29333Male did nothing less than open up seven new territories to our inhabitants; namely: Mercury, Venus, Mars, Jupiter, Saturn, Uranus and Neptune. In the great land-rush that ensued, thousands who were previously poor became rich.

"But, gentlemen, land which so far had constituted one of the main sources of wealth, was shortly to become valuable for individual golf courses only, as it is today, on account of another scientific discovery.

"This second discovery was, in reality, not a discovery, but the perfection of a chemical process, the principle of which had been known for many centuries. I am alluding to the construction of the vast reducing factories, one upon each planet, to which the bodies of all persons who have died on their respective planets are at once shipped by Air Express. Since this process is used today, all of you understand the methods employed; how each body is reduced, by heat, to its component constituents: hydrogen, oxygen, nitrogen, carbon, calcium, phosphorus, and so forth; how these separated constituents are stored in special reservoirs together with the components from thousands of other corpses; how these elements are then synthetically combined into food tablets for those of us who are yet alive—thus completing an endless chain from the dead to the living. Naturally, then, agriculture and stock-raising ceased, since the food problem, with which man had coped from time immemorial, was solved. The two direct results were, first—that land lost the inflated values it had possessed when it was necessary for tillage, and second—that men were at last given enough leisure to enter the fields of science and art.

"And as to the John Jones Dollar, which now embraced countless industries and vast territory on the earth, it stood in value:

2635 700 years	$912,000,000

"In truth, gentlemen, it now constituted the largest private fortune on the terrestrial globe. And in that year 2635 A.D. there were thirteen generations yet to come before John Jones the fortieth would arrive.

"To continue. In the year 2735 A.D. an important political battle was concluded in the Solar System Senate and House of Representatives. I am referring to the great controversy as to whether the Earth's moon was a sufficient menace to interplanetary navigation to warrant its removal. The outcome of the wrangle was that the question was decided in the affirmative. Consequently—

"But, I beg your pardon, young men. I occasionally lose sight of the fact that you are not so well-informed on historical matters as myself. Here I am talking to you about the moon, totally forgetful that many of you are puzzled as to my meaning. I advise all of you who have not yet attended the Solaris Museum on Jupiter, to take a trip there some Sunday afternoon. The Interplanetary Suburban Line runs trains every half hour on that day. You will find there, a complete working model of the old satellite of the Earth, which, before it was destroyed, furnished this planet light at night through the crude medium of reflection.

"On account of this decision as to the inadvisability of allowing the moon to remain where it was, engineers commenced its removal in the year 2735. Piece by piece it was chipped away and brought to the Earth in Interplanetary freight cars. These pieces were then propelled by Zoodelite explosive, in the direction of the Milky Way, with a velocity of 11,217 meters per second. This velocity, of course, gave each departing fragment exactly the amount of kinetic energy it required to enable it to overcome the backward pull of the Earth from here to infinity. I daresay those moon-hunks are going yet.

"At the start of the removal of the moon in 2735 A.D., the accumulated wealth of John Jones the fortieth stood:

2735	800 years	$17,400,000,000

"Of course, with such a colossal sum at their command, the directors of the fund had made extensive investments on Mars and Venus. By the early part of the Twenty-ninth Century, or the year 2821, to be precise, the moon had been completely hacked away and sent piecemeal into space, the job having required 86 years. I give, herewith, the result of John Jones' Dollar, both at the date when the moon was completely removed, and also at the close of the 900th year after its deposit:

2821	886 years	$219,000,000,000
2935	900 years	$332,000,000,000

"The meaning of those figures, gentlemen, as stated in simple language, was that the John Jones Dollar now comprised practically all the wealth on Earth, Mars and Venus—with the exception of one university site on each planet, which was, of course, school property.

"And now I will ask you to advance with me to the year 2920 A.D. In this year the directors of the John Jones fund awoke to the fact that they were in a dreadful predicament. According to the agreement under which John Jones deposited his Dollar away back in the year 1935, interest was to be compounded annually at three per cent. In the year 2920 A.D., the thirty-ninth generation of John Jones was alive, being represented by a gentleman named J664M42721Male, who was thirty years of age and engaged to be married to a young lady named T246M42652Female.

"Doubtless, you will ask, what was the predicament in which the directors found themselves. Simply this:

"A careful appraisement of the wealth on Neptune, Uranus, Saturn, Jupiter, Mars, Venus and Mercury, and likewise Earth, together with an accurate calculation of the remaining heat in the Sun and an appraisement of that heat at a very decent valuation per calorie, demonstrated that the total wealth of the Solar System amounted to $6,309,525,241,362.15.

"But unfortunately, a simple computation showed that if Mr. J664M42721Male married Miss T246M42652Female, and was blessed by a child by the year 2935, which year marked the thousandth year since the deposit of the John Jones Dollar, then in that year there would be due the child the following amount:

2935 1,000 years $6,310,000,000,000.00

"It simply showed, beyond all possibility of argument, that by 2935 A.D., we would be $474,758,637.85 shy—that we would be unable to meet the debt to John Jones the fortieth.

"I tell you, gentlemen, the board of directors were frantic. Such wild suggestions were put forth as the sending of an expeditionary force to the nearest star in order to capture some other Solar System and thus obtain more territory to make up the deficit. But that project was impossible on account of the number of years that it would have required.

"Visions of immense law suits disturbed the slumber of those unfortunate individuals who formed the John Jones Dollar Directorship. But on the brink of one of the biggest civil actions the courts have ever known, something occurred that altered everything."

The professor again withdrew the tiny instrument from his vest pocket, held it to his ear and adjusted the switch. A metallic voice rasped: "Fifteen o'clock and fifty-two minutes—fifteen o'clock and fifty-two minutes—fift—" He replaced the instrument and went on with his talk.

"I must hasten to the conclusion of my lecture, gentlemen, as I have an engagement with Professor C122B24999Male of the University of Saturn at sixteen o'clock. Now, let me see; I was discussing the big civil action that was hanging over the heads of the John Jones Dollar directors.

"Well, this Mr. J664M42721Male, the thirty-ninth descendant of the original John Jones, had a lover's quarrel with Miss T246M42652Female, which immediately destroyed the probability of their marriage. Neither gave in to the other. Neither ever married. And when Mr. J664M42721Male died, in 2961

A.D., of a broken heart, as it was claimed, he was single and childless.

"As a result, there was no one to turn the Solar System over to. Immediately, the Interplanetary Government stepped in and took possession of it. At that instant, of course, private property ceased. In the twinkling of an eye, almost, we reached the true socialistic and democratic condition for which man had futilely hoped throughout the ages.

"That is all today, gentlemen. Class is dismissed."

One by one, the faces faded from the Chromo-Visaphone.

For a moment, the professor stood, ruminating.

"A wonderful man, that old Socialist John Jones the first," he said softly to himself, "a far-seeing man, a bright man, considering that he lived in such a dark era as the Twentieth Century. But how nearly his well-contrived scheme went wrong. Suppose—suppose that that fortieth descendant had been born!"

KATS I HAVE KNOWN

HARRY STEPHEN KEELER

In *The Case of the Transposed Legs* a convict by the name of Big Rudy Uberholf plans a breakout, but details he needs for the escape are coded into a book by "Harry Stephen Keeler" which he looks for in the prison library. He's dismayed to find that Keeler is a "proscribed" author, whose works aren't allowed in the prison library system. Wishful thinking on Keeler's part, no doubt! Fortunately, for Big Rudy, he finds what he needs in a book that was written by Keeler, but published under the pseudonym, O. O. Orange. The text of the book makes up Chapters 23 and 24 of *The Case of the Transposed Legs,* two chapters that Harry didn't have to re-bust his cerebellum for.

Fender Tucker

This, I warn whomsoever may pry experimentally into its text, is a thin book!

A very thin book. Unable at all to stand up by itself!

It will not carry upon its binding the imprint of a famous publisher. For various reasons. A triangularly composed set of reasons, as it were. One is that books which do not carry thousands of words do not sell. Two, that its author will, in the course of its sparse text, be at all times strictly himself, instead of the bonny blue-eyed literary conformist that any regulation publisher would insist he be. And thirdly, that dissertations on such a prosaic subject as cats would not intrigue anybody except those rare persons who see in Mr. Cat something more than just—Mr. Cat!

No, this book will bear no publisher's imprint on its binding at all—for its type, the lead faces of which will doubtlessly be chipped a bit here and there, will be set in my neighbourhood printer's shop—and the sheets he prints from that type will be bound in a neighbourhood handbindery. 250 copies. No more. No less. But with bright blue end-sheets! 250 copies—which I shall give to just such of my friends as I wish. And many of these friends will, in due course, toss their copies aside—to wind up in the bins out in front of secondhand book emporiums, in hospitals, in Salvation Army reading rooms—and, perhaps, even in prisons, who knows?

But—wherever each book goes—there goes my own little story.

Cats!

Cats I have known.

I grew up more or less surrounded by members of the feline family—the larger ones of which are seen in public zoos as tigers, lynxes, leopards, and lions—and the smaller domesticated ones as just "cats." I have enjoyed the personal acquaintanceship of over a hundred cats—and have found that each of the hundred had a personality quite different from every other one.

For there have been, in my life, grouchy cats and genial cats; cats which got fat on nothing, and cats which stayed thin, no matter how much they ate; cats who were dandies, and cats who never put a tongue to fur; cats who spent three-quarters of their energies in creating purrs, and cats who never deigned to vibrate their purr chords; cats who possessed a perverted appetite, and cats who lived strictly along the dietary lines characteristic of cats; cats who would lie stretched out on a sun-heated covered garbage can, or perchance a cellar-floor flagstone warmed by some single beam pouring in a cellar window—apparently deep in sleep—yet able and ready to leap five feet into the air and disappear, did one even step within twenty feet of them; trustful cats who slept openly in a public alley, so that one could prod them with one's toe, wondering dimly if they were dead; cats who, when it came to such things as sleep, would, of an icy night, lie with one under the bedclothes, with the greatest of delight; and cats who—when gently insinuated between the bed covers—instantly scented a sinister conspiracy against themselves and struggled to get back into the gelid, but open, room; cats who were jealous and cats who welcomed other cats; cats who hated dogs, and cats who rubbed up against the chests of any old dog; cats who would fight a rat, and cats who would jump skyhigh and skip in terror at the sight of a grey mouse; cats who—but why go on? For, as I have said, I have known a hundred cats—and in so doing have met a hundred personalities.

The earliest actual cat I recall was one from around the time when I was five years of age. Lady Godiva Revere was her name. For, on the occasion of her first bath, when efforts were being made to ascertain her colour—she was a picked-up cat—she flew panic-stricken out from the bath tub, landing squarely on top of the flat shaggy back of a great black dog who was visiting us overnight, and who was enjoying her howls and terror no end; and she rode him terrified—it was he who was terrified, and who was howling now, for her claws were sunk deep in his fur and skin—rode him through at least two rooms. Lady Godiva Revere she became. It could never have been elsewise.

Lady Godiva Revere had been picked up in the famous old La Salle Street Tunnel which, in the early '10s, connected—under the Chicago River—Illinois Street and Randolph Street. Her coat was a hopelessly nondescript mixture of tan and black and white and yellow. Oh, Lady Godiva revealed that she had in her blood the blood of many, many cat families, and in Lady Godiva they all showed up. And did one disregard, as a cause, that first harrowing experience of hers, and assume it to be but an expression of her bare nervous system, Lady Godiva was what would have been called, by a cat-alienist, a "cat neurotic." For defective nervous system she did have. Or perhaps just an imbalance of the emotions, such as runs in people who drink too much coffee! Whatever the neurological cause, Lady Godiva, if she got excited beyond a certain point, lost her emotional balance, just as she did at the time of her first bath, and ran wildly all the way up the lace curtains to the curtain pole, clawed at the window pane on the way up, dropped back to the floor, performed circles thereon, jumped somersaults and carried on something terrible. In those days we used to just say—in our ignorance—that Lady Godiva was "having a fit"—and someone would immediately get accused of feeding her meat on the sly. In the light of the psychological knowledge of the present day I now think that Lady Godiva was, as I have intimated, simply over-emotional, and a fit specimen to be catapsychologized.

Amid the long vista of cats that followed—and with scarcely a break in the vista—I recall in particular Jerry. Jerry was a sort of a tweed, or homespun, mixture cat. Jerry used the home we offered him only to stretch out his tired body in the daytime, and recover from the bites received during the night.

Though no one knows where Jerry spent the nights. If the doors were locked on him after sundown, with himself inside instead of outside, Jerry raged and carried on like a mad-cat. Jerry was, however, a silent cat. The reason was that he never had a voice left when daybreak came. One could hear the wheezy shadow of a grateful cry when one's hand stroked him—and one could feel a dozen hard, scabby wounds inflicted by other cats. Jerry disappeared at last, and I suppose some disused yet well-aimed rifle put an end to the music of the night in which Jerry played no small fiddle!.

Then there was Tuffy, the unlucky. Tuffy was much like Jerry in appearance. But Tuffy was always "out of luck." Once, for an entire month, he cried pitifully—and appeared to be completely miserable, when one day one of us discovered that he had a needle sticking far in his side, and pulled it out. And Tuffy smiled again. (For cats do smile!) Then, another time, Tuffy got accidentally locked in the basement store room for over a week without food or water, and was rescued just as he was about to ascend into the cat heaven. His last accident, as I recall it, was sticking his tail in the open oven gas flame—and walking off with that appendix a blazing torch. He never did understand, nor forgive, the pail of cold water that was unceremoniously thrown on and at him!

Then there was Tommy o' the Drain, as we subsequently called him—the stray black and grey striped Tabby cat who was picked up, suffering from cat-pneumonia or something, in an empty drain pipe in the alley, and fed and clothed and cared for until he won the first prize—four years running—at the famous Beresford Cat Show. Tommy seemed to have a regard for only one person—our maternal parent—who had worked out his possibilities as a prize-winning, perfect cat. Other persons he would not tolerate.

And there was Snowball—with coat as white as flour, eyes pink, and ears totally deaf—as it is claimed all white cats are. At any rate, this particular Snowball couldn't hear a cannon cracker if let off just behind him. I recall how some well-meaning woman relative, visiting us, decided that there were too many cats in the house, and triumphantly informed us one day—a cold winter day, too, with the temperature far below zero—that she had hired a cab the night before and taken Snowball far out to the wilds of our city's great South Side, about ten miles from home, and there dropped him on the prairies.

Three days later, while we fumed with anger, Snowball was sitting on the back steps. His pink eyes said: "How goes it with you all? And—oh, how do we do it? Ah—that's the great mystery of Catology!"

And then there was Blacky—with the ebon fur and the yellow eyes, that rare thing—an all-black cat. Respectable cats, of course, always slept when the rest of the house slept, but Blacky preferred to run strictly on jungle schedule. A great blot of India ink he was, and on the whitest counterpane all day long—but he became Tarzan himself all night. Roaming the house—in lieu of an African river along which to prowl!—hither and thither, back and forth. No matter when one got up in the night, Blacky's big luminous eyes could be seen wafting eerily around in the darkness. They were the only part of him that could be seen. For he was, as has been said, an all-black!

Then there was old One-Ear—a tramp cat—who used to come close enough on our back porch to imbibe a little milk at our family's expense. Had One-Ear been an aeroplane he could never have performed a successful "bank"—for one of his great moth—eaten ears was completely gone—chewed off in a fight at some bygone time, and One-Ear was timorous about everybody and everything. He was suspicious as well as timorous. He surveyed a hand, holding out actual food toward him, with the same cautious speculative dubiousness with which a bank—president surveys the loan—application put in by a widow who requests, on a brand new $7,000 bungalow, an $800 loan at 7 per cent. interest. I remember well the day when, only a small boy, I tried to garner One-Ear in—and make him a member of our civilized home. He eluded me, however, by going to our second floor back porch. I followed him thence—and now, nicely trapped—he slunk on to the third back porch. I went after him, but at the third and top porch he went up the inclined ladder to the roof. I still followed him. And there on the roof—cornered as he believed himself to be—One-Ear promptly jumped off into space. His four legs crooked in a strange straddle. Killed? Injured? Not a sign of it. He hit the ground on four paws—and actually bounced. And he was lapping milk next morning right on schedule, having survived a jump that would have sent most cats—champion long—

distance "fallers" that they are—to the cat hospital, if not the little burial ground near the back fence.

Then there was Maltina, which sounds like a breakfast food. And Maltina was as grey as breakfast food tastes. She had been reared on a farm—and had learned how to knock eggs out of hens' nests and eat the broken contents. And—here, in the big henless city, Maltina performed the same stunts with eggs in the same way—knocking them off the ice-box shelf whenever the ice-box door was left open for a few minutes. At last, though, we solved the problem of Maltina's form of kinematical kleptomania. We pensioned her off with one real raw egg—served in a saucer—every day.

And then there was Whatzit. When we first found Whatzit, he was no bigger than a goose egg, sitting on the high sill of a stable window in our back alley, striped fearfully and wonderfully, and purring like a Rolls-Royce automobile. Was he a chipmunk?—or was he a squirrel?—or—or was he a skunk?—or was he just, perhaps, a tropical bird with four legs? We couldn't decide. "He contains," so we told our friends, "the elements of half a dozen different mammals!" He was too brilliantly coloured for a cat—indeed, his orange fur, instead of being fur, was actually plumage! So we named him Whatzit. Whatzit, growing up, would sit for hours thinking over—so far as we could determine—some cat mathematical problem; then he would leap into the air and wheel off at sixty miles per hour, doubtless having successfully solved for x in some equation where x was expressed in squared integrals of y. That Whatzit was a mathematician was proven by the fact that he reasoned very strangely in matters geometrical. For when he wished to "streak" from the parlour to the kitchen—at the sound of clanking kitchenware—Whatzit invariably ran across the huge dining-room table, instead of under. More often than not his terrific momentum—half skidding across the top as he invariably did—carried cloth and all to the floor. Just why Whatzit would not take the easier, simple path—under the table—we never knew.

And there was Nibby, a yellow cat—for whom we bought a pet turtle—to keep him company. Nibby would sit for hours next to that turtle, rapt, fascinated, ensnared, no more moving than if he himself were a bundle of clothing. The sight of that resplendent turtle head creeping out from under that great shell seemed to send Nibby into paroxysms of curiosity, and he would send out a cautious paw to touch the head—whereupon said turtle head would disappear back underneath the shell.

And—speaking of friendships between pets—there was Brownie, a brown cat who used to play for hours with a white rat, forgetting quite the social and military distinction existing between cats and rats.

And there was Mary Pickford, a beautiful specimen of cathood who was extremely conscious of her own dignity and breeding. She was a long—haired cat—a so-called Blue Cat—and was like a well—trained little lady who has been brought up to know that she is a thoroughbred and an aristocrat. Mary used to become a mother cat at stated intervals, but, just prior to the event, would become so excited that she would proceed to steal the kittens from a certain companion cat-mother living in the same house. Yet, just as soon as her own kittens would arrive, she would promptly discard such litter as she had purloined, and the despoiled mother would find her original batch back on her paws. Mary was undoubtedly born for silks and satins—not for kitten raising.

But I can hardly speak of cat-mothers without leaping nimbly catlike myself out of the long vista of cats remembered from those days when I lived with my maternal parent, and into the amazing sequence of cats subsequently owned by myself and her who was destined to be the other part of me. In brief, when it comes to mentioning cat-mothers, one has to mention—Alice-Come-Out-of-the-Kitchen. And her two offspring. A tragic cat family, all! Alice was a Siamese cat—worth, as such cats were at the time, $60—and had belonged, as the other half of myself and myself happened to know, to a rich family who had taken a temporary house up our street. The family went off one day to Europe, bag and baggage and cats, and, in the shuffle of bags and cats or else cats and bags, Alice got lost—and thus left behind—and we found her sitting on our back step, her chocolate-coloured face, paws, ears and tail contrasting oddly—in our experience with ordinary-marked cats—with her straw-hued fur.

Of course we took her in—knowing more than ever, as we did so, that our doorstep was marked in some cryptic way known to cats only—and Alice-Come-Out-of-the-Kitchen became one of us, and got her new name. For never would Alice—aristocrat amongst cats though she was—come into the parlour. She stayed ever back in the kitchen—a natural-born scullery maid—even when the kitchen was dark and cold, and the lights up ahead in the house proclaimed warmth and companionship—in the parlour. Alice had been bred, when we got her, to another Siamese cat owned by the same family—one whom we ourselves had named Hooey-Hooey-Sip-Soo, and which name the owners had gratefully adopted—Alice had been bred by Hooey, and eventually Alice presented us with two specimens of the genus Siamese cat. Funny little clowns both of them—after, that is, they grew out of kittenhood and got their little chocolate-coloured clown masks; and, before they became clowns, little monkeys determined to speed up all of America's hosiery mills—for each one invariably scuttled up the silk stocking of every woman visitor to the house.

One of the kittens we named Squawko, because he squawked in terror if he was lifted an inch off the ground.

The other kitten we named Squeako, because—

Exactly!

Well I remember the night I came home late—the other half of my family was at her mother's—and found that Squawko and Squeako had disappeared from the huge clothes basket where Alice-Come-Out-of-the-Kitchen had been keeping them. Though Alice herself was still there, however—meeting me at the door.

And well I remember how I searched the house, from top to bottom and back again. Since neither Squawko nor Squeako could then walk—much less get out of that basket—I knew that Alice, resentful of all the handling they had been getting, had hidden them. But—find them I could not! Even with Alice loyally assisting me. For she trotted along with me—all over the house—waving her chocolate-coloured tail encouragingly every time I pulled out an unthought-of drawer or up—ended a promising waste basket.

At last I had to give it up. Alice had beaten me!

And, beaten, I disrobed, climbed into my pyjamas, and went to bed. Went to bed, that is, so far as turning up the bedclothes went. For there—under the bedclothes—were the missing Squawko and Squeako!

But tragedy pursued the family of Alice and Squawko and Squeako.

For Alice—well, it is not generally known that cats are crazier about valerian than they are about catnip. And some out-of-town guest in our house, taking a few drops of valerian, had left her bottle of valerian in the bathroom medicine cabinet, and the cabinet door itself open. And Alice, reaching up from the wash basin, tried to pull the valerian bottle down. She pulled down, instead, a carbolic preparation supposed to be inhaled for lung colds and, of course, broke it. And walked in it, and then daintily licked it off her paws. If only—if only we had known then that cats always get poisoned from their own paws. She died a most tragic death.

Moreover, she bequeathed tragedy, it seems, to both her young.

For Squawko, long before her death, had got caught in a heavy swinging door—between dining-room and kitchen—and broke his back. Yet he lived for three years—a dwarf—and dragged himself gaily about by his front paws, the happiest, purringest cat we had ever known. Happy, that is, except for the time his mother died. For Squawko had always slept with his mother—in her very bosom, even when a big boy. And when Alice died we saw Squawko nestle in her cold fur.

The next two weeks we spent on our stomachs—rolling marbles in front of Squawko—dangling strings in front of him—so that the half-paralysed catlet would not miss his mother.

He made a splendid readjustment, except that he too eventually died—at least, the half of him that was still alive.

But his brother Squeako never got caught in the swinging door, No indeed! Foxy cat that he was—foxy from having his tail nipped once in it—he always stood high upon hind legs—shoved the door inward half a dozen inches—and then leaped agilely through the gap. Never so much as getting his tail nipped again. A perfect method—except that the wily Squeako always played safe—by leaping over all thresholds. Even when there was no door!

Finally the tragedy that pursued Squeako's family overtook him, too. It was inflammation of the bladder—nothing at all in humans, but in a cat, death.

But enough of sad things. By contrast, we think of Bill. Bill—the eternal watchdog! A reddish striped cat for whom we paid $8 cash to an ignorant Negro who believed Bill was a "Jonah" and that only if he tortured Bill to death would he get some luck. An $8 watchdog, Bill, so to speak. But with reservations. For Bill would sit all day, every day, on the back porch, waiting—just waiting—to glimpse the head of any luckless neighbourhood cat who might clambour up on the fence from the outside alley. And when that luckless cat showed, the placid Bill would turn into a streak of greased lightning—and thereafter only flying fur was to be seen. But Bill wasn't a vindictive, jealous, selfish feline, as one might imagine. For when he was watching for intruders, and a dog—any dog—came ambling through the gate, Bill would sidle down into the yard, and make love to that dog, rubbing and purring about the latter's legs; and the more dogs there were in the yard—or in the house—the more satisfied Bill was. Sometimes I wonder if Bill didn't think that perhaps he was himself a dog; or, better—and what is more likely—if Bill didn't decide to put it over the rest of the world and make them think he was a dog—instead of a cat?

Of course no remarks on cats could ever be complete without the mention of that stiffly dignified, stiffly English cat, Tobias, who lived in the Bloomsbury boarding house which, for a while, encased us whilst in London garnering atmosphere for a Bloomsbury boardinghouse mystery which, alas, never got written!

Not, however, that the establishment did not contain a mystery—all by itself. For it did! The mystery being not the so-fine, the so-colourful, the so-friendly, and so-o-o British folk who assembled with us each morning about the teapot—and of several of whom I shall have an affectionate word or two to say in a moment or so. No, the, mystery was the one boarder who did not fit—did not belong—the narrow-eyed South African—though obviously of German extraction—"tourist," who called himself Piddorp, or Bittledorf, or something like that, and who eyed us suspiciously from the very first breakfast time, and then—hm?—then—

Ah, Guilford Street. Gray's Inn Road. Russell Square. Bloomsbury. The folk about the breakfast table. Tobias. And Bittledorf. Who—what was Bittledorf, I wonder again and again.

Tobias, the so-stiffly dignified Tobias, was the pride and joy of Miss Diana Farmer-Whiffington, the elderly spinster who kept the establishment, and had been named after a husband-to-be of hers who unfortunately for her never got to be her husband-as-was.

Tobias, a great handsome muscular tabby, who used to sit on the stairs leading down to the dining-room, would accept pat on head or stroke on flank. But he would never extend muzzle for a nuzzle—never went into the usual up-and-down-bobbing ecstasies of catdom when the rear part of spine was stroked—would never come forward by even so much as a millimetre to receive a gentle touch—would never purr for anyone other than his mistress.

So, at least, she claimed; and so seemed plainly to be the case. Tobias's slogan appeared to be, with respect to the outside world, "Take all—give nothing." His entire cat-life had been spent in that quaint street with the high iron palings hemming in the dining-rooms where each morning we dined with the other lodgers, and a giant teapot stood on the table, and tongues, all around, became opened by the tea! The odd little clerk at the head of the table who looked exactly like the Mad Hatter in Alice in Wonderland, and whom we two Americans secretly called John O'London; the old gentleman with the white walrus moustache who resided normally at Ashton-under-Lyme, and who informed us with the most triumphant of hrrrmphs that we'd have to walk a demned long way, sir and madam, if we expected to see Robin Hood's Sherwood Forest, which we'd naively thought lay somewhere along the edge of London; the sharp- and narrow-eyed South African of whom I've spoken—the man Piddorp or Bittledorf or what, who eyed us suspiciously from the very first breakfast time, felt us out in cautious but utterly uncommunicative conversation, getting all from us and giving nothing about himself—and who then got out of the place within the next few hours, doubtlessly thinking we were American F.B.I. operatives, What was he, we still wonder even to-day? Crook or spy—which? What was—

But getting back to Tobias, the official cat of that quaint Guilford Street establishment, we often used to wonder whether he ever strolled up to the orphan asylum, then in Guilford Street, to see the little orphans who clustered at the tall iron fence. We hope, to-day, that he did; because, being so unattainable, so untouchable, so much a thing of that pure outside for which those little boys seemed to hunger—Tobias must have inculcated into those orphans, most of them, a liking and love for cats.

Nor would any remarks on cats be complete without a mention of Mimi Fanchon Fleurette, the cat who graced our lodgings in Rue Oudinot, Paris. Mimi Fanchon Fleurette was a tortoiseshell cat, with the usual fringe-like markings of golden brown, black, grey and what-not, and carried excess baggage on one of her ends to the extent that her name should rightfully and legitimately have been Gaston, or Henri. A fact! Mimi, if alive to-day, must still be causing brows to raise—most questioningly. Mimi had received her name—unfortunately, we must now be accurate, and say "his" name—because he was a kitten-stealer. Not a kitten-killer, nor a kitten-beater. A plain, kitten-hungry kitten-stealer. Some latent hidden instinct of motherhood, no doubt. That thing which will sometimes come out in cat male or human male.

Nor would mention of cats be complete without, say, mention of that tiny mite, with white and black markings and ridiculous clown face, taken away by us in Chicago from a gang of boys and named by us Kitten-Mitten. No bigger than a molecule, and threatening to remain the Tom Thumb of catdom, he evolved into a gigantic, waddling behemoth so huge that he had, finally perforce, to be called Fat-Stuff. But he remained a kitten to the extent that a daily rubber ball had to be bought for him, because he managed to hide every one. We often wondered, after we left the flat where Kitten-Mitten alias Fat-Stuff spent much of his life, what the cleaners-up of that flat must have thought when they found scores of rubber balls lying around in countless places.

And one must give mention to long, lithe, lean, lemon-yellow "Mistah" Jim—who preferred boiled navy beans to all food! We tried him out one day to see how many he could eat—and he wound up atop his back, swollen up like a balloon, four legs in air—but readying himself, as turned out to be the case—for another helping of beans!

And one can hardly ever forget Sir Fitz-Hubert Martingale, a doubtful white and yellow short-haired cat, plucked out of the bottom of a huge snowdrift after the biggest snow of the year, where he had melted a vertical channel clear to the bottom. Sir Martingale, who sneezed so badly, and so copiously, and for so many weeks after his rescue, that we had to have the flat re-papered. Indeed, during Sir Martingale's never-to-be-forgotten sneezing days, the single sight that could send us both flying back of the protecting backs of tall chairs was Sir Martingale with his white muzzle high, making the weird contortions of his face that showed he was about to let fly.

But this was not Sir Martingale's claim to position in our long vista of cats, no. His claim to fame, if any, was his mania for walking narrow ledges high above ground. And he—the undeftest cat ever born when it came to in-house movements! Where most cats, by that careful feeling with their paw-tips known only to cats, can stroll a parlour mantel full of Dresden china, in the blackest hour of the night, without knocking off a single piece, following the performance by a perfect one-point landing on the keyboard of the piano, and a triumphant burst of nocturnal orchestration, Sir Martingale could not cross the library table in full light of noon without knocking off at least one piece of bric-a-brac, and, from fright at the sound of its crash, falling off in panic himself; he could not spring up on the kitchen table without tipping over himself, and whatever plate or cooking pan he hopped into, on to the floor. But, just as one-legged people become Channel swimmers, and one-armed people billiard experts, Sir Martingale had to become a high-wire expert. For a two-inch wide stone ledge, broken only at intervals by scant three-inch wide window-sills, ran around the entire third storey level of the court of the flat building where we lived when me acquired Sir Martingale. We would often come home from downtown, or an afternoon movie, only to find about a hundred tenants and children standing in the court with bated breaths and faces turned upward—and Sir Martingale, who had invariably worked himself out and under one of our easily sliding screens, poised at some point of that long, narrow, two-inch stone ledge, yards from anything. He never fell during his several-year career as a cat, and, when he died, he died in bed.

And one must mention Josephus Satterwaite, a dirty black-and-white cat, who had a cleanly broken hind leg—broken at the very hip joint—when we picked him up—an injury said not to be healable or splintable. But the feminine half of our family—who indeed was our better half when it came to being unswayed and unconvinced by the dicta of "experts"—managed somehow to splint that leg, fearfully and wonderfully. It was a full afternoon's work, no less. And lo, Josephus did recover to the extent that his leg healed completely after some five weeks.

And one must mention Police-Call, who might, in view of his subsequent strange passion for candy—the only cat we ever knew who liked, candy—have been called Candy, or Jelly-

Bean. But Police-Call he became. He got named thus because, a short while after we acquired him, he caused the Police to descend on us, twenty strong, patrol wagon and all. For Police-Call, when we found him, was filthy to the point of nigrescence, and smelled like a pound of Roquefort cheese anointed with gasoline: the cheeselike component coming from goodness-knows-what plus general cat discouragement in trying to keep up with personal matters, and the gasoline component coming from some weird, sticky, tightly matting and cat torturing, petrol-smelling "goo" that some janitor had thrown over him, something no doubt specially compounded for the purpose of deviling cats. And so—wash Police-Call we had to do—first of all. If we were to find what lay underneath in the way of markings—and were, moreover, to be able ourselves to live with him, But, alas, he proved to be the coward of all cats when it came to washing—for cats, for the most part, and contrary to general belief, are fairly brave during this process of taking a bath—they give out, at most, faint plaintive mewing pleadings for their lives. But Police-Call, at the sheer indignity being offered him, and the threat of water to his existence, set up such a howling and yelling, such piercing screaming, that the tenants of the building—we were brand newcomers there then—the tenants excitedly phoned in, in twos and threes, to the Town Hall Police Station, one block off, that the strange newcomers, who had arrived that day with five typewriters and various strange coffinlike pieces of luggage, were beating up a defenceless child. And the police came thundering up the front hallway stairs, pounding with their sticks on the front door and shouting "Release that child—open up, you in there—open—up—in the name of the Law!"

And when we did open up, and they rushed in, there was, of course, in the apartment, only ourselves, with scratched bleeding hands, stinging soapsuds that had been freely kicked into our eyes, dripping Turkish towels pinned about our midriffs—and one very clean cat peering, with wet paws on the rounded bath tub rim, over the edge—too exhausted even to step off the folded Turkish towel on which it stood, and into which it had trailed gallons of ink—too exhausted, by far, to hop out of the tub—but not too exhausted, no, to be interested in drinking in the huge commotion it had set into being. Police-Call! He could never have been called anything else, after his induction into our family.

And one must not forget The Moll—who could not get along with the other sex in cats. Ever! We had to give her this name because she was a lady gangster, no less. Beautifully marked—a true tortoiseshell—she should rightfully have been called "Princess." She ran the fiercest and most dangerous Toms to the highest points in the room—out of the very apartment, indeed, if the sledding was clear—ran them up or out on immediate sight.

But The Moll's fierceness is counteracted, in our memories of cats, by one other lady cat, Mehitabel, the gentlest one we ever knew, who was an enigma in that she was mortally afraid of a single phrase—out of Mother Goose! Mehitabel, with snow-white breast and tabby markings, appeared one cold morning at our breakfast nook window, and was promptly pulled in. She became part of the family—at least for a while. She was often a nuisance at mealtime, standing up on her hind legs, and hooking out after bits of food going mouthward; but she could always be put in her proper cat-place by seven magic words arrived at by us by purest accident. The words, strangely, were "Fee Fi Fo Fum, I smell the blood of an Englishman." The moment these were uttered, even in a low, toneless, casual voice, Mehitabel skittered for her life to the further and darkest corner of the room, where she lay for the rest of that meal, her little bright green eyes taking in everything, but no more making a nuisance of herself.

Nor—now that we draw near the end—could this dissertation on cats be complete without mention of Little Dog, Big Boy, Talky Tommy and Pillbox. Little Dog was a deeply golden little tramp cat who, for a long time, could be brought no nearer than to be able to catch in his teeth a piece of liver tossed to him, and to speed away with it. By dint of long careful missionary work done on him, however, Little Dog finally became friends, and became in truth a "little dog." With deep indentation in spine like the back of a swaybacked old horse, and two front legs bowed out, almost in half circles, like those of a bulldog, he was rightly named; but even more rightly so, since he took upon himself to follow this scribe faithfully around the neighbourhood like a dog. Across the heavy automobile traffic of Addison Street he would trot at our heels, and clear to the Great Atlantic and Pacific Tea Company grocery store under the shadows of the Elevated Rapid Transit Road, where inside the counter sign proclaimed insolently, "No dogs or similar animals allowed inside here." Never, however, did Little Dog try to enter those precincts where "dogs or similar animals" were forbidden, but would wait outside, at the edge of the door, disregarding the many pairs of feet which would come out, and picking up our feet only when we had emerged and turned homeward.

And Big Boy! Sleek, long, tawny cat, so like a lion in so many ways, even to the grumbling, rumbling "jowelling" he used to emit. We clipped him so that he had a mane, anklets and a tassel on the end of his tail, and nursemaids and children scurried shrieking in terror when he lazily ambled down Fremont Street. A lion—small but unmistakable—on the loose. But Big Boy had not always been a cat. That is, he had not always had a cat-face. For his face, at the time we first met him, rescuing him from two fierce dogs who were finishing him off, was torn into ribbons, and our own veterinarian grudgingly consented to see what he could do with his needles and his adhesive tapes. And lo, Big Roy grew a beautiful new cat-face, even to the fur thereon, and emerged in the American Press in a countrywide syndicated story as "The Cat With the Plastic Face." And out of thousands of resultant petitions for him he went to two little twin Norwegian girls who have him yet to-day, and vie for his affections.

Coming rapidly now to the end, we think of Talky Tommy and Pillbox. Talky Tommy, a white-breasted lithe tabby, was of course exactly what his name implies: the talkingest cat ever to be found on land or sea, commenting vocally and interminably on everything, answering, querying, conversing as surely as does a human being. From Talky's vocabulary, and never-ending use of it, we succeeded in working out sixteen different cries, or intonations, that evidently constitute the language of cats. A philologist could have enriched his knowledge of language through a few minutes' association with Talky. But alas, a new resident of the neighbourhood shot Talky to death one morning with a revolver because, as the "man" put it, "the damn' little striped cat gave me the willies; every time I opened my kitchen door, there he was, a-talkin' at me as though he had the right to talk like us humans."

And now Pillbox!

Pillbox was a broad-headed Maltese with indefinable areas of black on him, plus a single notch of white down the middle of his forehead which made him seem to be always concentrating. Pillbox was a feline Chinese puzzle. Of all the many open cartons that were always about our place—and open boxes are what cats love—Pillbox would invariably select, to sleep in, one half a dozen sizes too small for him, so that he always leaked, dribbled, and poured out of his receptacle. Wherever a carton was to be found with four legs thrust stiffly at all angles out of it, one heavily overhanging tail, and one fast-asleep cat head half wedged atop one edge—and one perfectly packed sardine down within—it was Pillbox. He got his name because, one day, provided with a pill box because of a bet we had made that he would try to curl up in it, he tried exactly that—and got named for life.

And now we are indeed at the end, but not without mention of the Grand Old Man of all cats—Inspector Jones of Scotland Yard. He is still very much alive to-day. Inspector was a Siamese by breed, with a short tail and a kink at the end, and oblique blue eyes. He was always and ever the true aristocrat. He gave never a squawk when he was given a bath—though he knew each bath was his death knell. He never gorged any more food than his dainty cat appetite called for. He raised not the slightest eyelash at sign of a mouse, a bird, a moth or a butterfly. He was always willing to crack, with his powerful teeth, for any other luckless cat with sore gums who brought up a chicken bone and sheepishly set it in front of him, the joint of that bone, and expose the marrow for the cat who had brought it up. It sounds indeed like nature-faking, but the Inspector did that precise sportsmanlike act scores of times. Palsied during the last four years of his life due to a strange sickness which consumed eight and a half of his nine lives, inspector Jones lives to-day, a dignified patriarch, chocolate-eared and chocolate-faced head bobbing tremulously at any voluntary motion of it; but happy and intelligent. Unable any more to go up and down the single stairway in the house because of his palsy, his heart, and his arthritis, he sits at the top thereof—or the bottom—ever calm and placid—waiting for transportation down or up. He is as calm and unperturbed indeed, as the man who was found by the angry husband inside his wife's clothes closet, and who said "Believe it or not, sir, but I am waiting for a streetcar." For thus Inspector Jones waits throughout the day for his streetcar—that being someone who is traversing that flight of stairs in the direction he is going. And thus, riding under friendly arms, he travels up and down the stairs, all day long, with all the ease of other cats who can make it only on four feet.

And thus it has gone. A hundred cats I have known. And therefore—as inadequately delineated by this brief tract—a hundred distinct personalities have I met. For that is just it. No cat is like any other cat. Past, present, or cat-to-come future. No cat can possibly be presented in a dissertation dealing with cats "in general"; he can be set forth only in a biography of himself alone. He is the One—the Single One—out of the Billion in which he has to find himself classed.

And the lesson to be learned from all this is, of course, that cats are not cats at all.

They are Kats.

And that's—the difference!

Sunbeam's Child

Harry Stephen Keeler

This text was originally intended as Chapter VII of *The Strange Will*, but HSK rejected it with the scrawled notation, "This chapter stricken out by author. Too sexy." The typescript was given to Gerry Kroll by Thelma Keeler, and it is now owned by Chris Mikul. Chris kindly provided us with a copy, and Gerry did the work of transcription. Writes Chris, "a nice Keelerian vignette, I think (though it doesn't do much for HSK's credentials on race)." That's for sure—here's Keeler at his most racially grotesque. We must simply remember that he was also the author of such works as *The Wonderful Scheme of Mr. Christopher Thorne, Y. Cheung. Business Detective, Two Strange Ladies,* and *The Man Who Changed His Skin*—books that take the issue of race more seriously and come out looking much more appealing, though of course still bizarre.

Richard Polt

Howard Payne, archaeologist, seated in the luxurious library of his friend's home on Rich Man's Row, Cleveland, leaned forward in his chair and puzzledly knocked the ash off the rich perfecto he had been smoking.

"So you think this fellow Farrel Ivins in Central City," he queried perplexedly, "hasn't a chance in a million to escape being hanged—with that particular governor in the saddle?"

Arthur Gunton, the host to the youthful-appearing archaeologist, though older by ten years and clad this afternoon in beautiful blue silk dressing gown, shook his gray-thatched head firmly and knocked off the accumulated ash from his own perfecto. Answering the direct question at the same time.

"The fellow Ivins hasn't a chance in a billion, I'd say," he pronounced authoritatively.

Payne, as was his wont when sorely puzzled, cast his eyes about the library, with its bronze statuettes, its leather-backed books in their open shelves, the rich plum-colored monotone carpet, and back to the sunlight pouring from the cheerful vine-draped windows onto the polished mahogany table whose comer only, with elaborate bronze ashtray, separated the two men in their capacious leather-seated chairs. "You must know something, Gunton," he said significantly. "Something—on the inside?"

"I do," affirmed the older man but cryptically. "And all thanks to something I learned about that German governor in a passing conversation held in Lake Como, Italy."

"Lake Co—might I ask what the fact is? Something—you learned recently?"

"Heavens, no, Payne! No, I haven't been to Italy since—no, it was something learned in the long ago, when I was first married and before my son was born."

"Your son?" And Howard Payne shook his head. "And right here and now, Gunton, I'm going to digress a bit. Since you mention your son. Gunton, you're an unnatural father. Do you think that if I had a boy—17, 18 years of age—I'd keep him marooned in the care of a private family in England? Manchester, isn't it? Or is it Leeds? Though which town doesn't matter. The point is that—well, not for an instant would I do that. I'd have my son with me. I'd take him around to the theaters and cafés. I'd be his companion and pal. At any rate, I'd act like a real father. All you've ever done, though, is to write out a check every three months. I repeat my assertion, Gunton. Your attitude is wholly abnormal."

The older man removed his cigar from his lips and regarded the younger contemplatively. Indeed, Gunton's face bore a perplexed look which seemed to indicate that he was pondering over some exceedingly involved question. Finally, however, after a full minute had passed, he broke the silence.

"Payne, you've made that same accusation against me on several occasions during our seven years of acquaintanceship. Often, I've felt that I'd like to tell you more about the boy—and his mother—and other things as well. But it seems that something has invariably held me back." He paused and blew several smoke rings ceilingward. "This afternoon, though, since I've unwittingly put myself on record as being 101 percent certain Farrel Ivins will and must hang, there in Central City—at least with that governor in the saddle—and tell you I've authority for it—and you query me for that authority—and since the whole affair is all inextricably tangled up to the other—and I mean my keeping the boy there in England—well, it seems it's sort of in the bag for me to tell all. At one and the same time! So I will. All at one and the same time. You understand, of course, that my words are between the two of us only?"

"Have I ever violated your confidence in these seven years?" asked Payne almost reproachfully.

"No, you haven't—and it's for that very reason that I'm going to unburden myself." Gunton leaned forward and placed his hand on the other man's knee. "And the sole remaining reason," he added simply, "is because I've learned that you are my friend. Now listen."

And pausing scarcely a second, he drove on with his facts.

"I've never mentioned Sunbeam—my wife—to you. The circumstances under which we met were quite ordinary. I wasn't as well-off in those days as today—yet made a very good living. Her father was a business acquaintance of my uncle. She was the only child. We were introduced one evening at a private dance. And the result for each of us, I daresay, was love at first sight. Yes, the whole affair was quite ordinary—so I'll pass quickly to other things.

"As to the name Sunbeam: It was one used only, of course, by her family and her friends. And after I met her, by myself as well. Rather fanciful though, even for a pet name, eh, Payne?" The older man shook his head almost reverently. "But you should have seen her—to have understood. I'm sure that you've noticed those fragile little flaxen-haired dolls in the windows of the big stores around Christmastime? Well, just such a living, breathing human doll was Sunbeam. She was dainty—small—delicately featured. Her hair, which fell about her temples in the most entrancing ringlets, was the sunniest yellow. Her cheeks would have reminded you ineffably of the pink roses we see in the old-fashioned flower gardens. And her eyes—big and blue and trustful like those of a child. In fact, Payne, she was a child with woman's years, a beautiful unspoiled child, and when I was first introduced to her by my uncle, my peace of mind left me instantly. After I had known her for but a few weeks, I realized that I could never, never adjust myself to a life which did not include her. But my lucky star must have been in the ascendancy, for she gave me her love—and herself as my wife.

"I don't believe, Payne, that I shall ever forget the four weeks of our honeymoon. For quite a number of years, I had been enjoying a splendid salary, and I had saved the greater part of it. So just before we were married, I erected a charming little bungalow out in what was called Chesterhyde—today, of course, quite swallowed up with Cleveland's development and no longer exclusive and even newly built. In the rear of the bungalow I put up a small brick garage and purchased an expensive limousine. Then, after several wonderful days of shopping for furniture, we were quietly married and left for a leisurely tour of the East. We took in Boston, New York, Philadelphia, Baltimore, Washington. By the time we returned to Cleveland, our little nest was all complete, every piece of furniture was in place, and in care of it was a motherly woman whom I had engaged as a housekeeper.

"But now came the unpleasant part. I was compelled by the exigencies of my work to leave Sunbeam, since it was necessary for me to continue traveling for at least a year longer. I tell you, Payne, if you have never had to leave the woman you love for periods of time averaging a month, you cannot realize what a soul-grilling experience it was for me. It meant that I must go bumping about the country, enduring all sorts of hardships and inconveniences instead of being able to sit at home evenings in my big upholstered rocker with Sunbeam on my lap, her smooth pink cheek snug up against my own and her warm kisses coming at the most unexpected moments. But depart I must.

"Now at this point I must digress a bit in order to tell you about an individual who was connected with the events which followed. If only he had never existed, then.... But, after all, things are as they are; none of us must cavil at the immutable law of cause and effect.

"At any rate, to continue, this man's name was Dyke. Vincent Dyke. Did something in stocks and bonds, I don't know what. It seems that long before I had met Sunbeam, Dyke had been a regular caller at her father's house and had shown in numerous ways that he was anxious to ingratiate himself into her good graces. He was a blond and fairly good-looking chap in spite of the fact that there was a somewhat tricky look on his face.

"I have but one thing to tell about him. This I remark upon because you are always talking about the laws of heredity, the Mendelian theories and what not. Including the fact that cells, destined to occupy certain regions of a body, seem to somehow know they must reproduce certain stigmata and so forth.

Anyway, this fact I now relate to you constituted an oddity of nature which should interest you. Yes.

"For on Dyke's left temple, Payne, was a dark patch of red which had been there since his birth; it was a nearly perfect equilateral triangle and in size was perhaps that of a 25-cent piece. But the odd thing about it was that his father had borne the same peculiar mark in the same place. And to add to the strangeness of the fact, his grandfather too had carried a triangular patch of reddish skin at the left temple. This was true beyond any doubt, since there were many who had known Dyke's father and had seen the large tintype of his grandfather. So much for that. Explain it according to your theories or not, as you wish. I don't attempt to, you see. For—

"However, no sooner had I been out of town a week than Dyke made a social call on Sunbeam. By no means, Payne, do I wish to give you the impression that she concealed it from me. Almost as soon as I reached the house after my first trip, she met me in the hall, snuggled up to me on her tiptoes, and said, 'Dear, do you remember Vincent Dyke? While you were gone, he made a visit. And he asked whether he might drop in again sometime.'

"I tell you, Payne, a blind ungovernable rage seized me when I thought of that shifty-eyed, birth-marked Dyke daring to call upon my fairy-wife in my absence. Old stories that I had heard about him recurred suddenly to my memory. And then and there I mentally determined that if he ever repeated the action, he should receive a lesson which he would never forget!

"So after dinner that evening I made my way alone down to an employment office in the Black Belt, that portion of Cleveland lying between—but you know the region, I'm sure. Swarming, teeming with colored people then, as it is today. And I found just the specimen of a man I was looking for. Yes, powerful—the kind of man who would win hands down in any encounter with a white man.

"His name was Skoko—Skoko something or other—I've quite forgotten now what, since so many years—but no!—even that comes back to me now—Goodwillie—Skoko Goodwillie!—there's a good 24-karat Negro name for that author friend of yours who collects names.[8] Well, this chap was a gigantic, brawny apelike Negro, a veritable black Hercules. I'll warrant that there wasn't a nigger wench in existence that could have helped but go crazy over him. He was a typical African, Payne, with carbon-black skin, flat nose, flaring nostrils, great thick lips, and kinky hair. His long muscular arms, low forehead, and sloping cranium put me in mind of the stuffed gorilla that stands in the Museum of Natural History uptown. And—

"Here was the man I wanted, I told myself, mentally calculating what chance of defense Dyke would have if this black gorilla in human form ever began a chastisement! So I called him to one side and stated the details of the position for which I required a man.

" 'Now, Skoko,' I said, 'the manager of this agency informs me that you've been employed in the past as cook, chauffeur, and general caretaker. I require a man for those duties at my residence in Chesterhyde. I should expect you to drive my wife out on those afternoons when she wishes to take the air or to shop in the stores of the downtown district. So far, so good.

" 'There is one more duty—a very unusual one—and one which will never have to be repeated. If a man'—and I described Dyke very accurately in name and appearance—'ever comes up my steps, rings my bell, and asks for my wife, I want you to beat him within an inch of his life so that he'll never show his face around there again. And in such an event, I'll see that you're fully protected so far as the law is concerned.' Then I named a salary that caused that nigger to enter my employment on the spot.

"Sunbeam did not seem to be very glad when she learned that I had engaged a servant who could act as a combination chauffeur, housekeeper, and cook. But she finally agreed with me that it would perhaps be a more advantageous arrangement for her, since the man who had been coming every day to wash up our car and act as occasional chauffeur was proving to be very unreliable. So I discharged the woman housekeeper that night with two weeks of advance wages. The following morning Skoko was duly installed as general utility man and protector to Sunbeam.

---

[8] Like HSK himself, of course—who used the name "Skoko Goodwillie Tuck" in another tale.—Richard Polt.

"During the week I remained in Cleveland, he demonstrated that he was a very efficient servant. Hence, at no time did I regret the generous salary I was paying him. After that, while on the road, I was no longer preyed upon by the dread fear that Dyke might come around and worm his way into my household—as I felt instinctively he would if he could.

"Seven or eight months flew by. My trips on the road were now averaging but two weeks apiece, and my stays at home were of about the same duration. Apparently, Dyke had made no further attempts to call upon Sunbeam at the house, for she never made any mention of him again, and, in addition, catechizing Skoko elicited the fact that the only time she was ever out of his sight was for the two or three hours that she spent inside the great downtown stores. And I, very sensibly, never brought up Dyke's name again.

"Well, Payne, after these eight months had elapsed, I learned something that set me beside myself with joy. I had been at home for about a week when the family doctor called me aside one morning and told me the news—that later on there were to be three in our family instead of two. My heart leaped with gladness. Oh, how I longed for a boy—a little tyke with the yellow hair of his doll-like mother.

"Immediately I secured a leave of absence of a year from my firm. Then I made all the necessary preparations for taking Sunbeam over to one of the Italian lakes, where we could wait together in quietness and happiness for the great event to take place. Three days later I closed up the Chesterhyde residence. I paid off my faithful black, giving him a one-hundred-dollar bill as a bonus. When he left the house to return to the agency from which I had hired him, I tried not to show that my heart was heavy at breaking off from the home ties; and Sunbeam must have felt it more deeply than I, for the tears glistened on her eyelashes. And so, all this gone through with, we sailed for Italy.

"I rented one of the numerous villas that lie along the eastern shore of Lake Como. Built on the front of it was a long porch, where we used to sit together and watch the glorious colors of the Italian sunset. In fact, Sunbeam herself remained on the porch the livelong day, saying nothing, never moving, her face bearing the strangest, most baffling expression. From which often I'd have the hardest time to arouse her.

"And it was here that, speaking one day of Dyke—and his boyhood in some German family, who boarded him and brought him up for a few brief years—speaking quite casually, you see—came forth the single piece of information I referred to, to you, a while back. Something Dyke had told her or her father. And which she now told me. Namely, that the boy of that German family—the family's one son, that is—by name Gustav Homeier—used to hang his—rather his sister's—dolls."

"Oh-oh!" put in Payne. "Gustav Homeier, eh? And now governor—of an entire state! No wonder he attends all the executions in his state. Particularly those conveniently held—at Central City. Sadistic, eh? And with a complex on noose-ology! Well, well, no wonder then you figure Ivins's goose is cooked. Well, that riddle is out of the way. And now for the other riddle. So go on with the story, Gunton."

"Yes, I will. Well, as I say, Sunbeam used to remain on the porch of that Lake Como villa the livelong day, saying nothing, never moving, her face bearing the strangest, most baffling expression. And how that expression troubled me, Payne, for I knew that her heart must be worried. Then, as never before, did I do everything in my power to give her all the love and comfort I could.

" 'Dear heart,' I said to her one day, 'don't look so sad and forlorn. Am I not the same to you anymore—or is it the fear of the coming ordeal? You must not be afraid, my own. I promise you that we'll have the best medical attendants that the region affords, regardless of expense. And after it's all over with, we three will go back to our little Chesterhyde nest, and everything shall be just as it used to be. I'll get a car exactly like the one we had; I'll see that each piece of furniture is placed in the same position it used to occupy; I'll look up Skoko and re-engage him. We'll resume life again just where we broke it off.'

"On hearing that, her face lighted up, and she smiled a wondrous little smile—a smile, though, which proved to me that she was fearfully homesick.

"Upon seeing the smile, I added, 'There—how good it seems to see you smile again. Everything, darling, will come out all right.'

"And to my intense surprise, she burst into tears and replied, 'Oh, I hope so, how I hope so, how I hope so—and yet—I'm afraid. I'm afraid of—of—of—just everything.' And she commenced weeping so passionately that I almost thought her heart was breaking.

"Well, Payne, the months slipped by, one by one—until finally the great time arrived. Long before, though, I had installed two nurses in our villa, both English-speaking. I had secured the services of an extra servant as well. A most able physician and his assistant were in almost constant attendance. But, Payne, God must have intended her to give her life for her child, for she never breathed again after it was born. And I swear to you that later, when she lay in her coffin, I observed on her face the same strange elusive expression—a half smile—that had hovered there during the last months: of her life.

"But the child was a boy, Payne—a healthy, vigorous boy, just as I had hoped. But—but—but—how can I go on—?" His voice broke.

Payne leaned forward and placed his hand affectionately on the older man's shoulder.

"Dear old fellow," he said tenderly, "I feel that I know what you want to tell me. And which is that—that on the boy's left temple there was a—a red triangular birthmark?"

The older man gave a short, bitter laugh.

"By no means," he replied. "Nothing like that. From head to foot the boy was a dark copper color, with flat nose and exceedingly thick lips. I understand that later, when his hair grew out, it proved to be quite kinky."

Services of an Expert

Harry Stephen Keeler

It was close upon midnight.

I had just placed my silk hat on the rack that hung at the side of the room when I heard the slight sounds coming from the direction of the fire escape. Then I detected the shadow on the window pane.

I paused in the act of removing my gloves and felt quickly for my back pocket. My revolver was there.

So I stood very quietly in the darkness and watched the man on the iron framework outside as he fumbled a moment and then raised the window. Since a small patch of moonlight, now outlined on the rug, acted as a weak source of illumination, I drew further back in the shadow of the door.

After thrusting one leg over the sill, the intruder drew in the rest of his body. For an instant he stood, glancing with uncertainty at the raised window back of him.

Then it was that I slid my right hand carefully along the wall until my angers came in contact with the electric light switch. With my left I drew out the small, nickel plated revolver that I have always with me for cases of emergency.

"Hands up!" I said calmly—and snapped on the incandescents.

He thrust his hands instantly above his head and stood blinking in the sudden flood of light. I had opportunity then, for the first time, to survey him from head to foot.

He was a small and rather stockily-built individual, dad in a checkered suit; his face could be aptly described by the phrase "roly-poly." On his head reposed a derby hat and, dropping from his collar, was a gorgeously red tie that lent the final touch to his general appearance of flashiness.

"Well," I remarked, advancing toward him with weapon still extended, "what's your game, my man?"

He seemed to be yet dazed by the sudden turn of affairs for him. After a pause, he spoke.

"My game? Well—to tell you the truth—I don't just know. A minute ago I was sliding in that window back of me... and now... I seem to be... well... just waiting... for something to happen."

"Don't worry," I answered grimly, "It'll happen." I stepped toward the 'phone that stood on the table, watching him all the while. He didn't blink an eye. So I stopped.

"I suppose you're one of these fly-by-night birds known as second-story men, eh?" My voice took on a more sarcastic tone. "Or perhaps you're only walking in your sleep now. In a short while you'll wake up and declare it's some terrible mistake. Or possibly you've stumbled into the wrong house by error?"

His upraised arms were losing their rigidity. To satisfy myself as to whether he was armed, I stepped over to him and inserted my hand into each one of his pockets in turn. He had no weapons, however.

"All right," I said. "Let 'em dawn." I went over to the window, closed it, and drew down the shade. Then I returned to the table and dropped into the swivel chair, beckoning him at the same time into the straight-backed chair that stood directly across. "Sit down," I commanded. "Before I turn you over to the police I'll have a little talk with you. Do you know where you are? Do you know whose apartment you're in'"

"Well," he replied, "the name on the doorbell downstairs says Mr. Peter J. Dawson."

Probably I was goading him with my remarks far more than was necessary as I answered:

"You're quite observing, I'm sure, I presume then, that since the doings of successful private criminal investigators and their families are of such interest to our newspapers, you were merely one of many who happened to read in the *Chicago Despatch* that Mrs. Dawson left yesterday for Atlantic City, and that her illustrious husband, solver of the famous Wrangley counterfeiting case, the Abe Shaffner bond theft, the Cissy Rogers murder, and other bizarre little puzzles forming part of our social fabric, was to leave the city this morning to direct the work on the Clyley kidnapping case at Cincinnati. Put a little too much faith in newspaper data this time, though, didn't you? How could you be certain, for instance, that Millionaire Clyley didn't alter his plans the last moment about whom he'd employ to help him find his missing daughter? What could you know of telegrams that might have passed since that news story was published?" I paused. "Such nice plans as you have, too. Of course you made sure, by telephoning first, that the servant was away too—Heaven knows where?"

He bit out his reply in short, angry words. "Say! If you're going to turn me over, hurry up and do it. I'm not going to sit here and listen to all your gaff."

"Here, here," I said, "don't get huffy, my good sir. Even though I represent a phase of society that's not at all liked by your ilk, I can still be a very good fellow—a very good fellow at times—in fact, this is the one time of your life that you want to cultivate my friendship, of all persons." I watched him narrowly. Then I continued quizzing him.

"Confess, though, now... you just strolled in, as it were, to see whether any of the famous Dawson diamonds, achieved as rewards for an honorable career of hunting thieves much bigger than yourself, were lying around loose? They were most accurately described, I believe, in the newspaper account of the big dinner party last week, weren't they? How about it?"

His answer was non-committal, to say the least.

"I'm not confessing anything of the sort. Ring up the cops and be done with it." He laughed an odd little laugh.

"All the good cells'll be filled up with drunks in another hour. It's midnight now."

The more I thought of our unusual situation the more I felt that this man could possibly prove very valuable to me. My questioning now took on a definite trend.

"What's your particular specialty, if I may make so bold as to inquire? My experience, I'll confess, has been with a higher order of criminals than yourself. It seems really a rare treat to talk with a real second-story man; or are you perhaps a porch climber? or a lock-picker? Or a stick-up man? or maybe even a safe-blower?

"For example," I went on, "assuming that the jewelry you're looking for is over there in that iron box," and I pointed toward the massive safe that stood in the corner of the room, "just what, may I ask, was your method of procedure to be?"

"For the last time," he said wearily, "I'm telling you I'm not talking."

I was quite determined, though, to continue along the line on which I had already started.

"Ah, yes!" I remarked soothingly, "but you must talk. I feel a rather charitable impulse running through my veins this evening—an impulse that prompts me to be a trifle lenient with you. What do you know about safes?"

For the first time he betrayed a little interest.

"Oh, I know a little about 'em," he replied. "For instance—that one—over there—" He motioned toward the corner of the room. "I could tell you a few things about it—just from where I sit. That's one of the earlier ones put out by the International Burglar-proof Safe and Lock Company of Utica, New York. That's their type—" He wrinkled his brow and pondered a moment. "...36 B."

Things were shaping up better than I had expected. My voice must have shown the satisfaction I felt. "Good. You are quite an educated fellow in your line. Now that safe belongs to my wife. Not a soul knows the combination of it but herself. I frankly confess I don't. Is a safe like that really burglar-proof? Could you open it, all alone, unaided?"

He crossed his legs. "I daresay I could," he returned, gazing at me through eyes that had become mere slits. "For you see it happens to be all in the way you spin your dial around and listen for the tumblers dropping into place." He inserted his thumbs jauntily in his armholes and commenced to whistle a gay little tune. "But I don't intend to try," he added.

Obviously, this was the man I required. I dropped my tone of banter and spoke seriously.

"Now—as a sporting proposition—and because I've never seen such a person as yourself actually work in front of my eyes—if you could demonstrate your ability by opening yon strongbox in—say—five minutes—not a second more, you understand—I'd be careless—enough to shut my eyes and let you walk out of here through the same fire escape window you came in."

Exultantly, he rose to his feet. "Say—are you dead in earnest? Are you on the square about that proposition? D'you mean it? Will you let me walk out o' here if I can jiggle that combination open?"

"Certainly," I assured him "Of course I mean it. Can you do it?"

"I can make a try of it," he said, walking toward the safe. Then he glanced over it.

The silence was suddenly broken by the sharp ringing of the telephone bell which stood on the library table at the side of the room.

I ignored it.

Then it rang a second time.

The little man returned to the table and stood waiting, with his hands in his pockets.

"Going t' answer?" he inquired.

"Let it ring," I replied curtly.

He watched me closely, his face breaking slowly into a grin. Then he levelled his forefinger directly at me and launched forth into a scathing speech.

"Huh!" he exclaimed. "I'm a little next to you now. You're afraid to answer that phone. May I ask just why you don't want anybody t' know you were home in your apartment t'night—on the night of June the twenty-fifth—while the lady o' th' house is in the East—while you're supposed to be on a train going to a big case in Cincinnati? Eh? What's coming off here t'night? What's your game—Mr.—Mr.—Dawson?" At this point he evidently ran out of either breath or denunciatory ideas.

That cursed phone then rang for the third time. I was not only quite flustered now—but angry as as well. "That's enough from you," I growled.

His accusing forefinger was still pointed at me as the phone bell rang for the fourth—and what proved to be—the last time. He must have taken great delight in making me squirm, for he started off again.

"You're got something shady scheduled here for t'night. I always knew the police were as crooked as the crooks. You don't dare answer that phone. When you get ready t' let me into your little game, then maybe I'll do your dirty work. Not until." He sank into the straight-backed chair and stared at the window in back of me.

I glanced cautiously behind me, realizing that this rascal was perhaps playing for time. A suspicion crossed my mind that possibly a confederate was posted near the grounds. But we were quite alone. For about a minute I thought on the matter. This man had arrived at a crucial moment for me Without doubt, it seemed best that I render a detailed explanation to him if I wished to placate him—especially in view of the fact that the telephone bad complicated matters as it had.

So I leaned back in my chair and began, picking my words with care.

"I'm going to let you in on a family secret now. Of course, I'm quite safe—and, likewise, I don't have to do it. If I wish, I can turn you over any minute and the little tale you might tell I could brand as a lie, pure and simple. But in some respects you're a valuable man to me tonight. You can do me a big service. In return, I do you the bigger service—of saving you from five or ten years in the Joliet Penitentiary.

"Now pay attention," I commanded. "I'm looking for something in my wife's safe. No, not specifically her diamonds—except in a certain sense. It's a packet of letters—a packet that means more to me than the diamonds themselves. And I've got to get that packet.

"No doubt," I went on, "you've often read in the newspapers of some of the rich rewards I've received in the bigger cases I've worked successfully on. And I've been like a gambler, for when rewards were big, I've salted most of 'em away in diamonds. I made one fatal mistake, though: I gave all of mine, as fast as I accumulated them, to my wife. It's all she cares for—all she could ever see."

He was paying strict attention to my words; so I continued, punctuating my remarks with emphatic gestures of my clenched fists.

"That is, my friend, it's all she could ever see till—till these last few months—till she met this parlor lizard that she's fallen for. Oh yes, she's had an affair. She's received letters, and she's written them too; and the ones that she's written which have come back to her because of his being eternally on the move, she's faithfully put away in that private safe of hers till she could give 'em into his own dear hands. Fool that she was, to think she could carry on an affair under the very nose of a criminal investigator." I paused. "Well, to chop the story short, she's got my fortune—a hundred thousand dollars' worth in rings and geegaws—all hoarded up in that safe of hers like a miser. Sticking tighter to 'em than a barnacle sticks to the bottom of a mud scow.

"And I—well, I'm just a sucker—the benighted husband. Minus his fortune, minus the evidence to get a divorce with—for she's got to give me my freedom. I can stand most anything but this—being made a laughingstock of. I've still a chance to make a happy play for life with some good, right sort of girl.

"She—my wife—left this morning for a trip to Atlantic City. That part of the statement in the *Chicago Despatch* was quite true. She doesn't dream that I even suspect. The servant went to visit a sick sister And I—well, I'm on a train bound for Cincinnati to go to work on the Clyley kidnapping case... not!... are you wise now? Millionaire Clyley—my old friend—is simply helping me out a bit, that's all.

"Instead, I'm back here in the apartment tonight, reconnoitering—looking over the land—figuring out whether I could procure tools from some of the joints I know in the underworld, come back tomorrow night. and drill, saw, hack, punch or chisel my way into that strong-box and get that evidence that will give me my freedom—and those diamonds that belong to me—not to her. Oh, I'll take care of her all right. I'll be fair with her. I'll give her some sort of alimony. But I've got to protect myself." I paused. "That's the situation, my friend. And along comes yourself—an expert in your line. Do you see now what I need you for? Can you help me out? If you can, you're a free man." I leaned back and mopped my forehead. I had talked for five straight minutes.

If I had expected sympathy, however, I failed woefully in my expectations. He was coldly calculating—nothing more.

"You got some jane on the string that you want to marry, haven't you?" he said caustically.

"No jane," I returned.

"I doubt it," he said. He paused thinking. "Now I'm talking business," he added. "What's there in all this for me?"

So far as I could see, there was no necessity for me to dicker with this fellow, since it was quite evident that I had the upper hand. So my reply was short and to the point.

"Not a red cent."

He seemed still inclined to argue. "Pretty hard bargain, I call it."

I was becoming impatient. The unpleasant thought of a possible confederate, in the hope of whose assistance he was delaying matters, again entered my mind. "To my way of thinking," I remarked, "it's a pretty easy bargain."

"Well," he returned, "what guarantee have I got that you'll let me go if I do the job—that is—if I can?"

Really, the man's stubbornness was aggravating. "Numskull," I said, restraining myself with difficulty from shouting at him, "—if I can get at that property, which all came from my own pockets in the first place, it's to my decided advantage that you, the mysterious burglar, get away. I'll account for my possession of the divorce evidence by saying I bought it outright from the man who brought it to me. As for you, it's to your undeniable benefit to keep a quiet tongue in your head afterward. Then, too, haven't you my promise—my word of honor?"

He did not lose the opportunity to deliver a thrust.

"A lot o' faith," he jeered, "I'd put in the word of honor of a guy that'd steal from his own wife, so's to marry some jane he's struck on. I don't believe that story about Mrs. Dawson and this parlor lizard. You're making that up. Say," he finished with a leer, "aren't you yourself the Gay Lothario in this case? And aren't you one of those things called Indian-Givers?"

This was going just a little too far, I decided. I was commencing to feel decidedly wrathful, so I determined to use up no more valuable time discussing the offer. "We're wasting precious moments," I said sharply. "What do you intend to do? Is it this—or the police?"

Evidently he realized that he was hardly in a position to do otherwise than comply with my wishes.

"I'll make the best of it," was his reply. "My copper friend—you're a mighty hard man to deal with—and if anything goes wrong—don't blame it on anybody but yourself." He paused. "Well—here's where I get down to work. I never use tools. Too crude."

He removed his coat.

I watched him with interest, wondering how on earth he could open a supposedly burglar-proof safe without an instrument of any kind. I had heard of his kind, but never so far as I could remember had I met up with an authentic case of a "tumbler-feeler." He seemed, however, quite self-confident.

He folded up his coat and deposited it on the chair which he had occupied. Then he unfastened each cuff and turned it back, clear to the elbow. He glanced at me. "Say, friend," he queried, "if I can do it, don't I get one little jewel for myself—say a, little half-carat ring?"

Seeing the preparations he had already gone to, I had not been inclined to yield jot nor tittle. His persistency, though, had exhausted my patience.

I plunged my hand into my pocket and brought forth the only bill that there was on my person—a crisp, yellow fifty—

which I flung on the table without a word. He seized it cheerfully and tucked it in his vest-pocket.

After all—what did a mere $50 matter? The difference between his remuneration and mine was too great.

He walked slowly over to the safe and rapped on its sides and top with his knuckles. Then, with great mysteriousness, he wet the tips of his fingers, one at a time, on his tongue, and wiped them on his rolled up sleeves.

He stooped over.

Then he went through a series of puzzling actions. At times be spun the dial. At other times he worked it slowly, pressing his ear close to the iron door, and listening with a far-away look on his face. Occasionally he glanced in my direction out of the corner of his eye.

For nearly a minute I watched him. Then since it was summer time and the room had begun to feel stifling, I stepped casually over to the window, raised the shade, and opened it to its full extent, letting in a refreshing breeze from Lake Michigan.

This accomplished, I turned around to see how my expert was coming along with his task.

Great Caesar's Horn Spoon!—

While my back was turned he had quietly succeeded in swinging open the door of the safe and had extracted there from a huge blue-steel revolver which, in less than a second, he had raised, pointed in my direction, and fired with a thundering report great enough to wake twenty neighborhoods.

I dropped flat to the floor and lay still as a log.

Hurt? Not a bit of it! He probably missed me by a mile—but I was taking no chances of receiving another broadside from that villainous-looking weapon. While I lay prone, never moving, he stood stock still for a quarter of a minute. Then, with four giant strides, he cleared half the room and landed in the swivel chair with his back to me.

Cautiously, I raised my head. Silently, I regained my knees and feet. I tiptoed backward a step to the window and out on the fire escape, where I crouched down, watching the little man in the swivel chair.

Excitedly, he was jerking the receiver hook of the phone up and down. Finally he must have roused Central, for I heard him say: "H'llo—h'llo—'lo—North Shore Police Station, please—"

After the lapse of a few seconds he must have obtained his connection for he shouted into the transmitter:

"Station? Police station? North Shores? All right. Shoot an ambulance or a doctor and a squad in a red-hot hurry TO 725 Franklin Road—the second apartment—the Dawson's apartment. I've wounded 'r killed a man. Killed him. I guess. Nope, don't know him—was on my way to Cincinnati and saw the headlines in the late papers announcing the Clyley girl had been found—so came back on home—had lost my latchkey—came up by firescape—found him here—yes! yes! yes!—oh hello, Cap, sure—this is Dawson himself speaking—sure—yes, Peter J. Dawson—"

I had heard enough. I slid silently down the iron fire-escape ladder and hastened forth into the night, my last two dimes jingling as I ran.

Postscript: Once Keeler had found a good idea, he always reused it. Over two decades after writing this story, HSK would write an entire novel told by a mysterious narrator (*The Mysterious Mr. I*, Ward Lock, 1937; expanded into The Mysterious Mr. I and *The Chameleon*, Dutton, 1938-39). And the plot of "The Services of an Expert" is the seed that turned into one of Harry's wildest and strangest flights of fancy (so as not to spoil anyone's fun, I won't be more specific).

Finally, as Eric pointed out to me, we must give credit to Keeler for a very early use of the '...not!" construction (as in, "go to work on the Clyley kidnapping case ... not!"). Keeler was about 70 years ahead of his time on this one.

Richard Polt

Quilligan and the Magic Coin

Harry Stephen Keeler

Euphemistically speaking, Quilligan was suffering from the toxic effects of a common grain derivative. Mechanically speaking, his condition was such that it required the expenditure of more than the usual number of ergs to maintain his center of gravity directly above his point of support. Geometrically speaking, he was traveling along the path composed of a series of horizontal curves, each of which was halfway between a catenary and hypocycloid.

For the ninety-ninth time, Quilligan was drunk!

Possibly Arabian Nights adventures happen only to those who are drunk. Perhaps not. Very likely there was nothing mysterious about Quilligan's peculiar adventure with the magic coin, considering its prosaic outcome. And, on the other hand—

But, we reiterate, Quilligan was drunk.

It was eight o'clock in the evening. Since five that afternoon he had been wandering aimlessly back and forth through the mazes of the Loop, vainly searching for one person. He had inquired in all-night drug stores and fly-by-night auction houses, in ten-cent stores and Salvation Army soup kitchens; in pawnshops and penny arcades; in photo-postal studios and chop-suey restaurants; from traffic cops and blind beg- gars; from shooting galleries and home-scurrying shop girls; from chauffeurs and newsboys; from nickel show cashiers and street-corner shoestring merchants; from—

But the only result so far achieved had been the taking on of a cargo of the aforesaid grain derivative, each increment of which had drowned its inciting rebuff.

With such a rigorous search as this going on before our very eyes, it behoves us to investigate it a little more closely. Perhaps we can be of assistance—and thus stem the flowing tide of bitterness and booze that threatens to engulf Quilligan.

The object of Quilligan's search, it seems, was one Augustus Heinze Shutenthaler, a friend of his boyhood days. Exactly forty-eight hours before, Quilligan received over the general delivery of the postoffice at Kokomo, Indiana, a postcard which proved to be from Augustus Heinze Shutenthaler himself. In it the latter announced that in two days he was opening up his new and glittering palace of free lunch and fiery liquor, bowing bartenders and bottled beer, in Chicago's downtown district, and that he hoped to see his boyhood friend, Quilligan, there on the opening night. In view of the fact that the postal had eluded the argus-eyed Mrs. Quilligan, Quilligan was in Chicago ready to greet his old friend, Augustus Heinze Shutenthaler. But in view of the fact that he had forgotten to bring the postal carrying the address of the new and glittering palace of music boxes and matchless brew, brass railings and bottled rum, there was no Shutenthaler to greet—no Shutenthaler to find.

Earlier in the evening a sympathetic druggist had looked up the name of Shutenthaler in the city and telephone directories for Quilligan—and had found no entry whatever. So that trail, therefore, was nipped in the clue. Hence Quilligan was becoming discouraged. He longed to see Augustus Heinze Shutenthaler, with whom he used to paddle in the old swimming hole. He longed to see Augustus Heinze Shutenthaler's new and glittering establishment, and to imbibe a convivial glass with him. To return to Kokomo without seeing Shutenthaler would be no less than a—hic—crime.

For the ninety-ninth time, Quilligan perked up and approached a blue-coated traffic cop that loomed up in front of him from an alcoholic fog.

" 'S this way, ossifer," he murmured, " 'S m' fren' Shutenthaler. Shutenthaler—bran new s'loon—roun' here somew'ere." With a majestic sweep of his hand he indicated the whole 156 square miles of Chicago. "Here—somew'ere. Where'll I fin' Shutenthaler?"

"Now f'r th' third and last time," said the cop testily, "I'm tellin' ye it'll be roonin' ye in I will, do ye be troublin' me wid annymore quistions about y'r friend Shoohootenthaler. As I told ye wanst before, I know nahthing about anny Tootenshaler. If th' name's not in ather a 'phone directory 'r a city directory, thin I do be advisin' ye to consult a fortintiller—'r somethin' like that. Now be aff wid ye."

Sadly Quilligan turned away and resumed his wanderings along South State Street. Always the same. No one knew anything about Shutenthaler and the new saloon. What a—hic—fool he had been for forgetting to bring that postal with Shutenthaler's location on it. What a shame to have to return to Kokomo without seeing the old friend of his boyhood days. The cop had advised him to consult a fortune teller. If he didn't get any better results than he had so far, he might consider the idea and—

He brought himself gradually to a position of oscillating quiescence. He stared. In front of him was the entrance of a rusty looking building, placarded all over with dentists' signs advertising gold fillings for fifty cents—and up. And, crowning all the tooth scenery, was a sign that held great potentialities for Quilligan, It announced that

MADAME ASTRO
Revealer of the Hidden, Discloser of the Future,
Crystal Gazer, Trance Medium,
Is to be found in Room 202—Walk up.
Special for to-day:
Crystal reading with trance: 50¢

Swaying back and forth like an inverted pendulum, Quilligan read the sign from beginning to end. Then he dipped his hand into his trousers pocket and brought up all that he found there: two ten-dollar bills, a silver fifty-cent piece, and a return ticket to Kokomo. So far, so good. With punctiliousness he returned the two tens and the ticket to Kokomo. And with the fifty-cent piece clasped in his fist, he ascended a long flight of creaky, wooden stairs to a land of false teeth and gold fillings.

May heaven guard Quilligan and those two ten-dollar bills in his mad journey through the jungles infested by the tooth vultures. If he ever knocks at the wrong door he'll come out minus the two tens and plus a diagnosis of nothing less than pyorrhoea alveolaris. Ah—even heaven must be on the job, for he stops in front of Room 202. He knocks. Once more we draw a long breath, and pause while the story slides ahead out of the present tense.

A long delay followed Quilligan's knock. If he had been able to see through a wooden door panel he might have observed a huge, florid woman hastily hiding an ice-cold bottle of beer beneath a stand which carried a long black cloth and a great crystal ball. At the same time he would have seen her scrambling into a sombre robe covered here and there with white crescent moons. But finally the door opened.

"Lookin' f'r a Madame Astro," said Quilligan, bowing through a small and safe angle.

She bowed in return.

"I am Madame Astro, " she replied in clear, grave tones.

" 'S m' fren' Shutenthaler," he explained concisely. "Can't locate Shutenthaler. Augustus Heinze Shutenthaler. Been ever'wher'. Thought I'd—hic—try fortune teller. Last resort, you know."

"Be seated," she commanded, beckoning him to a chair which stood in front of the crystal sphere. He dropped into it. Whereupon she closed the door and seated herself opposite him.

"Already I perceive that you wish the hidden revealed. I, Madame Astro, seer into the far, student of occultism, unveiler of the mysteries of the Orient, stand ready to help you, Speak, layman, speak—and—er—cross my palm with the sum of fifty cents. What wouldst know?"

Quilligan dropped the half-dollar at the side of the crystal ball. Madame promptly performed the vanishing trick with it.

" 'S m' fren' Augustus Heinze Shutenthaler," he elucidated. "Star Shutenthaler," he elucidated. "Started new s'loon downtown. Jus' wan' fin' Shutenthaler. Thaz all. Thaz all."

Madame nodded understandingly and sympathetically. Madame realized that there was a victim, who, properly handled, was good for a double or even a triple fee. She commenced staring fixedly at the crystal ball. After a full minute had passed she began to sway gently from side to side. The swaying became more violent and then subsided, leaving her sitting stiff and rigid, her eyes glued mechanically to the transparent object in front of her.

Quilligan, rapt, watched her every movement.

Suddenly she leaned forward a trifle and commenced speaking in a dull monotone.

"I see—I see—I see—a—a—man. He is tall—and thin. He is clad in a checked suit. He is seeking vainly for—for—for—something. Ah!—what that is—I cannot see. He asks everyone. They shake their heads. He stops, He appears discouraged. He stoops. He picks—picks up—picks up—ah, nothing less than the magic coin—the all-powerful coin of the four wishes. Ah, fortunate, fortunate mortal, to hold in his possession the magic coin itself. Does he know that four wishes shall that coin give to its owner before it loses its potency? Four wishes! Wishes for health, for fame, for riches, for love, for knowledge, for what not else. Does he realize that he holds in his hand a coin that a king's ransom could not buy? (Either that bottle of beer has gone to Madame's head—or else she's spreading herself.) Four wishes! Wishes to be used wisely. Wishes to be used foolishly. Ah, fortunate, fortunate mortal. But will he remember—will he remember the number 4? The magic number 4? Will he remember? Will he—"

Quilligan reached over and gently tapped Madame on the shoulder.

"All ver' nize majick coin—four wizzes," he said thickly. "But how 'bout m' fren' Shutenthaler?"

Like a flash she relaxed. Her eyes opened wide. She stared stupidly about her.

"Idiot," she exclaimed, "you broke my trance. You snapped the most wonderful uninterrupted chain of vision I've had for a week. I could have told you everything you desired to know. As it is, it'll cost you another fifty cents."

Quilligan rose and pushed back his chair to the wall.

In Madame's second demand for cash he detected the faint creakings of a follow-up system. She was like all the rest. No one could tell him the answer to his problem: Where was Shutenthaler located? Without a word he walked to the door, opened it, and made his way down the squeaky stairs to the street. As for Madame Astro, however, she merely doffed her black robe, deposited her fifty cents in the Woman's National Lisle Bank, and resumed her bottle of cold beer.

Quilligan proceeded gloomily down the street. The clock on the corner of Van Buren and State showed the time to be 8:30 in the evening. Undecidedly, he paused, figuring whom to ask next. As he swayed to and fro in the breeze from the lake, the glint of something shiny met his eye. With infinite patience he stooped and picked it up. The light from the show-window of a nearby clothing store fell full upon it. A brief inspection showed him that his unsteady fingers held a bright metal disk on which the words were stamped:

"Remember the number, '4'."

"Odd that," Quilligan ruminated. The crystal gazer; her vision of a tall, thin man in a cheeked suit picking up a magic coin, her warning—"Remember the number 4"; her statement that the coin held exactly four wishes for its owner and then became valueless!

He scratched his head.

After which he clutched the metal disk in his hand and continued along the street, still picturing Madame Astro staring into the crystal sphere, All bunk, of course, he reflected. No such thing as a magic coin. No such thing as four wishes coming to a man in the twentieth century. And yet—well, he'd take a try at it.

"Lez see—lez see," he mumbled gravely to himself. "I wizz zat—zat—someone would—hic—walk up t' me and thrust a nize fat purse in my hand. Nize fat one, Nize fat one. Greenbacks—sparklers."

Scarcely had he covered thirty feet than a tall, thin young man with sandy complexion and a pair of steely blue eyes, stepped up behind him and apologetically tapped him on the shoulder.

"Beg pardon," he observed smoothly, "but—er—you must have dropped your purse. I came near holding on to it because of the hard times, but I've always—er—tried to be honest—so I want to hand it back. "

Quilligan wheeled sharply. With amazement he looked down at the slim young man. His eyes travelled to the latter's outstretched hand. Then they bulged out, for the hand was tendering him a fat leather purse, open just barely enough to disclose a bulky roll and a string of sparkling brilliants.

Only for a second did Quilligan hesitate. Then his own hand shot down into his trousers pocket and immediately reappeared, the fingers holding one of the two ten-dollar bills. With the other he reached out for the purse.

"You're the—hic—honestest man in the city, "he affirmed genially. "Don't see how I ever losht it. Ver' honest man, m' fren'!" He pressed the crisp ten into the slim young man's palm. The latter clinched it eagerly. "There's reward—small, triflin' reward—f' ver' honest young man." He jammed the bulging purse into his coat pocket and hurried around the comer.

As soon as he reached an alley he turned and made his way down it for a space of ten or twelve feet to a point directly beneath a hissing arc-lamp. Then he withdrew the purse and prepared to count the contents. But, to his dumfoundment, he found only a tight roll of narrow slips of green crepe paper—and a string of cut-glass beads.

"Beau'fully, beau'fully stung," he murmured, after the explanation had gradually sifted in on him. "Stung beau'fully. Ol' game—and caught Quilligan from Kokomo al' ri'. Well, got my wizz anyway—nize fat purse—but cosht me $10. That a majick coin, all ri', all ri'. Jus' goin' t' watch that coin."

He threw the purse and its contents in a dark corner of the alley; then he returned to the street.

He covered another block. By degrees he began to forget about the magic coin and to ponder once more about the question that had engrossed him all the evening: How and where was he going to find Shutenthaler?

Finally he stopped. The fact had dawned on him that it was high time to buy another drink—for there was still $10 left in the bank roll, But as he reached a decision in the matter, he caught sight of a big black negro, leaning nonchalantly against a doorway close by, Since the latter appealed to him as a possible source of information, he stepped over to him.

" 'S m' fren' Shutenthaler," he explained.

"Fren' Shutenthaler—"

"Shoot a dollah, sah?" interrupted the negro. "Yessuh." He peered carefully up and down South State street. Then he leaned over and whispered in Quilligan's ear: "Go straight to the fo'th flo' an' rap fo' times on the fo'th do'.—Jes' remembah the numbah fo', sah."

Quilligan began the long, wearisome climb. Evidently he was on the trail of Shutenthaler at last. In turn he came to the second, the third, and finally the fourth and top floor. There he paused and counted the doors from the top of the stairway: one, two, three, four. He went down the hallway and rapped exactly four times on the fourth door. Instantly it swung open as if operated by an invisible genie. And as he walked in, it closed noiselessly behind him.

He peered around, discovered that he was in an immense room. At the rear of it was a long, green baize table, presided over by a black moustached man. Around the edges twenty or thirty men were crowded, some sitting and some standing, but all watching intently the spinning of a roulette wheel. With a sinking heart Quilligan realized that the wires of fate had crossed once more—and that he was as far as ever from the trail which led to Augustus Heinze Shutenthaler.

As he stood there irresolutely, his attention was riveted by one of the spectators at the green baize table raking in a handful of silver and paper money. That was interesting. So he stepped over, wedged himself in the spellbound audience, and began to watch the ceaseless play on the black and the red, the odd and the even, the high and the low. Soon he caught sight of the great square which was painted on the green cloth and divided into thirty-six smaller squares, each of which was numbered with one of the numbers on the roulette wheel. He turned to a man at his side.

"Whaz nummers for?" he asked.

"Sh-h-h," whispered his companion. "Go easy, pal, on th' gab. They're runnin' under cover here. It's this way, friend. You lay your mazuma on any number. If that number comes up on the next spin of the wheel, you get thirty-six times your stake."

With an effort Quilligan steadied himself, for he suddenly remembered the magic coin in his pocket—the coin with three more unused wishes. And he recollected at the same time that his total wealth was reduced to a lone $10 bill and a return ticket to Kokomo. Since his mission to Chicago had failed, here was a heaven-sent opportunity to go back to Kokomo with a roll big enough to choke the postmaster's mare. So he turned to the man at his side once more and said, " 'F I—hic—put $10 on the nummer—any nummer—" He paused. More and more he began to see that he had nothing less than a half-Nelson on the Blind Goddess, for he possessed three A. No. 1 wishes as well as the red-hot hunch: Remember the number four. " 'F I put $10 on th' nummer four—an' th' nummer four comes up—do I get $360, fren'?"

"Righto, pal," said the man addressed, watching with unconcealed admiration an individual who, drunk or sober, contemplated risking a ten spot on a thirty-six to one chance, "It's thirty-six times your stake on a number bet."

Majestically Quilligan reached down into his pocket. He gave the magic coin an admonitory pat. Then he drew up his last $10 bill. A number of the players were depositing their stakes on the colored squares. Quilligan leaned over and placed his piece of paper money on the square marked "4".

"I wizz," he said sternly, to no one in particular, "that the number four comes up."

The black moustached man looked around. All the bets were placed. So he gave the disk an energetic twirl. It spun swiftly, the black and red merging instantly into a hybrid color, and the ivory ball giving a sharp rattling noise like a machine gun on the banks of the Yser. The wheel ran with undiminished speed for a quarter of a minute. Then it began to slow down. Quilligan looked on fascinated, steadying himself on the shoulder of his companion. Still more slowly it turned. The ivory ball now began to bounce several spaces at a time. Slowly and slowly the wheel revolved. And finally, with a last saucy leap, the marble dropped squarely into the slot marked "4".

"Well, by Hectofer," said the black moustached man, smiling gamely. "Stranger, you win. The first number bet placed to-night. Gentlemen, didja ever see the beat of it for sheer—" Crash!

An axe blade shivered the panels of the door, The shrill sound of police whistles and men cursing began in the outside hallway. Instantly confusion reigned supreme inside the room. The black moustached man sprang to the electric switch and snapped it. In a trice the room was plunged into utter darkness. Blow after blow continued to smash in the door. Amid the sounds of splintering wood and falling plaster, some excited person tipped over the roulette table. Men shoved, fought, struck out, kicked and tripped over each other in their wild efforts to elude the gambling squad that was breaking in the doors.

Quilligan, entangled in a mass of cursing, stumbling figures, found himself pushed and shoved through a small doorway. At once he felt a cool draught of air on his face. A second later he discovered that he was on a gravelled roof in company with twenty or more fleeing men. He descended hurriedly, swaying dizzily at every rung; but he clung on like a fly until he reached a dark alley. Here he threaded his way through a number of barrels and packing boxes, and finally came out on the brilliantly lighted thoroughfare.

He walked hastily in a northerly direction and soon found himself a block away from the scene of the excitement. Whereupon he leaned up against an arc-lamp post and made an effort to collect his fuddled wits.

At once he remembered that he hadn't had time even to collect his $360 winnings on his $10 bet. So he ruefully thrust his hand down into his pocket and drew up the magic coin.

"Y'r some majick coin, all ri', all ri'," he groaned. "Got m' firsh wizz—an' cosh me $10. Got m' shecond wizz—an' losh $10 more. Now I'm broke entir'ly." He paused, frowning at the coin. "Y're a big fake. Thought sho all th' time. Jus' a big fake, thaz all. I wizz I had jus' price of a drink—an' wizz I knew where I could fin' m' fren' 'Gustus Heinze Shutenthaler."

He flipped the metal disk idly over on his palm. Its reverse side read:

Remember the Number
"FOUR"
South State Street
Good for one drink at
SHUTENTHALER'S

Impressions of Hashees Drunk in Retrospect Written Day After, With Effects Still Somewhat On

Harry Stephen Keeler

This is a rambling essay written by Harry Keeler whose title should be taken literally. There is no date anywhere on it. I have no idea who Arrado is but he seems to be a friend of Harry's who supplied the hashees. There are a few references to Harry's cats in it, and there is a reference to Hazel Keeler at the end as "HVGK" (who possibly may have contributed to this essay in a flippant act of whimsy—see if you can figure it out).

There is some evidence that Keeler like to experiment with drugs. Some Keelerites in Chicago recently acquired some of his old belongings from the attic of a house he used to live in, and discovered an opium pipe hidden in a hollowed out book. Considering this work's subject matter, I transcribed this essay exactly as I read it. I included all typos, misspellings, and Freudian slips. Although Harry seems to have typed this on a somewhat defective typewriter, it was pretty easy to distinguish between the mistake of a wobbly mind and the mistake of a wobbly machine. There are a few spots with <brackets> around them, I used this to indicate where Harry went back and added hand-written edits.

The original type-written version of this essay is included in box number 15 of the collection at Columbia University.

Mark Allen

-page 1-

Same old thing. No effect. Will pay Arrado's friend two bucks for the two smoked; and turn the rest back. Two bucks out. Maybe worth it to be in Phillipine speakeasy. I speak to Arrado...I don't observe any effects...he smiles...man, you are terrifically under...can't you see it?.....no...but I do know that I am an actor..I can feel it in the deep, wellversed tones n my throat...William Collier...wonderful how I enunciate and how perfectly poised I am in every motion..I get up with cigarette and go over to cuspidor...my stride is perfect..I stand with elbow on electric conduit...should have been on the stage...my real self, the actor, has come out.......long gap.....have been laughing till the tears run out of my eyes. never laughed so much in my life...Arrado laughing too...Have staged the funniest vaudeveille act that could ever be put on....old hop head trying to get last bit of smoke out of hop....his actions could be spread over 30 minutes <act>...I have packed little bulls of Muggles in cigarette pipe, pried it out, stuck a pin on it, and gotten it down so low that I can't get my mouth on it...not a thing must be lost...god it is screamingly funny..and worse, I am losing the precious smoke because of bursting with laughter..God, I never laughed so much in my life.....am sick..despeately sick at stomach....I am sick, I tell Arrado...he says, you always do..you always get that way...blackness, sickness. close my eyes....open them Arrado says are you still stick..I say no, sickness entirely gone...he says, it always vanishes in a few seconds.......All idea of time has blown up..even space is scrooey...scrooey, that's what the word was invented

-page 2-

for..to cover a Mug l e drunkness...time and space, all scrooey......God, Arrado, I am seeing things..I would swear I saw a cat just now over there and there is no cat...well, what's the difference..other people have seen things..I'll get over it...he says, no there was a cat there..cat comes out under <t>gable ...Thank God...it is a real cat...Oh thank God..it looked so much like a phantom...Wait, Arrado, I will stage you the most wonderful lion hunt you ever saw..see, the ferecoisous beast, lord of the jungle...he shall be driven out of Africa....bang, bang.....lion is only playing possum....he rushes, he claws, daring hunter in danger of death....down lion....pussy, don't roll over..I will shoot you...daring hunter picks up lion and tosses it into saloon...so.....says Arrado, that's a dirty slam at that door...says I...always one must have a note of finality..I was talking kitty language...to a kitty the slam of a door means you're done..get out........I have been looking for hours at that man's coat on that hook, it covers acres, is all coat, coat coat, it is so black, so coaty..everything is that coat...all of a sudden the coat vanishes off into proper perspective and Arrado's voice is creaming into my ears like metal....he says, in an aneermous roar, like metal on glass...you know I tried so hard to get these muggles for you..tried many times....many months...have I contributed in a way to an author's knowledge....dirty little heathen..trying yo make me pay him some enormous sum...maybe ten dollars...I wll play possum....I won't admit that thery're worth anything to me.......time and space is all scrooey now...gone blown up......I have repeated over and over, he says, the same phrase...Boy, that's a bad rdgug....boy, that's a bad drug...he says I do nothing but repeat..but it's all so solemn

-page 3-

you have to repeat....oh God, life is awful... it is fearful. I am dygi from the horror of it...sordid, selfish...can't cry..can't do anything...well, it is all clear now...I see why these terrible crimes are committed...all terrible crimes are committed by drug fiends who wake up next day trembling in jail, and have to hang or to go to the pentitentiary....yes, that's it... I am going to strangle Arrado... there is no reason, it's a drug crime....we are here now...in five minutes I shall be sitting across from him. his head hanging on his neck....the police...East Chicago Avenue....God, what a stinking scandal...Author strangels Phillipino..Christ, what sordidness..what horror... is there any way I can avert it...if only people would come in....there is only us here....in fact, I have strangled him...I am sitting in the cell and the drug is making me relive the events.....I will get ten years...teh long years of prison life...how old will I be...should I kill myself first......I am now insane alright...of a sudden I see it all...hell is mental, in all my life I have never lived through such a mental hell...I have lived a thousand years... a thousand hells....Physical hell nothing.. it is mental..I would rather burn than live in hell and think thoughts as I think them now......God, I wish Arrado was big and could combat me if I strangle him... I am terribly afraid.... I am going out and get a cup of coffee next doors...he says "hey, don't get lost now. Leave your coat here..." I go out... it is raining.... my suit will have to be pressed.. should I go to a doctor and say I am poisoned on cannabic indica.... I am in restaruant... I have been here for a year...drinking a cup of black coffeee...no cups of black coffee... girl says a nieckel, and I pay her 15 cents...am going back... am back in speakseasy with arrado..time and

-page 4-

space all crazy... he is a mean, sordid little wretch... represents the rottones meanest little race in the Paciuific, garbage wagon on<f> all races... he is so hideous... ai never saw such ugliness.. he is so yellow... and he shows a horrible character, he is a snake in snake's clothing..... oh, I am in hell... Arrado, I have lived a thousand hells... a thousand hells.... a thousand hells.... I tell you I am frightened stiff.... there is something sinister in all this, this isn't just a companionable gift to a white friend of a chance to get some muggles.... this is a deep conspiracy...We have been here for hours and hours...he says let's go next door and eat... he's hungry... I am not hungry at all... we adjourn... <words x'd out: "we are in Greek restaurant."> we are looking for Greek restaurnat...listen may, why in Christ's name are we wandering around here for hours this way...... listen, Mr. Keeler, we aren't...it's only a few seconds since we came out....hours... hours...hours....where is this restaurant. where are we going......I see it...listen, damn it, I won't be a victim to this conspiracy.....what conspiracy he says.. what's the use of telling him... if it is, he knows it... he is an agent for a huge drug ring...he has roped me in on some terrible drug that I have a terrible craving for tomrrow and I am lost...lost...lost...he's not taking me to the Greek restaurant... in a moment two armed gunmen will come up, jam me in the ribs with guns. and I will be taken off for a ride to make a great scandal...kidnapping...how Dr. Read will laugh... he doesN8t like kidnappings... God, how cleverly this yellow man worked.... played for months to bring this about....no wonder the toverment gives

-page 5-

these devils a terrible sentence...it's worse than murder to do what has been done to me....we are sitting in Greek restaurant...Listen, Arrado, how many blocks is this resturant from the speakeasy....why Mr. Keeler, you've got a terrible dose...but it does that...it's just a couple of numbers... we spent only a few seconds in coming here.... No, I can't eat... I will eat... I will eat a dish of sliced tomatoes... I am looking abouta at the other diners....business men around Chicago Aven and Clark...ha. business men, shoveing in int..... no, I am insane... we are all insane tonight.... this is a lunatic asylum...X<I> can wait till later and go and speak to the other patients in the regular asylum or I can wander over to some of these people and ask them how they are getting along...insanity...Listen Arrado, we've been here for years... years....years... I feel so old..I feel terribly old beside you... I feel age opporessing me...<word x'd out: "ha"> oh-oh, foxy eh....that woman who just passed out took a glanace at me...detective all right.. can you beat it a woman detective... been spotting me for weeks.. knows that I am a drug firned... I will watch the man..I have seen that man watching me for weeks...he is going byu...have i seen him... I have seen that man a dozen times standing on curbs... he casts a glance at me...defective. both writing up individual notes.....God, I am hunhappy....Oh Arrado, if you only knew what I am going through... you have put me into a thousand hells today... you have added years to my back.... but I won't throw it up to you about the man and woman detective, because you know nothing about them... however, my man, you'll be followed when you get out of here.... you sure crossed my plot time at a bad time tonight..... we are out of the restaurant....can I get home,

-page 6-

Arrado is going to work... I will go to library... I get off Clark stret car at Randolph... I am in library, I spent thousands of hourw traversing each block, and I think I went all over loop.... it is seven thirty.... I will read SUNSET... I have been reading it for hours, turning the pages..but haven't read a thing..nor seen the pictures...well, it's time for the 10 o'clock bell to ring and we'll all be thrown out of here...I catch a look at the big clock..My God.....only teon minutes of eight....I am out on the street again... across from me is the Roosevelt Theatre... a little ahead.. but that was hors ago, I have walked many many blocks...hours ago I passed the Rooseveldt theatre... I look over my right shoulder... there it is, just a few feet in back of me now... I drink lots of orange juice and go home... a thousand miles between each stztion on the L -- but

I don't mind riding...when I think it's Belmont, we haven't even reached Chicago avenue.... it's like they pulled the L out like an acrodeon...very horrible... Well, I'm home at last...I will read the 10 story.....Now I can read so clearly... thr type is so black and my brain is so clear... I read two stories and-understand them better than I ever did in mylife... my cyclophoria doens8't bother me in the least....

I go to bed. Take 3 asprin tables. Hardly sleep 30 minutes all night. More coffee at brekfast. The disturbance is still very marked all right. Am goofy, scooey. Suppose it will linger another day. But I remember everything, even the wonderful lion hunt. And I sit here and write everything out in direct order the way it occurred in the right order. For many hoours, that must have been only an hour, I lived

-page 7-

through a hell so black that I believe many people would commit suicice...and I forgot utterly to releate that just prior to my going out for coffee, there was a tingling down my arms, on the under side, to little fingers, and on my legs.. and this was very horrible....space had a way of jumping about, it is true..but time was what went utterly blooey.

HK

-page 8-

<hand written note: "2nd draft">

Boy, did I go under, I'oll tell the world I did go under christ, hours since I wrote the first line. Pheew Phew uw what can a a man doo, doo, doo, doo she shewne tot powe po eww

I got the lauggies-- the jolly jolly laughied

By, I want to write on the machine that it's onl

I don't know what I started to strite above; I will now say that I want tokeep a record, arerecord,a r reocor,

I want to kep ar rcorcon you a own tum tum I wantto iee a recor di I a recrco l t on t no t l ty pyupemty tumtutytt TUM! Now you write one)h shit I'll sign it al right eee heehheee But i shallneverthe lwss wtite onethat would have been a r. Ho yob'. yob' Yob . <hand written note, illegible, looks like "IT'S,">

You didn't siggntthis, up to to t o m you didnd't singn this As the leave bevan t o fal Ingeneanard, aIN Why in the hello don't you sing

Oh ingegard, my own. (Nit not mine,thankG) Klinch number $ 4 : Harry says to me "Gee kid you mever saw you look so nice before -- prettitest girl I ever saw in my life ; awful lot nice, says he. signed HVGK to keep Harry from forging my sig.as before -- which shows that my memory, my inter mug memory so to speak -- is good.

-page 9-

But I really can remeber well and think clearly

Sort of Like Harry

Z. NARVIK: NORTH POLE MANHUNTER!

Ken Keeler

I.

Tick... Tock... Tick...

One forty-three and 30 seconds AM... One forty-three and 31 seconds... 32 seconds...

Through three sets of steel bars, two-and-one-half pairs of eyes followed every barely-perceptible twitch of the Wallinghaus Noiseless Electric Clock's near-motionless hands—five eyes belonging to three men doomed to hang at sunrise — hang even more silently and motionlessly than the Wallinghaus Noiseless Electric Clock hanging on the wall of the insulated quonset hut that formed their prison!

And small comfort indeed that, at this extreme Polar latitude, the sun would not rise for some 4 and 1/2 months!

"Dam' that ol' bastahd Luther Madigan anyhow!"

From Cell Number One, a colossal rustic whose rude burlap overalls left no doubt of his sub-Mason-Dixon-Line origins spat on the floor.

"Oi now, an' don't ye be about blamin' our-r-r tribulations, Gilyard, on the agricultural Professor whose research in the late 1990's produced the cold-resistant crops and livestock that made it econom-m-m-ically feasible to far-r-r-rm the Arctic Ice Cap." The speaker was a wiry erythristic of perhaps 50 years, whose puckish grin and extensively-hyphenated speech confirmed his Irish heritage.

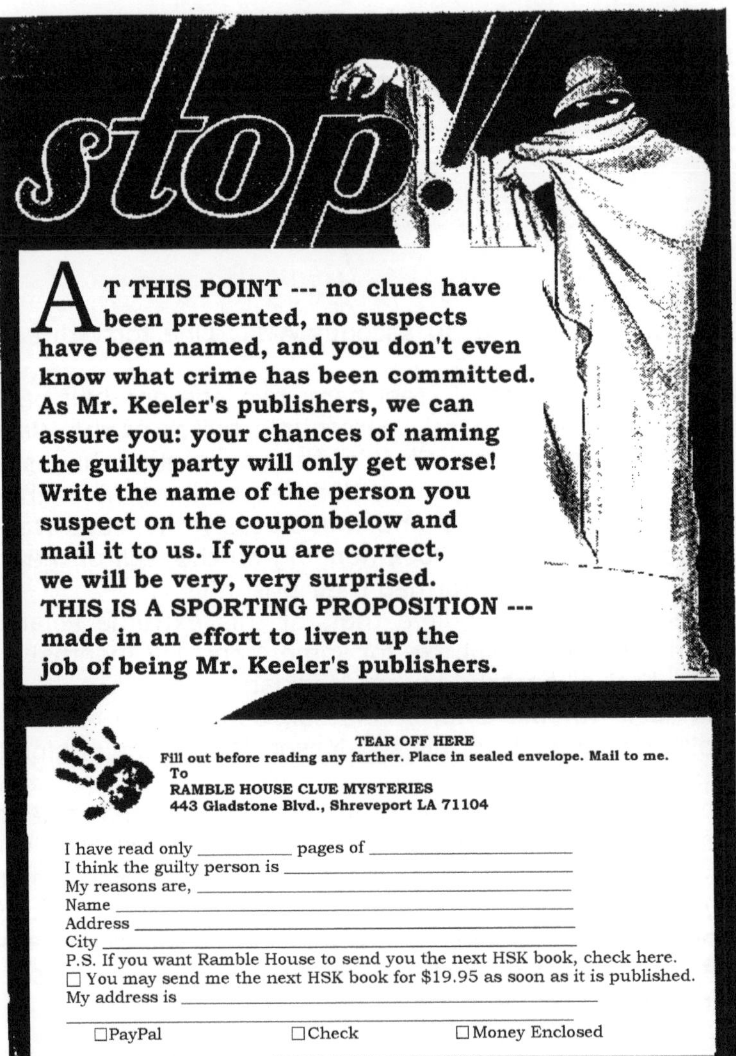
stop!
AT THIS POINT --- no clues have been presented, no suspects have been named, and you don't even know what crime has been committed. As Mr. Keeler's publishers, we can assure you: your chances of naming the guilty party will only get worse! Write the name of the person you suspect on the coupon below and mail it to us. If you are correct, we will be very, very surprised.
THIS IS A SPORTING PROPOSITION --- made in an effort to liven up the job of being Mr. Keeler's publishers.
TEAR OFF HERE
Fill out before reading any farther. Place in sealed envelope. Mail to me.
To
RAMBLE HOUSE CLUE MYSTERIES
443 Gladstone Blvd., Shreveport LA 71104
I have read only __________ pages of ____________________
I think the guilty person is ____________________
My reasons are, ____________________
Name ____________________
Address ____________________
City ____________________
P.S. If you want Ramble House to send you the next HSK book, check here.
☐ You may send me the next HSK book for $19.95 as soon as it is published.
My address is ____________________
☐PayPal ☐Check ☐Money Enclosed

"Why th' hell not, One-eye?" shot back the giant. " 'F'twere-n't f'r Madigan developin' th' ice cabbage 'n' th' polar boar, 'twouldn'ta been no fa'mwo'k to luah none of us three up heah pas' th' Arctic Circle... 'n' 'twouldn't none of us nevah uv been convicted uv Ol' Man Farnuthin's murder!"

"Arr!" the third prisoner, a pirate—if his black beard and eyepatch were any indication!—interjected from his cell. "Stop callin' the Irishman 'One-eye'. His name is 'O'Neeye'!"

"Sorry, O'Neeye," grumbled the Southerner. "Didn't mean t' imply y'all had one eye, since you clearly got two."

"And the real reason we're here, damn ye," barreled on the buccaneer, "is the Polar Republic's Reduced-Burden-Of-Proof Statute, stating that, due to the small number and crucial role of the Arctic farming population, homicide is so heinous a crime that up to three defendants can be convicted of the same murder, so long as the evidence indicates at least one of them *must* have committed it!"

Gilyard spat again. "I reck'ns, Coalbeard, that y'r ri't. Incidentally, though, I'm damned if'n I knows why you wears that eyepatch—when y'r eyes are both perfeckly good—unlike mine." And he rubbed his empty left eye socket sadly.

A complete cross-section of mankind they were —the Irishman, the pirate, and the giant one-eyed hillbilly—trapped like convicted rats as a blizzard howled on the polar ice outside!

O'Neeye shivered. "If only, boyos, whichever of us shot Old Farnuthin, not twenty miles from this prison at the exact magnetic North Pole, leaving no clues, would ow-w-w-n up, the other two could skip—but haven't we been all thr-r-r-rough that, Coalbeard an' Gilyard, and isn't it that we were the only three strangers north of the 89th parallel that night, and isn't it that that circumstance alone was sufficient to convict the three of us under the Arctic Reduced-Burden-Of-Proof Statute, and isn't it, finally, none of us who'll be confessin' now if we haven't already."

"Avast, yes!" rumbled the one called Coalbeard. " 'Twould take a detective the likes of Z. Narvik himself to find the guilty party and stop young Warden Hank Farnuthin, sleeping even now behind yonder private door, from marching two innocent men up those gallows steps like—like plank-walking mutineers!"

Gilyard spat twice. "Don't be denigratin' Warden Hank Farnuthin. F'r don't he take us'ns out twice a week fo' a taste o' freedom on the dogsled—ten mile south, then ten mile east, and then ten mile north—back right here to jail? And ain't that a whimsical touch, seein' as how th' No'th Pole's the onliest place on Earth where's a fellah could do that?

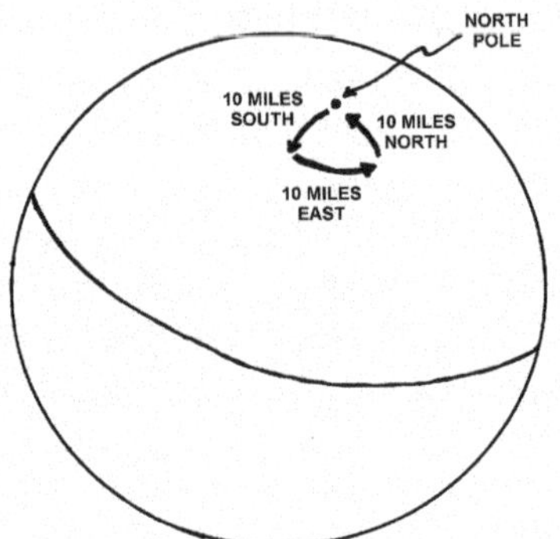

"Faith, but doesn't that same Hank Farnuthin, Gilyard, spend each trip a-cursin' us for murthering his blessed father?" shot back O'Neeye. "The Divvil take him! Why—"

But the Hibernian's oath was cut as short as a dwarf who had been put through some sort of machine that makes you shorter by the slam of the insulated front door as a bulky figure in a parka burst in and forced the door closed against the driving blizzard, then took off his hood as the pirate pointed at the stranger in amazement.

"By Neptune's beard—'tis Z. Narvik himself!"

"Da very zame!" grinned the outsider, whose straight, jet-black hair and ponderous consonants branded him unmistakably as an Eskimo.

O'Neeye gaped. "Zunderkind Narvik? The Polar Republic's top crimebuster?"

"We-all was only jes' sayin' how it'd take a detective of youah brains to get us out of this heah jam we'uns is in. Or, two uv us out, anyhow."

Narvik—for it was indeed he!—arched his heavy brows.

"A dedegdive buzzle? By all meanz, dell me aboud id." And, so saying, he doffed his parka, abstracted a gigantic dead salmon from its pocket, sat down, and took a bite.

II.

"Arr, and it's like this," began Coalbeard. "We three be sentenced to hang for murder in just four-and-one-half months—a murder that only one of us committed—"

"Though none of us knows which, and none of us will confess," continued the Irishman.

Gilyard pointed at the Inuit sleuth. "But su'ely y'all musta heahd, Narvik, 'bout th' murder of Old Man Farnuthin?"

The salmon dropped from the Eskimo's shocked fingers. "You mean you—you dhree are de varmvorgers gonbigded ov de Varnudthin murder under de Argtig Reduzed-Burden-Ov-Broov Sdadude?"

"Sure and who else, me lad, would be rotting away here in this isolated prison at the exact North Pole?"

"Dhe egxagt Nordth—vaid, vaid. Led me dhingk..." The burly Northlander began to pace the room in his heavy mukluks. "Iv you are here, dhen—Aha! Yez!"

So fast that it took the prisoners' breaths away, Narvik turned and thrust his heavy round face up to the bars of Coalbeard's cell.

"I gan zolve diz grime and releaze the innozend men vid dwo guezdions!"

III.

"Two blasted questions? Arr," growled the freebooter, "Ye're a son of a scurvy seadog, you are! But have at us!"

"Vhat is dhis zgurvy zeadog dhat—bud never mind. Guesdion Number One: Have any ov you been zigk ladely?"

Three cellbound jaws dropped like three astonished bowling balls onto a newly-polished alley; clearly the canny Inuit's shot had landed. "Why, yessuh," Gilyard recovered. "We all contracted Polar Fever jes' one week aftuh ouah conviction—that is, on April 21st, 2001."

"And lay senseless nearly six months, Narvik, while Warden Hank Farnuthin nursed us back to health!" the redhead chimed in.

Narvik smiled. "Az I zuzbegded. Guesdion Dwo: Vhad day iz id?"

Gilyard sighed. "Fellers, I's afeard ol' Narvik's battier than one of Luther Madigan's Ice-Bats! F'r don't the tear-off calendar, over on Warden Hank Farnuthin's desk there, clearly say that today's the 10th o' November, 2001—jes' seven weeks into the six-month-long Arctic night?"

"Den diz mysdery iz zolved," grinned Narvik. "For I know dwo vacts dad you do nod—namely A, dad doday iz only May 12th, 2001, and B, dad diz iz *nod de Nordth Bole!'* "

IV.

Three gasps emanated from three cells like three overinflated Wallinghaus "Wear-Ever" tires springing three simultaneous leaks!

"De Nordth Bole Brizon," continued the moon-faced polar gumshoe, "vaz vound abandoned dwo veegs ago, and every lawman in de Argtig haz been seegking you vellows ever zinze. Und now id's obviouz vhad habbened: Varden Hangk Varnudthin—whom I now invfer iz dhe drue giller ov hiz own vadher—avraid dhad hiz guildt vould be dizgovered, bud zo gommidded to hiz dudy az Varden dhad he velt gombelled to exegude you as diregted by de gourt—drugged your vood, zpirited you avay in hiz Vallinghauz Driple-Engine aeroblane vid ids vreeze-brotegded vuel dangk, buildt a dubligade brison here, dore rouvghly one-hundred-and-eighdy bages ovff ovf hiz dezgk galendar, and gonvinzed you dhad you'd been zigk vor zigx mondths!"

"Begorrah, man, but it *has* been six months!" expostulated O'Neeye. " 'Twas just a month or so into the six-month-long Arctic day when we took ill, and you can plainly see we're well into the six-month-long Arctic night!" The Irishman pointed to the tiny window, through which could be seen the polar dimness outside.

"Dhad, my vriend, iz de zigx-mondth-long *Andargtig* nighd!" chuckled Narvik. "You see, bagk in the Argtig, id'z zdill daydime!"

"But—but—" Coalbeard sputtered. "D'ye mean to tell us, you salty scowscupper, that we're in the *Antarctic* right now? For if so, ye're plain barmy!"

"Barmy? Berhabz. Bud gorregt? Devinidely! Varden Hangk Varnuddin buildt dhiz imidadion brizon brezizely here zo dhad you vould never know you veren'd sdill ad de Nordth Bole!"

"Y'all are nuttier than—than a pecan what's convinced it's Napoleon!" exploded Gilyard. "They ain't no doubt, Nahvik, that we's at th' exact No'th Pole, for twice a week we takes a sleigh ride ten mile south, ten mile east—"

"And den milez nordth, and end ub righd bacg here—gorregd?"

"Correct—and as any schoolchild knows, the No'th Pole's th' onliest place on Earth where— What's that? How do we navigate those trips? Well, *by my own compass*! An' befoah you gets the bright idea, Narvik, that th' Warden opened my compass and repainted the needle backwards—so's it read South f'r Noath and West f'r East—let me tell you that it's military issue—which means it's *hermetically sealed* to protect 'gainst enemy soldiers doin' jes' that, to confuse our boys. So's you see, we cain't be nowhere else but the goldurn No'th Pole!"

"Vell, yez and no. Vor regardlezz ov vhat 'any zgooljild knowz', dere's odder blazez on Eardth dhad dhe zame dhing gan habben! A vagd!"

And with that, the squat Northlander went to the desk, scribbled a diagram, and showed it to the three incarcerees.

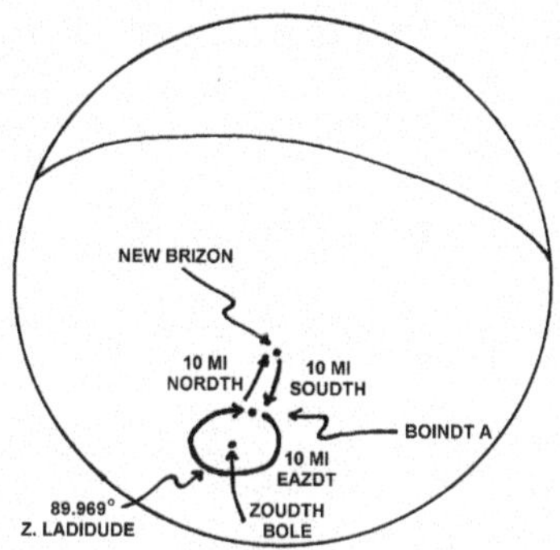

"You vellows are here—abbrogximadely eleven-boint-zigx milez nordth of dhe *Zoudth* Bole. On your zleigh dribs, you go 10 milez zoudth, to here—ad vhad ve vill gall 'Boindt A'—aboud one-boindt-zigx miles avay vrom de Bole—ad aboud 89.969 degreez Zoudth Ladidude. Vhidch line of ladidude iz exagtly 10 milez long az id zirglez de Bole. Zo vhen you go 10 milez eazd—you zirgle the Bole and *gome bacg do Boindt A*—vrom vhidch you go 10 milez nordth—bacg along the bath you game by—and arrive again ad dhis zubzdidude brizon!"

"By Neptune's hoary beard, it all makes perfect sense!" gasped the buccaneer.

"But ain't y'all, Narvik, got no *di-rect* evidence 'gainst Warden Hank Farnuthin?" inquired the behemoth.

"N-no..." ventured the salmon-toting private eye. "But gan you dthingk ov a more ligely egxplanadtion?"

The three men looked at each other in helpless surrender to the detective's relentless logic. Then a look of triumph crossed the emerald Islander's ruddy face.

"Ah, but explain *this*, me bucko! If we're really only eleven-odd miles, Narvik, from the South Pole, then what the Divvil are you—a *North* Polar Republic detective—and an Eskimo to boot!—doing in the Antarctic?"

The Asiatic's obsidian eyes twinkled.

"I'm on vagation!"

THE CRACKSMAN WITH THE TRANSPOSED HANDS

Jim Weiler

Chapter I

Depressed and despondent, Habberton Singlebody looked out the hospital window at the dregs of another dreary, gray January day in Chicago, then down in dismay at his hands. Why in the Six Hells of Sumatra had he gone ahead with his decision to have his left hand attached to the right arm and the right to the left vice-versa-wise? When he tried to make a fist, his hand opened. Painlessly, correctly, but exactly the reverse of—*how in the Third Hell of Heliopolis am I going to read a book or wipe my butt?* he thought.

"How are we doing this morning, Mr. Singlebody?" A perky blonde nurse who Habberton definitely did not recognize—there could be no forgetting that angel face!—sashayed into the room and checked his chart. "Ready for your physical therapy?"

"Still can't make a fist without concentrating on it," he replied, his funk forgotten in the presence of perfection. "Are you new?" *Geeze, what a lame line! There go my chances with her.*

"Everybody's new here, Mr. Singlebody. *The Chicago Center for Frivolous Elective Surgery* has only been open for business for 45 days. I'm Miss Pfaar. I've been working in the west wing for the last month—helping the mouth widenings adjust to their lip grafts. Let's see how our bones are mending, shall we?"

Sweet, petite Loreli Pfaar leaned over the bed. Habberton Singlebody smelled Ivory soap and Johnson's baby powder—his mother had always smelled like that. Nurse Pfaar grasped Habberton's right—or was it the left?—hand with both of hers and gave it a sharp, twisting tug. Cool hands and searing agony. *Strangely erotic,* he thought. *I gotta marry this girl.*

Chapter II

Detective Pinckley Malone stood near the bed in Chicago General's room 303 and listened to the rhythm of the heart monitor. The doctors said their patient, a security guard for Southern Illinois Gemstone Exhibitors, definitely wasn't going to make it. The stiletto blade which three times had entered Dolfus McDermish's heart had exacted too heavy a toll on the tissues and there was no time to arrange for a transplant. He might regain consciousness, but he wouldn't last the night. So Detective Malone stood vigil, hoping to speak—however briefly!—to the sole witness of the biggest gem heist in Chicago's history—bar none!

Six hundred million dollars worth was a lot of precious stones to keep in one place. But security had been tight: a computer-controlled setup admitted just one person—one and no more!—at a time to see the gems on display but required two to open the door. The person entering put his right hand on a right-hand-shaped sensor on the door while the guard, five feet to the right, turned the pass key. Heat and motion sensors prevented any of it from working if there were more—or less!—than two people in the anteroom. The doorway leading to the anteroom wouldn't open to admit another as long as the gem-room door was open, which it must remain while the guest viewed the exhibit. At any hint of mischief, all the guard had to do was turn the key back and the gem-room door would close—ker-swoosh!—trapping the culprit in a room that could not be opened from the inside. Southern Illinois Gemstone Exhibitors touted it as "the most secure exhibit since the Treasures of Tut."

Yet one man had entered, overpowered the guard, single-handedly opened the gem-room door, pocketed half a billion dollars in jewels, and quietly left. It was all on tape except—as usual!—the perp's face. No alarms had gone off because both guards watching the monitors—the selfsame guards who were to have given such an alarm should foul play transpire—had already been killed in their sleep.

Security guard McDermish stirred on the bed. His eyes fluttered open. The heart monitor skipped a beat. *It's now or never*, Malone thought. *Our love can't wait. Dammit! Now that stupid song will be playing in my head all night.* "Lie still, McDermish," Malone said. "You're sliced up pretty bad. Can you tell us who did this to you?"

McDermish shook his head no. "Sss-sss-fsss," he breathed.

Malone leaned closer. "What was that? I couldn't make it out."

Rallying his strength McDermish tried again, louder, though still hissing. "Sssih... sssih... fsssssss......"

Detective Malone blinked and searched his mind for a match. "Sisyfus?" he asked.

McDermish nodded, exhaled and closed his eyes, his strength gone. The alarms on all the monitors went wild and the room filled instantly with hospital staff— leaving no space for the detective, who stepped quietly out of the way. From the hall where he stood in thought Malone heard the shouts of "code" and "clear" and finally "I'm calling it." In twelve years on the force he'd gathered his share of deathbed evidence. *Why can't they ever give you a clear answer?* he thought. *Why is it always one cryptic word? That old woman who sat up and shouted—"bosco!"—we never did get to the bottom of that. And last month—when that Shakespearean actor Mortimer St. John Pugh died from gunshot wounds—his only word to the police had been "Yorick." As it turned out, his agent, Horatio Alger had owed him money and killed him to eliminate the debt. Why couldn't he just have said "Alger?" Now this. "Sisyphus." The Greek king who was condemned forever in Hades to push a stone to the top of a mountain only to have it roll back down—Gem stone?— Is that the connection?—Endless labor?—Condemned —why? For chaining Death—Thanatos, to be exact. Futility?—Vanity of Vanities?—Ecclesiastes? It's April Fools Day—maybe he was joking... This is getting me nowhere.*

Pinckley Malone whipped out his cell phone, hit fast-dial. "Hubbard? Malone here. We got nothing. McDermish is dead. All he said was 'Ssih Ssih Fsss.' " ..."Yeah, that's right. I thought he meant the Greek king damned to rolling a rock forever uphill." ... "No. I don't see any connection either. I think we've got another 'bosco' on our hands. See you in twenty at the scene."

Chapter III

Detective Elron Hubbard was hopping around the Southern Illinois Gemstone Exhibitors exhibition anteroom in full rant. "This security system is a joke! Sit over there and watch, Malone." Placing his right hand on the door sensor Hubbard reached for the key with his left hand, crossing it under his right arm and stretching as far as he could. "This is what the designers intended," he said. "Can't reach the key—can't open the door, right?" Malone nodded. "Now watch this—" Hubbard said. Keeping his right hand on the sensor he turned his back on the door. He could easily reach the key with his left. Hubbard clicked the key and the door swung open. "That's not all!—" he shouted, warming as he always did at the myopia of design engineers. Reaching into the pocket of his trenchcoat he withdrew a human hand. Not a real hand. One of those battery-powered rubber gag hands that moves on its own. From another pocket he extracted a roll of duct tape and ripped off a ten-inch length. "Think it'll work?" he asked. Malone shrugged. Hubbard taped the rubber hand in place on the door and stepped over to the key station. Click! The door opened. Click. Click. Click. Close. Open. Close. "The morons used air-flow sensors instead of heat sensors. Now watch this—" He ripped the rubber hand off the door and pitched it into a corner, keeping the duct tape. At the key station he turned the key. Two steps to the door. He put his hand on the sensor. The door opened. "And this!—" He tore off little squares of tape and plugged the sensor holes on the door, then turned the key. The door opened. "Any five-year-old could bust into this room in ten seconds. The two-bodies bit works, though. None of these tricks'll work if there aren't two warm bodies in here."

"That's some great stuff, Hubbard," Malone said, "but I watched the security tape from beginning to end, from start to finish, from A to Izzard and back again. That ain't how it was done. The perp came in, stabbed the guard, put his left hand on the door and turned the key with his right. A fact! Give that a try, why don'tcha?"

"Never thought of that," Hubbard admitted. He picked the tape out of the sensors then put his left hand on the door and turned the key. Nothing.

"Make your hand fit better," Malone suggested. "Thumb in pinky slot—pinky in thumb—"

Hubbard tried to make his hand fit. But there were seven sensors. One for each finger and two for the palm. There was no contortion of the left hand that could block all seven sensors at once. The door stayed closed.

"Curious," said Hubbard. "You're sure this is how he did it?" Malone nodded. "Musta been some kinda mutant—" Hubbard muttered. "Let's get breakfast and a beer. I got some thinkin' to do— And I want a look at that security tape."

Chapter IV

Habberton and Miss Pfaar sat eating a cold sandwich lunch in Singlebody's shabby third-floor walkup, drunk with yesterday's success and with Jack Daniels, laughing.

Habberton laughed because he'd pulled it off. He was going to be one of the richest men in Brazil. And, lame line, reversed hands and all, he'd got the girl. Of course the diamonds had helped. It still surprised him how quickly Lori—dear Lori!—he called her that now, not Miss Pfaar any more—had responded to his hints of limitless wealth.

Loreli was laughing for reasons altogether different. This schmuck actually thought she was going to marry him and follow him to Brazil. Not! As soon as they fenced the gems she would knock off dear old Habby and skedaddle to the land down under with the loot.

Lost in their separate reveries, neither heard the approaching footsteps. But both jumped a full six inches at the sudden pounding on the door and the shouts of "open up—police!"

Chapter V

"All right, Elron—" Pinckley Malone said over beers that evening, "I dig that after looking at the tape you could make out that the perp—" Malone checked his notes. "—Habberton by name—had his hands reversed, the left on the end of his right arm and the right on the end of his left. I dig that they could only be arranged that way surgically. But how in the Five Hells of Santa Monica did you know exactly which hospital to call?"

"Elementary, my dear Pinckley—" Elron Hubbard said. "There are only three hospitals in Chicago that perform this type of surgery: *Lakeshore Lost Hand and Foot Hospital, Mother Hitton's Severed Extremities Clinic* and *The Chicago Center for Frivolous Elective Surgery*. The latter is more commonly known by its acronym, CCFES. Cee. Cee. Fsss. Q.E.D.

"Now, tell me more about that Greek king you alluded to this morning..."

THE SKULL OF THE STUTTERING GUNFIGHTER

Francis M. Nevins

Xenophon Cheung, half-Greek, half-Chinese honors graduate of Canandaugus University School of Law and legal representative of the Tong of the Warty Toads Who Sing Sweetly in Mating Season, rose from the leather swivel chair behind his highly polished double-sized teakwood desk—with its inlaid pen set flanked on the left by an ornate bust of Socrates and on the right by a no less ornate bust of Confucius!—and strode past several shelves of lawbooks to the comfortable leather couch on which sat his three oddly assorted visitors, staring at the coffee table on the glass surface of which sat a skull. And not just any skull but one that gleamed forth in bright gold, plated upon the sconce long ago by secret method known only to the master goldsmiths of the Toads Tong, and the gold plating itself studded with rare and precious gems, with the result that at a conservative estimate the said sconce was valued at three million of Uncle Sam's dollars!

"As executor of the estate of my grandfather, The Honorable Wing Sing Cheung, who was the supreme exalted chieftain of the Toads Tong until his death early this year at the age of 99," began Cheung, "it is my solemn obligation to carry out the mandate in Paragraph 37(b) of his will. " He paused, and withdrew from the breast pocket of his sharkskin suit a blue-backed document which he proceeded to unfold and then to turn from one of its multitudinous pages to the next until he had located the passage he sought.

"You gentlemen, " he said, "being descendants of the famous figure from the colorful history of the American Old West whose official name was Daedalus Didymus Digby but who was known colloquially as the Stuttering Gunfighter, are presumably familiar with the biography of your ancestor, and with how in his youth he was the protector of the many Chinese railroad workers who were so frequently robbed and beaten and exploited and murdered by that crowning glory of human civilization, the white man. Therefore—since it is and ever has been a point of honor among my people to repay a hundredfold whatever good deed might be done for us—when Mr. Digby was hunted by corrupt white lawmen for his perhaps at times technically illegal activities in defense of the Chinese, it was the Toads Tong—headed at the time by my honorable great-grandfather Wong Sung Cheung!—that gave him shelter and protected him in turn for as long as he needed protection. When it was safe again for him to travel, he left our Chinese community and roamed all over the United States—winning several female hearts during his peregrinations!—but after many years he returned to his adopted people and stayed with us until in peaceful old age he died of natural causes. Long after his death, when mother nature had stripped the flesh from his bones, our Tong leaders had his skull exhumed and, as a mark of the reverence in which all true Toads hold him, plated said skull with gold from our treasury and imbedded therein the assortment of precious jewels you see before you. But my grandfather Wing Sing Cheung concluded late in life that after his own death the skull of the stuttering gunfighter should be given to—and here I quote from Paragraph 37(b) of the will itself!— ' to whichever direct descendant of the said Daedalus Didymus Digby shall be deemed, in the judgment of the executor of my estate, most worthy to possess the same. ' "

The first of the oddly assorted trio to reply to Cheung—and by far the most diminutive, so much so that it was clear to Cheung, who read himself to sleep each night with medical treatises, that he suffered from the malady commonly known as dwarfism!—wore a pin-striped suit of undoubted European cut plus a shirt of brightest Kelly green that perfectly matched the color of the beret he had deposited on the richly figured carpet at his feet. "Ah, begorra," he squeaked in his abnormally high-pitched little voice, "and 'tis a foine specimen of sconce, messieurs, n'est-ce pas? Nevair have I seen such a one. She will have ze place of honneur in my pied-a-terre overlookin' the river Liffey in Dublin town or me name ain't Pierre Etienne FitzRourke! Naturally I reserves for meself the right to dejewel and ungild the old bhoy should I be needin' the money. "

"Your claim is indeed a strong one, " said Cheung, striving with true Celestial politeness to keep his face from showing his disgust. "For the investigations I have undertaken in order to fulfill my honorable grandfather's bequest have established that you are indeed a grandson of Daedalus Didymus Digby, through his marriage to the French actress Colette Yvette de la Modette, which produced a daughter, Jeannette-Odette Digby, who in her turn married the dwarf Irish poet Seamus FitzRourke, which marriage in due course produced yourself! "

The man seated next to FitzRourke leaned forward in his seat on the office couch and touched his finger—one of the six that graced his right hand!—to the delicate little mustache that graced his upper lip. Above his richly figured bolero jacket and trousers graced with a bright crimson silk stripe rose a perfectly square head with hair cut in a stiff bristly military style that suggested nothing so much as a Prussian Junker. "Halten Sie bitte, amigo!" he said, lifting his hand as if to stop a motorcade. "It zhould nod be forgodden that ich too—ich, Juan Diego Jesus Maria von Heiligenstein, ze most fearless boolfighter in der vorld, known in all Mexico as Der Eleven-Fingered Torero!—but also der vaquero who vill make der besd use of the mucho dinero the skull weel breeng, seence I weel use der money to zupport veeveezection of tousands of gottverdammte schweinhund kats!—that ich too bin ein grandson of ze deesteenguished Senor Digby. "

"And indeed it will not be forgotten," responded Cheung, again struggling—for he was a passionate lover of every cat that ever pawed the earth!—to conceal his disgust under a mask of Celestial impassivity. "For your lineage has been traced back to Mr. Digby through his later marriage, after the sad death of his French wife at the hands of a murderous Apache—not a noble warrior from the American tribe of that name, I should add, but a sociological monster from the Parisian underworld!—through his later marriage to the Spanish flamenco dancer Rosita Lolita Carmencita, which produced a daughter, Gatita Estrellita Digby, who in her turn married the German industrialist Gustav Adolf von Heiligenstein, which marriage in turn produced you!" Remembering some of the tomes on psychology with which he often whiled away the hours before sleep, Cheung wondered if the felino-hatred that obsessed the stuttering gunfighter's Germano-Hispanic grandson might be connected with the fact that his mother's first name translated into English as pussycat!

At which point the third of the motley trio—and perhaps the most colorfully attired man in the room since his raiment consisted of a purple velour derby that he had not troubled to remove upon entering the office and a screamingly checkered suit that might have adorned any costermonger hawking his wares in London's famed Whitechapel district but failed utterly to conceal the fact that the man was a hunchback!—rose from the couch and planted himself squarely in front of Xenophon Cheung, his biscuit-dough chin quivering with his emotion. " 'old yer 'osses, myte! " he demanded in a voice that established beyond peradventure his origins within the sound of London's so-famous Bow Bells. "H'I—H'Alfred 'enry 'arbinger, h'if yer please!—H'I 'ave some clyme to the bloomin' sconce meself, yer knaow! H'in't H'I halso a hair to this bally H'American 'atchetman or gunfighter or whatever the bloody 'ell 'e woz? H'indeed, h'if the truth be towld, H'I 'as the strongest clyme of h'all, 'unchback though H'I h'am, bein' h'as 'ow nothin' runs in me vynes but one 'undred p'cent pure H'Angry-Saxophonish blood, syme as what run in the vynes of me granther!"

With the politeness inborn in his race, Xenophon Cheung took two steps back from the furious little Cockney and rubbed his own well-shaped chin thoughtfully. "I concede the purity of your bloodline," he said, "my investigation having established that your mother, 'Annah—pardon me, your accent seems to be contagious!—that your mother, nee Hannah Hepsibah Digby, was the daughter of the final marriage of Daedalus Didymus Digby—after his Spanish wife was trampled to death by a mad bull during the annual running of the bulls at Pamplona!—said marriage having been to a young Englishwoman named Helen Hetherington-Henley. And in the fullness of time, the marriage of Hannah Hepsibah Digby to Herbert Harrison Harbinger produced you. However, as one of mixed blood myself, I fail to see on what basis the absence of such admixture in yourself gives rise to any clyme, er, claim of superior right to your grandfather's skull." He paused and cleared his throat judiciously. "Indeed, in my capacity as arbiter of the skull's ownership I have concluded that each of the three of you has no greater and no lesser claim to the skull than any of the others. Therefore I rule that Mr. Skull belongs to—none of you!"

A chorus of protest in a veritable polyglot of tongues arose from the three dumbfounded claimants. Cheung distinctly heard a high-pitched "Faith an' ma foi!" and an anguished " 'oo does 'e think 'e h'is?" and, most distressing of all, an outraged "Madre mia, der gottverdammte Chink!" Finally one of the trio, seemingly taking it upon himself to act as spokesman for them all, addressed Cheung himself directly.

"Now see 'ere, myle," said Alfred Henry Harbinger, "h'as h'I h'understand 'ow things stand, yer cahn't legally do what yer just did. Yer grandfather's bloomin' will h'obligates yer to turn h'over the skull to one of h'us 'ere in this h'orffice."

"I am bound to turn over the skull to a true descendant of Daedalus Didymus Digby," replied Cheung, "and as a true Chinese—though one with the blood of the great Socrates thrown into my veins as a bonus!—I am faithful to my obligations. If any of you wish to retain an attorney to challenge my decision, please do so. Now, gentlemen, I would be most appreciative if you would stand not upon the order of your going but take your respective departures instanter."

Mumbling imprecations in half a dozen commingled tongues, the furious threesome trickled out of the office, leaving Xenophon Cheung alone with the skull of the stuttering gunfighter. Standing over the said skull, he proceeded to announce his official decision.

"In the judgment of the executor of my grandfather Wing Sing Cheung's estate—namely myself!—the direct descendant of Daedalus Didymus Digby—namely yourself!—who is most worthy to possess your skull, is—Xenophon Cheung—namely myself!" He made a slight bow in the direction of the gold-plated jewel-encrusted sconce. "For am I not also your direct descendant? While you were being sheltered by my great-grandfather Wong Sung Cheung, did you not take as your first wife the beautiful Katina Melina Kakageorgiou who was employed as a teacher of Greek language and culture in the Chinese schools of the American West? And was not the fruit of that marriage a daughter, Cassandra Melandra Digby? And when Cassandra Melandra Digby became a woman, did she not marry the distinguished Chinese-American Federal judge George Cheung, son of the very same Wing Sing Cheung who had sheltered his now wife's father a generation previous? And was not the result of that union the very same Xenophon Cheung, Esquire, who stands here before you? Ah, how true are the words of the great Confucius, echoed in ancient Greece by the philosopher Xenocrates: Life is indeed an amazing web!" With great reverence he lifted the bejeweled skull and bore it in stately procession to his double-sized teakwood desk, on whose blotter he set it down.

"And it will be my pleasure," he said, smiling, "at the earliest possible moment, to return you to the Toads from whence you came! Oui oui, si si, jawohl, yuss and yowsah!"

THE FAMILY TREES OF THE CHARACTERS

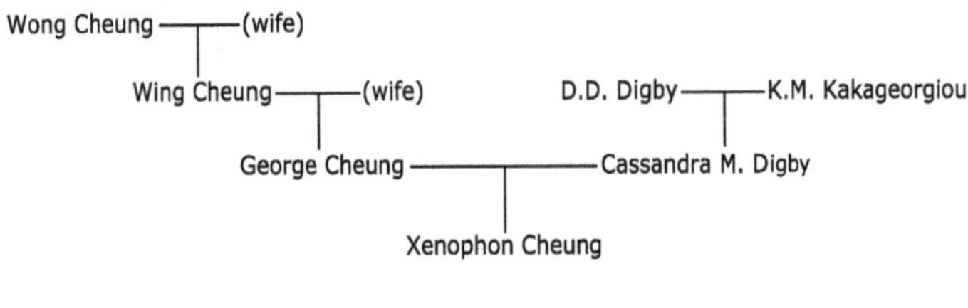

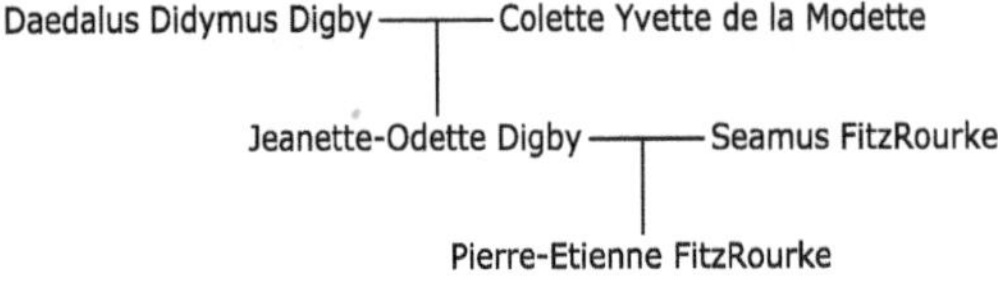

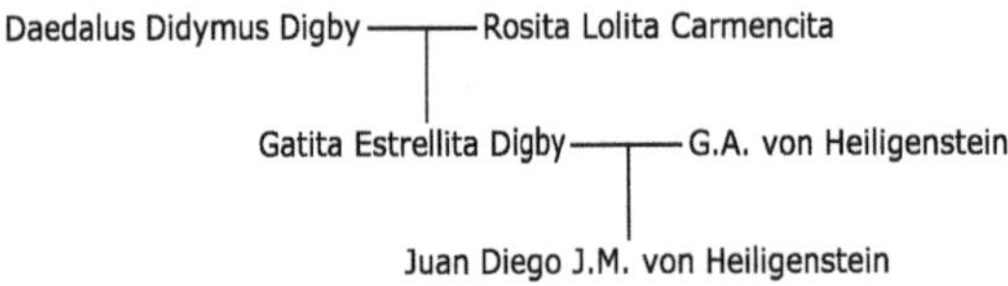

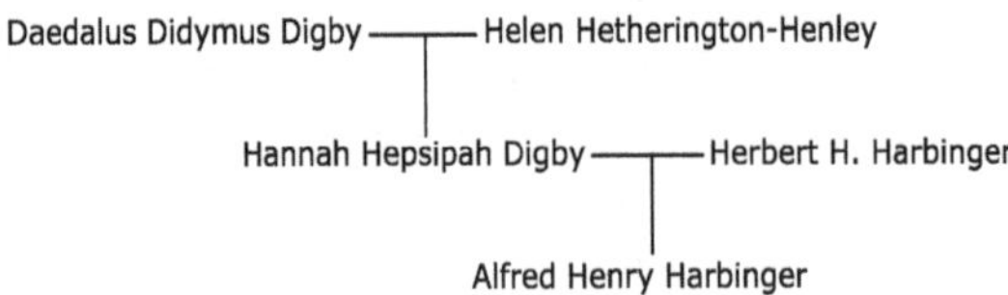

THE MAN WITH THE PLASTIC SKULL

Fender Tucker

Chapter I

A DISTURBING TELEGRAM

Philo vunPtaffholster leaned back in the specially-designed car seat of his brand-new 1960 Metropolitan convertible and once more regarded the telegram that had just arrived from Mora Bora, informing him that like it or not, he was *not* the only man on the planet with a plastic skull!

He was on his way to spend an hour or so with the most beautiful woman in the world—bar none!—and now, as he pulled out of his driveway into the slow-moving 5 P.M. traffic, he began to read the message from the far off Pacific that threatened to strip him of his fame, his fortune, and more importantly, the most beautiful woman in the world—nuff sed!

MORA BORA 5:13 A.M. JULY 5, 1960

FROM: DWIL SPROCKET
TO: PHILO VUNPTAFFHOLSTER

PHI, OLD FRIEND, I'VE GOT BAD NEWS. A NATIVE OF MORA BORA, ONE MANUEL AMANO, IS GOING TO REVEAL TOMORROW AT HIGH NOON THAT HE TOO HAS A PLASTIC SKULL LIKE YOURS.

Philo swerved around an 18-wheeler that was making a wide right turn, then drove on.

NOW, AS YOU KNOW, YOU'VE MADE QUITE A NAME FOR YOURSELF IN PAST YEARS AS "THE MAN WITH THE PLASTIC SKULL", EXHIBITING YOURSELF IN TRAVELLING MO-

TORCADE CIRCUSES, ALLOWING PEOPLE TO FEEL AND MANIPULATE YOUR NON-RIGID SKULL.

A car in the right lane cut Philo off and he had to slam on the brakes, sending the car into a tight, well-controlled spin. Straightening out, Philo once again turned to the telegram and drove on.

I'VE MANAGED TO FIND OUT THAT THE OPERATION ON AMANO WAS PERFORMED BY A DOCTOR WESLEY TOOTH-WELL, WHO PRACTICES AT PEPPERDUKE UNIVERSITY, JUST DOWN THE ROAD FROM WHERE YOU LIVE IN NORTHEAST CHICAGO. HE'S A, WHAT DO YOU CALL IT, BONE SURGEON.

Philo pulled into a service station and told the attendent to fill'erup. The attendant gave a toothy grin and shuckled, "Gawsh, Mr. vunPtaffholster, anytime!"

"How did you know my nam—" Philo shot back, but immediately realized his mistake—he was one of the most well-known and beloved circus performers in the Tri-State area.

"Wa-all, Mr. vunPtaffholster, it's writ' raght thar on th' sida yer car!"

"That's right," Philo thought, "I forgot that I had a sign painter come over and paint:

PHILO VUNPTAFFHOLSTER
"THE MAN WITH THE PLASTIC SKULL"
A Circus Near You

on both sides of my car." He paid for the gas, got back in the convertible, and picked up the telegram as he started the car, and drove on.

THERE IS MORE TO TELL YOU BUT THESE TELEGRAMS ARE, WELL, EXPENSIVE. I'LL WRITE YOU A LETTER AND SEND IT TO YOU VIA THE U.S. MAIL.

A policecar pulled up alongside the Metropolitan, which was going about fifty, and the policeman who was not driving held his billy club up and, through the closed window, thumped it against his gloved left hand once, twice, three times, all the while gazing at Philo with a sleepy grin on his face. Philo winced, and felt the skin on his hump loosen. He knew what those three thumps meant—the third degree! Then he saw the cop's eyes drift down to the sign on the side of the car, and the cop's face went ashen. He yelled at his partner to speed up and to Philo's astonishment, the policecar sped on ahead and was soon out of sight.

Philo breathed a sigh of relief and resumed his telegram-reading. Once again he drove on.

I GUESS THAT'S ABOUT IT, PARTNER.

DWIL

Philo put down the telegram and thought about the implications of another person having a plastic skull like his. And how? Philo had always been told that it was ol' Doc Winkerdoll that had saved his life by removing his heavily radar-active skull back in 1954, replacing it with a skull prosthesis made from Plastene, a new form of plastic the doctor had invented, a form that was actually more like a soft rubber with incredible tensile strength. It wasn't the whole skull, but just the bowl-shaped top part, from the tops of the eye orbitals up.

But ol' Doc Winkerdoll was killed not long after performing the operation, and never revealed the secret formula for Plastene. He left a note saying it was hidden in a 2-inch Plastene sphere, but the four government agents who killed Winkerdoll searched every inch of his office and home and never found it.

At this point in his ruminations Philo pulled into the posh driveway of the Smith-Smythes, where dwelt the most beautiful woman in the world, Confessa Smith-Smythe.

Chapter II

CONFESSA WORRIES!

Confessa met him at the door as she always did, giving him a warm kiss while rubbing his hump for luck. But she had a look of worry on her pretty face.

"Oh, Phi, oh Phi, oh Phi," she bewailed, "I've just had the most dreadful news!"

"Me too! You first," Philo countered.

"Well, you know that Daddy has had some bad luck in the market lately, and he just found out that unless he pulls a big score with Plastene, Inc. the company that you and he started in anticipation of the day when the formula is found, he's dead broke! And you know we can't get married until he can afford to pay for the lavish wedding ceremony!"

"Gosh, Confessa, that *is* bad news. My news isn't quite so bad, but it's sort of in the same category. I just found out that there is another person who now has a plastic skull, and that may put a damper on my circus career. As the only man on earth with a plastic skull, I was quite a draw, but with this Amano guy—"

"Oh Phi! What are we to do? You've always been so resourceful. In fact, it was because of your hump that Daddy was happy for us to become, well, an *item*. He always said, 'If a man can grow up with a handicap like a huge hump on his right shoulderblade, and still not be bitter with the world, that man is good enough for my daughter!' Of course I've come to love you in spite of your hump—although it does get in the way of our lovemaking sometimes and I *do* wish it could be removed—but that's not to mention your brave experience with your radar-active skull."

"We-ell, Confessa, I feel the same way about your father. As for my skull, you remember how I discovered back in 1954, quite by accident one day when I wandered too near an army air force installation, that my original osseous skull was hypersensitive to those new-fangled radar waves used by the military since WWII. I got an excruciating headache that knocked me out and it was only through the good luck of being found by Ol' Doc Winkerdoll that I survived. Apparently, the radar waves caused my skull to contract, giving me the horrible headache. So he removed the top of my skull and replaced it with a Plastene facsimile. I was in a coma for a month afterwards but came out of it in good condition."

"Oh, Phi, if only he had told you what he did with your old skull, we might be able to help Daddy. I've heard that the military and the police are very interested in any material that can detect radar-waves. Of course it's obvious why the air force wants it, but—"

"—why would the cops want it? I know what you mean, Confessa, it's a real mystery."

He pulled her close to him for another kiss, then snapped his fingers. "Hold it! I just had an idea. Can I use your 'phone?" He reached for the telephone and dialed 0. "Operator, connect me with Professor Wesley Toothwell at Pepperduke University!"

A few minutes later a voice answered. "Toothwell here."

"Doctor Toothwell, my name is Philo vunPtaffholster. Did you just perform surgery on a Mora Boran native, giving him a plastic skull?"

"Why, yes, I did. Did you say, 'vunPtaffholster?' "

"Yes I did. I'm the original Man with the Plastic Skull. Er—ah—did you use Plastene for your skull?"

"No I didn't, Mr. vunPtaff—"

"Just call me Philo, please."

"Thank you, Philo. No I didn't use Plastene. As you know, the formula is still unknown and the Plastene in your head is the only bit of it known to be in existence."

"That's right, Doctor. May I ask two questions? One, is the man you operated on planning on travelling around, exhibiting his skull in circuses? And two, was the operation difficult? I mean, would it have been easier if you *had* had some Plastene to work with?"

"Well, Mr. vunPtaff—er, Philo, the answer to your first question is, absolutely not. Mr. Amano has an abject fear of circuses, especially clowns, and wouldn't get near a circus. In fact, he leaves his village in Mora Bora whenever a circus comes to town, and lives on another island until the carnies leave town for good. As for the second question, the answer is yes, yes, yes, and double yes, yes! The qualities of Plastene, as exhibited by the hundreds, if not thousands of circus-goers who have seen and manipulated your Plastene skull, show that it is a much better material for skull-fabrication than the hard bakelite I used. The formula for Plastene, when it is finally found, will make mill—"

"That's what I wanted to hear, Doctor! I think you'll be hearing from me again—sooner than you think. Thanks for everything!" With that Philo hung up the phone and turned to his Confessa. "Darlin', I think I've got the answer to all of our problems!"

Chapter III

All Strings Tied Up

Bong Hai, leader of the tong, the Fat Black Lemurs, leaned back in his *papa-san* chair and tamped down another bowlful of his tong's best brand of opium. He lit the pipe and took a long, slow pull, gazing at the wall as if it were ten miles away. He set the pipe down and settled deeper in the chair, then reached up and rubbed his skull vigorously, with both hands. He pushed with both hands, squeezing the sides of his head until they receded about an inch. Then he pushed the top down, squeezing the sides out. He had a plastic skull!

The sensations Bong Hai felt as the inner side of his Plastene skull rubbed against his brain, even moving it a bit, were exquisite. He simply could not describe the pleasures to anyone who did not have some good opium and a Plastene skull.

He thought about how he got his new skull. His photographic memory had it all down in detail and the opium was making it seem especially real. His lips mumbled soft words as he drifted into the warm, rolling clouds of nepenthe.

"It began wi' that 'Melican fella, vunPtaffholstel. He velly smalt. He have filst plas'ic skull. He got skull in fi'ty-fo' because he fin' his skull contlac', get smallel, w'en he get neal ladal."

Bong Hai chuckled to himself at his pitiful attempt to say "near radar". And drove on.

"But he luckily foun' a bone sulgeon docta'—fella name' Winkeldoll—who lemove skull an' leplace it wi' Plastene. Docta' also hid folmula fo' Plastene at 'loun' same time. Folmula not foun' until day six yeals latel, w'en vunPtaffholstel get blight idea w'ele it be. He kill two bilds wi' one lock! He fin' folmula fo' Plastene an' fin' his ol' skull w'ich contlac' w'en neal ladal. All in same place!"

The wizened old tong leader smiled to himself as he continued to manipulate his Plastene skull with much pleasure. His softly spoken ruminations continued.

"He get bone docta' name' Toothwell to op'late on his hump and *he* fin' that oliginal docta' name' Winkeldoll, aftel lemovin' skull an' leplacin' it wi' Plastene skull, also lemove hump an' leplace *it* wi' oliginal skull! T'en he hide folmula ball *inside* skull-hump! Why? Because he know govelnment agents wan' to kill him fo' bot' seclets an' will sealch offices flom A to Izzald."

He took another pull on the opium pipe and continued to manipulate his Plastene skull, which he got at the *Chicago Center for Frivolous Elective Surgery,* or CCFES. Once the formula was released by Plastene, Inc. to much public hooplah and unheard of investment by the stock market class, Bong Hai, thanks to his huge fortune amassed from opium sales, was one of the first to receive a new skull.

"So much pleasule I get. Make me glad vunPtaffholstel get lich flom Plastene, get lid of hump an' mally sweethealt, an' sell impoltant ladal-sens'tive skull to militaly so they can tell if ladal bein' used 'gainst them."

Bong Hai's eyes glazed over with extreme joy as he mumbled one last question.

"Nevel did figule out w'y cops wan'ed ladal-sens'tive matelial. Cops nevel use ladal 'gainst own cit'zens, would they? Aftel all, 'tis 'Melica, lan' of flee, light?"

GREY-SCALE PLATES

Keeler by Design

Gavin L. O'Keefe

When it comes to book cover designs, there are three main aspects I feel strongly about: their suitability, aesthetic appeal, and textual faithfulness. In many cases, both in older and modern days, cover designs have appeared which either didn't reflect the author or the contents of a given book.

The blame for such mismatching between a book and the front cover that presents it to the world can usually be firmly placed at the door of the marketing department of the publisher, which has declared that 'commercial' packaging for the book is necessary. This seems to have been a traditional solution used by publishers for many decades, especially for authors whom they felt couldn't be easily classified into a given trade genre.

The admittedly ambitious aim of the genuine book cover artist (in my opinion) should be to create a design which is not only faithful to the author and their book, but which also gains the attention of the author's converts and non-converts (the latter may have never encountered Author X, but a sympathetic cover design might open their eyes to give an appealing-looking book a try), whilst presenting a design which is strong, aesthetically-pleasing, and interesting. Truly a wonderful juggling act if all the above can be achieved successfully!

Harry Stephen Keeler seems to have been one of those authors whom publishers found awkward to categorize into a genre. True, the dustwrappers of his books declared his novels as mystery fiction from the start; Keeler's books *are* mysteries, but they are also a lot more than that besides. This uncertainty regarding Keeler's place in the literary field seems to have been conveyed by the very unevenness of quality found in the dustwrapper art to his books throughout his publishing career: some artists depicted realistic cracksman, courtroom or murder scenes, some went for the melodramatic, while others got bogged down in web, skull and 'Fu Manchu'-type symbolism.

Certainly, the Keeler books published by Phoenix Press in the US feature fairly token artwork. Some of the cover art on the Spanish editions of Keeler, published by Reus, is adapted from the US or UK editions of the same books, though the majority of covers feature original illustrations ranging from the inventive and striking to the just plain odd. More justice seems to have been done to him by his British publisher, Ward, Lock & Co., where there are more cover art highpoints than low. The art on the books published by Dutton in the US is fairly consistent, though with progressively more focus on creative lettering and Art Deco-style design than pictorial representation. Early highlights would be *The Spectacles of Mr. Cagliostro* and *Find the Clock* (the latter apparently the work of Mahlon Blaine), while covers like those for *The Face of the Man From Saturn* and *10 Hours* are rather poor.

Perhaps what Keeler needed was a dustwrapper artist on the same imaginative wavelength as himself (if such ever existed). There are certainly good examples of this having happened in recent literary history: Richard Chopping's idiosyncratic but immediately-identifiable designs for the bulk of Ian Fleming's books, Tom Adams' polished and evocative covers for reprints of Agatha Christie, and even, in a more fantastic vein, Josh Kirby's artwork for the covers of Terry Pratchett's 'Discworld' novels. There are probably many more examples of such 'published collaborations', where the authors' books are given rich, imaginative and faithful covers by artists who themselves must surely feel as rewarded in reading the books and creating the cover art.

When Fender Tucker invited me to devise dustwrapper designs for the Keeler titles being issued by Ramble House, I was excited at the prospect of being involved. My experience of reading HSK was in its early days at the time, but I'd read enough of his books to be completely hooked! From my viewpoint as a book illustrator, few and special are the occasions when I discover a writer whose literary works truly inspire; the last time I had been similarly inspired was fifteen years ago when I was discovering H. P. Lovecraft and Lewis Carroll for the first time. With Keeler, I've found such inspiration again, and the process of designing covers for his books is proving to personally be one of those special 'collaborations'. The question of whether readers like my Keeler cover designs will be answered in the fullness of time.

I find Keeler's books exceedingly rich in characters, plot, humour and atmosphere, and I have no trouble finding inspiration in them for artwork. There are also highly-suggestive elements of surrealism in his novels: strange juxtapositions and, of course, amazing coincidences. An added bonus for me has been Keeler's regular inclusion of references to Australia and New Zealand in his books, and these antipodean asides seem to make the Keelerian world as much alive in Melbourne as it is in Chicago.

Most of my HSK jacket illustrations to date have been drawn and painted, the finished art then being scanned and retouched in a graphics editing application. If not already hand-lettered, I will insert specific digital lettering into the design. Though all of these designs are my own invention, I'm mindful of those designs and designers who came before me in their own cultural climates, and find it occasionally fitting to 'tip my hat' their way. I was quite impressed with the effectiveness of the original Dutton art for *The Mysterious Mr. I*, and deliberately followed its colour scheme, with the calligraphic red title redrawn in my own manner. I doubt whether any of my Keeler designs look like they were executed in the 1930's or 40's, but I hope that I achieve somewhere a subliminal acknowledgment of the times when these books were first written.

There is the additional element for me of restoring some artistic justice to those Keeler books that had received indifferent cover art treatment when first published. Just as one would prefer one's brother to be dressed in a tuxedo rather than rags at his wedding, so I would prefer Keeler's books to be adorned in fitting jackets which reflect the magic of his novels. I promise to continue striving to do that for as long as possible.

I have the greatest admiration for the work being done by Fender Tucker and Jim Weiler, not only for reprinting the numerous out-of-print Keeler titles, but also for publishing first editions of those works surviving in manuscript form and issuing the original English texts of books only previously published in Spanish or Portuguese. With the addition of pertinent introductions by authorities Francis M. Nevins and Richard Polt to selected titles, the Ramble House program is a passionate and concentrated effort to bring Harry Stephen Keeler's literature back to the world. I, for one, will remain ready to contribute with brush and pen.

Publisher's Note: The first edition of A TO IZZARD, made by Ramble House, had color plates of eight of Gavin's Keeler covers. This edition has eight different, grey-scale covers. All Ramble House books have beautiful colorful covers.

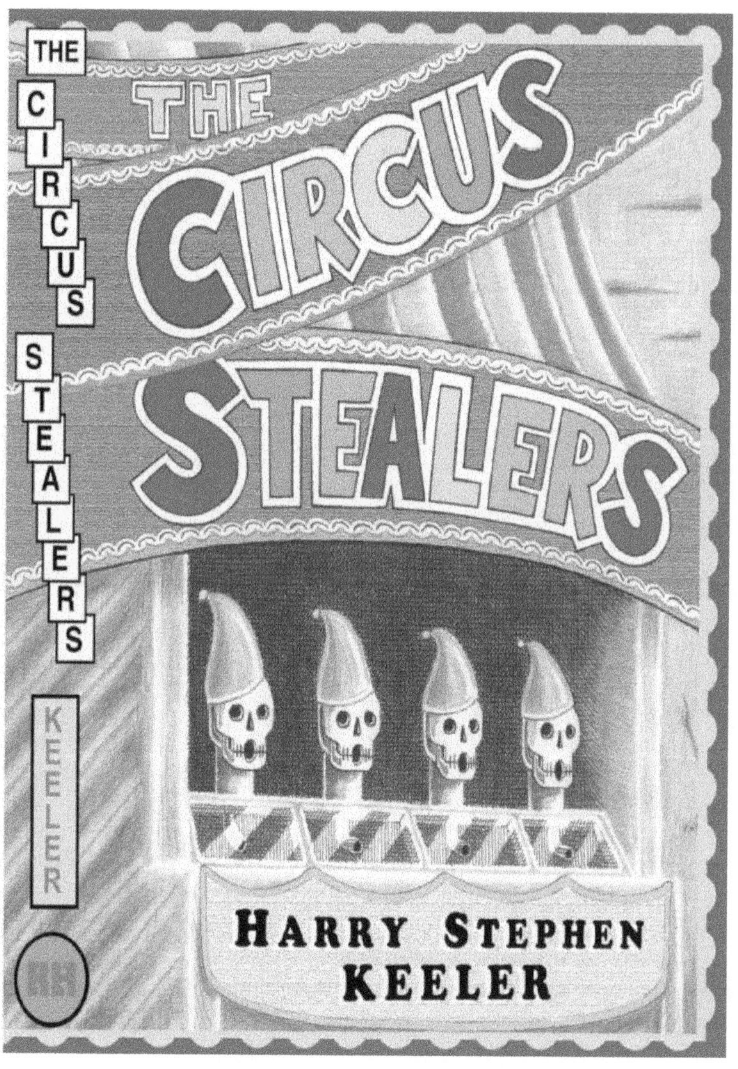

Grey-scale version of the cover and spine of THE CIRCUS STEALERS.

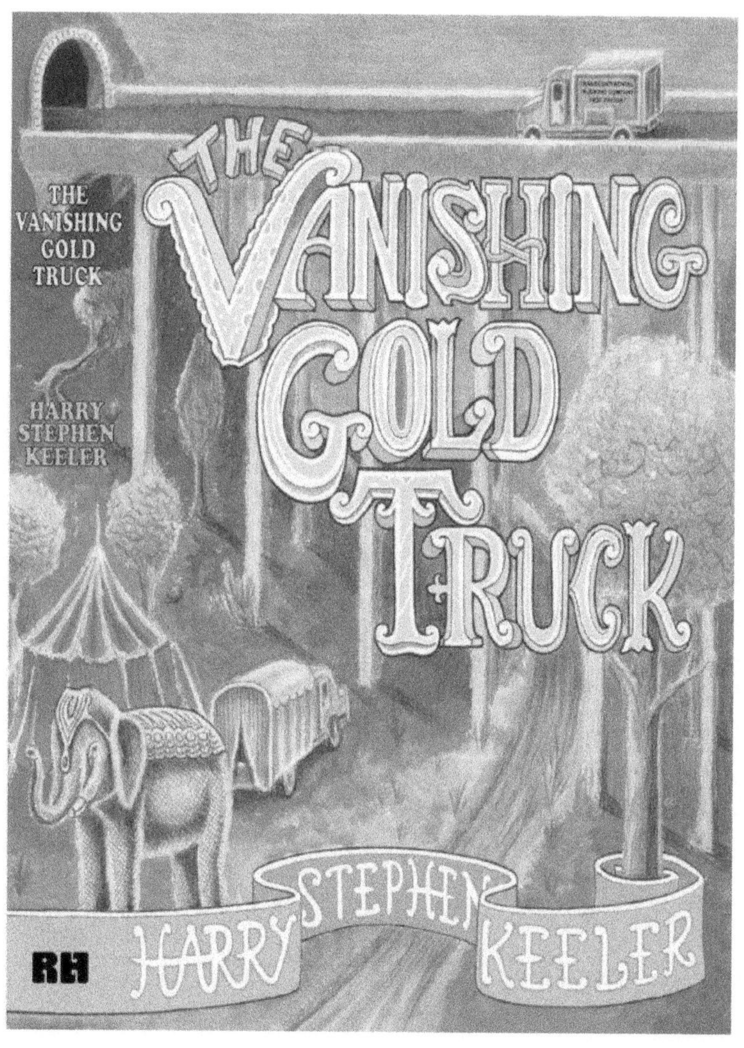

Grey-scale version of the cover and spine of
THE VANISHING GOLD TRUCK.

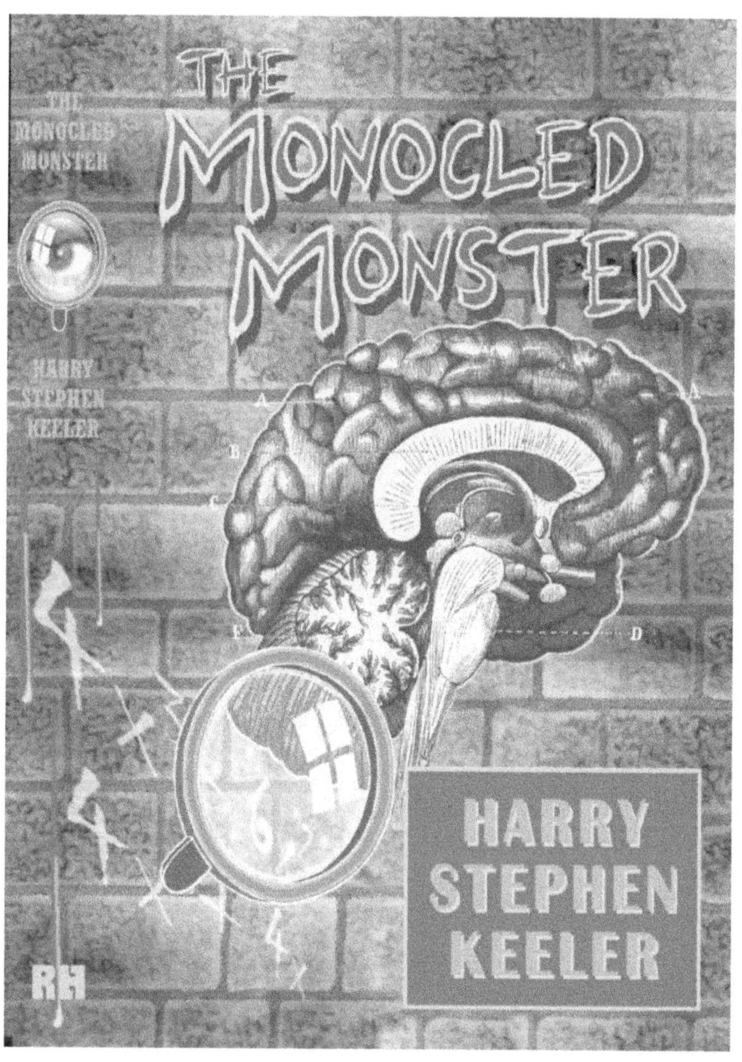

Grey-scale version of the cover and spine of THE MONOCLED MONSTER.

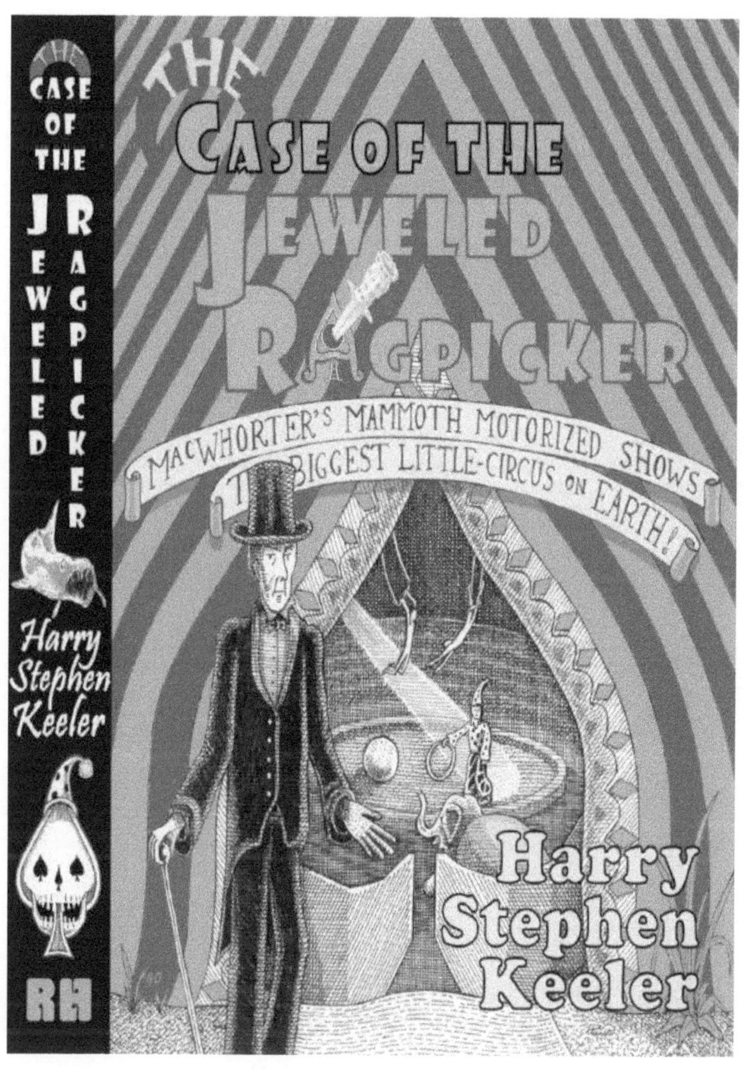

Grey-scale version of the cover and spine of
THE CASE OF THE JEWELED RAGPICKER.

Grey-scale version of the cover and spine of THE STRAW HAT MURDERS.

RH

Harry Stephen Keeler

The Riddle of the Wooden Parakeet

Volume One

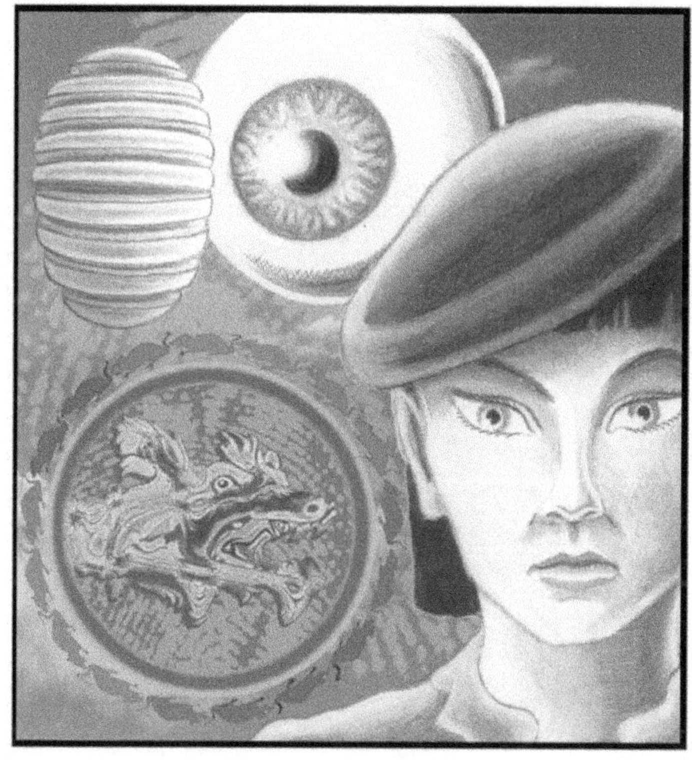

Grey-scale version of the cover of
THE RIDDLE OF THE WOODEN PARRAKEET.

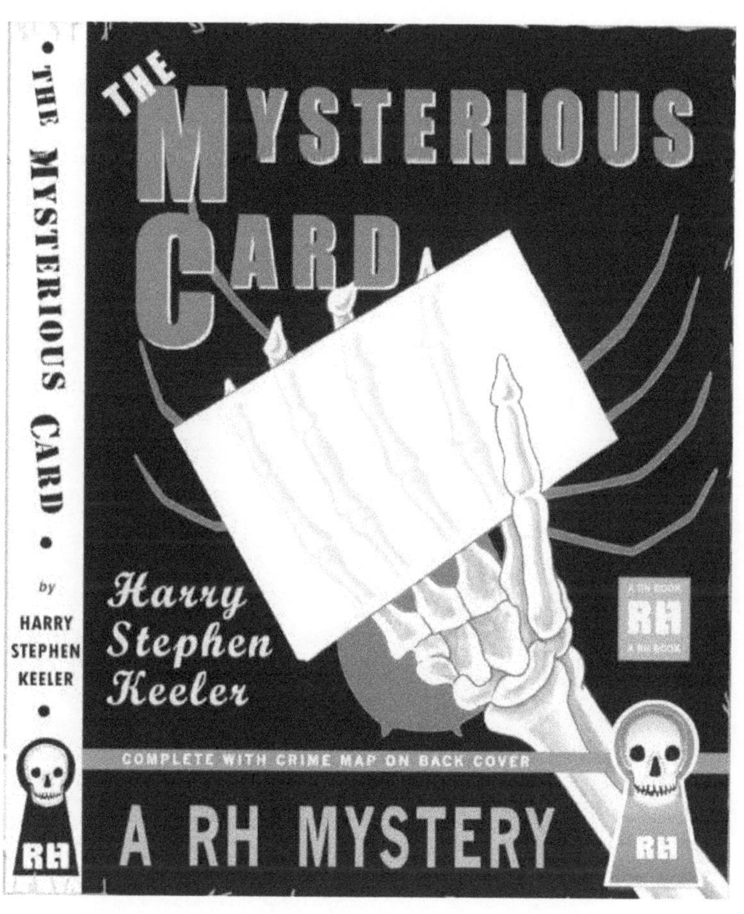

Grey-scale version of the cover and spine of THE MYSTERIOUS CARD.

Grey-scale version of the mapback back cover of THE MYSTERIOUS CARD.

KEELER BIBLIOGRAPHY

NOTE: As of July 2005, all of the novels that Harry Stephen Keeler finished have been reprinted or published by Ramble House, except THE SIGN OF THE CROSSED LEAVES. All are available from the Ramble House web site:

www.ramblehouse.com

The RAMBLE HOUSE List o' Keelers

(Published in English)
Edited by Fender Tucker
Taken from Francis M. Nevins' Harry Stephen Keeler bibliography in Richard Polt's *The Keeler News*

The Ace of Spades Murder

Written in 1946. Published in Britain by Ward Lock in 1949. Published by Phoenix in 1948 as *The Case of the Jeweled Ragpicker*. British version is substantially longer.

The Amazing Web

Written in 1921. Published in Britain by Ward Lock in 1929.

Behind That Mask

Written in 1932. Published in Britain by Ward Lock in 1933. Later expanded into *Finger, Finger* and *Behind That Mask* and published by Dutton in 1938

The Black Satchel

Written in 1915 as *The Michaux Z-Ray* and expanded in 1931. Published in Britain by Ward Lock in 1931. Published in the U.S. by Dutton in 1931 as *The Matilda Hunter Murder*. The British version is greatly cut from the U.S. version. A Tuddleton Trotter book.

The Blue Spectacles

Written in 1924. Published in Great Britain by Ward Lock in 1931. Published in the U.S. as *The Spectacles of Mr. Cagliostro* by Hutchinson in 1926 and Dutton in 1929.

The Book with the Orange Leaves

Written in 1940. Published in U.S by Dutton in 1942. Published in Britain by Ward Lock in 1943. One of *The Way Out* books.

The Bottle with the Green Wax Seal

Written in 1939. Published in U.S. by Dutton in 1942. Third and final in the series that began with *The Portrait of Jirjohn Cobb* and *Cleopatra's Tears*.

The Box from Japan

Written in 1932 by adding 270,000 words to the original 50,000 words of "*Renegades Rampant*", a short story published in 1917. Published in U.S. by Dutton in 1932, and in Britain by Ward Lock in 1933.

By Third Degree

Written in 1940. Published in Britain by Ward Lock in 1948. Published in U.S. by Dutton in 1941 as *The Sharkskin Book*.

The Case of the Barking Clock

Written in 1946. Published in U.S. by Phoenix in 1947. Published in Britain by Ward Lock in 1951 as *The Barking Clock*. The British version is 8000 words longer than the U.S. version and was reprinted in 2001 by Ramble House. A Tudleton Trotter book.

The Case of the Canny Killer

Written in 1944. Published in U.S. by Phoenix in 1946. Published in Britain by Ward Lock as *Murder in the Mills*. British version is substantially longer.

The Case of the Flying Hands

Written in 1947. Published in 2001 by Ramble House. A collection of three Quiribus Brown novelettes. Has an introduction by Francis M. Nevins.

The Case of the Ivory Arrow

Written in 1942. Published in U.S. by Phoenix in 1945. Published in Britain by Ward Lock in 1943 as *The Search for X-Y-Z*. British version is substantially larger than the U.S. version.

The Case of the Jeweled Ragpicker

Written in 1946. Published in U.S. by Phoenix in 1948. Published in Britain by Ward Lock in 1949 as *The Ace of Spades Murder*. British version is substantially longer. Takes place in the Screwball Circus world.

The Case of the Lavender Gripsack

Written in 1940. Published in U.S. by Phoenix in 1944. Published in Britain by Ward Lock in 1941 as *The Lavender Gripsack*. Fourth and final segment of the Skull in the Box series which includes *The Man with the Magic Eardrums, The Man with the Crimson Box* and *The Man with the Wooden Spectacles.*

The Case of the Mysterious Moll

Written in 1942. Published in U.S. by Phoenix in 1945. Published in Britain by Ward Lock in 1944 as *The Iron Ring*. British version is substantially longer than the U.S. version.

The Case of the 16 Beans

Written in 1943. Published in U.S. by Phoenix in 1944. Published in Britain by Ward Lock in 1945 as *The 16 Beans*. One of *The Way Out* books.

The Case of the Transposed Legs

Written in 1947. Published in U.S. by Phoenix in 1948. Published in Britain by Ward Lock in 1951.

The Case of the Two Strange Ladies

Written in 1940 with a working title of *Enigma from the Swamp*. Published in U.S. by Phoenix in 1943. Published in Britain by Ward Lock in 1954 as *The Two Strange Ladies*. One of *The Way Out* books.

The Chameleon

Written in 1936. Published in U.S. by Dutton in 1939. It's the second half of what was published in Britain in by Ward Lock in 1937 as *The Mysterious Mr. I*. In the U.S. the first half is called *The Mysterious Mr. I*.

Cheung, Detective

Written in 1936. Published in Britain by Ward Lock in 1938. Published in U.S. by Dutton as *Y. Cheung, Business Detective*.

Cleopatra's Tears

Written in 1939. Published in U.S. by Dutton in 1940. Published in Britain by Ward Lock in 1940. Second of series that began with *The Portrait of Jirjohn Cobb* and ended with *The Bottle with the Green Wax Seal*.

The Crilly Court Mystery

Written in 1933, expanded from a 50,000 word story of the same name written in 1916. Published in Britain by Ward Lock in 1933. Published in U.S. by Dutton in 1933 as *The Face of the Man from Saturn.*

The Crimson Box

Written in1938. Published in Britain by Ward Lock in 1940. Published in U.S. by Dutton in 1940 as *The Man with the Crimson Box*. Third segment of the Skull in the Box series which includes *The Man with the Magic Eardrums*, *The Man with the Wooden Spectacles* and *The Case of the Lavender Gripsack*.

The Defrauded Yeggman

Written in 1934 as part of the *Vagabond Nights* opus. Published in U.S. by Dutton in 1937. First half of combo with *10 Hours.*

The Face of the Man from Saturn

Written in 1933, expanded from a 50,000 story, *The Crilly Court Mystery,* written in 1916. Published in U.S. by Dutton in 1933. Published in Britain by Ward Lock in 1933 as *The Crilly Court Mystery*.

The Fiddling Cracksman

Written in 1933. Published in Britain by Ward Lock in 1934. Published in U.S. by Dutton in 1934 as *The Mystery of the Fiddling Cracksman*.

Find Actor Hart

Written in 1938. Published in Britain by Ward Lock in 1939. Published in U.S. by Dutton in 1940 as *The Portrait of Jirjohn Cobb*. First of series that continued with *Cleopatra's Tears* and *The Bottle with the Green Wax Seal*. Reprinted in 2002 by Ramble House as *The Portrait of Jirjon Cobb.*

Find the Clock

Written in 1921 and serialized in six installments in *People's Magazine*. Published in Britain by Hutchinson in 1925 (expanded from original). Published in U.S. by Dutton in 1927.

Finger! Finger!

Written in 1933. Published in U.S. by Dutton in 1938. First half of combo with *Behind That Mask* in the U.S. In Britain both were published by Ward Lock in 1933 as *Behind That Mask*.

The Five Silver Buddhas

Written in 1934. Published in U.S. by Dutton and in Britain by Ward Lock in 1935.

The Fourth King

Written in 1921 and expanded in 1929. Published in Britain by Ward Lock in 1929. Published in U.S. by Dutton in 1930.

The Green Jade Hand

Written in 1919 and expanded in 1930. Published in U.S. by Dutton and in Britain by Ward Lock in 1930. British version is cut down from the U.S. version.

The Iron Ring

Written in 1942. Published in Britain by Ward Lock in 1944. Published in U.S. by Phoenix in 1945 as *The Case of the Mysterious Moll*. British version is longer than the U.S. version.

The Lavender Gripsack

Written in 1940. Published in Britain by Ward Lock in 1941. Published in U.S. by Phoenix in 1944 as *The Case of the Lavender Gripsack*. Fourth and final segment of the Skull in the Box series which includes *The Man with the Magic Eardrums, The Man with the Crimson Box* and *The Man with the Wooden Spectacles*.

The Magic Eardrums

Written in 1937, expanded from short story "Services of an Expert" (1914). Published in Britain by Ward Lock in 1939. Published in U.S. by Dutton in 1939 as *The Man with the Magic Eardrums.* First segment of the Skull in the Box series which includes *The Man with the Crimson Box* and *The Man with the Wooden Spectacles* and *The Case of the Lavender Gripsack.*

The Man Who Changed His Skin

Written in 1959. Published in Spanish by Reus in 1966 as *El Hombre Que Cambio de Piel.* Published in English in 2000 by Ramble House.

The Man with the Crimson Box

Written in 1938. Published in U.S. by Dutton in 1940. Published in Britain by Ward Lock in 1940 as *The Crimson Box*. Second segment of the Skull in the Box series which includes *The Man with the Magic Eardrums*, *The Man with the Wooden Spectacles* and *The Case of the Lavender Gripsack*.

The Man with the Wooden Spectacles

Written in 1938. Published in U.S. by Dutton in 1941. Published in Britain by Ward Lock in 1941 as *The Wooden Spectacles*. Third segment of the Skull in the Box series which includes *The Man with the Magic Eardrums*, *The Man with the Crimson Box* and *The Case of the Lavender Gripsack*.

The Marceau Case

Written in 1935. Published in U.S. by Dutton and in Britain by Ward Lock in 1936. First segment of combo which includes *X. Jones-Of Scotland Yard*.

The Matilda Hunter Murder

Written in 1915 as *The Michaux Z-Ray* and expanded in 1931. Published in the U.S. by Dutton in 1931.Published in Britain by Ward Lock in 1931as *The Black Satchel*. The British version is greatly cut from the U.S. version. A Tuddleton Trotter book.

The Monocled Monster

Written in 1945 with the working title *The Strange Case of Professor Adolph Witherpool.* Published in Britain by Ward Lock in 1947.

Murder in the Mills

Written in 1944. Published in Britain by Ward Lock. Published in U.S. by Phoenix in 1946 as *The Case of the Canny Killer*. British edition is longer.

The Murder of London Lew

Written in 1951. Published in Britain by Ward Lock in 1952.

The Murdered Mathematician

Written in 1947, expanded from part of *The Case of the Flying Hands*. Published in Britain by Ward Lock in 1949. A Quiribus Brown novel.

The Mysterious Mr. I

Written in 1936. Published in Britain by Ward Lock in 1937. Published in U.S. by Dutton in 1939 as the first half of a combo with *The Chameleon*. British version contains complete story.

The Mystery of the Fiddling Cracksman

Written in 1933. Published in U.S. by Dutton in 1934. Published in Britain by Ward Lock in 1934 as *The Fiddling Cracksman*.

The Peacock Fan

Written in 1940. Published in U.S. by Dutton in 1941. Published in Britain by Ward Lock in 1942. One of *The Way Out* books.

The Portrait of Jirjohn Cobb

Written in 1938. Published in U.S. by Dutton in 1940. Published in Britain by Ward Lock in 1939 as *Find Actor Hart*. First of series that continued with *Cleopatra's Tears* and *The Bottle with the Green Wax Seal.*

Report on Vanessa Hewstone

Written in 1957. Published in 2001 by Ramble House. Takes place in an alternate circus world. It has an introduction by Francis M. Nevins and an afterword by Richard Polt.

The Riddle of the Traveling Skull

Written in 1933. Published in U.S. by Dutton in 1934. Published in Britain in 1934 as *The Travelling Skull*. Reprinted in 2000 by Ramble House with an introduction by Richard Polt.

The Riddle of the Yellow Zuri

Written in 1922 and expanded in 1930. Published in U.S. by Dutton in 1930. Published in Britain by Ward Lock in 1931 as *The Tiger Snake*.

The Search for X-Y-Z.

Written in 1942. Published in Britain by Ward Lock in 1943. Published in U.S. by Phoenix in 1945 as *The Case of the Ivory Arrow*. British version is substantially longer than the U.S. version.

The Sharkskin Book

Written in 1940. Published in U.S. by Dutton in 1941. Published in Britain by Ward Lock in 1948 as *By Third Degree*. One of *The Way Out* books.

Sing Sing Nights

Written in 1927. Published in Britain by Hutchinson in 1927. Published in U.S. by Dutton in 1928.

The Six from Nowhere

Written in 1958. Published in 2001 by Ramble House. Takes place in the Screwball Circus world.

The 16 Beans

Written in 1943 with a working title of *The Paradine Murder Case*. Published in Britain by Ward Lock in 1945. Published in U.S. by Phoenix in 1944 as *The Case of the 16 Beans*.

The Skull of the Waltzing Clown

Written in 1934 as part of *Vagabond Nights*. Published in U.S. by Dutton in 1935. Expanded from the British version of *10 Hours*.

The Spectacles of Mr. Cagliostro

Written in 1924. Published in the U.S. by Hutchinson in 1926 and Dutton in 1929. Published in Great Britain by Ward Lock in 1931 as *The Blue Spectacles*.

Stand By—London Calling!

Written in 1950. Published in Britain by Ward Lock in 1953. The last title to be published in Britain in his lifetime. Takes place in the Screwball Circus world.

The Steeltown Strangler

Written in 1949. Takes place in the same steel mill featured in *Murder in the Mills/The Case of the Canny Killer*. Published in Britain by Ward Lock in 1950.

The Strange Will

Written in 1948? Published in Britain by Ward Lock in 1949.

Ten Hours

Written in 1934. Published in Britain by Ward Lock in 1934. This is the one-volume edition which was split into three U.S. books and two other British ones.

10 Hours

Written in 1934 as part of *Vagabond Nights*. Published in U.S. by Dutton in 1937. Second half of combo with *The Defrauded Yeggman*.

Thieves' Nights

Written 1914-1930. Published in U.S. by Dutton in 1929 and in Britain by Ward Lock in 1930. Contains about ten short stories written earlier and wedged into the text.

The Tiger Snake

Written in 1922 and expanded in 1930. Published in Britain by Ward Lock in 1931. Published in U.S. by Dutton in 1930. as *The Riddle of the Yellow Zuri.*

The Travelling Skull

Written in 1933. Published in Britain in 1934. Published in U.S. by Dutton in 1934 as *The Riddle of the Travelling Skull.*

The Two Strange Ladies

Written in 1940 with a working title of *Enigma from the Swamp*. Published in Britain by Ward Lock in 1954. Published in U.S. by Phoenix in 1943 as *The Case of the Two Strange Ladies*.

Under Twelve Stars

Written in 1917 and expanded in 1933. Published in Britain by Ward Lock in 1933. Published in U.S. by Dutton in 1933 as *The Washington Square Enigma*.

The Vanishing Gold Truck

Written in 1940. Published in U.S. by Dutton in 1941. Published in Britain by Ward Lock in 1942. Takes place in the Screwball Circus world. One of *The Way Out* books.

The Voice of the Seven Sparrows

Written in 1922. Published in Britain by Hutchinson in 1924. Published in U.S. by Dutton in 1928.

The Washington Square Enigma

Written in 1917 and expanded in 1933. Published in U.S. by Dutton in 1933. Published in Britain by Ward Lock in 1933. as *Under Twelve Stars*.

When Thief Meets Thief

Written in 1934 as part of *Vagabond Nights*. Published in Britain By Ward Lock in 1938.

The White Circle

Written in 1954. Published in 2001 by Ramble House. It has an introduction by Richard Polt.

The Wonderful Scheme

Written in 1935. Published in Britain by Ward Lock in 1937. Published in U.S. by Dutton in 1937 as *The Wonderful Scheme of Mr. Christopher Thorne.*

The Wonderful Scheme of Mr. Christopher Thorne

Written in 1935. Published in U.S. by Dutton in 1937. Published in Britain by Ward Lock in 1937 as *The Wonderful Scheme.*

The Wooden Spectacles

Written in 1938. Published in Britain by Ward Lock in 1941. Published in U.S. by Dutton in 1941 as *The Man with the Wooden Spectacles*. Third segment of the Skull in the Box series which includes *The Man with the Magic Eardrums, The Man with the Crimson Box* and *The Case of the Lavender Gripsack.*

X. Jones

Written in 1935. Published in Britain by Ward Lock in 1936. Published in U.S. by Dutton in 1936 as *X. Jones—of Scotland Yard*. Segment two of *The Marceau Case* duology.

X. Jones—of Scotland Yard

Written in 1935. Published in U.S. by Dutton in 1936. Published in Britain by Ward Lock in 1936 as *X. Jones*. Segment two of *The Marceau Case* duology.

Y. Cheung, Business Detective

Written in 1936. Published in U.S. by Dutton in 1939. Published in Britain by Ward Lock in 1938 as *Cheung, Detective.*

Keeler Spanish Originals

All published by *Instituto Editorial Reus* of Madrid
(Taken from Mike Nevins' bibliography
in The Keeler News)

El casa del reloj ladrador (1947)

Keeler completed this long novel in July 1946. After its Spanish publication he broke the manuscript into two unrelated novels which were published as *The Case of the Barking Clock* (Phoenix, 1947; Ward Lock, 1951, as *The Barking Clock*) and *The Case of the Transposed Legs* (Phoenix, 1948; Ward Lock, 1951).

El caso Jaarvik (1957)

Spanish version of *The Monocled Monster* (Ward Lock, 1947), with about 15,000 extra words which Keeler added to the manuscript in 1954.

Noches del verdugo (1957)

Keeler completed this novel on May 16, 1951 but it was never published in English. At various times he referred to it as *Two Nooses at Dawn, Four Nooses at Dawn* or *The Strange Case of Alfred Crofts-Hartley* but its final title is *Hangman's Nights*.

28 sospechosos (1958)

Spanish version of *The Steeltown Strangler* (Ward Lock, 1950), with about 30,000 extra words which Keeler added to the manuscript in 1954.

Ladrones de circos (1958)

One of several Angus MacWhorter novels into which Keeler divided his huge 1946 manuscript *The Ace of Spades Murder* after failing to find a publisher for the original version. He completed this 69,000-word novel in 1956 but it was never published in English. Its manuscript title is *The Circus Stealers*.

El cubo carmesi (1960)

Keeler completed this 100,000-word novel in 1954 but it was never published in English. Its manuscript title is *The Crimson Cube.*

Una version del Beowulf (1960)

Another of the Angus MacWhorter books carved out of the *Ace of Spades* manuscript. Keeler completed this 75,000-word novel on July 15, 1957 but it was never published in English. Its manuscript title is *A Copy of Beowulf.*

La misteriosa bola de marfil de Wong Shing Li (1961)

Keeler completed this 90,000-word novel on January 27, 1957 but it was never published in English. He first referred to it as *Performance for Mr. Wong* but its manuscript title is *The Mysterious Ivory Ball of Wong Shing Li*.

El casa de la mujer transparente (1963)

Keeler completed this 63,000-word novel on October 26, 1958 but it was never published in English. He sometimes referred to it as *The Case of the Transparent Woman* but its final manuscript title is *The Case of the Transparent Nude.*

Yo mate a Lincoln a las 10.13 (1964)

Keeler completed this 484-page manuscript on June 25, 1958 but it was never published in English. He first referred to the novel as *Put Out Those Lights!* but its final manuscript title is *I Killed Lincoln at 10:13!*

El circulo blanco (1965)

Keeler completed this 75,000-word novel in his Ramble House series in 1954. It was accepted for publication by Fantasy Press, a small publishing house that went out of business before the book could be issued. Keeler never found another English-language publisher for it. Its manuscript title is *The White Circle.* Ramble House came out with an English version in 2001.

La calle de los mil ojos (1966)

Keeler completed this 100,000-word novel on February 27, 1956 but it was never published in English. He referred to it at times as *14 Trinidad Street* and *Danger Street* but its final title was *The Street of a Thousand Eyes.*

El hombre que cambio de piel (1966)

Keeler completed this 77,000-word novel on June 15, 1959 but it was never published in English (until Ramble House came out with its edition in 2001). He first referred to it as *Nigger Nigger Never Die* but its final manuscript title is *The Man Who Changed His Skin.*

Keeler Portuguese Originals

O caso do cadaver endiabrado

Lisbon: Editorial Seculo, publication date unknown. This is another of the Angus MacWhorter books Keeler carved from the *Ace of Spades* manuscript. He completed the 60,000 word novel on April 2, 1954 but it was never published in English or in Spanish either. He referred to it at times as *A Nightgown for Johanna* or *A Girl Named Patch* but its final title is *The Case of the Crazy Corpse.*

???????

(Portuguese title and date of publication unknown.) Keeler completed this 125,000-word novel in 1960 but it was never published in English or in Spanish either. He referred to it at times as *The Riddle of the Wooden Canary Bird* but its final title is *The Riddle of the Wooden Parakeet.*

SERIAL KEELERS

Compiled by Richard Polt and Francis M. Nevins

Tuddleton Trotter Series
The Matilda Hunter Murder
The Case of the Barking Clock
The Trap (Unpublished manuscript)

Marceau Series
The Marceau Case
X. Jones—Of Scotland Yard
The Wonderful Scheme of Mr. Christopher Thorne
Y. Cheung, Business Detective
Murder at Little Ivington (Unfinished manuscript)

The Mysterious Mr. I
The Mysterious Mr. I
The Chameleon

Vagabond Nights
Ten Hours
The Skull of the Waltzing Clown
The Defrauded Yeggman
10 Hours
When Thief Meets Thief

Hallowe'en Nights
Finger! Finger!
Behind That Mask

Adventures of a Skull
The Man with the Magic Eardrums
The Man with the Crimson Box
The Man with the Wooden Spectacles
The Case of the Lavender Gripsack

The Big River Trilogy
The Portrait of Jirjohn Cobb
Cleopatra's Tears
The Bottle with the Green Wax Seal

Circus Series

The Vanishing Gold Truck
The Case of the Jeweled Ragpicker
Stand By—London Calling!
The Case of the Crazy Corpse
The Circus Stealers
A Copy of Beowulf
Report on Vanessa Hewstone
The Six from Nowhere
The Case of the Two-Headed Idiot

The Way Out Series

The Peacock Fan
The Sharkskin Book
The Vanishing Gold Truck
The Book with the Orange Leaves
The Case of the Two Strange Ladies
The Case of the 16 Beans

Steeltown Series

The Case of the Canny Killer
The Steeltown Strangler
The Crimson Cube

Quiribus Brown Series

The Murdered Mathematician
The Case of the Flying Hands (Published 2001 by Ramble House)

Hong Lei Chung Series

The Strange Will
The Street of a Thousand Eyes (Spanish only)
The Six from Nowhere (Published 2000 by Ramble House)
The Riddle of the Wooden Parakeet (Spanish only)
The Chinese Ticket Murder (Unfinished manuscript)

Ramble House Series

The White Circle (Published 2001 by Ramble House)
I Killed Lincoln at 10:13! (Spanish only)
The Purple Room (Unfinished manuscript)
Strange Journey (Unpublished manuscript)

"Call me Gonwyck."

A Collection of Opening Lines from the novels of Harry Stephen Keeler, arranged chronologically by date of publication, showing how his introductory style changed (or didn't) over the years.

Compiled by Fender Tucker
with help from Richard Polt and Mike Nevins

1924 (year of publication)

The Voice of the Seven Sparrows

Mr. Harry Fosgrove, senior partner in the firm of Fosgrove and Fosgrove, Engravers to the Publishing and Printing Trades, looked up with annoyance from his flat-top desk in his private office at the timorous young lady-clerk who stood at attention in the doorway.

1925

Find the Clock

His unscrupulous blue eyes gazing over his half-moon spectacles, the lean fingers of his left hand reflectively stroking the short, crisp beard flecked with grey, Doctor Victor Flandrau bowed out of the tiny side door of his office his last patient, a pasty-faced "dope-head."

1926

The Spectacles of Mr. Cagliostro

One hundred and twenty miles more—two hours at the most—and he would be in Chicago, at the end of this strangest of all journeys that had carried him exactly half around the terrestrial globe.

1927

Sing Sing Nights

In the large, square death-cell a sudden peculiar quiet had fallen upon four men of different nationalities. McCaigh, the American—he whom the newspapers, during the progress of the strange trial, had dignified with the appelation of "The Iron Man"—paced slowly up and down, his wideset grey eyes roaming vacantly from the heavy oaken door, with its tiny barred window, to the solitary electric lamp which casts its shaded rays over a chamber fitted only with stout mission rockers, square mission table, couch and rug.

1929

The Amazing Web

Al Lipke, his sleek black hair parted in the middle, his checked suit pressed to fit every curve of his well-shaped form, his lone valise unpacked and its contents placed on the bureau, took from the bellboy of the Hotel McAlpin in New York City, the Chicago newspaper he had just sent out for, and dismissing the boy with the usual gratuity went over to the tiny desk at the window which looked out on Broadway.

The Fourth King

J. Hamilton Eaves, seated in the leather-lined swivel chair of his private office in the National Industrial Securities Company, gazed down curiously at the small and inconspicuous parcel the mail-carrier had just delivered along with the rest of the afternoon's letters.

Thieves Nights

The one dirty window of the barren little room on the corner of Halsted and Maxwell Streets, Chicago, looked out on a scene that, to Ward Sharlow, its only occupant, resembled nothing so much as that noisy Maelstrom in London known as Petticoat Lane.

1930

The Green Jade Hand

It was just past noon on a cloudy, gloomy Saturday in September, the year of our Lord 1931, that old Amos Carrington, eccentric collector of precious odds and ends from all over the world, spender of a fortune on his fad, and with a fortune yet to apend, sat in his curio room in his big residence on Chicago's Lakeshore Drive, tapping the floor nervously with his foot.

The Riddle of the Yellow Zuri

Clifford Carson, seated this sunny morning before the mail that covered his desk in the tiny office of his unique two-room suite on the 24th floor of an American skyscraper, found himself for some strange reason reflecting that it was a long, long call indeed from East India Dock Road, London, to this dignified niche high up in the 333 Building on Michigan Boulevard, Chicago.

1931

The Matilda Hunter Murder

Evidently four of the five patients in the emergency ward of the Nurse Cavell Memorial Hospital on West Superior Street, Chicago, considered that the excitement was over for the evening, for they all settled back resignedly on their beds and commenced staring at the shaded electric light bulbs that had just been lighted.

1932

The Box from Japan

Carr Halsey, coming up out of the dark subway, this bright morning of Sol 18, 1942, first glimpsed the huge hand-lettered placard in the window of the Associated Express Companies.

1933

Behind That Mask

Yin Yi, expert wax worker, gazed reflectively over the waxen head he had just completed for Captain Barraby's Dime Museum and Chamber of Horrors, of Davenport Iowa.

The Washington Square Enigma

To Ford Harling, seated on the cheerless wooden bench in Washington Square, Chicago, the knock of Fortune came at first as a pronounced shock.

The Face of the Man from Saturn

It was one minute to four in the afternoon when Jimmie Kentland sprang from a Madison Street car on the west fringe of Chicago's great Loop.

1934

10 Hours

The defendant finished his story. His story, by which, beyond any doubt whatsoever, he was to live—or to die!

The Mystery of the Fiddling Cracksman

Billy Hemple, dozing in his big comfortable over-stuffed chair after his long wearisome trip back to Chicago from New York, opened his eyes with a start and sat stiffly erect, his nerves tingling with the shock of his sudden awakening.

The Riddle of the Travelling Skull

I knew full well, when the Chinaman stopped me in the street that night and coolly asked me for a light for his cigarette, that a light for his cigarette was the last thing in the world he actually wanted!

1935

The Five Silver Buddhas

Penn Harding, newspaperman—late of the *Chicago Tribune,* though now "at leisure" as the Thespians term it!—stood on the dingy sidewalk of "Honkey-tonk Row" this October evening at 13 minutes of 6, and stared at the huge red-painted cloth sign that surmounted the gaudily bedecked South State Street store which was confronting him.

The Skull of the Waltzing Clown

Wharf 16, Honolulu—to No. 16 Russell Square, Chicago. What a long jaunt that had been! And now I stood on the sidewalk, in front of what was presumably No. 16 Russell Square, my three pieces of hand luggage strewn each side of me, and cast my optics over the place.

1936

The Marceau Case

Have just received a tip here in London that some new man at Scotland Yard, by the name Xenius Jones, has the solution of some allegedly world-famous murder mystery known as "The Marceau Case" virtually in his mitt.

X. Jones of Scotland Yard

Thanks a million times for the check-up of the fingerprint in Nebraska. I may now say conclusively that I have the basis for the solution of the Marceau Murder Case sufficiently in my hand that I hope ultimately to hold the full and complete solution itself.

1937

The Wonderful Scheme of M. Christopher Thorne

Kwan Yung, his frayed woolen cap drawn down well over his eyes, gazed fearfully up Broadway as he came slowly around the corner of Ann Street, and paused a bare second at the entrance of the old St. Paul's Building, with its slitlike windows.

The Mysterious Mr. I

It was exactly 4:10 in the morning—at least by the greasy clock in the window of the all-night Greek restaurant close to the street intersection—as I hopped off the Clark Street car at Chicago Avenue to size up the offices of MacLeish MacPherson, M.D., to try to estimate just what luck I might have on the morrow in my strange mission to him.

The Defrauded Yeggman

The three hobos who squatted around the little fire, staring silently into its dancing flames as though visioning better and happier days, appeared quite in ignorance of the strange events which had enmeshed the tiny town lying in the inky darkness scarcely a quarter mile to their west.

1938

When Thief Meets Thief

My name is Jerry Hammond. J. Hammond, yeggman, in the vernacular of gangsterdom and the underworld, safe-cracker in everyday English.

Finger! Finger!

John Walsh passed his hand through his greying hair, tilting his khaki hunter's cap as he did so, and looked half-heartedly at the diminishing duck he had just beautifully missed.

Y. Cheung, Business Detective

Y. Cheung, lone passenger on the little rumbling, tumbling Indianapolis streetcar, now passing interminable dark blocks of bungalow-like residences, turned in his seat as the conductor, who had come up behind him, tapped him on his shoulder.

1939

The Man with the Magic Eardrums

It was close upon 9 o'clock in the evening when I first met that gifted—and yet pitiful—individual, "The Man with the Magic Eardrums."

The Portrait of Jirjohn Cobb

The Sheriff, seated on a partly flat boulder, suspiciously eyed the three oddly garbed men who, likewise seated off the dampish earth on boulders that were more or less flat, defiantly faced him—and each other.

The Chameleon

$100,000 reward! In cash! To the person—or persons—who should return Gilrick Sandringham, escaped lunatic, to Birkdale Insane Asylum, Kaskawa County, State of Illinois, before midnight tonight!

1940

The Man with the Crimson Box

Convict No. 53,784—known on the records of the Northern State Penitentiary at Moundville, Illinois, as Gus L. McGurk—in the Chicago newspapers as "Big Gus"—and amongst crookdom as "Muscle-In", stopped short in his mopping of the lower cell walk in Old Cell Block.

Cleopatra's Tears

Yoho TenBrockerville, seated this early afternoon in the office of the Managing Editor of the *Buffalo Transcript*, making his seventh application in that city for a newspaper berth, reflected grimly that, in his three decades of existence, ranging all the way from being a millionaire's only son to selling 10-cent novelties at back doors, he had encountered plenty of adventure of a sort.

1941

The Man with the Wooden Spectacles

Mr. Silas Moffit, loaner of money to the Chicago judiciary and members of the Chicago bar, carrying his usual black cotton umbrella without the like of which—rain or shine!—he never went about, and dressed in the same rusty black suit and black string tie he invariably wore, dismounted in great haste from a Yellow taxicab in front of the old Prairie Avenue residence of Judge Hilford Penworth, and hastily paying off the driver with a handful of nickels, dimes and pennies—but which handful of change included not a single 5-cent tip for the driver!—went up the crumbling soapstone steps two at a time.

The Case of the Lavender Gripsack

Elsa Colby, criminal attorney, just turning up the high soapstone steps of the dark old mansion where was to be held, within less than thirty minutes now, the first case she should ever defend in actual court—the State of Illinois in re grand larceny and murder in the first degree!—noted that she was at least not going to have to ring the old-fashioned saucer-sized bell at the top to gain entrance!

1942

The Peacock Fan

Gordon Highsmith, pacing the floor of the big whitewashed death cell of Capital City's Municipal Jail and Prison, and listening, as he paced, to the clock ticking inexorably away in his ears, realized that he was tonight in a bad, bad spot indeed!

The Vanishing Gold Truck

Jim Craney, driver for the MacWhorter's Mammoth Motorized Shows, brought to a stop the huge lion cage on wheels in which, back of the gaudy gilt and crimson circus-wagon panels which covered it tightly, lay the show's big lioness and her five newly born cubs.

The Bottle with the Green Wax Seal

Derek Wingblade, ambling this evening along New York's notorious "Honky-Tonk Row" in the flamboyant Mexican regalia specially provided him by the City Editor of the *New York Courier*, hoped against hope that he was going to work out successfully the particular feature story he was after.

The Book with the Orange Leaves

As Stefan Czeszcziczki, rapid calculator, ran lightly up the stone steps of Chelsington City's Parkway Hospital this early afternoon, he felt a curious presentiment of evil and foreboding.

1943

The Search for X-Y-Z

Ezra Jenkins, waiting restlessly on the little unroofed train-boarding platform for the Wiscon City Limited, looked up suddenly from the distrubing letter he was re-reading for the 19th time.

The Case of the Two Strange Ladies

Tommy Skirmont, Yankee reporter on the *Southern City Democrat*, gazed in sheer desperation at his superior, the owner, publisher, and editor of the *Democrat.*

1944

The Case of the Mysterious Moll

Margaret Annister, waiting death in the gas-execution chamber of Nevada City's prison, had little hope that her last desperate appeal to the governor for reprieve or commutation would succeed.

The Case of the 16 Beans

Boyce Barkstone leaned forward in his chair, aghast. "And do you mean to tell me," he repeated, unbelievingly, to the attorney seated facing him, "that my grandfather left me only a handful of beans—out of an estate of practically $100,000? And left the $100,000 itself?—or nearly so—to that fool Academy for the Proving of Social Theories?"

1945

The Case of the Ivory Arrow

Ezra Jenkins, proceeding troubledly along busy Auffenberg Street, in that famous city of America known as "Little Berlin," came to a full stop—in front of Number 444.

This was it!

This was were reigned the man who intended to send him to the penitentiary!

1946

The Case of the Canny Killer

Noah Turnbo, electrical construction and transportation superintendent of the Tippingdale Steel Plant, slammed the desk telephone over which he had been talking viciously down on its cradle base.

1947

The Monocled Monster

Barry Wayne, seated on the edge of the small white-painted hospital bed, and all dressed and in readiness to leave this place where, as he understood matters, he had been lying unconscious for 3 days, gazed in astonishment at the grave-faced, middle-aged, white-capped nurse who stood in front of him.

The Case of the Barking Clock

Joe Czeszczicki, whose name had been woefully mis-pronounced as "Zicky" all through his recent trial and conviction for murder, rose swiftly from his chain-hung pallet as the two blue-clad, brass-buttoned prison officials stopped in front of his barred cell gate.

1948

The Sharkskin Book

Ogden Farlow knew that he was about to break! To confess—something—anything. Even, if necessary, the actual murder of Peter van Dervelpen.

The Case of the Jeweled Ragpicker

Detective Sergeant Frank DuShane, temporarily assigned as ordinary plainclothesman to the Depot View Police Station, on the down-at-heel south fringe of Chicago's great downtown district, was just about to go off duty for the night—it being 10 minutes after 6 in the morning—when the telephone call for him came.

The Case of the Transposed Legs

Warden Westman Pembroke, of the Northern State Penitentiary, stared incredulously at the opening lines of the brief purple handwritten communication which had just come in with his afternoon's mail.

1949

The Murdered Mathematician

Quiribus Brown, his 7½ feet of giantism causing him to tower high above all the pygmy-like humans about him, his vivid plaid lumberjack's short jacket and blue-and-orange-striped tightly-fitted knitted cap turning him into a literal blaze of colour for the inhabitants of such a drab city as Chicago, paused uncertainly at the unsavoury down-at-heel corner of Harrison and State Streets.

The Strange Will

Farrel Ivins, standing on the gallows trap of Central City's Municipal Prison, his hands tied tightly behind him, his feet strapped firmly together, the black execution cap lying in readiness loosely across his right shoulder, the noose about his throat with its cunning handman's knot snugly against the back of his neck, grimly surveyed the sea of faces gazing stiffly, steeply, up at him.

1950

The Steeltown Strangler

Amos Kittredge, warden of Northern Penitentiary, gazed thoughtfully from the heavily barred window of the Records Room into the great cobbled courtyard of the prison, where a quarter of a thousand grey-clad convicts were engaged, under burly blue-uniformed guards, in setting-up exercises.

1952

The Murder of London Lew

The expensively clad man with the rakish grey fedora hat, and one-carat diamond gleaming from his purple foulard tie, who was piloting the black limousine—rather, carefully inching it, with all lights doused —along the dark, tree-enshrouded dirt road that led towards the river, had a grim, determined look on his face.

2000

The Man Who Changed His Skin

Clark Shellcross, striding fiercely up the steps of the charming little white-painted cottage at 242 Flower Street, wondered what in heaven's name he was going to say to this lovely being inside who had given him the ultimatum of ultimatums!

The Six from Nowhere

Eli Kettlebone, elderly Chief of Police of the town of Whistle Stop, jerked from the rickety ancient typewriter standing on the kitchen table in front of him, the special criminological report he had just finished.

2001 and Beyond

The Case of the Flying Hands

Quiribus Brown, 7½-foot-high giant, ascending the narrow low-ceilinged staircase that led upstairs to the "Restaurant of the 99 Blackbirds Returning to the Nest, Prop. Hung Fung Lee" in Chicago's Chinatown, realized that this heavily adorned and ornate place, smelling of weird though fragrant incense, must undoubtedly have been constructed, and was being run, for the delectation of people visiting Chinatown for a thrill.

The White Circle

Kirk Solfedge, hopping out of the yellow taxicab that had brought him to the corner of Cotton Tree Road and Fordyce Boulevard, Washington, D.C., examined carefully under the bright globe-shaded street light piercing the early-December darkness of 7 in the evening, the dollar bill he was about to extend to the driver.

Report on Vanessa Hewstone

D. Appleton Hepplegarth, Chief of the famous United States Bureau of Crime Prevention, troubledly scanned the opening of the highly confidential letter he had just written, without aid of any secretary or stenographer from whom its contents could ever possibly leak to the outside world. Bearing at its top the single embossed heading U.S.B.C.P., with underneath but the simple words, Washington, D.C., but gleaming brilliantly in the splotch of bright morning sunshine lying on the foolscap-sized sheet, and typed in green ink, the letter, with its single-spaced lines only, began:

HANGMAN'S NIGHTS (1951)

In the large, square wood-floored death-cell of the small American Mississippi River town jail, a sudden hopeless silence had descended upon two men of utterly unlike descriptions.

THE GALLOWS WAITS, MY LORD! (1953)

Kedrick Merijohn, scheduled to be hanged in four days for a murder he had not committed, gazed bitterly out, from the window of his cheerless death cell in El Cabildo Prison, Republic of San Do Mar, on the prison-yard gallows on which he was to die.

THE CRIMSON CUBE (1954)

Lord Jeffrey Stillingfleete, Earl of Kislingbury, richest man in the entire world, gazed troubledly down at the slender American milltown girl, in cheap black cotton dress, with 10-cent-store white trimmings at the neck and elbows, whom he held fast in his arms.

THE CASE OF THE CRAZY CORPSE (1954)

Captain Phideas O'Lay, chief of the Water-View Police Station, Milwaukee, stared down at the long narrow slimily-wet white-pine box, tightly wired by stout wire that criss-crossed upon itself at dozens of points, and thus ran in every direction. The 3-foot length of snapped-off chain attached to a powerful steel eyelet sunk in one end of the long box showed that it had been affixed, at some time, and not far back either, to a heavy weight; perhaps a yawl anchor—perhaps only a 6-foot-or-so length of heavy I-beam. Brought here to the station-house but a few moments before by the two husky, powerful fishermen who had found it bobbing on the surface of the lake near their launch this sunny early September morning, it waited now but a wire-cutters.

THE STREET OF A THOUSAND EYES (1956)

Blonde, 17-year-old Eadgyth Whitchurch, London trans-Atlantic telephone operator, lying bound hand and foot, on the upper floor of the ancient dun-brick house in Limehouse, knew that within but a few hours now—at least conscious hours, anyway!—she was to find herself gasping her last in the Thames.

THE TRAP (1956)

The finely dressed man in the purple velour hat, and sparkling diamond stickpin in his purple foulard tie, facing the open illumined doorway at the side of the darkened Chinese laundry on the dark outskirts of Comanche, Oklahoma, repeated his question to the younger man who stood in that doorway, more or less silhouetted against light from a ceiling bulb.

THE CIRCUS STEALERS (1956)

Jules DiValo, Demon Illusionist of the MacWhorter's Mammoth Motorized Shows, irritably rattled the receiver of the ancient wall-phone in the flyspecked glass booth in the town pharmacy at Pricetown, where the "Biggest Little-Circus on Earth" had arrived but three hours before.

THE MYSTERIOUS IVORY BALL OF WONG SHING LI (1957)

Jarth Kilgo, standing out in front of the big 3-story stone mansion on Fordyce Parkway, Chicago, this sunny early-June morning, proceeded to re-read, once more—and troubledly!—the telegram from his lawyers in Buffalo, New York. Before making the plunge that would, he gloomily realized, get him nowhere fast—on saving $100,000!

A COPY OF BEOWULF (1957)

The elderly owner and proprietor of the Biggest Little-Circus on Earth, touring America's Southwest, did not realize, as he sat in his personal trailer, a full hour after the close of the evening's show, how rapt and puzzled he was as he gazed at the opened-out yellow telegram on his knee.

THE STOLEN GRAVESTONE (1958)

Fife MacDuff, cemetery inspector for Peaceful Rest Cemetery, Omaha, strode troubledly, worriedly, along the winding walk of the cemetery that led in front of him.

I KILLED LINCOLN AT 10:13! (1958)

"Sorry, young man, but I can't give you even a walk-on part in this new show of mine. For you're the spitting image of John Wilkes Booth—you know who he is, or rather was, don't you?—and the audience, seeing you, would start to scratch its collective head—and lose track of the plot of *my* play. And then—"

THE STRAW HAT MURDERS (1958)

Chief of Homicide Investigation Huntoon Cambourne, parking his light car under the Chicago Elevated-Traction Road this cool, early-fall, grey-skied afternoon, realized grimly that the straw hat murderer must have struck again.

THE CASE OF THE TRANSPARENT NUDE (1958)

Helmon Hobersteed, Chief of the Homicide Investigation Division of the Chicago Police Department, scowled angrily, blackly, as the phone on his broad mahogany glass-covered desk gave a significant five short jerky rings.

THE AFFAIR OF THE BOTTLED DEUCE (1958)

Police-Captain Michael Simko, day-chief of Chicago Avenue Police Station, raised the telephone on his battered desk as it rang raucously.

"Chicago Avenue Police Station," he said wearily.

A male voice, suggesting itself strongly, somehow, to be Italian, answered.

"I wish to report a suicide, if you please."

THE MYSTERIOUS CARD (1959)

"Pinky" McHarg, burglar and safecracker, frowningly swung his gaze from the white card which he held in his fingers—his sole takings in last night's safe-burglary—to the strange want-ad that had appeared in this morning's paper.

THE PHOTO OF LADY X (1959)

Damascus Bayley, Editor of the Central City *Morning Star*, strolling through the down-at-heel part of the city that lay just off of its downtown section, stopped at a tall curbside waste-paper box to dourly read, for the dozenth time, the typed memo in his coat pocket. A memo from no less than—the owner of the STAR!

THE SIGN OF THE CROSSED LEAVES (1959)

Not available at this time.

THE RIDDLE OF THE WOODEN PARRAKEET (1960)

Death-guard Smithertree Biggs, of Pentonville Prison, the glass of whiskey in his hand by which the condemned American criminal could be made to walk to the gallows by himself, surveyed troubledly the latter, in the big whitewashed death-cell, lighted only by its ceiling light. The guard, a big middle-aged man, and redfaced, was in his blue prison uniform. The condemned man, a slightly-built individual of about 35, was in brown overalls and open-throated shirt, rendered thus for expert placement of the noose later. Toward Biggs the convicted man stared bitterly. And why not, when his life could no longer now be said to contain even one remaining hour.

KILLER (1960 unfinished)

Superintendent Charles Mayhew, head of the Central Illinois Hospital for the Criminally Insane, was fast asleep in the bedroom of his bungalow, across the road from the hospital itself, when the phone at his bedside shrilled loudly. As he came to full awakening, to the bell's strident and repeated call—*and* fairly quickly at that, for, as superintendent of such an institution as he was, he had to be ever on the *qui vivre* for complications of strange and maybe even dangerous nature!—the grandfather's clock in the corner of the bedroom gave forth with a preliminary tri-tinkle, then a single sonorous tuned-down "bong" that stated the time to be 1 in the morning.

THE CASE OF THE TWO-HEADED IDIOT (1960)

"Well, Lura-Lora, the double-headed idiot girl, for whom we'd pay our souls around here to get hold of for a few minutes, is alive! A—L—I—V—E, and not dead and buried—as claimed! Nor merely dead, period, as recently hypothesized by—well, you know who! So what to do—now?"

THE SCARLET MUMMY (1965)

Don Langdon was disheartened, dispirited, perhaps a bit disillusioned too, this snowy morning in February, as he climbed up to his two by four bedroom on Chicago's ancient Washington Square, and flinging his hat and overcoat fiercely on his narrow iron bed, sat down to consider the situation with which he was confronted.

STRANGE JOURNEY (1965)

Chapter I, "Finale," was written by Thelma and reads as follows:

Alma Quarnborough and her husband, Alfred, ate breakfast in silence. The only sound in the small, sunny breakfast room, overlooking Connecticut Avenue, N.W., in Washington, D.C., was the chirping of the buttercup-yellow canary in its brass cage which hung next to the big tiny-square-pane windows. There was no other sound except the drumming of her heart. Al, too, was trying to act as though nothing was amiss, but she became aware that he was suddenly unable to stand the tension any longer. She thought in amazement, he seems like a stranger to me. She noticed that he had cut his chin in shaving, right at the cleft. His nose looked more pointed than usual this morning, and his eyes, normally a blue-grey, now looked like grey ice. As usual, when he was exasperated, he furrowed his high forehead. he spoke finally.

The rest of this extremely long book is by Harry. Here's the opening of Chapter II, "Bombshells Two!":

Bakerby Kell, seated at his huge maple desk in his private office in the offices of Rowbottom, MacWalterman and Palay, Business Analysts, was conscious, by the tone of the ring on one of the two phones standing in front of him, that the call just coming in was coming in on the private wire which did not go through the company switchboard; was, therefore, *very* private, *very* confidential; indeed, that number was vouchsafed to but few people, and for very select situations.

RAMBLE HOUSE's

HARRY STEPHEN KEELER WEBWORK MYSTERIES

(RH) indicates the title is available ONLY in the **RAMBLE HOUSE** edition

The Ace of Spades Murder
The Affair of the Bottled Deuce (RH)
The Amazing Web
The Barking Clock
Behind That Mask
The Book with the Orange Leaves
The Bottle with the Green Wax Seal
The Box from Japan
The Case of the Canny Killer
The Case of the Crazy Corpse (RH)
The Case of the Flying Hands (RH)
The Case of the Ivory Arrow
The Case of the Jeweled Ragpicker
The Case of the Lavender Gripsack
The Case of the Mysterious Moll
The Case of the 16 Beans
The Case of the Transparent Nude (RH)
The Case of the Transposed Legs
The Case of the Two-Headed Idiot (RH)
The Case of the Two Strange Ladies
The Circus Stealers (RH)
Cleopatra's Tears
A Copy of Beowulf (RH)
The Crimson Cube (RH)
The Face of the Man From Saturn
Find the Clock
The Five Silver Buddhas
The 4th King
The Gallows Waits, My Lord! (RH)
The Green Jade Hand
Finger! Finger!
Hangman's Nights (RH)
I, Chameleon (RH)
I Killed Lincoln at 10:13! (RH)
The Iron Ring
The Man Who Changed His Skin (RH)
The Man with the Crimson Box
The Man with the Magic Eardrums
The Man with the Wooden Spectacles
The Marceau Case
The Matilda Hunter Murder
The Monocled Monster
The Murder of London Lew
The Murdered Mathematician
The Mysterious Card (RH)
The Mysterious Ivory Ball of Wong Shing Li (RH)
The Mystery of the Fiddling Cracksman
The Peacock Fan
The Photo of Lady X (RH)
The Portrait of Jirjohn Cobb
Report on Vanessa Hewstone (RH)
Riddle of the Travelling Skull
Riddle of the Wooden Parrakeet (RH)
The Scarlet Mummy (RH)
The Search for X-Y-Z
The Sharkskin Book
Sing Sing Nights
The Six From Nowhere (RH)
The Skull of the Waltzing Clown
The Spectacles of Mr. Cagliostro
Stand By—London Calling!
The Steeltown Strangler
The Stolen Gravestone (RH)
Strange Journey (RH)
The Strange Will
The Straw Hat Murders (RH)
The Street of 1000 Eyes (RH)
Thieves' Nights
Three Novellos (RH)
The Tiger Snake
The Trap (RH)
Vagabond Nights (Defrauded Yeggman)
Vagabond Nights 2 (10 Hours)
The Vanishing Gold Truck
The Voice of the Seven Sparrows
The Washington Square Enigma
When Thief Meets Thief
The White Circle (RH)
The Wonderful Scheme of Mr. Christopher Thorne
X. Jones—of Scotland Yard
Y. Cheung, Business Detective

Keeler Related Works

A To Izzard: A Harry Stephen Keeler Companion by Fender Tucker — Articles and stories about Harry, by Harry, and in his style. Included is a compleat bibliography.

Wild About Harry: Reviews of Keeler Novels — Edited by Richard Polt & Fender Tucker — 22 reviews of works by Harry Stephen Keeler from *Keeler News.* A perfect introduction to the author.

The Keeler Keyhole Collection: Annotated newsletter rants from Harry Stephen Keeler, edited by Francis M. Nevins. Over 400 pages of incredibly personal Keeleriana.

Fakealoo — Pastiches of the style of Harry Stephen Keeler by selected demented members of the HSK Society. Updated every year with the new winner.

RAMBLE HOUSE's OTHER LOONS

The Master of Mysteries — 1912 novel of supernatural sleuthing by Gelett Burgess
Dago Red — 22 tales of dark suspense by Bill Pronzini
The Night Remembers — A 1991 Jack Walsh mystery from Ed Gorman.
The Organ Reader — A huge compilation of just about everything published in the 1971-1972 radical bay-area newspaper, *THE ORGAN*.
Old Times' Sake — Short stories by James Reasoner from Mike Shayne Magazine
Freaks and Fantasies — Eerie tales by Tod Robbins, collaborator of Tod Browning on the film FREAKS.
Four Jim Harmon Sleaze Double Novels — *Vixen Hollow/Celluloid Scandal, The Man Who Made Maniacs/Silent Siren, Ape Rape/Wanton Witch* and *Sex Burns Like Fire/Twist Session.* More doubles to come!
Marblehead: A Novel of H.P. Lovecraft — A long-lost masterpiece from Richard A. Lupoff. Published for the first time!
The Compleat Ova Hamlet — Parodies of SF authors by Richard A. Lupoff - New edition!
The Secret Adventures of Sherlock Holmes — Three Sherlockian pastiches by the Brooklyn author/publisher, Gary Lovisi.
The Universal Holmes — Richard A. Lupoff's 2007 collection of five Holmesian pastiches and a recipe for giant rat stew.
Four Joel Townsley Rogers Novels — By the author of *The Red Right Hand: Once In a Red Moon, Lady With the Dice, The Stopped Clock, Never Leave My Bed*
Two Joel Townsley Rogers Story Collections — Night of Horror and Killing Time
Twenty Norman Berrow Novels — *The Bishop's Sword, Ghost House, Don't Go Out After Dark, Claws of the Cougar, The Smokers of Hashish, The Secret Dancer, Don't Jump Mr. Boland!, The Footprints of Satan, Fingers for Ransom, The Three Tiers of Fantasy, The Spaniard's Thumb, The Eleventh Plague, Words Have Wings, One Thrilling Night, The Lady's in Danger, It Howls at Night, The Terror in the Fog, Oil Under the Window, Murder in the Melody, The Singing Room*
The N. R. De Mexico Novels — Robert Bragg presents *Marijuana Girl, Madman on a Drum, Private Chauffeur* in one volume.
Four Chelsea Quinn Yarbro Novels featuring Charlie Moon — *Ogilvie, Tallant and Moon, Music When the Sweet Voice Dies, Poisonous Fruit* and *Dead Mice*
The Green Toad — Impossible mysteries by Walter S. Masterman - More to come!
Two Hake Talbot Novels — *Rim of the Pit, The Hangman's Handyman.* Classic locked room mysteries.
Two Alexander Laing Novels — *The Motives of Nicholas Holtz* and *Dr. Scarlett,* stories of medical mayhem and intrigue from the 30s.
Three Wade Wright Novels — *Echo of Fear, Death At Nostalgia Street* and *It Leads to Murder*, with more to come!
Four Rupert Penny Novels — *Policeman's Holiday, Policeman's Evidence, Lucky Policeman* and *Sealed Room Murder,* classic impossible mysteries.
Five Jack Mann Novels — Strange murder in the English countryside. *Gees' First Case, Nightmare Farm, Grey Shapes, The Ninth Life, The Glass Too Many.*
Six Max Afford Novels — *Owl of Darkness, Death's Mannikins, Blood on His Hands, The Dead Are Blind, The Sheep and the Wolves* and *Sinners in Paradise* by One of Australia's finest novelists.
Five Joseph Shallit Novels — *The Case of the Billion Dollar Body, Lady Don't Die on My Doorstep, Kiss the Killer, Yell Bloody Murder, Take Your Last Look.* One of America's best 50's authors.
Two Crimson Clown Novels — By Johnston McCulley, author of the Zorro novels, *The Crimson Clown* and *The Crimson Clown Again.*
The Best of 10-Story Book — edited by Chris Mikul, over 35 stories from the literary magazine Harry Stephen Keeler edited.
A Young Man's Heart — A forgotten early classic by Cornell Woolrich
The Anthony Boucher Chronicles — edited by Francis M. Nevins
Book reviews by Anthony Boucher written for the *San Francisco Chronicle,* 1942 - 1947. Essential and fascinating reading.
Muddled Mind: Complete Works of Ed Wood, Jr. — David Hayes and Hayden Davis deconstruct the life and works of a mad genius.
Gadsby — A lipogram (a novel without the letter E). Ernest Vincent Wright's last work, published in 1939 right before his death.

My First Time: The One Experience You Never Forget — Michael Birchwood — 64 true first-person narratives of how they lost it.

The Incredible Adventures of Rowland Hern — Rousing 1928 impossible crimes by Nicholas Olde.

Slammer Days — Two full-length prison memoirs: *Men into Beasts* (1952) by George Sylvester Viereck and *Home Away From Home* (1962) by Jack Woodford

Beat Books #1 — Two beatnik classics, *A Sea of Thighs* by Ray Kainen and *Village Hipster* by J.X. Williams

Murder in Silk — A 1937 Yellow Peril novel of the silk trade by Ralph Trevor

The Case of the Withered Hand — 1936 potboiler by John G. Brandon

Invaders from the Dark — Classic werewolf tale from Greye La Spina

Fatal Accident — Murder by automobile, a 1936 mystery by Cecil M. Wills

Corpses Never Argue — 1938 Australian hardboiled novel by David Hume

The Devil Drives — A prison and lost treasure novel by Virgil Markham

Dr. Odin — Douglas Newton's 1933 potboiler comes back to life.

The Chinese Jar Mystery — Murder in the manor by John Stephen Strange, 1934

The Julius Caesar Murder Case — A classic 1935 re-telling of the assassination by Wallace Irwin that's much more fun than the Shakespeare version

West Texas War and Other Western Stories — by Gary Lovisi

The Contested Earth and Other SF Stories — A never-before published space opera and seven short stories by Jim Harmon.

Tales of the Macabre and Ordinary — Modern twisted horror by Chris Mikul, author of the *Bizarrism* series.

The Gold Star Line — Seaboard adventure from L.T. Reade and Robert Eustace.

The Werewolf vs the Vampire Woman — Hard to believe ultraviolence by either Arthur M. Scarm or Arthur M. Scram.

Black Hogan Strikes Again — Australia's Peter Renwick pens a tale of the outback.

Don Diablo: Book of a Lost Film — Two-volume treatment of a western by Paul Landres, with diagrams. Intro by Francis M. Nevins.

The Charlie Chaplin Murder Mystery — Movie hijinks by Wes D. Gehring

The Koky Comics — A collection of all of the 1978-1981 Sunday and daily comic strips by Richard O'Brien and Mort Gerberg, in two volumes.

Suzy — Another collection of comic strips from Richard O'Brien and Bob Vojtko

Dime Novels: Ramble House's 10-Cent Books — *Knife in the Dark* by Robert Leslie Bellem, *Hot Lead* and *Song of Death* by Ed Earl Repp, *A Hashish House in New York* by H.H. Kane, and five more.

Blood in a Snap — The *Finnegan's Wake* of the 21st century, by Jim Weiler and Al Gorithm

Stakeout on Millennium Drive — Award-winning Indianapolis Noir — Ian Woollen.

Dope Tales #1 — Two dope-riddled classics; *Dope Runners* by Gerald Grantham and *Death Takes the Joystick* by Phillip Condé.

Dope Tales #2 — Two more narco-classics; *The Invisible Hand* by Rex Dark and *The Smokers of Hashish* by Norman Berrow.

Dope Tales #3 — Two enchanting novels of opium by the master, Sax Rohmer. *Dope* and *The Yellow Claw.*

Tenebrae — Ernest G. Henham's 1898 horror tale brought back.

The Singular Problem of the Stygian House-Boat — Two classic tales by John Kendrick Bangs about the denizens of Hades.

Tiresias — Psychotic modern horror novel by Jonathan M. Sweet.

The One After Snelling — Kickass modern noir from Richard O'Brien.

The Sign of the Scorpion — 1935 Edmund Snell tale of oriental evil.

The House of the Vampire — 1907 poetic thriller by George S. Viereck.

An Angel in the Street — Modern hardboiled noir by Peter Genovese.

The Devil's Mistress — Scottish gothic tale by J. W. Brodie-Innes.

The Lord of Terror — 1925 mystery with master-criminal, Fantômas.

The Lady of the Terraces — 1925 adventure by E. Charles Vivian.

My Deadly Angel — 1955 Cold War drama by John Chelton

Prose Bowl — Futuristic satire — Bill Pronzini & Barry N. Malzberg .

Satan's Den Exposed — True crime in Truth or Consequences New Mexico — Award-winning journalism by the *Desert Journal.*

The Amorous Intrigues & Adventures of Aaron Burr — by Anonymous — Hot historical action.

I Stole $16,000,000 — A true story by cracksman Herbert E. Wilson.

The Black Dark Murders — Vintage 50s college murder yarn by Milt Ozaki, writing as Robert O. Saber.

Sex Slave — Potboiler of lust in the days of Cleopatra — Dion Leclerq.

You'll Die Laughing — Bruce Elliott's 1945 novel of murder at a practical joker's English countryside manor.

The Private Journal & Diary of John H. Surratt — The memoirs of the man who conspired to assassinate President Lincoln.

Dead Man Talks Too Much — Hollywood boozer by Weed Dickenson

Red Light — History of legal prostitution in Shreveport Louisiana by Eric Brock. Includes wonderful photos of the houses and the ladies.

A Snark Selection — Lewis Carroll's *The Hunting of the Snark* with two Snarkian chapters by Harry Stephen Keeler — Illustrated by Gavin L. O'Keefe.

Ripped from the Headlines! — The Jack the Ripper story as told in the newspaper articles in the *New York* and *London Times.*

Geronimo — S. M. Barrett's 1905 autobiography of a noble American.

The White Peril in the Far East — Sidney Lewis Gulick's 1905 indictment of the West and assurance that Japan would never attack the U.S.

The Compleat Calhoon — All of Fender Tucker's works: Includes *The Totah Trilogy, Weed, Women and Song* and *Tales from the Tower,* plus a CD of all of his songs.

RAMBLE HOUSE

Fender Tucker, Prop.

www.ramblehouse.com fender@ramblehouse.com

318-455-6847 443 Gladstone Blvd. Shreveport LA 71104

Lightning Source UK Ltd.
Milton Keynes UK
UKHW012014180722
406026UK00001B/126

9 781605 431253